# GRIG

# GRIG

by

## H. B. CRESWELL

with drawings by
ANTHONY GARDNER

FABER AND FABER LTD
24 Russell Square
London

*First published in January Mcmxlii*
*by Faber and Faber Limited*
*24 Russell Square, London, W.C.1*
*Second impression January Mcmxliv*
*Third impression December Mcmxliv*
*Fourth impression November Mcmxlv*
*Fifth impression February Mcmli*
*Printed in Great Britain by*
*W. Taylor & Co. (Printers) Ltd., London, E.9*

To

MY WIFE

# CONTENTS

Page numbers refer to the Sections concerned with leading persons and incidents, as follows:

9

# PREFACE

" John Grigblay " will be recognized as the name of the builder prominent in *The Honeywood File* and *The Honeywood Settlement*. What follows is from a record Grigblay kept when he was lapsing into retirement and had leisure to amuse himself by recalling the past and commenting on the present.

No further introduction is necessary, as the ensuing narrative is in no way pendant on the old, and " Grig " may be left to tell his own story in his own way.

H.B.C.

*Hampstead*
1941

It doesn't seem like a year gone since I retired with my son-in-law to carry on the old firm—but not the old name, for I have taken good care of that name, and am not ashamed of it, nor ever have been; nor yet of any building work I have set my hand to, first to last, and so I do not choose to make a present of it to any other to take care of it for me. My son-in-law—the husband of my eldest girl, and the nearest to a son I ever had—is a smart young fellow, and his only trouble is that he thinks himself a bit smarter than he is, and goes ahead till he is stepping over the edge and has to use all his smartness to get back again, like Mickey Mouse on the films, so that I have to keep a sharp look-out to see what he's about. But Arthur knows what is what by the years he was under manager with Brookner & Swurt, for there's not a better builder in the country than Dick Swurt—Brookner died twenty years ago and more—unless it is myself. I can see the new board on top of the old one when I look out of my bedroom window, skew-ways, across the yard: "Arthur Ballard & Co. Builders and Contractors, late"—and then comes the old board—"John Grigblay, Builder" that has not been repainted these nine years, and is beginning to fade out the same as I am beginning to fade out, and I tell Arthur he can have it to make my coffin when the time comes.

Arthur wants the old board down, like he wants a lot of things he can't have, and the new—"Grigblay & Ballard",

13

for I have held a controlling interest in the business, and keep an eye on things without interfering too much with all these rare new clever ideas that are going about, as though we never did anything the right way to make it last three hundred years, but must do it better with bits of rabbit-netting in the joints, and telegraph wires and gas pipes in the concrete, to skewer the lot together so that it will stand up for fifty. I know things have got to change, and that I am too old to change with them; but when it comes to little squidgy five-storey blocks of flats with shop windows below of fine thick plate glass to hold the lintel up, like we have just finished in Hedderton Market Place—by Arthur fretting to send in a tender—all of nine-inch brickwork notched to a little wobbling spindle-work of steel H irons—well, I say that the old way was the better way for use and for lasting and as a job of work; and if it took a bit longer and cost a bit more, the time and the money were well spent and gave better value than the gimcrack affairs architects ask us to tender for nowadays. If the architects get any satisfaction out of that class of work they are the only ones that do, for no tradesman does and no craftsman, nor yet any right builder, except for the profit to be had which has nothing to do with the merit of the building. It is the satisfaction in a good bit of building that has made my work worth doing for me and for the half a dozen of trusties who have worked along with me for twenty years—and longer, some of them —and been more like one family with me than "master and man", as they call it. The most of my men have always been non-union; and when any Union Officials have come about asking questions and thinking to get more members—well, often as not, it has meant my men leaving their Unions instead of the other way about, though they can please themselves unless they start making upsets, and then —out they go.

14

# A QUARREL

Now, here I am rambling along—which is another sign I am getting on in years—and have not finished what I started out to say, which is why I would not have it put up "Grigblay & Ballard". Arthur wanted it, but I said to Art.: "No, my lad. Your Dad will be in another star some day", I said, "and does not want to look down through one of the dainty, fascinating, ultra-super telescopes they will likely have up there, and see his name on a big sign all illuminated and jumping in coloured lights, with arrows jerking in and out at the front door in case any should try to get in by the windows so as to be in time to accept a tender. Nor I don't want to see," I said, " 'Grigblay's Cosypalace Period Super-Chalets', flood-lighted side of the arterial road in case any motorist should run by in the dark and miss the chance of buying one at thirty-seven pounds and fourpence down and the rest by instalments over twenty years, when there won't be any but the repairs left standing to pay on," I said.

Of course Arthur laughs, and says he will never have to do with truck of that sort—and no more he would in my belief, though I am well aware he doesn't hold with me, and thinks he knows best to go with the times and take things as they come, and a lot more of it; but I said: "What about our successors?" I said. "How do we know there will not come to be my name pushed high in the air advertising Cosypalace Chalets with real glass sun-parlours all sides—so that the owners can live nice and cosy like flies in a bottle—and with walls of beautiful five-inch "Squiffo" blocks, lined with quarter-inch "Bunko"—to soak up the damp—clout nailed to make a pretty pattern of rust stains on the wall-paper? How do we know?" I said.

"And what if it is?" says young Art.

"Because my name's John, and not Jerry," I said, "and I mean it shall be respected after I am dead the same as it is now I'm alive:—and, come to that," I said, "why do you want my name hitched to yours, except it is to recommend you where your own won't?" I said.

"Well, Dad," says the boy, "you belonged to the times when you began, the same as I belong to mine, now. I'm starting and you're finishing."

"I'll let you know when I'm finished," I said; "but I'm not finished *yet*, and there are sound and craftsmanlike ways of building, and there are speculative and shoddy, and always have been, and always will be," I said.

"Yes," says Master Arthur Ballard thinking to sauce me, and I should not be surprised. "Those are your ideas, I know."

"And they're dam' well going to be your ideas, too," I said.

"But we must build what we're asked to build, Dad, and keep ahead in modern ideas, or else go out of business altogether," he says. And then he starts off with why won't I have him tender for the gasholder tank? "That's honest building, anyhow," he says.

"I've told you why twice over already," I said—for so I had done—"but I'll tell you once more, over again, for a third time, to make a finish," I said. "It's an engineer's job, and an engineer's job is not my job, and never has been and never will be," I said. "The Gas Company's Engineer may be captain of your cricket and a good sort to play penny nap with in the train; but it's not my idea of business to tender to a dear old pal you can trust faithful to see you through, and who trusts you faithful to see *him* through, and, directly there is trouble from his sloppy ways, puts you in the soup so as he can keep out of it himself," I said. "There are no Quantities supplied, and the Specification is just a mug-trap, as you can see for yourself. What's the ground like all that way down, and no trial pits? Suppose we come to a fine old hard-as-rock sewer to blow out with dynamite

16

so long as we don't make any noise! And suppose we find water and have to pump, and Bagshot crops in and we pump sand and undermine the face! And what about planking and strutting, that are not specified, let alone measured! Who's going to pay for the pickle? We aren't Tolmichael's, Sonny!" I said.

"You suppose this and suppose that, Dad; but there's risks in all contracts. You can't expect profits if you don't face risks," says the clever lad.

"I didn't take you in for partner to learn something no-one ever knew till you were special born and taught to talk so as you could tell me," I said.

"I've got a right to my own opinions," said Master Art, getting a bit pink in the cheeks with it.

"You can have as many opinions as you like as long as you don't act on any of them," I said.

"I know you differ from me in lots of things, Dad . . ." but I wouldn't have him to go on:

"What you mean, my young cock, is that it's *you* that differ from *me*," I said: "and there is another matter you differ from me about that you don't know, by appearances, and that I can tell you of the same as I can tell you a lot else you don't know," I said, "and that is—you are surprised we don't agree; but I'd be surprised if we did." On that the boy must get his shirt out and say:

"At any rate there's one thing you know thoroughly well, Dad; and that is how to be offensive." Him answering me back that style, and one thing on top of another, with a bit of blood-pressure I suffer from sometimes when excited, made me so wild that I shouted at him to get out before I chucked him out. However, that night going along past his house I happened to see in, and there was Ellie had brought the two boys down in their little pyjamas to say good night, and pretty it was to see when I remembered my own young time; but it looked to me Art was a bit quiet and subdued,

17

tickling them and rolling them on the floor, and I hadn't gone ten yards by before I had turned back and gone straight in with the kids halloaing and rushing at me to climb up my legs. I gave Art a nod and, after, he came to the door with me and I told him to go ahead with the Tender and I would look into things and make safe; so now the Tender is accepted, and maybe I shall be building sewage works before I finish!

## COMING EVENTS

Well, that's the reason Arthur is carrying on in his own name with me as "Co." to keep close at hand to watch out what the boy is at; and a lucky boy he is, for my old trusties, Tweedle, Snoop and old Fred Bloggs and the others, are well content; and Arthur sets store by them, as he ought to; and we can depend on them to do us credit with the special jobs we tender for by the opportunity given us by architects I have built for in the past who invite us knowing the good performance we can give, and who we can rely on for fair treatment. Mr. James Spinlove, F.R.I.B.A., has been a good friend of mine for many a year, spite of the rare bothers and upsets we had, first start off, with Honeywood Grange by Marlford, for Sir Leslie Brash, those years when he had first set up and knew a lot more than I could tell him and a bit more than he knows now: but Mr. Spinlove was always a fair-spoken and fair-dealing gentleman, I will say that; and many a fine job have I carried out for him since, and shall again, I hope—not big work, but particular, that takes up a lot of his time and a bit too much of mine, once or twice. It was only last year we finished the new wing to Dulkington for him, beautiful! All panelled out and wonderful ceilings and lead-work, and there's no better masonry, new or old, in the country, and so I told the Earl when all was done. I don't think I ever took more pride in any work, and do now when I see his fancy chimneys sticking up in the trees, going by in the train. Only a fortnight ago, when I went to his office for the settling up, he told me he was about restoring Belhampton Castle, a place half in ruins by what I hear and now brought by some new Croesus or other. Mr. Spinlove was most kind in hoping we might give him a tender; but it's a bit far afield for us and we would be biting off more than we could chew, and so I told him, and I think he felt the same though sorry it was so. Ten years ago it might have been different—and there is another sign I am getting old.

However, I am an active man yet, and must be at something or another directly I am up in the morning, though not ready for the bustle and racket I enjoyed in my younger days; so here I have started this Journal, as they call it, that I can write in when I feel I want to blow off steam; for I have done a rare lot of writing in my time, what with all the letters and press-copying with my own hands in early days —and late at night, often—long before the girls with typewriters and shorthand notebooks came on the scene to rattle off so many letters that you have to lick your thumb turning over for a half-hour to find what you could learn in two minutes before the new inventions. I saw in an exhibition a letter of a half-sheet of notepaper, written in his own hand by Sir C. Wren, ordering a forest of oak-trees to be thrown and logged for Saint Paul's Cathedral, and saying just what it had to be and the price; and so it was done, we may be sure, without two hundred and fifty letters written, and telegraph boys knocking on the door and telephone bells going. It is my belief that when typewriters are made to type when you talk at them, and we all carry a wireless telephone on the other end of our watchguards, and everything has reached absolute perfection by all the new clever

19

inventions—no-one will be ever able to get anything done at all unless it is by machinery. Lucky I was able to stop Arthur buying the patent filing cabinet that was pretty near as big as a church organ. "That's a fine thing, Art, my lad," I said. "A company of chimpanzee monkeys out of the Zoo, that could recognize capital letters and numbers when they saw them, could work it easy; but our girls are not a pack of nit-wits," I said. "They can think now and again, and remember once or twice in a week, and they will be better going on practising their brains that way, for passing on to their children when they get married, than come to breeding chimps themselves by pushing those knobs in and out all day long," I said.

There is a thing I've got to see to, and worries me a bit; and that is Fred Bloggs has been giving trouble again. I've been a bit too tender with the old chap and Arthur can't do anything with him, but I did think, after the last time, we should have no more of it, and he's been quite his old self these fifteen months past. Well, I've got to hear what he has to say, but it goes to my heart having to talk rough to old Fred, for he sets no end of store by me and, first to last has always worked to please me same as if it might be to please himself, and no trouble has ever been spared by the old chap, who can never do enough to make sure all is kept safe, as if it was him to look after me instead of me him. Many and many a time have I found out that old Fred was at work, on the quiet, to prevent some awkwardness or mix-up coming about, not knowing that I was busy in the same direction; and it is so with him that he is terrible hurt in his feelings if he thinks I have any complaint against him.

## FRED BLOGGS

Fred never was in any trouble till after his wife died. I know what that means, and don't forget in eleven years, and me with grown-up daughters at home; but Fred seemed to go all numb with it as if he couldn't believe such a thing could happen to him. They never had any children—which wouldn't be Fred's fault—and lived in the little "Farm Cottage" in Farm Lane, that was—now written up "Porchester Avenue" and all broke out in little red five-room semi-detached, like the measles—where Fred still lives; and you could not anywhere find a happier pair. If Fred wasn't at the Yard and wasn't working in the nice bit of garden they had, you could be sure he was sitting inside with the Missis; and three or four times when I had to send him in charge of jobs far afield, he would have her to be with him in apartments—a thing you would scarcely hear of anywhere, in my experience.

Fred came to me just forty-one years ago. He was early foreman bricklayer, soon to be general foreman on small jobs and then on big ones, and if I have cause to be grateful to any who have worked for me it is to Fred Bloggs. A stocky, powerful man he always was, and now grown to be more so; and one of the few I have known who could work right- and left-handed, just as suited best, and not to be beat as a craftsman. He was always quiet-mannered to me—though apt to get excited if things went wrong—and a proper bulldog that never let go when he took hold, so that I don't think I ever asked him a question on any matter he was concerned with, without getting a clear answer. Fred always kept what he wanted where he could easy come by it, and that was inside his head or by knots in a bit of string he kept in his pocket; and, though he was never much of a hand at writing or cyphering, he was not troubled by the want of it, nor was I. He had the clearest head of all I ever had about me, and is the most energetic and the best organizer, and many an awkward corner have I got round by having Fred Bloggs at my back; and though I was a bit shy of trying him as yard foreman when poor Perkins was killed by the lorry being lost control of—for he had grown to be a bit impatient and violent when upset—I liked the idea of him being settled down at home, and, first start off, it looked to be the best day's work I ever did. His energy livened up everybody; the stuff came through the shops quicker than ever it had done before; and all went as merry as bad language could make it—nothing low, but choice and varied beyond belief. Whether it's in the family I can't say; or perhaps it's "inspiration", as they call it; but, when he is thoroughly rattled, I will say there is not a more verbose man in these islands than Fred Bloggs. They tell me he never says the same twice over, scarcely; and his eloquence is a thing no one would credit unless they heard him at it, as I know by the few times I have been within hearing when he was letting fly at them for something or another done wrong or not done when it ought. The men are afraid to provoke him; but Fred is a great character, and, in spite of his impulsive ways when things don't go smooth, he is the most popular of my men, for all of them—except those he is telling off—love to hear him at it.

Well, as I say, when his wife died, four years after I had put him in the Yard, the old fellow changed altogether. He kept close to his work, but seemed all cast down and had none of his usual fizz and bang; and, though no harm came of it, by the men being sorry for the old chap and not taking advantage, I felt a bit uneasy as it looked he might go off his head if he didn't cheer up; and then, after four or five weeks, he *did* cheer up, and it came near to being his ruin—and would have been, too, if he had had any other to reckon with but me—for what must old Fred do all of a sudden but take to football.

There were a good few in the Yard at it, in a quiet way, but when Fred started he became the leader of a gang that were supporters of the Buckleton Pirates. The first I knew was one day when I saw Fred, then fifty-seven years of age, blowing a penny squeaker and waving a black skull-and-crossbones flag, breasting along to the railway with ribbons in his cap on a Cup-tie Saturday at the head of a troop with rattles and paper hats and mouth-organs. I was afraid he would lose authority with the men, carrying on that style; but the harm was that he began to jolly himself with beer—a thing he had never taken too much of in all the years I had known him. I made a guess at what might be when I heard of him roistering with a crowd of them in the High Street one night so that the police had to take a hand; and all just because the Pirates had won a goal off the Vampires, or some such silliness. Then he began to come back to the yard after dinner so that it was noticed by some; and the next was when they told me in the office one afternoon, that Fred was squiffy and carrying on in the machining like a lunatic.

I went across, and there was a clatter and roaring in the shop the like of which was never heard; with all the machines standing, and the shop foreman and all of them gaping at Fred who was laying a ten-foot against the linings for the Infirmary we were then building, that were stacked ready for routing, and pitching them over his head and all ways and shouting and cursing so as it was a wonder to hear him.

"Now, then, what's all this?" I said.

"Scald your tail, sir!" he roars out. "I've got to learn

these lousy cow-droppings here!"—and so he went on, taking no heed of me standing behind him, and seeming as though he would do murder, soon as not, with his red, sweating face and glittering eyes. He is grown a thick hefty man with arms as big round as his legs, pretty near, and I knew it was a bit risky; but I didn't believe he would start in on me, and so it was. When I stepped up and laid my hand on his elbow he spun about as though he meant to floor me; but, when he saw me, his arm fell and he stared in my face; and then his eyes dropped and he turned his head and began dragging his fingers along the smooth of one of the linings. I stood for a time and then I said: "You come along, Fred," and walked out of the shop; and there wasn't a sound but my own steps until I heard him following. I went in my room and sat at the table and left him to shut the door when he came in, after.

Well, no one could say he was rightly sober, nor yet that he was anyways drunk. It had been growing on him to get violent if things went wrong; and there had been a stupid mistake notified from the job by a messenger, just before dinner, of linings sent 3 in. short of length, and Fred was worried to know what harm was done, and so had taken more than he should to hearten him and make him feel ready to tackle the muddle and give hell to those who had caused it. It had come about by a dimension 8 in. being read 5 in., so that all the linings got out and thicknessed were the same, and there was no sense whatever in Fred carrying on in the style he had done, and so he admitted standing there with his cap in his hands; but he said he had done it to give them all a lesson so that they should have a better care and mind what they were about next time.

There didn't seem much sense in that, either, and so I told him; but I couldn't feel angry with the old fellow however much I wanted to be, though I talked to him serious, and good reason to, or the whole place would be at sixes and sevens with such goings on. I got out of him that he had only taken five pints.

"That's more than a stoker or a navvy has need of to his dinner," I said. "Two pints is your proper mark, Fred, doing the light work you're on," I said; "so hold to it."

He promised me he would keep off in the future. "Yes, and so they all promise," I said, but was sorry when I saw his look; for Fred is no boozer, and I have an idea that the old fellow is getting past his work and does it just to keep up his energies; and that is the whole cause, and nothing else, in my opinion. However, I had to tell him I couldn't overlook it; and he had a proper start when I said he would have to stay away for a week: "but", I said, "you can go sick, Fred, for sick you are in your head or your guts, or both," I said, "to behave the way you have done; and you'd better take a holiday," I said. "I'm not going to make a disgrace of you this first time and lay you off the same as I would any other. You can draw your pay," I said.


## A WINDFALL

The old chap was grateful and went quietly off, and I thought we should have no more of it; and, sure enough, he was good as gold for nearly a year, except I had to look at him pretty straight one day when we were having that trouble of scribing window-bars to suit the ideas of the late Sir Oswald Pursefoot, F.R.I.B.A., F.S.A.—who carried a pair of microscopes on his nose to make sure nothing was done that would look amiss to any high-art flies that might chance to crawl over—and Fred had took an extra pint, as I could smell him, to sharpen his eyesight and keep his vocabulary running full bore; and then one Friday, just after knocking off and the men paid, there came a shouting and hurrahing that brought me to the window pretty quick, and what was there but a crowd of them round Fred Bloggs cheering and clapping him on the back; and, when I asked, it turned out that one of them had brought in some weekly paper or another, and, lo and behold! if old Fred hadn't won a football competition prize—£75, by what I remember. He was gone off before I could have word with him, or things might have been different; but that old fellow no sooner came in for a nice bit of money for the first time in his life, than he must set about to get rid of it as fast as he knew how; and before midday on the Monday he had run through the lot and was petitioning me to sub him £8 to see him straight, and such goings on as never were heard of. I can't help laughing whenever I remember, spite of the nuisance and worry it was to me at the time.

The first thing he did—and he never got to the second thing—was to stand treat. He must have found the draft waiting by letter when he got home that Friday evening, for he did not come to the yard on the Saturday, but sent an excuse instead, and a lot more did not clock on; and, soon as the bank opened at 9.30 and he could get the cash, about thirty started off with flags and mouth-organs and cases of Worthington on a beano to Brighton. They did not contract for a coach; Fred must have taxis, seven of them, for his friends to travel like gentlemen, all ticking up 9d. a mile each way and waiting on the clock, like enough, with the drivers joining in the fun and having their beer with the rest. They had a rare dinner at the Rampart Arms as I heard, and what they did after I don't know; but it was past one on the Sunday morning when they got back, singing and cheering and blowing bugles; and then Fred, and four along with him, must have his own little private jollification to blow off steam and make a finish before spending the night in the beautiful new police station then just

26

finished building in Radnor Street; and that was by chasing through the residential quarters—Plankton Way, Selina Close, Penzance Crescent and all over—singing and halloaing and throwing bottles of beer at the houses and through the windows—which is what he aimed to do, without a doubt.

First I heard was at nine o'clock on the Monday, when Mr. George Trencher, the solicitor, rang up for me to come to the court; and lucky I was at hand to say a good word, or Fred would have been jailed, certain. The magistrate pulled a long face, but gave Fred the option—ten pounds or twenty-eight days—and by the time he had paid the fine and court and solicitor's charges, he was pretty nearly cleaned out, and couldn't have found what he still owed if I hadn't seen him straight.

I was properly bothered, and thought I should have to lay him off for good and all; but that would have hurt me as much as it would him, pretty near; and he was so puzzled and upset at what he had done—being primed up at the time, no doubt—that, after I had talked to him and seen the tears trickling down his cheeks, I let it go as no concern of mine; but I paid off two I could do without, for notice to all and sundry to be on good behaviour out of hours as well as in, or take themselves off to get a job with Nibnose & Rasper, if they like, where they can keep pots of beer under their benches, by what I hear, with Mr. Dirty Johnny Rasper to take a pull at now and again when he comes round the shops—and I wouldn't be surprised. Mr. Johnny will not forget, yet awhile, the sharper's trick he played on me two years back—only it didn't come off—when he made one of his clever accidental mistakes and took away ten tons of Green Line Cement, consigned to us, from the Goods' Yard dock, because his own ten was away in the siding and not to be got at; and then had to load it all back again and lorry it to me free, gratis; and two bags short—

27

by another of his clever accidental mistakes—that he was made to pay for!

Well, this is all past history and best forgot; but last night there was Fred on the mat with me again, after fifteen months without any complaints, because Arthur can't do anything with him by reason of his obstinate ways, not doing what he's told, but the way he thinks best, instead; and carrying on disgraceful for the men to see, answering Arthur back—which I will not have any more than it was myself—and perhaps a drop of beer mixed up with it that had better not be there. I thought best have him round for a talk, private, after Arthur complained about him, and I sent round to his place for him to come and see me; and, after supper, there the old fellow was all dressed in his Sunday clothes and hair brushed, a bit pale and downcast—and good cause to be—and looking so as no-one would ever credit the games he's been up to. I came near laughing to see him, for I love the old chap spite of the trouble he's been to me, off and on, these last years.

It is pretty clear that the old fellow has a bit more than he can do; and these new machines Arthur said we must have—and I agreed—and that Fred doesn't like and won't make the best use of, is the last straw. I told him I would have another to help him and be responsible for the machining when he had seen to the marking off. The old man began to cry, but I am used to that, and he dried up and was ready to fight directly I said "Rube Johnston". He wouldn't have Rube, he said; and when I asked "Who?" it was Alf Rumble that has never done other than what he has been told, except teach Sunday School. Fact is, Fred thinks Rube is too strong, and will cut him out; but I said: "There it is, Fred. You think it over. There's no other way this time. If you don't like it you can take your benefit," I said; and off he went with his head hanging down so as it hurt me to see him; but that's the best I can do, or Arthur

28

will have me clear him out altogether unless we send the old fellow away on some job or another, as might perhaps be now Mr. Spinlove has written asking me, over again, if I will tender, with three others invited, for alterations and additions to Belhampton Castle for Sir Ezra Gotsnitz, Bart. It pleases me having Mr. Spinlove want us on such a particular job, but Arthur fights shy. It wants a bit of thought.

## THE NEW CASHIER

I don't fancy the cut of this young man, Oswald Snape, Arthur wanted taken on and has now made assistant cashier and wages clerk in place of Sennock, gone to the Prime Costing Office. He is a lot too polite and kindhearted for my tastes, and there is something lays behind, when you look straight in his eyes, I don't care about; and, also, he's afraid of me when he has no call to be: but Arthur seems pleased with his "Certainly if you wish, Mr. Ballard," and "Not if you don't like, Mr. Ballard," and "Shall I close the window, Mr. Ballard, in case of the rain coming in, as it seems likely it may do, Mr. Ballard, and perhaps wet all your papers, Mr. Ballard," as I heard him a while back. He's not the style I want about the place, and so I told Arthur first start off, with his sticking-out ears and permed hair mixed up with a bit of ladies' scent that is too pretty to put a hat over in case someone might lose the chance to see it and smell it. Arthur says he is quick and clever with the pay sheets and register and bagging up, and Saunders—that is responsible—is well satisfied; but I have seen something of this widowed-mother's-only-son idea before now, and it does not carry so far with me as it does with Arthur that the old lady suffers from the rheumatics and that her husband went broke:—and why wouldn't he go broke? I can remember Sidney Snape as one in business at Laverly with a wash-basin and bits of lead pipe coiled, and rolls of wall-paper spread out, in his front parlour window—and a wonderful lot more stored away in the hen-house at back, I've no doubt, if anyone ever guessed—that tendered lowest against me and some others for road drains in that bit of a layout they had there, and got to work so quick for an early Certificate that he had the sewer and manholes and gullies of the first street done and cleared up in no time, all beautifully finished with the falls the wrong way ready for testing and breaking up and doing different. Happened, I went in to have a word with Saunders to-day, and there was Son stretching his ears a bit further out to hear what we were saying—as I could see him, clear enough—and directly I turned, he jumps up and scrambles to the door to open it.

"Good morning, Mr. Grigblay," he says, like as if he was one of these affable floor-walkers at Biggin's drapery.

"You'd better take your cue from the way you see others behave, young man, or the day will come when I shall have to say 'good morning' to you," I said. "I don't want any dancing footmen here," I said, "and I learnt to open a door all by myself when I learnt my name off by heart without any needing to tell it me," I said, "and that was seventy

30

years ago, and I haven't forgotten yet," I said—when what must be but Arthur, just coming in, that heard it and must follow his Dad down the passage to say not upset the young fellow just as he was feeling his feet.

"He'll damn-well feel *my* foot if he don't have a care, my son," I said "A running kick at his behind end is the best cure to keep him out of hospital at Wandsworth or Wormwood Scrubbs," I said, and gave a nod that made Arthur to stare as I passed along—but there! It makes me sorry seeing things different to Arthur, for it makes him unhappy; but what can I do other than just take a hand on the quiet to help keep things straight, and drop a gentle hint now and again?

## A LESSON FOR ARTHUR

The contract from the Gas Company is a fine bit of work by Art's dear old friend P. J. Parkin, Esq., A.E.S., for P. J. Parkin's dear old friend Art. I covered our Tender with a letter setting out what we included for and what we did not include for—which is why we came out lowest, without a doubt—but it seems Mr. Friendly Parkin didn't think to read it! However, I rang up and asked could I see the Manager about signing the contract, and, lo and behold! there was a board meeting Thursday, and would I please very kindly be so obliging as to attend at 3.30 p.m.? So I took Arthur along to see the fun and make his innocent young eyes to stare a bit, and a nice hole we should have been in if I had not taken charge, as he sees now clear enough.

All the Directors were there: Mr. Treadwell, Chairman, in his white beard with the coffee stains it always has; Mr. Prudnor, Secretary, now quite well of his operation and pink in the cheeks with it; Mr. Bonor; Mr. Percy Turner; Mr. Viner, the Grocer and Provisions—that I had a word with about the ham he sent round last week and he said he would inquire; and Mr. Friendly Parkin, sitting and biting his nails by reason of what Arthur said aside to him as we came in—and I should not wonder.

Well, there we all were, sitting cosy round the table with tea getting ready at the side; and two of them with their keys for Prudnor to unlock the seal brought from the safe; and the agreement, Conditions, Spec. and Drawings all laid out. So then I just asked a little question, and that was: had anyone thought to read the letter pinned on our Tender, by any of those queer chances that will come about now and again when no-one expects?—only I didn't put it quite that way. On that Prudnor says to Friendly: "I handed you the tenders as received, Mr. Parkin," and Friendly P. says, Oh, yes, he thinks he remembers there was a letter, and off he goes to get it; and then we had a pleasant chat about all these gas-oven suicides lately—and I asked how much they read on the meter, which none seemed to know—till Friendly came back with the letter, and Prudnor read it out aloud while I gave Art a nudge to have him take notice. Next the Chairman says:

"I should like to ask the Company's Engineer why this letter was not before the Board at the time the tenders were considered?"

The Company's Engineer did not seem quite to know the answer to that one; but said that the letter was of no consequence as he was satisfied the face would stand without any shoring necessary, by what he heard tell of the tank built seventeen years ago 45 feet deep, but this new one only 33 feet by the telescopic gas-holder it is to take; and he was

32

satisfied there would not be any water met with; and satisfied there were no old foundations below, as the site had never been built on, for certain.

"So you recommend the Company should enter into this Contract?" says Treadwell.

"Oh, yes, certainly," says Parkin.

"Satisfactory to you?" says Treadwell, looking under his spectacles down the table at me and Arthur with his beard pointing at us.

"Quite," I said.

"Well, then we are all agreed, I think," says Treadwell, pointing his beard round at them in turn with his eyebrows raised to catch their nods; and so we proceeded to sign, seal and deliver, Mr. Friendly Parkin being too well-pleased at escaping awkward questions to tell his employers that if all tenders had been priced with the limits of liability I had fixed in our letter, a much lower one might have been had—as it certainly would. Also, in my letter I wrote:—"Day-work to be charged time and material at prices to be agreed," but neither Parkin, nor any other, pointed out that the Schedule of Prices ought to be settled *before* contract signed, and it was no part of my business to tell them; so now, if any daywork is necessary, they will have to pay at the rates we think well to charge.

While my letter was being typed and the words put in the agreement to attach it, we had tea and hot toast and plum cake and cigars served—all paid for out of the gas and no cost to anyone—and a nice chat; for they are all friendly to me by long acquaintance, and pleased they were going to get a good job with no trouble, and not a scamped one by any chance—and Parkin along with the rest, no doubt.

"So you see," I said to Arthur, coming away, "your friendly young friend would have put us in a hole, first start off, if I hadn't made safe and pushed him in instead," I said. "The Company's Engineer won't like to have to pass a big account for daywork extras up the table if it happens that that great eighty foot excavation has some surprises brought to light before we finish," I said.

Arthur was properly polite to me about it as he had ought to be, but there! all just for a little thing that might happen any week in the year! Fred Bloggs would be up on his hind legs soon as ever he put on his spectacles to spell out the Specification, but Art noticed nothing amiss—which is one of the ways old heads are better than young, now and again.

## TROUBLE WITH DRAINS

Here is Arthur has managed to get on to the wrong side of Bargate, Surveyor to the Urban District Council, for a change! who has written in a pretty stiff style, for him, in answer to the letter Arthur sent when we had notice the drains at the School were not passed by reason of losing water. Arthur made a mistake earlier on, before drains were covered in, by complaining to Bargate because that new assistant of his, Cornshaw by name, refused to pass them. He is an obliging young fellow, dancing attendance, as he does, to help us along, with nothing lacking but a bit of experience; and Arthur could have easy proved to him, with a little patience, that the ⅜ in. drop at manholes, under the test, was due to absorption and nothing else, and had no call to make complaint to Bargate—and so I told him at the time. Well, now, after covering in, there is real trouble at last by three of the five lengths of drain being fractured, it seems; and it makes me ill, with the trouble we've had before by careless filling in and punning cracking the joints, and Tolpenny in charge, too! So there we are, and have got to uncover more than 100 yards four foot down—most of it—to find where the faults are; and—in case we should not have enough to do—part is overlaid by the foundations for the playground and will have to be broken up! Arthur is down on Tolpenny for that, too; but I tell Art it's no good being heavy on Tol: we are behind time and Tolpenny has been pressing on all he knows, like we told him, and we can't blame him because he did not hold back and wait till Cornshaw had passed the drains. Cornshaw would have managed it a week earlier if Arthur hadn't made him sore by his complaint; and now young Art has upset Bargate by complaining of Cornshaw keeping us waiting! I never had any trouble with Bargate myself all these long years I have known him; for if he's strict with one he's strict with all, and he is bound by the Bye-laws just as us that build are. I tell Arthur that when a Municipal Surveyor is educated with letters after his name—as they all are nowadays, in a general way—and knows his business, and is a straight clean fellow like Mr. Bargate, he ought to make a fuss over him the same as if he was some dear old Auntie he had expectations from. There's no way of getting round if Bargate stands in the way: you've got to do what he says and stand aside and wait with your hat in your hand till he gives you leave. Well, I'll take an early chance to see Bargate and put things straight with him, for I wouldn't have him rattled on any account after the many times he has gone out of his way to help me along.

# A PARTICULAR JOB

Now here, come to-day, are the Form of Tender and Bills of Quantities of Belhampton; as tricky a thing as ever I saw, with little bits of all sorts—gilding on stone, silvered bronze, different marbles from all over, and odds and ends I never heard tell of before. Old Tinge is the Quantity Surveyor, and that's good seeing, for his Provisions are always full; but some of the Labours I don't know what they mean! What's "circular skew face twice sunk moulded on diagonal" and "do. but square on return", in Mason? and what's "ft. run Spanish mouldings $1\frac{3}{4}$ in, girt out of solid three times mitred chevrons to panels of mahogany doors"? What Mr. Spinlove has been at this time I can't make a guess till I see the Spec. and drawings. I shall get Spedder, of Bright & Spedder, the Quantity Surveyors, to price out and take care of us. It's not the sort of job to get in a mess with or we shall never get out again. I will give a straight tender, as I promised Mr. Spinlove I would do; but there are three against us, and, like enough, we shall be cut out by one of these big organizations—"Byldquyk" or another—that can swallow a job the size of this one without tasting it scarcely.

It will be best I go down to the Castle with Spedder—which is pretty much of a ruin by what I make of it—after we have seen the drawings; and then there are references to the gentleman's house where he is now living—Tallon's Dyke, in Hants—for patterns of this, that and the other; so it looks as though we ought to visit there, as well, as it lies on the way to the site—a queer style to set about things, for certain, but it's a very particular job as I can see well enough. Sir Ezra Gotsnitz, Bart., is, I hear, Chairman of the Gotsnitz Multiple Dry Stores, Ltd., that there was all that shouting about in the papers a while back; and it seems as though he had so much money he don't know the best way to spend it without Mr. Spinlove, or another shows him how to:—w.c.s lined with Rouge Garonne, and lavs. dished in Welsh Agate that we used (Gosby & Son, Sub. Contractors) in Mr. Spinlove's Chapel at Westminster Cathedral, and is like green bottle-glass and near as hard. Three baths to be brought from Tallon's Dyke weigh seven and a half tons and are likely jasper or alabaster; and the Provisions make it look that the taps are to be gold-plated with perhaps a few diamonds and rubies, top of the screw-downs, to show them off! Well, we shall know a bit more later on.

## THE VICAR IN NEED

I came near to laughing right out in his face before I knew, when I met our good vicar to-day, that stopped me by St. Andrew's Crescent in the worried, undecided way he has, and hawed and hummed and then said he had quite decided it was most desirable to set about doing some more building at St. Andrew's, and he thought perhaps best to make a beginning by speaking to me, first, as I had always been such a good friend to the Church in times of need and anxiety; and he looked up and down the Crescent and didn't seem to care much about a grocer's boy with a basket on his arm coming along; and appeared to think better of what he was going to say; and then began, fresh, about the difficulty of collecting the money wanted, and could I tell him how much it would cost, exactly?

I said I would have a try at making a rough guess if it was a small matter and he would say what was wanted so that I could measure the existing, settle what best to be done, and run out quantities and estimate of cost. On that he looks over his shoulder and round about to be sure no-one would overhear, and says he wants to make the vestry more convenient because things are very inconvenient the way they are now; and how that the Archdeacon has said it will not do to ask the Bishop to come to dedicate the new roof unless things are made different: "And the Bishop means more than a hundred and fifty pounds at least!" he says, with his eyes wide open at me, "and perhaps a lot more!" he says. When I asked what did he want done to the vestry? he came closer up, so as to be more secret, and said there was added convenience necessary; and when I said "what sort of convenience?" he looked at me and I saw he meant a w.c., but ashamed to say it out loud in the open! I could have told him a few less shy words if he had asked me—but there! A grown man over forty years of age and not able to own up to a w.c.!

Our late Vicar, Mr. Hillary Benson, now retired these six years to a bath-chair at Penzance and whose Church-warden I was for fourteen, was a very different sort; and it's just this—that our good Mr. Peebles frets at not being a gentleman in blood like the other; and is always thinking how best to behave the way he thinks a gentleman would do, and so is never sure what he'd better say next; but that does not prevent him wheedling money out of those who haven't got any, as well as out of those that have.

He won great fame—and preferment to St. Andrew's as well, like enough—by buying the land and building a church at Cobartney, where he was Curate-in-Charge; and he collected such a wonderful lot by fourpence here and two-and-ninepence there, that in no more than only eleven years he had come very near to paying off the debt. First thing, when he came here, he had it in big print in the Parish magazine—"PROPOSED MEMORIAL TO OUR BELOVED LATE VICAR", and went on how delighted everyone would be to know that the proposal had been made, et cetera: and, of course, it had to be supported and carried through with old Mr. Benson reading the Parish Magazine in his

38

bathchair each month, and seeing the list of subscribers and how many shillings and half-crowns they had given since last time, so that he could keep count and know how much he was beloved and who loved him the most.

Happened, I met Richard Trundell, the carver, in the way of business, that belonged to this place and knew Mr. Benson who had helped him along when he was a lad. I told him of the memorial font-cover proposed, and he said he would like to make it and present to the Church, and would I give Mr. Peebles the message to see if it was acceptable—and very handsome and neat it looks with its gilt counterpoise and all. When I told the Vicar, he stared in front and looked worried and began biting the side of his finger, not knowing what to say next, by appearance.

"A considerate thing of Mr. Trundell to do, don't you think, Mr. Peebles?" I said. "He hasn't been to the place for nearly twenty years," I said.

"Oh, most, most," he says. "Do you think he would give a screen for the baptistry arch, also?"

Well, that took me aback and no mistake, for I didn't know our Vicar at that time; and he didn't ease off with the subscriptions, either. He had Mr. Ramsden make him a silver ewer, with great polished garnet for thumb-hold, that cost £67 and is now kept there on a chain, like it might be some dog, in case anyone should have a mind to run off with it; and tarnished all colours, soon as cleaned, by leak of coke-fumes up the grating. The next—in case he should get out of practice begging money—was the roof wanting to be done new, though the Church has not been built above a hundred years or so, I dare say, for all it is starting to come to pieces the same as if it had been standing three hundred.

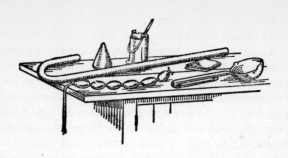

## WAYS AND MEANS

We had been used to go up on top most years, by the old trouble of the clever new-invented Gothic Architects of a hundred years ago knowing such a lot more than any tradesman could tell them, and making the slope nice and steep to throw off the water quickly in case any should lie too long; and also laying the lead in beautiful long, pretty strips, so as it would expand easy down the slope when the sun got on it, and stretch away from its fixings—instead of contracting up the slope—when it went off so as to be a bit further down ready for a new start next time; but all very slow and gradual so that the lead would not tear away to let in water till the Architect was buried and out of the way, and his name carved up "R.A." in gold letters at the Royal Institute of British Architects.

I told our Mr. Peebles the roof would stay twenty years with a bit of attention now and again, but "Oh, No, No! Better renew at once. Must uphold the fabric. Cheaper in the long run"—so he went on and carried the Council with him; and then it was: could he look to me, that had been such a very kind and valued friend of St. Andrew's all these many years past, to lend my aid to see him through his troubles?

Well, of course, I was Vicar's Churchwarden fourteen

years and Sidesman before that—as I am still—and have attended to upkeep and repairs at the Church as long as I can remember, almost; and I offered to do all, and charge only the prime cost. I don't know what he expected, but he didn't seem to think much of that, as though I was giving only what cost me nothing! I should have pleased him better, and saved my pocket as well, to have charged the fifteen per cent overhead and profit, and put my name down for £250 subscription:—but that was not the end of it.

After we had stripped the roof; made good where rot had started; put in new troughs with proper falls and cesspits, and relaid; there was the account, £2,342—which was a bit more than I had made a guess it would be by the tarpaulins to maintain, and the men coming off and on to suit his church services, and dodging the weather, and loss marketing the old lead; and so there he was wringing his hands at me—as if it was my fault!—with: "Oh dear, oh dear, whatever is to be done!" whenever I met him. By the end of two years he had paid £1,900 odd—mostly in driblets—and didn't know however he would find all the rest; and then he started, in extra big letters, "FOR MR. GRIGBLAY," in the Parish Magazine; and "Urgent appeal to wipe off this heavy burden": with list of latest subscribers: "Mothers' Union (Special Eastertide Effort), 11s. 7d. St. Andrew's Boys' Brigade (Second Offering), 5s. 4d.," and all the rest of it.

Well, reading this every month didn't agree with me any too well as I am not in the money-lending myself; nor yet one of these terrible sad cases of the deserving poor; nor yet a decayed gentleman that has seen better days; and the whole thing made me a bit angry for it seemed the game was to sicken me off; so I made up my mind to give him a lesson in better manners, and help him to be a good boy next time, by extracting the last halfpenny off him; and I even got near to telling him he would have to pay me interest on balance outstanding. However, what finished me was the "SPECIAL COLLECTION. ROOF RESTORATION" after morning Service, second Sunday in each month; with me, as Sidesman, holding out the plate for the sixpences and threepennies and coppers saved up for Mr. Grigblay, all to be added together in the Vestry for paying to me later, and me not knowing where to look! I could not face it after the second time, and gave receipt in full; but I had the Vicar print it in the Magazine what my contribution had been (including the 15 per cent knocked off the account), to put things right all round. It was £541. 11s. 2d. exactly; so when His Grace the Lord Bishop of Tanchester comes to dedicate the new roof and help pay off overdraft our Vicar has at the bank, I shall get adequate return made me at last, certain, by being introduced to the Bishop in top hat, et cetera, and my photo in the London evening papers, as well —with a bit of luck; and, the way things are going, if I keep on in the same style until I am sold up, like enough I shall get an O.B.E. after my name and live happy ever after.

Well, Arthur shall look after the new convenience to the Vestry, and a good experience for him to see what *he* can do with our good Vicar! It will tickle me to see how Mr. Peebles puts it in the Parish Magazine when he makes appeal for subscriptions, for it is sure to be "A crying need" or "A long-felt want" to talk about. However, he has learnt better than try his alphabetic list of the Church Workers' Guild again, pinned up in the porch and that went after this style:

| | |
|---|---|
| Miss Ablet | 4s. 6d. |
| Mrs. Badcock | Nothing |
| Mrs. Dormidge | Nothing |
| Miss Druce | £1   1   0 |
| Miss Gradgley | Nothing |
| et cetera | et cetera. |

42

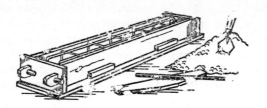

## OBSTRUCTION

Here is Arthur tells me he thinks his friend Parkin looks like a box or two of cigars would please him. "To make your friend a bit more friendly, is it?" I said. Arthur laughs and says he's getting things straightened out to make a start, and just as well keep on the right side of Parkin.

"Well," I said, "that will be all right come Christmas and a bit of pleasantness and conviviality all round; but Christmas is more than two months away," I said, "and your Mr. Friendly will have to play at 'trust' like a dog with a bit of sugar on its nose, for a few weeks," I said.

However, Art. seems a bit bothered by the fellow getting in the way of the arrangements he has in mind—and that's a matter I have got to look into with him when he's ready with his levels, and so on—and all I said to Art. was to stand his friend treat and act up to keep right with him, but not to give any sort of a present or promise of one; and so he gave me his word he would do.

Arthur is all for hiring a Grab and Caterpillar Tractor and Lord knows what else, just for that bit of digging for the Tank! In my belief the boy will never be happy until he gets one of these bricklaying machines; and a machine for cutting his hair and shaving his chin any time he likes to put his head inside and knock over the switch; and another for lacing his boots and blowing his nose—by the look of things! "You're for bringing an elephant to pick up a needle," I said; but he holds to it we shall save cost and time; and he has written for quotes from the Blagdale Excavating Company and two others, so now we shall see! He has got all his levels and everything laid out, and knows what he's about, clear enough; and his chief trouble is his dear old friend Parkin going sour on him and getting in the way to trip him up—for a change—by showing sulky, and not to be bothered to get approval of his Directors for us to stand our lorries out of the way just inside the Company's gates, against the fence, instead of us making our own track right across the field with a gate in, and arranging with Bargate for a draw-in over the footway and having all the bother we had at the Schools over again, by clay falling off the wheels and mucking up and rotting the highway—and how could we help it?

No wonder it made me to open my eyes when I had a look at the petty cash, Wednesday! From what Arthur tells me, it seems he walked into Parkin getting off the train at Victoria, Saturday evening; and they got talking business and had dinner together—all fresh over again—at the Trocadero Restaurant; with oysters to begin, and brandy to their coffee at the finish—which they had forgot to have at home, one o'clock—and cigars, and stalls at the Hippodrome, and supper at Spondini's, and taxis everywhere, and home sweet home at half-past one in the morning, and Arthur paying the lot! Arthur had a word with his friend about our lorries standing, when he was primed full with contentment and other details; and Arthur says he turned huffy; and said he had got us the contract with all risks accepted by the Company, and us to be paid daywork at our own rates for shoring and pumping, and that the more he did for us the more we wanted; and he couldn't go to the Directors, again, with more new proposals to help us, etc. —which is all so much nonsense, as Arthur agrees, for there will be no trouble to the Company by our standing

44

inside the gate, and we will cart away and pay for that lot of clinker they have heaped at the place, and allow value of reduced length of trackway as well; so it's clear enough that Mr. Friendly Parkin is out for a bit of bribery and corruption, as they call it; and with that I'll have nothing to do, nor ever have.

"I'm not going to let a twopenny-halfpenny fellow like that put me wrong," I said to Arthur. "If the Gas Company likes to see their engineer with his legs under their Contractor's table," I said, "I don't mind," I said, "and you can be as friendly with your friend as you think wise to be, and he can have his Christmas-present cigars along with others when the time comes," I said, "but that's all he's going to get," I said. "I've known the Company's Chairman, Mr. Treadwell, along of 'The Hand and Heart' and 'Bulls of Bashan' as long as I can remember,' I told Arthur, "and you can drop a friendly hint to your friend," I said, "to let him know that—however much you would wish to reward him for his kind and charitable actions that deserve he should wear a crown of glory here below without waiting to go up and get it like the rest of us—your old stick-in-the-mud partner—you say to him—is a sly, malicious old devil that will do a dirty thing sooner than a clean—you say —and has ruined many a young man, let alone old ones, long before now, and will do again, certain, if he gets the chance. And you tell your friend," I said, "that your pesky old partner, that had ought to be dead and buried long ago, has the ear of the Company's Directors; and if that old curmudgeon—you say—that never parts with a penny he knows how to keep safe in his pocket, gets any idea that money is being paid other than what could be claimed in an action at law, there will be a rare lot of squawking and uproar, you tell him," I said.

Arthur wrinkled up his forehead and looked properly bothered listening to me; and then he started off saying it

45

was no use following that line, which would only put Parkin's back up, first start off, when we wanted all the help he could give us. There was good sense in that, of course; so I said to Arthur that I would write to the Directors, or go to see Mr. Treadwell on the quiet, and get it sanctioned for us to stand inside the gates; but Art. was up against that, too.

"That idea's no better than the other, Dad," says the boy. "You know as well as I do that the Directors can only refer the question to Parkin. They have no technical knowledge, and are bound to give better attention to his ideas than to ours; and, even if we succeeded in getting what we want, Parkin would be upset at us going behind his back, and make trouble by obstructing and objecting, right from the first, and it would be a fight with him from start to finish."

That was good sense too, in my opinion, and a pleasure it was to see the boy so clear-headed and forcible with it.

"Yes," I said. "It's clear we've got to keep friendly with your Mr. Friendly Parkin." On which Arthur must jump out with:

"Never mind that, Dad. He's a good sort of fellow"—and I had a word or two to say about "good sorts" being, often as not, "bad lots", which he didn't much care about hearing, I dare say; and then, after a bit more talk, it was settled for Arthur to keep at it and stay the right side of Parkin and hold out the carrot in front of the donkey like as if we might perhaps—all well, and who can say?—build him a little house at a nominal charge, but not to make any promises, and to keep me informed just how things went; and, when all was safe finished and settled up, I would step in with: "Hulloa! What's all this?" and learn the dirty fellow where he stood so that he should know better next time and could put it on his gentleman's visiting cards:—"Mr. P. J. Parkin, Esquire, A.E.A. (B)" with the "B" added on in brackets, for "Bilked"—but I didn't say it that way to Arthur, him being a little tender with it all.

46

## GREAT OPPORTUNITY

This Belhampton job will be the most remarkable in all my experience if I live to be a hundred years; and "pretty" no word for it by what I saw of Mr. Spinlove's drawings, and the perspective picture he showed us—all in colour with the landscape painted in like real life—when me and Spedder called at his office, first thing Tuesday, after I had stayed the night at the nice little place Spedder has on Ditton Green.

I had never heard tell of Belhampton Castle before, nor yet had Spedder, and no wonder! When we got there, early in the afternoon, ten miles from Dorchester and the last two along an accommodation road with five gates to open—all to be remade—there was just a farmhouse—now to be pulled down—with a great lot of shabby old barns, cow-houses and stables and all sorts, higgledy-piggledy; with the ground everywhere up and down; and nettles; and a great marshy, stinking pond all trodden mud; and more muck and muddle than ever I saw—though a dirty farm is a profitable farm, as they say: and then, beyond, on far side, there was just the top of a great ruined tower—which is about all there is to call it a castle by except what is covered over and botched in with the farm buildings and not to be seen.

However, when we went out at the side and down in front, we could tell, clear enough, what Mr. Spinlove is after; and such a view of sea and downs as never was: with Saint Alban's Head just poking out East beyond Wey-

47

mouth Bay and Portland; and the whole stretch of Chesil
Beach clear in front; and right away west beyond Burton
Bradstock, to Lyme that was like a little grey smudge laying
there; with the blue sea going out of sight in the distance,
and blue sky with knobbly white clouds floating—enough
to take your breath with the sudden sight of it all.

The great tower stands out on the steep slope of the
down—734 ft. up by the map we had—and, butting on the
side of it is a straight stretch one hundred and seven feet
long carrying the roof of the barn—the level at back being
"made ground" and eighteen feet above—except against
the tower, where twenty feet run, or more, stands high,
with the old battlements carried clear of the wall-face on
great brackets, so that those defending could pour molten
lead and boiling filth on the heads of those thinking to
ladder the wall; and keep it ready, all hot, we may be sure,
in case any *others* should fancy having a try to see what it
felt like, for *their* turn; or the old lot come back again for
more by not getting enough to please them the first time.

Mr. Spinlove is going to carry up the tower to a finish
with a flat roof and telescope-observatory in the centre; and
a great room, forty-one feet diameter, under, with windows
looking all ways; and, on the floor below, it is divided up
for dining-room and service and sitting-room all on same
floor as the bedroom wing, running the length of the
straight bit, which is carried over on brackets—the same as
those carrying the battlement—with roof of Purbeck slabs
butting against the tower. Down below, he has all the offices
and servants' quarters, and this and that; and the great
entrance hall, in the tower, has a staircase, all solid
masonry, that will be a sight to see; and the whole ground
floor opening on the enclosed north side: so there will be
the south front rooted on the slope of the down like a great
grey cliff—ninety feet and ore to parapet of tower, and
near seventy to eaves and sixty to window sills—with the

48

house, except servants etc., at top; and the old surrounding walls at back, three feet and more thick, to be pulled about and made uniform, eighteen feet high measuring from the level of the new courtyard and gardens that are near four acres in extent, and the whole place not far short of half a mile to walk round on the outside of the walls, in my judgment.

One of the three "bastion towers"—as they call them—is to be the gatekeeper's lodge; which is where the guard always was, without doubt, for bits of the old gateway—to be restored back—are there; and the other bastions are for garden houses. Mr. Spinlove has barred openings here and there in the surround wall to look out by; and the spring, where the pond now is, made to serve for water supply and a great swimming pool also, with the overflow to run out through the walls into a kind of dell—now all cow-slop and duck-feathers—where he has cascades and rock-and-water-gardens and all sorts; so that, what with a skittle alley and badminton, squash-rackets and lawn tennis courts and a kind of gymnasium affair; and electric panel-heating; ventilation with air-conditioning boosters; Turkish bath, water-softening, lift, electric plant with power plugs everywhere, and organ and cinema projector, and a garage with hydraulic jack:—it will be hard to say what has been left out that had ought to be in, unless it is an aerodrome; or a cable railway from top of the tower so that the gentleman and his lady friends can easy go bathing in the sea when they want—and a very beautiful sight it would be, and not to be missed:—the gentlemen and ladies travelling high in the air in a cage, with their sunshades and naked backs and gramophone-music and shouting and cocktail-shaking and all.

## A FRIENDLY RECEPTION

Me and Spedder stayed the night at Dorchester for calling at the gentleman's other house on our way home; and next day we got off the train at Brockenhurst to see the gentleman's house, Tallon's Dyke, and hired a car and went seven miles, and up a long drive banked up each side with rhododendron shrubs, till, all of a sudden round a bend, there it was close to—a long, low house with no end to it, standing on high ground backing against pine woods and looking south over great terraced gardens across the Solent to Yarmouth, with the Needles and Osborne to right and left. It is built of Bastingstoke facings below, and the first storey solid quartered oak timbering, with fancy nogging, and pierced and carved bargeboards everywhere all weathered silver colour. There are great fancy chimneys—spiral, octagonal fluted-faced and moulded, all in special-mades—running up clear above the trees; the work, sixty years ago, of Mr. Norman Shaw, and one of the great things he is known by, I understand—and small wonder, too! We reached there a bit before twelve, and, by a big motor standing at the front, thought best go round to the trades' entrance, where was a great garage yard with four or five chauffeurs and washers at work, and a fellow like a

50

naval officer, with his jacket unbuttoned and smoking a cigar, that seemed the boss of them.

The back door was standing open on a wonderful dirty passage with a stink of sinks and nastiness that was surprising; and, after we pushed the bell, a slut with her hair in a mess put her head out of a side-door to know what we wanted; and, just when Spedder had told her, a fellow in sooty overalls—just been inside the flues to clean them, by appearances—came out by a door further along; so the slut beckoned him, and we told him all over again, fresh, and he sloped off down to the end of the passage and pushed a door covered in green baize with brass nailings, and then a tall fellow came through in silk breeches and stockings and dancing shoes, with a tailed coat sewn in braid and buttoned over; and great silk ropes and tassels hanging across his chest that had come off the window curtains to loop them back—by appearances. This fellow came up close and looked over our heads at something across the yard while Spedder said it over again; and soon as curtain-tassels had seen all he wanted, he jerked his head sideways for us to follow, and we went along through the baize door into a dingy kind of inner hall with the back stairs going off, where another tasselled dude—spit and image of the other—was hanging forward in a chair with his hands dangling between his legs, grieving over something—by the look of things; and a tall, portly gentleman in evening dress with starched front, white tie and two medals on, was standing in an open doorway to the left.

I had a surprise, and no mistake, when he stepped forward, but couldn't for the moment, recognize who he was; and then he smiled, and it was Henry Curt, Louisa's cousin, that I had not seen half a dozen times since our wedding thirty-three years ago, and not set eyes on for over thirty; for we lost all patience with the fellow, then turned sixteen, with his swagger and lah-de-dah, and " Me and the Princess were driving in the park, Thursday," and all the rest of his nonsense—as if he was one of the Royal Family himself, just by being a Tiger, as they call it, to sit back of the young Royal Highness's dogcart with arms folded across his chest, dressed up with pink turnovers to his top boots and a cockade to his tall hat. He thought all the women were mashed on him, and he couldn't stomach chaff; so when I said it was time a smart young fellow like him had ought to try for a promotion with feathers to his hat, and he asked "What?" and I said: "The job of a dressed-up monkey sitting to crack nuts on an organ," it didn't please the young man any too well, and we saw no more of him. He was going to be head of Buckingham Palace by his own accounts; but he didn't get there, nor yet to be King of England. I heard of him first as valet to some great lord; and, after, as butler to the Marquess of Brandt, and I had no idea he had shifted; and now here he was! a big yellow fellow with his waistcoat buttons straining to hold up his belly; and two chins arrived and a third on the way; and his front hair gone right back over the horizon. However, he was glad to see me, and friendly and affable with it though a bit haughty in his slow style of behaviour. He asked a lot of questions about me and the girls and Louisa—that was; and nothing would do but he must show us over, himself, before the gentleman came back, and that we should stay dinner; and he gave one of the tasselled fellows a nod to go off and see about it.

## A GENTLEMAN'S HOUSE

We went through the house, and a rich place it is with all the new improvements—marble columns, carving and gilding everywhere; ceilings painted all clouds and fairies —naked, or near to—skirmishing about with tambourines and fiddles and pink ribbons; and the walls the same, some of them. Spedder checked over with the Bills while I talked to Henry about old times. He shook his head when I asked was he married? and said he "saw enough of 'em without" —just like his old swagger. He said he parted with the Marquess eight years back as he didn't like the way things were, with the family growing up.

"I heard tell of a play, *Lord Richard in the Pantry*," he says, "but I had Lord Richard and Lord Ernest and Lord Alfred and Lady Rachel and half a dozen more of them and their friends in *my* pantry," he says, "me financing their bridge debts," he says, "and getting up at three in the morning to find sandwiches and sausages and beer for them, and the tips left out," he says; and so he told the Lady he couldn't stay with it, and he called her "the old cow", which didn't seem to me a polite name to call a Marchioness by!

He took me into the gentleman's bedroom—which was all got ready for the lying in state of the Shah of Persia, by what I could make of it—and then into his dressing-room and into a room opening off it, all built round with wardrobes, with a fellow brushing and folding at a table, and a younger to stand by and look on at him; and, beyond, was a room with a great cloth over the floor that went up to the ceiling when Henry pressed a button; and there you saw the gentleman's boots all laid out in alleys—dozens and dozens of them, all the kinds one could think of and others besides. By another door from the dressing-room, was his toilet; with a bidet and weighing machine, and electric "liver-joggler"—Henry called it—and couch for masseur, and marble slab for shampooer, and a Turkish bath affair to sit with your head out and sweat when you had a mind to it. I never saw the like of it in all my days, with the marble walls, and floor patterned in marble slabs with mats about; and the ceiling painted gloss black; and electric-light gadgets, all special-made, that never were before. The bath

53

was a solid marble block—by what I could see—with three steps down, all Siena, or similar to; and a shower with sitz, plunge, and douche, built up solid, at the end. Along the side, in niches, were flasks with liquid soap and bath crystals and all sorts; and, set in the middle, a great cut-glass bottle, like in a chemist's front window, to hold three gallons and more, half full, with a bluey shine in the liquor; and, when I asked, Henry said "Florida water", which is a kind of eau-de-Cologne, by what I can make of it.

"He'll put near the whole of that lot in to-night," says Henry. "Would you like some to try it?"

Well, that was a new idea to me, but Henry says: "Oh, that's nothing; he tried milk a couple of years back, but didn't like the skin that came on it; and if not hot he didn't like that, so milk is off," says Henry, "and a good job, too, or I should be off," he says. This is one of the baths to go away to Belhampton; and Henry says it is because he fancies a silver one, gilt, to keep the heat—as if no-one could ever tell that marble stays cold, without fitting up to try it, first!

According to Henry, Belhampton is wanted just for him to take his friends to Weymouth in the Turbine Yacht he has lying at Lymington, so that there is a place for them to go ashore to when they get there.

"And the half of us will have to go too," says Henry, "and that will be the time for me to step off," he says, "and start a nice little hotel at Brighton or some other flash place, for I like my home comforts and don't care for racketing from one place to another," he says.

He took me down to his own quarters, built out one side of a back passage, with a nice little sitting-room, and bedroom off it with great safes built in along one side, and windows barred. He pushed aside a picture of a racehorse, head of the bed, and, lo and behold! it was a recess behind, with a magazine pistol laying.

"The old toad will have it so; but he doesn't know it isn't loaded," says Henry; which didn't seem to me a polite fashion of speaking, with one of the flunkeys standing by to hear him. "The gentleman who was here before me slept in along with the sinks where the safes were," Henry says; "but I've had enough of that before, and I had him to add on; so now the plate has to be carried across from the pantry." He opened one safe, and there was a solid gold service of forty covers, with casters, and flagons and epergnes and candelabra and a gold statue of a pretty young naked girl with bow and arrow shooting at you; and barbed oyster forks, as well, with a great pearl set in the handles. "A jeweller's job to keep in order," Henry says.


## THE OWNER APPEARS

When we went to the back hall, after, there was a motor horn outside; and then a queer noise of screaming and squawking came in at the window.

"Not the right time of year for the peacocks to be calling out," I said.

"There are no peacocks," Henry says. "It's him talking to the gardeners."

He made a motion to the pair in tassels and followed them through into the front hall; and then put his arm across for me to stand back, and went forward to the middle while the other two waited each side of the entrance. Then the double-hung doors were swung back and the gentleman came in—about forty-five; average height; a bit thick in figure, but quick and alert, with big brown eyes and shaven blue on a yellowish face; and with black hair, a little frizzy front of his ears, and a bit the look of a ram about him. He had small feet in buttoned patents, and little plump hands with a diamond ring; and there was a jewelled tiepin—big as a brooch, pretty near—in his black satin stock:—not the sort I would take for a Baronet, I will confess. He handed his hat and umbrella, one each side, to the flunkeys, and Henry helped him off with his overcoat that was lined astrakhan to show on his collar and sleeves. As he turned he saw me and asked of Henry, who answered him; and then he called across to me, quick and sharp:

"Have you begun yet?"

"Well, we're just seeing about making a start," I said.

"I told Mr. Spinlove I wanted it begun at once—understand? It's got to be finished by July the 1st: the Prince of Monaco is coming to stay with me. It must be finished by July the 1st—understand? Understand?" and off he went out at the other end with the flunkeys, side by side, on his heels, without waiting for me to answer him; and another with curtain-tassels, I had not seen before, was standing to open the door for him. This one came and took his coat off Henry's arm like it was a baby to be baptized.

"Now for dinner," says Henry. "Quarter to one is my time. He has his lunch at half-past, but a bit later to-day with the doctor waiting to see him."

"What's wrong with him?" I asked.

"Nothing that I know of," says Henry. "Sir Ramsden Scatterley comes from Wimpole Street every Thursday week to test his blood pressure and his water and his heart and all the rest of his inside works, and stays, lunch, to talk it all out and say what his chances are. Seventy guineas for telling him to have tapioca pudding to his breakfast! Wish I could earn such easy money," says Henry; and when I asked how he came to be made Baronet—"Bought it," says Henry, which does not agree with my ideas of such things, I must say.

56

# THE BUTLER ENTERTAINS

Spedder, who had seen all he wanted, was waiting at the back; and we went to a comfortable room where was a very genteel lady—"Mrs. Brewster" by the name Henry introduced her—who was near to being Royal blood herself by the style she talked of the great people she knew all about, and the kind of hair-grease they used, and what the ladies had on underneath, et cetera. It was a first-class dinner, I will say, with one thing after another; from soup to a frothy kind of cheese pudding, and grapes to finish, and coffee and cream after. Henry asked us what we'd take, and went off himself to bring a bottle of Hock that he said was A1; but a bit salty to my taste. Mrs. Brewster sipped at a glass; but Henry took nothing and, when I asked "Why not?" gave a couple of slaps on his stomach and says "Gas", which made Mrs. Brewster to pull her shoulders back with "You forget a lady is present, Mr. Curt," at which Henry tipped me a wink on the sly.

We had to get along to catch our train, and I said to Henry that it would be impossible to get finished for Belhampton to be occupied by July the 1st; but Henry says— "Oh, you mustn't pay any attention to him. There's no Prince going to stay with us; President of the Cat's Meat, more likely," and then, passing the telephone in the back hall, he seemed to notice something and picked up and smiled, and held out to me, and said: "He's on now if you want to hear him."

I scarcely knew who it was till I took hold and there was his quick, snappy voice—"You stupid ass!" and he hung up.

"Who was he talking to?" I asked.

Henry shrugged. "His architect, maybe."

"Mr. Spinlove wouldn't allow it," I said. "Does he talk to you that style?"

Henry began to joggle up and down, which is his way of laughing, and waggled his head at me; and a tasselled beauty that had come after with a great basket, grins at me and says with a side-nod at Henry: "He knows a bit too much!"

Henry took the basket and handed it to me with: "Here you are; something to remember us by;" and, when I looked under the napkin on top, there it was full of grapes, and a great pine, and, actually, a chip basket of strawberries and another of peaches, and it near the middle of October! There was a champagne bottle as well, but Henry says:

"Not fizz. That's the Florida Water for you to try."

I felt a bit shy with it, especially when I asked about the basket and the napkin and he said: "That's all right; you needn't bother."

Our car-driver had had his dinner in the servants' hall, and there he was! all red in the face with it and none too steady on his legs, and all surly in his manner as well.

Henry was very friendly saying he would come and look us up some time, and see the girls and the little boys, standing the while in the doorway all dressed up with his medals on, with the flunkey to shut us in, just like any lord might behave, and one of the most surprising things, in its way, that has come under my notice. Spedder said the same, and I gave one or two pounds out of the Muscatels to him to take home, which he fancied above the Hamburgs.

I must say it made me surprised to see the sort of gentleman we have got this time, for I am not one to put up with such an ugly style of behaviour; and by what I know of Mr. Spinlove, he would not pass it over for a moment, either; but as he has managed to get the plans settled to please the gentleman, perhaps we shall manage the same for building.

## THE CASHIER HAS SOMETHING TO SAY

I have not felt like going across to the office after the long days with Spedder, and was kept properly fidgety by a letter handed in by Saunders, marked "Private and Confidential" that he would call, on chance, to see me, quiet, after dark; for, though he is a silly, chicken-headed fellow, that is not the sort of message anyone would ask to get from his cashier! He was shown in after supper, with his hat twisting about in his hands, and started to apologize for troubling me.

"You should have thought of that before, and waited to see me at the office, if that's how you feel about it," I said; for he makes me impatient with his shilly-shally.

"Oh!" he says, looking startled at me. "But I thought best to see you, private, so as no one should know," he says.

"Well, put down your hat, and there's a chair, and let's hear what it's all about," I said. So he lays his hat on the floor, and makes to point with his behind at the very edge of the chair, as though he was too polite to put it fairly on; and then he must lean forward to be nearer, till the chair tips up and nearly lands him on the floor—as if he had changed his mind, of a sudden, and had an idea to say me his prayers, instead.

"Here! Hold up!" I said. "What's the matter with you to-night? What does it all mean?" I said, being a bit nervous at the way he was carrying on. So then it all came out, and he told me that someone had been monkeying with the

Kitty—eighteen pence a fortnight ago, and now a bob missing.

"You and your Kitty!" I said—being made all hot by the scare he had given me, with no reason. "You ought to know by this time that the Kitty is *your* affair and no concern of mine," I said, "and if you can't make do with the pound you had for a private float, first start off, with nothing to do but just square with the auditors once a year, you've got to make good yourself, or we shall have to fetch away the mangle and the stair rods, or the new drawing-room curtains, to strike a balance," I said. "You never hear of Lloyd's, or the National Provincial, or Bank of England calling out about their Kitties," I said; "and you know well enough that when a bank clerk hands over half a crown in mistake for a florin; or two notes stuck together instead of one; or a few pounds too much by the sponge they wet their fingers with, counting, being on the dry side, it is *you* that have made the mistake. No bank cashier ever makes a mistake, as you know well enough. They balance up exact to the penny, every time, without running about like so many loose dogs yapping about their Kitties"; I said, "and you'd better take and turn a new leaf, and let me hear no more of *your* Kitty," I said.

He told me he had it hid away in his lock-up drawer with a note-book to keep tally.

"Well," I said, "if it doesn't suit to keep it in the safe, and you can't keep it in your lock-up drawer with a tally; you'd better keep it in your pocket without a tally," I said. "And if you can't keep safe in your pocket by having holes in it, you'd best ask your wife to sew them, and not come running to me, all hours, every time a sixpence or a three-penny slips down the leg of your trousers," I said.

He looked rather sick with it all, sitting there; and the corner of his moustache began twitching up and down, by him having no proper bone in his back—as they say. However, I felt I had been a bit rough with him by getting rattled, so I asked him how it all was—for he is a careful, exact fellow that goes running along, year in and year out, like some tram that can't turn aside off the rails if it wants. And then he made me so wild and angry at him as I never was with anyone before; and I came over all red in the face by the blood rising, and felt near dropping with it, when he told me he had suspicion it was young Syd had somehow managed to help himself—that good, clean little lad that is the son of Bert Wallace, who was my leading foreman mason seventeen years—till he crocked up—and the whole family proud, decent folk, and doing well. I put the little chap in with Saunders to do office-boy, and messages, and sticking down the bags, for a start. My word, but I let Saunders have it all right; I don't know when I've been so worked up.

"It's damned lucky for you, my man," I said, "that you came in time for me to tell you that the first I hear of a word of suspicion against young Sydney Wallace out you go as fast as I can get my hand on your collar to run you across the yard and kick you into the road," I said, "and no going-away party with 'For he's a jolly good fellow', and a pretty silk umbrella with silver band and your name engraved, *I* promise," I said.

"Here's this proper little pink, wholesome lad, all cocked up with his modest self-respect and respect for his elders and ambition to do well by them, that is just starting out in life, full of belief in right things—yes, I've watched the way the boy carries himself," I said; "and you'd break his heart, and dirty the soul that looks out of his brave, happy eyes, with your lumbering stupidity that understands no further than any bullock in a field would do, and all because of your fumbling and muddling with your damned shillings and halfpence," I said.

"You ought to know by this time," I said, "that the first

step to making a thief out of a little innocent like that boy, is to suspect him of being one. And what will his father say? If I know Bert Wallace right, he'll heave himself out of his chair and come on his crutches and knock your silly block off," I said, "and a damned good job if he did do, and I'd travel ten miles to be there in time to see him," I said. "Don't you dare ask that boy so much as one question," I said, "for he'll see you don't believe him, and that is the first step to making a liar of him. I would have thought better of you, Saunders—of your heart and your head," I said. "You! A grown married man with young ones of your own—if they are both girls!" I said. And there he was, sitting and looking as if he might start off blubbering any minute! He is so weak and sloppy away from his figure-columns that he has no mind of his own, scarcely.

Then, no sooner had I said a quiet word to cheer him up than, lo and behold! if he wasn't ready actually to start off again with the reason why he had thought Sydney to be the one! but I stopped him pretty quick.

"If you've got so much to say as hurts to keep bottled up inside your pudding head that's only fit for boiling and throwing in the dustbin soon as finished," I said, "you'd better talk it into the hairy ear of the next jackass that claims acquaintance; and take good care there is no one overhears, or it will be a black day for you, Saunders," I said:—and I do not remember when I have ever been so talkative, being full of my feelings at the time and fair sweating with it, so that I had to go up after and change my shirt.

Saunders waited to see if there was any more coming to him, and then got on to his legs very cautiously, so as to be sure he wouldn't do it any way wrong, and began twisting his hat about for a chance to say good evening; but I had him sit down again by an idea coming into my head—as well as not forgetting the rumpus we had twenty years ago by that pilfering scamp, Lupmann, setting everyone by the ears—and that was remembering the new assistant Saunders has by Arthur's choice, Oswald Snape, that I do not like the cut of. So, after a bit of thought, I said to Saunders to keep on just the same as he had done; and give no sign of anything noticed; and say no word to anyone, but let me know, private, how things kept. Saunders said he had not dropped a hint to any—as I fully credit; and I said I would let Mr. Arthur know how things were—which I shall remember very careful to forget to do, for the fewer there are mixing up clever ideas in a business of this kind, the fewer sleepless nights and grey hairs there will be in the world.

## CHECK TO THE GAS ENGINEER

Here is a lucky thing happened, which just shows how matters will come about when you don't expect! Arthur, it seems, has been dancing round his friend Parkin and skirmishing and wagging his tail and wriggling his back with his tongue hanging out, like he might be some dog with his master; and yesterday, as things chanced, he came on Parkin at the very place, inside the Company's gates, where we want leave to stand our lorries. However, Friendly Parkin was all sulky in his manner, and saying the Directors do not allow any traffic, other than their own, inside; and how it was no good Arthur going on at asking, because it was already settled against him—as though Parkin had asked the Directors and got a refusal, when he had not asked and did not mean to ask, either!

Just then, who should come to pass out, but the Company's Chairman, Mr. Treadwell, walking out of the office, all cheerful and smiling—like enough because it is just given out the gas is to go up a penny, next month. He stopped to have a word with Arthur. "Arranging to make a start with your contract?" he says. Arthur replied to him— "Yes," he was; and how at that very moment he was asking leave of Mr. Parkin for us just to stand our lorries up at the side, out of the way, against the fence, after carting away and paying for the clinker heaped, so as to start the sooner and get finished the quicker.

"Certainly! Oh, certainly!" says Treadwell. "There's the watchman to open the gate early as you like, and you won't be in our way," he says. "My regards to Mr. Grigblay," and off he goes.

So, now, Parkin has got to make the best of it; and Arthur says he pretends to be glad on our account and quite agreeable to help us—as though he had not been playing his own dirty game to spoke our wheel and have us to grease him! Arthur says Parkin has never dropped a word about our offer to allow the value of the reduced length of trackway; so it seems Parkin means to make us a present of that bit so as to qualify for the sleight of hand with packets of notes which he is getting ready for, by appearances. I told Arthur to notify the omission directly he had occasion to claim an extra, and so blight the young man's budding hopes, first chance. Arthur seems to think better not, but rather let it wait over till final settlement of account. He says Parkin will think he is holding it over us that he can claim the omission, and that that will help to keep him contented. Well, I'm glad Arthur is beginning to see the hang of things, so let the boy do what he likes with his friend; but not a penny is he going to profit from us, and I have Arthur's word there shall be no hanky-panky with the fellow, for I have set my face against that sort of thing, since the beginning, and have never had anything to do with it, first to last, and so I will continue as long as I keep going.

64

## AN IMPORTANT MATTER

Spedder came down to-day with the Belhampton Bills he has priced, for me to settle our Tender; for there is no time to spare with tenders due at Mr. Spinlove's office, Tuesday, next week. We sat two hours, with Arthur popping in and out between whiles, but the young man is all for what he calls "straight jobs", and thinks this Belhampton business will be more trouble than it's worth, and show precious little profit when all is done. I shall have to take it on my own shoulders, that's clear, like old times; and a good finish-up for me if I never handle another job, for it will be a fine thing to have to one's credit, and I take it very kind of Mr. Spinlove to have invited me so particular, as he has.

I sent Bloggs down to Dorchester to have a look round, and inquire into lodgings and local labour available; for we shall need to keep on a rare lot of men with all the ground-work and preparation and pulling about there is. Bloggs brought back a good report, and, as for lodgings, there are villages round about that will save us journey-money; and we shall get in first, and all that crowd of specialists there will be, later on, can look after themselves.

Well, Spedder made it £65,000—which was a bit more than I had guessed it would be; but he has had an easy job with all these Provisions for Specialists, and the Labour Provisions—pages and pages of them; and if old Tinge is a bit short in any of his Provisions, there will be plenty of savings on others, sure enough. I had a close look at the wages rates Spedder has set down, for, with all these labour-provisions and the rare lot of extras and variations there will sure to be, we shall be hard hit if we are not careful to cover for journey- and lodging-money; and, like enough, lorrying men in and out of Dorchester, and providing messing sheds on site, also, that Tinge—for a wonder—has forgot all about. In the end I had Spedder put an increase that added close on 7 per cent to his total allowance for labour. That brought the total up to £67,420, and, one thing and another, by what Spedder thought, I fixed on £67,000, which Spedder said he would price out the bills to suit, but would make it £66,987 14s. 7d. or the like—a way Spedder has because he thinks it looks like closer pricing; but seems to me just so much tommy-rot, for, stands to reason, if anyone wanted to make a push to put in a low tender he would cut the tail off his total of items and offer at a round figure. However, Spedder is doing the best he knows to help us, so, if he thinks to be more clever than anyone else, it suits me well enough.

The next thing was the time. Mr. Spinlove's covering letter said: "Firms tendering are asked to note that an early date for completion is hoped for." I know Mr. Spinlove by this time—or ought to do—and I know he never will have any racing and scrambling to get done. Not once, but three times over have I seen him with his clients cursing in all the polite ways they knew how to, because the work was behind-hand by the different orders given and alterations made; all just by reason, like enough, of their wives wanting to give a party, or whimpering and fretting because the wall-creepers would have to wait till next year—as though they might be darling little spoilt misses in need of turning up for a spank or two, which I have often felt like offering to give them myself—but Mr. Spinlove not turning a hair with it. He was like any mule for obstinacy in refusing to have us race the work that time the Blagport Town Hall was building, and he had the Council and the Chairman and the local paper on his back because of delay by changed ideas on the Council and quarrelling over what the clock-tower ought to be, half-way through, and putting us back. At this Belhampton job there are sure to be delays by all the specialists there are treading on each other's heels, and chaffering, and pushing one another aside each to be fore-most; or the whole lot standing back for the others to get ahead and make room—all in the usual style, and a rare mix-up it will be, I expect, with the site that long distance away. We shall have plenty time to get our work on the house done; and then we can tackle the groundwork and rebuilding, round and about where we shall not be in the way, and not have our plasterer obliged to stand on the heating engineer's stomach to reach up to run a door-head! It seemed to me fifteen months was about right; but Sped-der reckoned thirteen safe enough, and Arthur agreed, so there it was settled—£66,987 14s. 7d. and thirteen months; and Spedder is going to get the bill straight and confirm by 'phone for me to post our Tender, Monday.

There was one thing we talked about quite a bit, and that was the approach road, 3,192 yards, that we have to main-tain and remake with new hand-picked pitching, and 2-in. metalling, with the old filled on top and heavy rollered. Spedder made it £4,884. It seems a pretty good road as it is now, and it must have carried big wheel-loads, time to time; but a little carelessness with heavy lorries passing one another and getting to the side, in all the wet weather now coming, might land us in a rare mess. Arthur says: "Build passing-places and flag them, and have the lorries keep middle of the road"—which had ought to do well enough in my opinion, by what I saw of things when I was down there; and we can let our sub-contractors and all and sundry know that if they break the rule they can pay the damage.

So that's all cleared up; and if our tender is lowest I shall have something to keep me pretty busy for a year.

## BLOGGS AGAIN!

It has come to my ears, just by a chance, that Fred Bloggs had a row, Wednesday, with Rube Johnston that I put in charge of the machining to relieve Fred. No-one seems to know what it was all about that made Fred shape as if he was going to land Rube a clip: but Rube's not the man to stand for any of that stuff, and he had a bit of two-by-four ready in his hand that made old Fred think twice till the others got between them. It was Billock told me when I asked him—by a hint picked up by overhearing one of the men; and he's friendly with Rube and with Fred also. It seems the whole shop was ashamed at it; but Rube and Fred made friends before knocking off, and all goes smoothly again, so best let well alone. I hope nothing comes to Arthur's ears, for I know things are not according to his notions of how they should be, and I can't keep dancing in between him and Fred much longer. If this Belhampton job comes off it will be just the thing for Fred to go down and look after it, where he can be cock of his own walk with plenty to keep his head busy, and will be safe out of mischief and away from his football and silliness.

Fred was always a bit too ready with his fists, in old days, but I was content to let him manage his own way, except only when I heard of him at it with Bert Wallace that became my foreman mason and is now laid off for good, poor old chap. It did not please me to have my leading hands knocking each other about; but, hearing they were the better friends after, I let be.

68

## DISAPPOINTMENT

To-day there came the letter from Mr. Spinlove to say he cannot recommend our tender on the score of price, and there we are, nearly bottom of the list! It was a chancey job, and difficult to estimate, and it seems I was too cautious. Well, I did my best to give Mr. Spinlove a low tender, like I promised him I would do; but it leaves me a bit surprised—when others invited, special, with me, are first-rate firms that know the particular care and high-class standard required—to find I tendered the highest of the lot, for the bottom on the list funked the job, clear enough, or else he had no mind to take on more than he had already in hand. I should like to know who they all are, but Mr. Spinlove never gives the names. I always have to get that information out of Tinge, later on, for he generally comes to know.

1. £61,000—twelve months.
2. £62,420—fifteen months.
3. £66,987 14s. 7d.—thirteen months (our tender).
4. £80,000—eighteen months.

Well, it may be all for the best, for one never knows what lays in store, and I'm not so young as I was to enjoy wrestling with things; but, however I think in my head, it somehow lays heavy on me all the time when I am not thinking of it, so that I keep wondering what is wrong with me. Arthur seems glad enough, however, and he is full of all his clever notions for tackling his gasholder pit, with quotes for derricks and grabs and tractors, till he's like some bullet-headed boy going to get a Meccano toy for his birthday to wind it up and let it down again all day long. I've got to inquire into his arrangements to-morrow, for time is getting on, and we ought to be at work.


## A SURPRISE

Here is a proper startler! A wire was sent to the house after I had left the office, Wednesday, just before knocking off: "*Will you stand by your tender Belhampton letter in post please wire or phone morning early Spinlove.*" There was something queer happened, clear enough, that I couldn't make out the meaning of. Arthur, who looked in on his way home, thought that it seemed Mr. Spinlove wanted to accept our tender by the other two below us withdrawing theirs! It was difficult to see how that could be unless both cancelled their tenders after the Architect had written reporting results and accepting the lowest of them, but before they received his letter. It seemed time must be short for Mr. Spinlove to telegraph notification that he had written, which might just be to secure that his letter should have attention, first thing; so I went over to the office before breakfast to get his letter, and a busy time I had of it one way and another, for the letter said:

Dear Sirs,

I enclose confirmation of telegram sent you this afternoon, and have to inform you that my client, Sir Ezra Gotsnitz, has instructed me to accept your Tender of October 21 for £66,987 14s. 7d. if you are prepared to stand by it, in which case I will ask you to send me a letter formally renewing that Tender.

In the event of your being willing to so renew, I shall be obliged if Mr. Grigblay will himself ring me up between ten and eleven to-morrow, Friday morning; or, if that is not possible, that you will notify me at an early hour.

Yours faithfully,<br>
JAMES SPINLOVE.

Well, that did not tell me any more than his telegram had done; but just on ten o'clock when I was about going across to the office, there was Mr. Spinlove put through to the house! After thinking things over since the evening, I was willing enough to stand by my tender, and so I told him. He thanked me, but could I run up and see him early in the afternoon to talk things over? And so it was fixed, and I knew nothing of what it all meant till I got to Mount Street at two-fifteen, as appointed, and then it all came out.

## AN EXPLANATION

It seems that when Mr. Spinlove had reported on tenders to the building owner and recommended the lowest, which was £61,000, by Blackington & Pollard, Ltd., the gentleman rang up and said he would have *us* build; and when Mr. Spinlove began to explain the rights of the matter, he wouldn't hear a word; so then Mr. Spinlove went to his office and saw him to talk to.

It is always Mr. Spinlove's way to write to all firms directly tenders are opened and to notify the first on the list that he is prepared to recommend their Tender for acceptance; but it seems the gentleman argued that it was no part of the Architect's business to pledge his employer; that the Tender set out that the building-owner was at liberty to accept any tender he had a mind to, and none at all if he didn't choose, and there was no more to be said. So then, that same day, Mr. Spinlove wrote him what he had tried to tell him by word of mouth—only he wouldn't hear a word—and he showed me the letter where it was quoted from Emden & Watson's Book, and I remember the words he put: "There is something of the nature of a moral obligation upon the building owner to accept the lowest tender."

However, that was to no purpose, either; for the next day the gentleman rings up and says he will have *us* to build for him, and no other; but contract time to be twelve months, instead of thirteen, because if one builder could undertake to finish in twelve, another could do the same; and a start to be made at once as he had been kept waiting beyond all reason with nothing begun to be done yet—by which he meant that no time had ought to be taken up making drawings and Spec. and taking out quantities, et cetera!

Mr. Spinlove told me he was glad enough to have us do the work, but that he was bound to hold the balance fair among all; and the awkwardness for him was that it might look like he had favoured us by not pressing the claims of Blackington & Pollard (it being known we had built a lot for him for many years past); or even that he had put others to the trouble and expense of tendering just only as a check against the price we would offer at. So now he has to write and explain to B. & P. and apologize for what was no fault of his and not to be avoided; with them, like enough, not believing the half of it, and acting crusty, and also not too pleased to tender the next time.

Mr. Spinlove was so rattled telling it all over to me that he let fly a curse or two—which he can do, in style, now and again when he likes—and, knowing me so well this long time, he is not so shy of doing it when I am by as he would be with another. It looks to me Mr. Spinlove is not so deep-fallen in love with his client as to need to creep close up, a-tiptoe, to steal him a kiss when he don't expect. I said to

72

him: "Why not have the gentleman to draw B. & P. a cheque for £150 just to pay their out-of-pocket expenses on preparing their Tender, and which would sweeten the bitter pill for them?" and Mr. Spinlove said it was quite an idea, and he would think about it.

The reason for the whole upset, as Mr. Spinlove sees it, is just this: that Sir Ezra Gotsnitz came to Mr. Spinlove because he is Lord Rainsport's Architect. Sir Ezra was at some Bazaar held in the gardens of Dulkington where Mr. Spinlove carried out the alterations with the great new wing we added on to make it near as fine a house as any in the country; and he is all out for blood and social climbing by hobnobbing with the great gentry, and so he would have the same architect as the Earl, and now is out to have the same builders and so get to be the equal of any Earl himself—in his own estimation.

Well, I agreed for twelve months, for it is not us that will be accountable for the delays there are sure to be, but all the Specialists crowding in like it might be an excursion steamer to Margate in August. And also I agreed, by Mr. Spinlove asking me, to get men down on the site clearing away and making ready, just for a show, in a week's time, for there are barns and outbuildings to make shift with for a start: and so it was all settled in half an hour, and we shook hands, hearty, like I have done with him these many times at starting, and also at settling up; for if there is a fairer or more nice-spoken gentleman for an architect than Mr. Spinlove, I have never met him yet; and if he takes good care of his client—and I have seen something of that —he takes good care of his builder also, to see he gets fair treatment, and the subcontractors and specialists the same —so long as they act up—which cannot be said of all F.R.I.B.A.s and F.S.A.s and R.A.s by a long chalk, some being ready enough to get clear of the mess they have made for themselves by pushing the Builder under foot to walk on top of him, clean and dry, to firm ground; and the Builder out of pocket and out of face, with nothing to strike balance with but hope of the Architect's future favours.

## A PLEASANT MEETING

Just as I was going out at his door, there was a lady walked in with a pair of young boys; and it was Mr. Spinlove's lady that I remember for a wild young slip of a girl running up and down ladders, and all over, the time we were building Honeywood Grange for her father, Sir Leslie Brash. She recognized me, after all the years past, before I did her; for she has changed in figure and filled out in the face, but a comely one she is still and laughs the same as I remember, for all she is grown to be more sedate than she had used to be.

I heard, at the time, of the sorrow they had when their eldest, a young girl, died; but these two boys—Leslie and Jim are the names they are called by, the one twelve and going to Winchester next year and the younger one seven, that had come for their father to take them all to the Zoo— are fine young limbs, full of their freedom, and a frank open style with them.

"Are you going to be an architect like your Dad when you grow up?" I asked of the elder.

"Well, I don't think I've quite decided yet," says the young man.

"And what are you going to be?" I said to the other.

"Oh, Jim's going to be an engine-driver," says Mr. Spinlove; on which they all laughed out, and the boy must rush and tackle his father like a footballer, and punch him in the stomach as well, till Mr. Spinlove says: "That's enough, Jim," and he gives over.

The lady said her father was well, though getting on in years, and still acting chairman of his firm and going up to Town every week or so; and her mother is all taken up with flying, and can't get carried high enough to please her, and is all for stunting, it seems—which was a surprising thing to hear that I could scarcely credit, for she cannot want many years to sixty and was at all times wonderful mixed in her ideas and feathery in the head, by what I saw of her. I would scarcely have believed it; but Mr. Spinlove, hearing what passed, must be reminded to tell me that Sir Leslie has it in mind to get advice and perhaps build a little house with run-way and aeroplane hangar down in bottom field, so that his lady can have her private machine and a pilot of her own to take care of her, instead of her running off to Brooklands, any time it hits her fancy, to be taken up in the clouds, or get a bit closer to the moon on a fine night—and, like enough, keep Sir Leslie at worrying that his lady wife won't come dropping down the chimney, of a sudden, when he doesn't expect! Well, there it is; and the longer I live the more I can't make a guess at what strange things will not happen next, for Lady Brash, when I had to do with her fifteen years ago, was all fancies and worrying, and getting everything upside down and topsy-turvy to make a fuss over, and crying about nothing, poor woman, and going away to be cured;—though she was always a most kind nice lady that everyone would be sorry for and try to please if they could. To have her perking up to turn skittish in her old age and take to a dangerous game like aeroplanes, is the last thing anyone would expect to hear of.

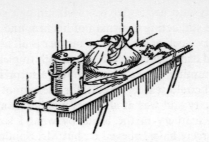

## GOOD AND BAD NEWS FOR FRED

I had plenty to think about on my way home with drawings and Spec. spread out on the seat; and I felt a bit
tired with it when I reached the house, and so I had Meg to
get tea set out; and then I 'phoned for Fred to come over
and see me, as I want to act up for an early start to oblige
Mr. Spinlove, and also because of telling Fred the news to
please him, for he had been cast down by hearing we were
all out with our tender.

I was back of the room, facing the window, when there
he was, coming across, and I could have laughed out loud
to see him if it hadn't taken me the other way, too; for
there was Fred Bloggs looking like the whole world had
come to an end for him and he was going off to hang himself and no relish for that, either! What he's been up to *this*
time I don't know—words with Arthur again, like enough
—but, Oh! I did feel sorry. Such a fine, straight man as he
is, through and through, and no fault in him, but all just
happened by reason of misfortune in his life and by the way
things have come about so that he doesn't fit in. The most
brave, loyal, honest soul that ever breathed is old Fred, that
would give his life for me and not think twice. By the look
of things, he had made up his mind that he had been
fetched over to be paid off for good and all.

I had a chance to tell the girl fetch another cup and plate
76

before she opened to him, and I was all impatience, waiting; but he took a lot of time making up his mind to come in the room, though the door was standing open for him; and then there he was! all slow in his steps and looking on the floor.

"Come along in and have a cup o' tea, Fred," I said; "I've got some good news for you."

That made him to look up at me, quick, standing there in the door; and he was a study to see, for he is such a simple old fellow that his face reads the same as any child's would do.

He was taken aback, and no mistake; looking at me pretty straight to be sure I meant it, and then going a bit breathless and stammering with it—as is his way when he is puzzled or put about: but I had no curiosity to know what was amiss, for whatever it is will be cured by him being sent to Dorset; and soon, there he was sitting cheerful enough with four lumps in his cup and his thumb hooked round the handle of the spoon—instead of taking it out—which is his way. Before he went off I had it arranged for him to go down to Dorchester, Monday; with Saturday and Monday morning to go over the drawings and get his things together; and I will go along off on the Tuesday night and see him straight for a start, Wednesday.

Soon as letters opened this morning, Arthur came along for me to look into his gasholder arrangements for an early start—and time enough! I could see something was amiss directly he came in, and there it was, just as I guessed! He can't do with Fred any longer by Fred going contrary to orders to suit his own ideas; and Rube complaining he does not have the chance to put the stuff through the machines the way he's expected; and the men at the benches discontented, and even the smith not knowing what he'd better do next.

Arthur says it looks like Fred is doing it intentional to

show he can carry on better by himself with Rube to do what *he* tells him, instead of the way it is fixed for Rube to answer direct to Arthur; but that I do not credit, as I had Arthur to know, pretty quick. It is just because of the old fellow being cast down and bothered at not having the full authority he had before; and by not allowing that Arthur knows better how things ought to be done than *he* does—which is true enough, come to that!

However, Arthur has been looking into the books with Jedbury, in charge of the prime costing; and Arthur says the work coming through the shop is costing more than it should do, spite of the new machines. The last straw was yesterday morning while I was in Town, by a lorry standing three-quarters of an hour and the doors for the school not loading; and Rube telling Arthur the sand-papering machine is so much waste the way he has had it standing idle, and now is all stacked round with stuff wanted faster than it can be put through; and how he has to re-set a machine for a new job, and then alter back to the other; and how he gets all cluttered up with one machine, while another is standing that ought not—and a lot more of it.

So then Arthur went to have word with Bloggs to get him to organize differently; but Bloggs showed as if he had no mind to listen, and turned aside and said something Arthur could not hear, but knew to be pretty ugly by the shamefaced way half a dozen, near by, looked across at Arthur. So then Arthur said—"That's cooked your goose for *you*, Fred Bloggs," and walked off; and I agreed it must be the end, for I will not have Arthur treated different from myself; and, while I respect him, all and sundry shall do the same or they can pack up and be a good riddance. It was lucky for Fred I was in London yesterday; and I feel all the more angry at him for sitting at my table as if nothing was the matter—however, that's all over and done. I told Arthur I was shifting him to Dorset, Monday, to look after

78

the Belhampton job, and said I would have him apologize to Arthur; on which Arthur says:

"The fellow can keep out of my way and I shall be glad if I never set eyes on him again"; but I said:

"Not so, Arthur lad! Just you go in the shop ten o'clock to-morrow morning, and if Fred Bloggs doesn't speak up handsome before everyone and apologize to you in proper language for all to hear him, I'll clear him out neck and crop straight away for good and all," I said, "and you can answer him back just as rough as you know how and think wise," I said—so I was careful to tell Fred to do it.

Arthur agreed, for he is very sensible at seeing things the right way and at not being rattled and put out—which has always been my way, also.


## THE VICAR'S "CONVENIENCE"

Arthur told me he had agreed proposals for Mr. Peebles' "convenience" by a $4\frac{1}{2}$-in. wall across the end of vestry for a little lav. with w.c. off; and a two-light window to match the existing, with cross-partition butting against mullion. There will be just a trapped gully with salt-glazed channel—along with soil drain and fresh air inlet with mica flap—connected to a disconnecting chamber with clearing-eye, benched 60 deg. in cement—set and trowelled to a nice polish—and white-glazed channels and special junctions; finished with solid, cast iron, galvanized cover pressed down, in best cart-grease, into rim of solid, cast iron galvanized frame according to the Bye-laws—the same as we put at the Police Barracks and Saint Julian's Hotel; and that, with a bit of a 3-ft. by 6-ft. impervious cemented cess-pit for pumping out, domed over for another solid cast-iron galvanized cover, cart-grease and frame, et cetera, had ought to do well enough, in my humble opinion—with a hole knocked in the bottom soon as passed—any time the Bishop comes along and has a mind to ring the bell—taking into account, of course, the heavy cast-iron spigot-and-socket-run-in-blue-lead-and-caulked 4-in. vent pipe, treated Angus Smith Solution and carried up three feet above gable with copper wire dome to look pretty in the picture postcard-views sold inside, by the Verger, price 2d. each; and make Bargate, the Sanitary Inspector, feel proud whenever he passes that way. The cost of the lot, Arthur says, will be £60, paid in coppers as time goes by, no doubt.

Arthur let fall he was ordering lav. and closet fittings out of Bonnerswat's catalogue—for we don't stock such things now; but I laid my hand on his arm for a caution:—

"Don't you do it, Art., my lad," I said. "A gentleman like Mr. Peebles hasn't enough things to attend to without he thinks out some extra; and the smaller a job is the more he thinks, so that if you put a spire on top of the tower it might be too big for him to see it, almost; but if it was a new coat of varnish on the alms box, he will study to find the leg of a fly stuck in it to write a letter about," I said. "If *you* choose these fittings, first thing will be the screw-down is too stiff, and there is a pimple in the glaze, and the rubber ring on the pull-handle slips off, and the W.W.P. goes on singing after the organ has stopped," I said. "You just have our good Vicar to choose for himself at Branks's West-End showrooms," I said, "and be careful he lets Branks note the patterns he wants, for *us* to order them," I said. "For if not, we shall have an S-trap sent down when we want a P; and left hand when we want right; and a lav. just exactly the right size to prevent the door swinging; and enamelled copper fall-pipe with bends made ready for fixing the W.W.P. in front of the window," I said.

Well, of course, Arthur always knows it all before he is told except when it happens he is *not* told: but there! I was the same in my young days, and we all have to learn by our own mistakes and not by other people's.

## THE TANK AGAIN

After that, Arthur got out his papers and drawings for the Gasholder Tank, and a rare vexation it all was. The boy seems to think he is building a dry dock for the *Mauretania*, and we came near to quarrelling before he would give over with his new-fangled clever ideas to do everything the way no one ever did it before, and hear reason. He was all for starting off with digging a trench round, eight feet wide and thirty-two deep, open-planked with walings and struts, and filling in solid with concrete at back of the retaining wall fast as it went up, with new struts off face of wall across trench, put in as fast as the old pulled out. After all building finished, he was for having a grab get out the spoil in middle, with the wall-face all mucked up for cleaning, after; and damaged by the grab swinging up against, as well, like enough!

"Why," I said, "I would do the job just with picks and shovels and horses to cart up a ramp, and get finished quicker and at less cost," I said.

"My way is the proper way they set down in the engineering books, I know that, Dad; and the Tube engineers do the same way," says young Art., as if he had said the last word and time to go off home to bed.

"Yes, and that's about all you *do* know," I said: "and what you know is only fit to make you a professor yourself," I said, "to let hair that ought to be on your head grow on your chin, and write books to teach it all over again for others, that come after you, to go on at writing bigger books for them that are not yet born or on the way, to copy out in a few dozen more books, yet," I said. "My business, just now, is to dig a hole by the way I know how to; and no time to waste running about asking orders from those who never tried and don't know the way to begin," I said.

"It's all very well, Dad, for you to go on talking to make fun," says young Art. "But we've got to get the thing straightened out. You know we can't work with horses and carts, so what's the use of talking? And you have forgotten all about the planking and strutting."

"I'm not talking to you to make fun," I said. "I'm talking to you to make sense, as you will find out pretty soon, my lad," I said, "and about time *you* began to talk sense yourself," I said, "and *think* sense too, for a change," I said, "and not make a quick guess that I have forgotten about shoring the face when I have been remembering not to forget to shore faces every week of my life since long before you were born," I said. "You would do better to make a wiser guess, which is that I said nothing of planking and strutting for the reason that there is not going to be any planking and strutting," I said.

"What!" said Art., all of a surprise. "Thirty-two feet to go in that ground and no planking!" he shouts out.

"Don't you start bellowing and roaring at me," I said. "I've lived long enough in the world to know what I'm talking about without you to throw up your hands every time I open my mouth," I said.

Well, so it went on till we got to the question of cost, and I had Rumble come in with his taking-off sheets, and that made young Arthur to shut up his tongue in the box where it belongs, at last, and this is how it all was—just by a comparison of excavating costs.

The whole of excavating and filling into lorries we made to be worth £275.

Then, if we went to work Arthur's way, the trench with

planking complete, would be £485, which, added on, made £760; and filling at back of wall with 7 and 1 concrete, £300; so the total by Arthur's ideas of going to work was £1,060 for comparison with my ideas: which were:

Excavating and filling into lorries as above, £275. Add excavating to break back on 60 deg. incline, and filling and ramming to back of wall, cost £84, makes total £359 against Arthur's £1,060; and less work handling the grab, for while Arthur was for having it travel three-quarters way round, by *my* way it would stand on the ground to be excavated and start at the far rim to excavate in the shape of a new moon, just traversing a few yards right and left the while, and dropping into lorries drawing up behind; and so go on, backing slowly away from the hole, as it might be some polite lady curtseying to a throne, till the new moon was grown to a full moon and the grab finished with and only the throwing back and ramming to wall to be after done. So there at last it was settled by figures we all agreed, that make the cost of the job by Arthur's proposal considerably over Rumble's estimate, and a useful lot below by mine.

I had a bit more to say that had not come into Arthur's young head—by all the busy thinking it was doing, I've no doubt, how to bring in a conveyor-belt to carry off the spoil, and aeroplane to deposit concrete on bottom—and that was for him to get Parkin to agree to extra of £100— which is the value (£84 est.) of raking back and filling in— instead of the shuttering he has contracted to pay for; and if his directors do not like to pay *one* hundred, then they can pay *eight* for Arthur's trench idea, and stand and look on for an extra month to see how it is all done by professors writing in books instead of by the proper way, and learn something useful they did not know before.

However, one thing Arthur agreed without arguing it, and that was: better, after all, for us to have our own gate in, and track-way; and the lorries to come up behind the grab instead of delivering into tip-wagons running on staging to discharge into lorries standing in the company's yard. So now the thing is all settled for making a start; and enough talking and argument with it as would go to the building of a lunatic asylum for Arthur to go inside, soon as finished, to live there for good—and so I told him. But he's a kind-thinking young fellow and like a son to me by the way he puts up with my irritations and shouting.

## MAKING READY

I got down to Belhampton just on dinner, Wednesday. Our little two-ton lorry was standing, but no one else about, by appearances, till I let go a shout, and there was old Fred put his head out of a calf-house like jack-in-the-box, and a pair of labourers looked round the corner to see what was up. Trust old Fred to make himself comfortable, first start! There he was with a bench knocked together of old stall-boards, and the Drawings and Spec. and Quantities laid out; and a barrel cut about for a chair, made comfortable with a bit of old sack with straw stuffed in it; and a picture-almanack nailed up; and his mac. hanging; and a hole broken for light with an old window botched in. There was a box for cupboard-shelves fixed up, and, of course— the first thing Fred always does—a great stove, picked out of some junk shop, near red hot, and the place like an oven. He was at frying a pair of fine pork chops on the blade of an old shovel, thrown away; with a feed-tub, upside down, laid out for dinner, with loaf, teapot, sugar, and a bit of cheese on a newspaper, and Fred as happy as a king. Not a bottle was there, as I should have seen if it had been, for Fred would never hide anything away; so there it was, all just like old times come back!

" You seem to have settled in all right, Fred," I said.

"Yes, sir; I shall do well enough till I can get straight for the start," says he.

He had his cat curled up front of the stove on a nice sack folded in an old sieve picked up. He is an ugly old cat—though you mustn't say it out loud—but his tail makes Fred proud, for it is a curiosity that might be the top joint of your thumb growing hair there, as if pussy had been close shaved by some express train. Actually, it is nothing but a touch of Manx in the blood; but no other in that litter, nor in any other, was like it—so Fred tells.

"He feels strange up in the village," says Fred, "but he travels comfortable in a bag on my handle-bars, and likes to push his head out in fine weather to see where he has got to—don't you Tom?" he says.

I had a good look round with the survey plans, and all seems clear enough. I like the look of the job, I will say, more than I did first go off; for the most of it is just pulling about and making good, and new bits here and there, all over, and a great part on day-work schedule. We got in with good prices, and Fred being in charge will make safe, and all will be plain sailing by what I can see. The Tender was near on my limit; but, now the schools are about cleared up, we have no heavy commitments, and Belhampton will be like a lot of little jobs bunched together, to my way of looking at things.

I stayed the night at Dorchester, and went over again, Thursday morning, along with a surveyor and assistant from the place; and arranged for the main bench-marks—that I will have solid concrete with no chance of shifting—and the clearing away for sighting through and laying down axis lines, so that Fred can get along with his setting out. In a week we can have Mr. Spinlove to come down and approve, I dare say.

# A VISITOR

I had a fashionable caller to-day, with me sitting in my shirt-sleeves by the mild weather it was and the heating over-stoked, when a gentleman's visiting card was brought in by Smith—without any silver salver to lay it on—that read: "Mr. Vernon Pollard, The Cedars, Partingham Road, Beckenham, Kent."

"Who is he?" I asked of Smith.

"Some big commercial swell, I should say, sir," says Smith, who never gets anything right, poor little man, except the filing and records and typists he looks after.

"Well, you can show him in," I said, not having anything particular for attention at the time; and then I caught the bonnet of a great Packard round the edge of the window. Next, a tall, youngish man was walking in with yellow gloves on; and a green-colour hat, shape of a pie; and yellow and brown checkwork coat put on over a dark blue collar and shirt; and greenish flannel trousers hanging free down his legs in pleats like they might be ladies' clothes— pulled off his wife for the day, by the look of things. He had a little bit of a moustache like his nose was dirty underneath; and a shiny tie all blue and green zigzags, to make you look at it twice over so as not to forget—just the swanking sort I will have no truck with, nor ever have.

"Mr. Grigblay?" he says.

"Sitting here," I answered him.

Then he nodded at me and I nodded back at him and waited for him to say was it a motor fire-engine or just a couple of threshing-machines he wanted me to go in for?

"I am Mr. Vernon Pollard, of Blackington & Pollard, Ltd.—Mr. Pollard, Junior," he says.

"Well, I didn't make a guess it would be *senior*," I said, not caring for his ladylike behaviour and drawing up a chair before he was asked; and, as he hadn't thought to take off his hat, I gave a shout for Smith, and had him give me mine off the peg.

"Oh! I beg your pardon," he says, and takes his off, when, lo and behold! he was bald on top, and hadn't wanted me to know he was. So then I threw mine across on to the side-table. "I must apologize for my unceremonious attire, Mr. Grigblay," he goes on. "I just called in on my way to see my son, who is at Willchastar Collarge," he says, which was the way he talked all the time, being so special-educated to be the real gentleman careful to speak beautiful, that he went on like one of these comic dudes on the music-halls that I never quite believed in before.

"You can come in your swim-clothes any time you're out for bathing, if it suits, and all the same to me," I said; "but you haven't said what you've come about yet," I said —though I had made a right guess directly he gave the name of his firm.

"Well, in point of fact, Mr. Grigblay," he says, "our Managing Director requested me to interview you to gather whether you can tell us why our tender for Belhampton Castle was passed over the way it has been," he says.

"That's for the Architect to tell you," I said.

"We do not like to have these things happen," he says. "In point of fact, they never do happen with us—except once before," he says, "and we think we ought to have a clear explanation of the meaning of it," he says.

"The Architect can give you an explanation that had ought be clear enough for *you*, the same as it is to *me*," I said.

"In point of fact, our Managing Director has himself interviewed Mr. Spinlove, but he feels there is something else laying in the background which we ought to be informed about. We are aware you have worked in association with this particular Architect for many years. You are not a member of the County Federation of Builders, I understand, Mr. Grigblay."

"I am able to take care of myself without any Federation to nursemaid me," I said; "and," I said, "I have just one short word for you to hurry back home and pass on to your Managing Director so as not to keep him waiting too long," I said, "and that word is: 'Them that stinks is the worst smellers'."

"I beg your pardon?" he says, like as if he didn't hear right.

"Them that stink is the worst smellers," I said a bit louder and more slow, for him to remember it better.

"I do not understand you," he says.

"I dare say your Managing Director will improve your learning for you soon as you get back home," I said. "But to ease your mind so as you will not be worried thinking over, it means: because them that stink think everything stinks the same as themselves, like any gas-fitter might do," I said.

"You speak in riddles, Mr. Grigblay," he says, staring at me like he was trying to remember if he had ever seen me before.

"Well, that's all for to-day," I said, and got out of my chair to have him clear off and no more of it; but there was a sample brick approved for the Gasholder Tank laying on the table—one of these great, smooth, greasy, salmon-colour engineering bricks out of Kent, or near by, harder than a Staffordshire Blue and full as heavy—and, my eye falling on it, I had a mind to joke him, seeing the sort he was.

"What do you think of that brick?" I said, on which he looks at it as though it might jump up and bite him.

"Sample facing approved for Mr. Peter Piper's new Christian Science Church, Whitechapel," I said. "Would *you* use a brick like that?" I said. "Just smell it and tell me what you think," I said.

He began to stoop over to sniff it, but I picked up and handed to him. He took hold of it by his fingers right at the end, so, when I let go, it swung down and he had to snatch at it with his other hand to save it falling. Then he put it to his nose.

"Notice the sulphur?" I asked of him.

He didn't seem sure whether he did or not, so I took hold and spilled some water on it out of a little flower-vase I had there. "*Now* you'll smell it," I said; so he had another sniff, and says:

"Oh, yes. You're quite right," he says, and puts it down pretty quick, by his gloves being wetted.

"Well, it's just what I say," I said. "There's sulphur in that brick as you can smell it yourself," I said; "and it means that the peroxide of hydrogen will start coming out soon as the carbolic acid in the air gets in by the water evaporating; and after a year or eighteen months we shall have blue and green mould standing out three-quarters of an inch all over the face, and washing down in streaks soon as it comes on to rain, and a new crop starting to grow soon as it stops," I said, "and no end to it for, maybe, fifteen or twenty years, as you know well," I said.

"Yes," he says. "It's a very difficult question we always find," and he stooped down to have another sniff to prove he knew it all beforehand.

"What would you do about it yourself?" I asked him.

"Well—in point of fact—have you—why not—have you told the Architect?" he says, not knowing what to say first.

"Told the Architect!" I said, half-way to shouting at

him. "It is the Architect himself specified the bricks and approved the sample!" I said. "How can I go and hold out to the Architect that I am better at smelling sulphur than *he* is? You make me laugh!" I said, and so I pretended to do, and he joined in with me to show he knew he had made a funny mistake. Then off he went to tell the masters at the school be sure learn his boy to be a perfect gentleman the same as Dad is; and never to have any dirty low ideas like knowing one end of a brick from the other; but to grow up a polite ladylike contractor dressed in his wife's trousers, to keep clear of any dust or mud that's going and sit at a Board meeting smoking a cigarette till tea is laid out.

## A FRUITLESS ERRAND

I wondered, passing by, when I saw our good Vicar, in company with Vint and Billington, bustling along to the station, two o'clock, Saturday; and to-day, from what Pember—Peoples' Churchwarden—told me, they were the Sub-Committee of the Parochial Church Council, off to choose a pretty lav. and water-closet at Branks's Show Rooms for the new "convenience" in the Vestry. I can't keep from laughing to think of them hurrying not to be late to catch the next train; and watching out of the window, as they ran through Clapham, the shoppers crowding all the streets; and then, after getting on a No. 25 at Victoria and driving out of the Yard, it was: "Hullo! Oh dear, Oh dear! Whatever is happened? Has someone gone and died, then?" by the streets all empty and shutters up like it might be a Sunday. I shall pull Vint's leg properly when I see him— forgetting early closing is not at mid-week in the West End. I do not doubt our Vicar had them get off in Oxford Street to have a try, by kicking on the door, to fetch Mr. Branks

or the old lady or some of the family down to let them in
out of consideration for all the long way they had come;
and then it seems they went off to Tassaud's Waxworks, by
our Vicar never having had a chance to see the Chamber of
Horrors before; and I dare say London was short of a bun
or two, as well, by the time they started home. Well, the
Sub-Committee will have to report a failure at first attempt,
and get it confirmed for them to make another try; so
better luck next time, let's hope!


## A MYSTERY

There will never be an end with this gasholder tank of
Arthur's, far as I can see. Now, just as we are about
starting, there comes a letter from the Company for us to
hold back for a few weeks as the site is going to be shifted!
I asked Arthur what it meant, and he told me Parkin is on
with drawings of a great range of buildings along at top
end: bunkers, retort-house, condenser, purifier and a new
meter-house—as if they hadn't any gasworks already!
Arthur sketched it down, and it means the gasholder will
be pushed more than sixty feet south.

"Well, it won't be sited *there*," I said, "because that is
just on the line of the old two-foot, brick barrel sewer from
Gayton to the sewage farm other side of the railway," I
said—which it happened I chanced to learn of one day
when I called in to see Bargate to smooth over the upset at
the schools. I mentioned we were building a tank south of
the gasworks, on which he went across and pulled down a
great survey he had fixed up like a roller-blind on the wall,
for me to point him, where.

"That will be all right, then!" he says, and he showed me
the sewer marked, red ink, running across on south.

" Parkin knows all about it," says Arthur. " I mentioned the sewer after I had word of it from you; and I told him again, two days ago, when he showed me the plans pencilled out on his drawing-board," he says.

" Well, what did he answer you?" I said.

" Nothing; he just winked at me," says Arthur, with a queer look.

" Out with it! What's it all about?" I said.

" Of course I'd tell you if I knew, Dad; but I can't even make a guess. It looks to me as if he is hiding something on his sleeve," says Arthur: so there's some funny game up, and we shall have to wait and see. I have written the Company that we can hold off for a bit if they will give us ample notice when to start; but lucky it was not a week later or we should have been tied up with our own contracts for grab and special plant.


## A PROPHECY FULFILLED

Here we are, just what I thought! I happened on it by a chance Arthur would be glad enough to have had me miss, I dare say; and that is: Branks has sent the fittings for the vestry "convenience" Mr. Peebles and sub-committee went to London, special, to choose; and, lo and behold! if the lav. isn't big enough to bath a baby, and won't let the door swing—just exactly as I made joke to Arthur it would be—and, also, the flush-tank has got to be sent back, too, for some reason or other, after the whole unpacked and lorried to the job and plumber and mate sent over to get at fixing! I warned Arthur how it would be; but Arthur says he told Mr. Peebles to let *us* order—as I advised he should do—and it seems Mr. P. thought to save a bit of money (by us losing it) if he bought for himself—us paying the bill, no doubt—and diddle us out of our discount! Well, our good Vicar will find out different and learn something he did not know before when he gets our account; and he will also know exactly what the cost of freight three times over instead of once is, and how much the traffic we have had handling and unpacking and repacking, etc., amounts to. I am glad enough to put my hand in my pocket for a subscription to the "Vestry Fund", as he calls it; but our Mr. Peebles has got to learn, same as any other, how not to be too smart getting the better of builders who are doing the best they know to help him.

Reminds me of the upset we had when we built that little house down in the Weald—Fenderton, A.R.I.B.A., architect—for Major Cockrane, D.S.O.—"Andananapandarana" he named it, after some battle he was in—and the gentleman thought he would do his pocket a good turn by going to departmental stores and furnishers and decorators all over the place, and buying the whole of the papers for himself, having first been very clever at getting to make notes of the measures of the rooms, and the prices out of the spec. in our foreman's office, without Jonas tumbling to what he was about. So there we were, and a nice old muddle! with the staircase and hall bought twice over, different patterns; and no knowing which paper was for which room; and the most sent many pieces too much except when short—just for a pleasant change. I could have worked it so that he paid catalogue price with our $33\frac{1}{3}$ per cent added on top; but that is not my way, and Major Cockrane was always the gentleman, and was only trying to be clever in all the clever ways he thought it clever to be clever in.

## THE BUILDING-OWNER LOOKS IN

There was a bit of delay—but not to hamper us—before Mr. Spinlove could come to Belhampton to approve setting out and arrange with us to go forward the way he wants; and I took Arthur along, for I shall want him to keep things going in the office—and on the site, too, if I get any of my winter troubles and have to stay indoors—and because it was well for Mr. Spinlove to meet Arthur while I was by, for he has not done before. He took a fancy to the young man, clear enough. Arthur was chipping in with questions to be settled that Mr. Spinlove was glad enough to decide about; and a nice, modest, quiet way with him the boy has, though firm at holding on till all is made clear so that there will be no loose ends left hanging about to trip someone later on, and lead to things being done the way they ought not or forgot all about, or other mistakes made that are never anybody's fault at all and can't possibly be helped! Mr. Spinlove stepped forward and shook hands, hearty, with Fred Bloggs directly he saw him, having had him to look after his work many a time before; and what must old Fred do but go pink with it, right over the top of his forehead, like he might be any young girl just caught a kiss from somebody extra she didn't expect.

We had a rare lot to get done in the time, with it starting to go dark so early; and then, what should happen close on half-past three, but the gentleman himself must arrive in a great limousine with a large-size pink-and-yellow lady in-side—who kept seated—and two up in front, the one to drive and the other to stand to open the door and, after, follow round at his master's heels like he might be some great dog. It was a good thing we had finished our work, or the day would have been wasted by the style he went on in: asking questions of Mr. Spinlove quicker than there were answers for them; and saying this, that and the other had got to be so-and-so, without waiting to know what he was talking about; and saying the same thing the other way round, backwards, over again, often as not; and all the time—"Understand? Understand? Understand?" It was the ugliest style of carrying on I ever saw a gentleman behave in, and not often them that are not gentlemen.

It seems he thought to find the place crawling with men and the walls going up, instead of just the pulling down we had in hand, and shacks going up and plant being got together. I had Arthur to draw aside with me, but I could follow all that passed. Mr. Spinlove behaved very stiff and cool and slow in his words, waiting till the other had said all he wanted before answering him back; and—when Sir Ezra chipped in to interrupt—starting to say it all over again more slow and clear than the first time, till at last the other began to keep quiet so as to hear him out. However as the gentleman had got mixed up in what he said before; and couldn't find the right words for what he wanted to say so that no-one knew what he was talking about; and couldn't understand which direction he was looking, or remember East from West, or make out what was drawn, clear, on the plans; it was just so much foolishness and waste, as if we were all got into some lunatic asylum of a sudden. However, he had to cut it short by the light going; and the last was, he must walk into one of Fred's concrete "benches" standing in the grass, and look to be going to land on his conk, which gave him a fright same as if someone had let fall the baby; and such fussing—with the flunky going down on his knee to see if his patents were scratched

—as could not be credited. Then, the next thing was, he would have paths made and planks laid down so that he could walk round, safe and dry, on the level, next time; with: "Understand? Understand?" till off he went at last, after he had made us to miss the express, so that Arthur and I stayed the night at Weymouth, instead. Mr. Spinlove went on in his car to a Bridport hotel, so as to look round at a bit of church restoration he has near by, come the morning.

## TWO NEW JOBS

Here is a letter from Mr. Rupert Blenhassett, A.R.A., asking to have us tender for terraces, pergolas and garden pavilions at Prior's Franklyn for Col. the Rt. Hon. the Viscount Blades, V.C., etc., the same that is heir to the Marquess of Calverley and has his speeches printed in the papers. I do not know where Mr. Blenhassett got our name to ask us to tender for what is a very special job, by the look of things, and the kind of work this architect is particular known by. At any rate, it will be a nice thing to get finished next year along with Belhampton; and I tell Arthur that, what with the Earl at Dulkington and the Viscount at Prior's Franklyn, I shall end up by being a Duke myself one of these days!

However, Arthur is all for us getting the contract for the Sausage Factory on the Halliburton Byepass, with F. Billington Snadge for architect—the fellow who puts the letters L.R.I.B.A. on his headings done Gothic style for the L. to read as an F., as I read it myself all the time we were building the little row of shops he designed for falling down when the wind changed if I hadn't had him to strap and bolt his hips and ridges. Arthur says we must be sure and get to build factory buildings or we shall be left behind the times; so there it is, and Spedder is pricing out for us, and if we are lucky we shall have a great board high up in the air— that Arthur sets great store by—lettered in beautiful style with our name and address and telephone number and who we are, for the motorists to read and take to heart as they run by, so as always to remember and never forget that it was us, and no other, built the place that shouts where to buy sausages by the best new-style architecture of a row of plaster pigs, sitting along the parapet, with pink glass eyes for lighting up and winking at night, and a double-size pig on the gable—judging by what Spedder says of it. This idea was invented by the architect when he was sober, I make no doubt; but I found him, most times, half-tight or waiting ready to be made so along of the hotel round the corner and the representatives belonging to the patent floors, and the special roof-bitumen, and the heating boilers; or else, if not, it would dam' well be different floor and a different roof and different boilers, next time—so look out! A cheap, rubbishy fellow and no mistake—but there! Art. says it is a straightforward job we can do ourselves some good with; and the boy has got to learn his own business to carry on the way he thinks best when I am forgot, and it is no good worrying to have him do any different; so now we shall see what will happen, and what good or what harm will come of it if we get the contract—which I hope we shall not, but that I keep a secret to myself.

Last evening, no sooner supper finished and me nicely settled in front of the fire, when Meg must tap on the door and it was Saunders come!

"Well, what's it about *this* time, Saunders?" I said, on opening the door of my room where he had been shown in. "What's wrong *now*?" I said, being none too glad to see him.

What was wrong was a pound missing out of the petty cash, and Saunders seeming all smug with it as though he was a good boy come to tell the master sneak-tales out of school!

"Well, and whose fault's that?" I said. "Are you the one responsible for the Petty and Subbing, or have I got to bring in a policeman to look after things?" I said, so as to give him a jolt; and on that he must get all white in his cheeks and start his moustache jumping up and down at me, and his Adam's apple diving in and out of his collar like he had a fish-bone on the way—the silly little man.

"You've paid out and forgot to book it; so don't begin singing the song about hanky-panky like you started off last time you came, unless you have the proof," I said. "Your Kitty is not troubling you again, is it?" I asked, and he says it was not.

"Well," I said, "you can try the same medicine for the Petty that cured the other," I said. "Things were kept straight enough with Sennock to lend a hand, so why not now?" I said; and he agreed it was so except for the usual slips to put right, and he said he was carrying on with Snape same as he had done with Sennock.

"So Snape's the matter, is he?" I said.

"Oh, no!" he says. "It was Snape told me when he checked over, first thing, Tuesday; and only a fortnight back it was Snape that discovered a deficit of ten shillings and he kept in a rare stew for three days trying to find out what was wrong, till there was a ten-shilling note shut between the pages of the book, and it was smart of him to think to look there," says Saunders.

"Well," I said, "your Mr. Snape has got to be a bit smarter in future, so as not have such things happen," I said. "Seems as though you are all the time playing at paper chases together with the notes," I said. "Have you looked under the carpet?" I said, "in case of anyone thinking to lay a false trail and forgetting he had done; or up the chimney, by any chance, in case of the wind blowing it?" I said.

He didn't like that, of course and, by what I make out, it may happen to be Saunders, or it may chance to be Snape, pays out and enters up; and, also, there are too many coming in and out of the office all the time; so I said I would have a hatch put in the panel of the door, and Snape to have charge of the cash and the book and to be responsible to Saunders for balancing up, Friday mornings; and a good lock to be put on, new, to his drawer, and duplicate key kept in the safe; and I told him I would have a private word with Master Snape.

"I will have no balance struck till that pound is found in the books or wherever else it has got to," I said; "and if not, you can sing your song to the auditors in May, Saunders, and we shall hear what they think of the cashier of Messrs. Arthur Ballard & Co., Builders and Contractors," I said; and, when I showed him out at the front, there he was going down the steps like as if his tail was dragging in the dirt and he not heeding whether it was or not; so I gave a bit of a whistle to have him come back.

"Don't you be cast down, Saunders," I said. "I'm well enough pleased with the way you carry on, and there will be a raise for you come the New Year. We all have our share of troubles we don't deserve," I said. On that he must come back up the steps and say:

"Oh, sir, I don't mind troubles so long as you think well of me."

"Thank you, Saunders," I said. "That's a proud thing for anyone to have said to him," I said. "Hope your wife is prospering," I said; for I knew he had another on the way. So off he went, wonderful perked up all of a sudden.


## A WORD WITH MR. SNAPE

I sent a kind invitation this morning, first thing, for Master Snape to pay me a call in my room; and soon there was his tap on the door.

"Come in," I said, and kept at my writing to give him time to admire the furniture and make a good start with any guessing he had a mind to try. I heard the door close very gentle and polite, and then there was the smell of whatever it is he carries about in his hair, like as if some old tom-cat had made a mistake next door.

"Well, Mr. Snape," I said, making to blot the sheet very particular, "I've been having a word with Mr. Saunders about you," I said; and then I sat back in my chair and looked at him pretty straight, standing there, to judge how he was feeling about things; but, except that his eyes always have a wrong look, you couldn't say what.

"Oh, yes, Mr. Grigblay?" he says, smiling with it like he was eager to hear a bit of good news he had made a guess was coming his way.

"Yes," I said. "Mr. Saunders has been telling me what a clever young man you are, and how careful letting him know, always, directly the petty cash don't balance by a note or two mislaid, instead of waiting for him to ask questions," I said.

"Yes, Mr. Grigblay, I was always a one to be careful

where money is concerned; you may rely on me, Mr. Grigblay," he says.

"So I understand," I said; "but I am glad enough to hear you say it, so that I may know for certain, and not be kept in any doubt," I said. "Well, after what Mr. Saunders has told me, I am going to give you plenty chances to show how careful you know how to be, and that is by promoting you to have charge of the Petty and Subbing and be responsible," I said.

"Oh, thank you, Mr. Grigblay! I never should have expected I deserved it, Mr. Grigblay," he chips in.

"Mr. Saunders was special pleased at the smart style you found that ten-shilling note that went astray, by searching a matter of three days for it," I said.

"Yes, I did, Mr. Grigblay, by thinking and thinking wherever it could have got to; for I said to myself, 'None coming into the office could be so light-fingered as to think to slip a temporary loan off of the petty cash by me not keeping a sharp eye'; for so I always do just from habit, Mr. Grigblay, by the way I was taught wherever money is concerned, Mr. Grigblay," he says, all in a breath and letting the cat out of the bag, clear enough.

"What's that I hear about slipping a temporary loan?" I said.

"Yes, Mr. Grigblay, so as to pay back on the sly without me knowing, Mr. Grigblay," he says.

"Is that what they did where you were taught to keep such a sharp eye?" I said.

"No, Mr. Grigblay; I only know hearsay, by a friend telling me private, Mr. Grigblay."

"And so you think the ten-shilling note was slipped for a temporary loan by somebody, and afterwards hid in the pages of the book, do you, Mr. Snape?" I said.

"I'm sure I could not say, Mr. Grigblay; it is all so mysterious, Mr. Grigblay," he says.

"Well, there's going to be a hatch fixed so that there will not be so many coming about to distract you," I said.

"Oh, yes, Mr. Grigblay; it distracts me all the time more than you can think, Mr. Grigblay; so no wonder I can't be——"

"Quite so," I said, having no mind to hear his jabber; "and then you will be able to think a bit more close about this new mystery of where the pound is gone, and show us you can be as smart at finding out where, as you were the last time. It is only five days gone, so far," I said, "and, if you keep at it the way you have begun, you will have plenty time to put all straight before we have the auditors come to pull ugly faces, and the police offering to take a hand," I said, looking at him pretty straight.

"Yes, Mr. Grigblay," he says; "and you can rely on me, faithful, Mr. Grigblay, never to let anything interfere where a discrepancy is concerned, Mr. Grigblay," he says, and, by the way he looked, no-one could say whether he is hiding something, or whether it is just his fanciful way of carrying on, and the general cut of the fellow, that makes me shy of trusting him. Perhaps getting the creeps inside me the first time I ever set eyes on him, puts me off from fair judgement; but I have found it all through my life that when, after months and years, I have by gradual experience come to know the whole insides of a man so that I can guess right, every time, the way he is feeling and thinking and how he will act, it has always been just the same as what I knew when I first clapped eyes on him, without me knowing I knew; but if it was the case of a woman—well, I wouldn't like to say, or else there are some might get a sight of this writing and cry out how perfectly idiotic Dad is! though I have no mind that any should read in my Journal, which is just to keep me going, and to hark back when I feel like it.

# A LETTER FROM FRED

Here is a letter come for me in a separate private envelope along with Fred Bloggs' returns and reqs. from
Belhampton. It is old Fred all over; so I have pasted in to
keep by me in this journal.

*Mrs. Ballard Coy.*
*Building*
*at Belhampton*
*Dorchester*
*Monday 7 tht*
*(December)*

Privit.

Mr. Grigblay.

Sir,

I think best tell you how it come about before he say.
Neare on elleven was a tall lanky chap come in a hire car
out of Weymouth has I thought to be on the cadg pokeing
about to ask of the men. So I whent along over to learn
waht he want an he says why wasent this done an thother
made a start, and when I ask he says he was C. of W. by the
gent's orders to see has we got a moveon. An I say I hadent
aerd nothing an we dont want no fatt C. of W. has dont
know know better than too order my men I says. He wehnt
on like hiteytitey so I say get along off double quick lousy
or I will drown them off of you in that there pond so has
you will go home missing them an all I said for I was care-
full not to be rued in my words has you wouldent have me
be. But he take offense an talk back an I add 2 labs show
him his rode and he kep at it over his sholdier so has I follow to have him behave more respectably to us. An if he
complain, he say has my mother was a biche before I say
anything what he was an it led to words but I am very sorry
what I said to him but it come off of my tongue before I
reckoned an I kep on so has he shd not have the last word
at us an it was enough before he drove off an the men will

say. They behave polite and cheered and shouted after if he like to come back for more of it. He let fall his name was Barnakkle an say he wd bloddywell let you know so he will spell the correct letters and please say if he is to come on next time or be put off again has thother time before and kindly oblige thanking you kindy Sir

Yours humbly
FRED.
Privit.

As I was on the 'phone with Mr. Spinlove, I told him how things were at Belhampton, and went over one thing and another to be sure we were carrying on the way he would have us to do; and then I asked him how soon was the Clerk of Works coming on the job to answer questions for us, and made bold to give him old Fred's account of a Mr. Barnacle walking on to the site to give orders and finding he'd come to the wrong shop, which set him laughing over the wire.

Mr. Spinlove said he never heard of Barnacle nor any other, and the gentleman had no business to fix on a Clerk of Works. Mr. Spinlove told him he would recommend a suitable man for Clerk; but, happened, he had not been able to get Bainbridge, and Joe Dawson was booked, so he was looking about to inquire who. Mr. Spinlove seemed real wild when I told him, and said if he couldn't have his own man to be responsible to carry out his orders, he would refuse to go on; and so it looks as though we shall get things fixed the way he wants. He said Fred had acted correct not allowing any on the site except by proper orders. I suppose we shall be hearing from Mr. Barnacle before long, about his little trip to Belhampton Castle.

# A CLERK OF WORKS

I called at Mr. Spinlove's office, to-day, about signing the Belhampton contract. There were fifteen drawings attached—the most I ever saw—with $\frac{1}{2}$-in. details, and all sorts, to cover the odds and ends and separate bits there are, so Tinge has been able to get down close with his quantities, and we shall know where we are and have straight sailing, I don't doubt.

Mr. Spinlove said he had seen the gentleman about appointing a clerk of works, and it seems the fellow Bloggs showed off the site is one William Barnacle by name, that is in the gentleman's regular employ to keep at running round to see after upkeep and alterations at all the shops the Gotsnitz Company owns. Putting two and two together from what Mr. Spinlove let fall, Mr. Spinlove has had a bit of a hullabaloo over the gentleman sending his man down to Belhampton behind Mr. Spinlove's back. However, they seem to have managed to shake hands in the end, for it is fixed up for this William Barnacle to live near by and act Clerk of Works; and Mr. Spinlove has had him to his office for a talk over, and it seems he was formerly Clerk under architect's orders before he was taken on to be supervisor of the Gotsnitz Company's property; and so he understands his duties, though, by what Mr. Spinlove said, he has never had to do with the class of work we are now at. It seems Mr. Spinlove told him pretty straight he was being employed to carry out the Architect's orders and be responsible to the Architect and to no other; and that if he did not give satisfaction he would be cleared out and another appointed.

Mr. Spinlove was upset about it all, clear enough. "The fact is, Grigblay," he said to me, confidential, "Barnacle is appointed as a spy to report to his employer behind my back, or it looks very like it," he says; and he went on that, soon as ever, for the very first time, he has trouble of that sort, or by the Clerk running counter to him, he will have a man of his own choice instead, or else he will himself resign from the work—"but", he says, "I would rather drop any two of my other jobs than Belhampton," he says.

"That will never happen, sir; don't you be afraid of that," I said. So he laughs and says No, he doesn't suppose it would do, but it was all extremely unpleasant, he says.

I said to Mr. Spinlove I thought well for me to go down and see Barnacle and Bloggs safe started on a proper understanding, or we should have bloody noses handing round and the Mayor of Dorchester racing out on his bicycle to read the Riot Act before we knew where we were, I said; and Mr. Spinlove agreed it would be the best thing, but it will not be for a fortnight or more, by the arrangements made, he says.

## AN OFFICIAL ARCHITECT

These final figures of the School that Jedbury, prime coster, with Sennock helping, brought in to me this morning, are a proper facer, though I knew the account was all on the wrong side. Rumble, that priced out the bills of quantities, has been dodging in and out of the Prime Cost Office, to see the worst, these many months past; and fretting more than I have ever known him before. Contract price, £14,490; add balance of variations, £327; equals £14,817 to be paid us. Prime Cost Jedbury makes to be £14,632, which means about £100 or more out of pocket, in addition to some £2,000 profit and overheads, so we shall show a loss in the books of over £2,000.

I can't blame Rumble—and glad enough not to, good little man as he is. I have got to blame myself; first, for knocking 5 per cent off Rumble's total pricings before filling in Tender Form—and even then we were only £74 below the next; and, second, I must blame myself, over again, for letting the option on facings from Vince & Brandington's yard run out, just only four days, by the time taken accepting our tender, but, lo and behold! they had contracted to supply Nibnose & Rasper for their loco. house on the new siding in the meanwhile, and none could be ready for us in time. I have had plenty facings from Vince & Brandington in the past, and it doesn't seem like them to give me the go-by without a reminder that the option was running out; but, like enough, Mr. Dirty Johnny Rasper got at them with a higher offer to cook my goose, like he has tried it on to do many a time before, so there we were! and we had to go to Peterhanger and pay 8 per cent more money, and lorry sixteen miles instead of two!

A great part of our loss, however, was no fault of mine nor of Arthur's, nor of any responsible to us; but was just by a misfortune that might happen to anyone, and that was having an engineer-surveyor-sanitary-official-architect in charge, who had not enough nerve left over from all the terrible fighting to get through his examinations, to be able to act on his own discretion and fair judgement; but must look to the strict words of the spec., like as if he was being examined over again to be sure not to make any mistakes, or was some lawyer out for splitting hairs, instead.

The gravel aggregate for all those hanging concrete floors and roof there are, was specified "to pass a $\frac{3}{4}$-in. mesh"—

just as I am used to; and I got a quote for the lot from the Gayton Pits, and gave them the order after sample was approved. It is what they call their "second underbed", and I have used it under same spec. twenty times over, I dare say, and never heard any complaint yet. There are a few flints get in that don't belong, size of an egg some of them, and we have the men throw aside any that matter as they spade into the mixer, and, if any should get by, those at spreading on the shuttering throw them out, and no harm to anyone.

Well, young Mr. Bertram P. Dumbler, B.Sc., A.M.I.C.E., A.S.L., A.I.S.E., just new out of college, with special-shape spectacles to make him look clever, passed the sample; and then, all of a sudden, when we had near two hundred yards tipped, ready for a start, it was: "Not up to sample! Must pass $\frac{3}{4}$-in. mesh." Tolpenny, in charge, looked surprised at him and let it pass; but next time His Royal Highness Professor Brains, Esq., came on the job, Tol. 'phoned through to the office, and me and Arthur went over like the fire brigade was wanted. We had Bertie with his back up in a corner so he couldn't run away home to tell mother, and the pair of us talked at him till he didn't know which to answer first; but would that fellow see sense? No, not for one moment!

There was no good us saying we would pick over careful: it was not so written down in the spec. It was no good us saying we were acting up to our contract, and that if screened ballast was wanted it had ought to have been specified "*Screened* to pass a $\frac{3}{4}$-in. mesh" for us to put in a price to cover. "To pass a $\frac{3}{4}$-in. mesh. To pass a $\frac{3}{4}$-in mesh," he kept saying, over and over, as if everyone was deaf. It was no use saying we were supplying to sample approved, because the sample was mixed in, instead of kept aside, and so we couldn't prove it—but who would ever think, all being the same grade out of the same pit!

Arthur says: "Well, sir; you don't get screened ballast unless it *has* been screened," he says; but the other:

"I don't ask for screeded ballast, I ask for ballast all to pass a ¾-in. mesh as you contracted to supply, and it is nothing to do with me," he says, "whether the ballast is actually screeded, or whether it is capable of passing a ¾-in. mesh without screeding," he says, like any professor chopping logic, as they call it; and all the time saying *screeding* instead of "screening" by not knowing what he was talking about. Arthur answers him that the spec. did not say "*all* to pass," but just "to pass", and then Bertie must argue on that like some school teacher that is always right; and so it went on.

I couldn't put it on to the Gayton Pit, for we had ordered "second under-bed", just as usual; so there we were, landed; and I admit I felt bitter about it at the time, and so do now. We had to order the rest of it screened, which brought the price up 20 per cent, and we started screening what we had on the site; but throwing against a screen stops the half of what will go through the power-screen they have at the pit, so at last we used some of it to mix in with the rough ballast for the ground concrete-spread, and the rest still lays there till we can find a use somewhere else. It would have cost too much to lorry to the pit for screening and then back again to site; but if Tolpenny worked any of it in for the hanging floors on the quiet, without me knowing—well, I can't blame him. I dare say we dropped near two hundred pounds over it just by Pa and Ma being special pig-headed for handing on to darling Bertie so as he might learn to know everything from examinations, like a good little pig-headed lad, and keep on at being pig-headed after.

# A RIVAL

Here is a queer state of things I had a talk over with Arthur to-day, arising from our tender for the Sausage Factory which has lost us the contract just by five pounds, exactly. The figures in the Architect's letter run like this:

| | | |
|---|---|---|
| Nibnose & Rasper, Ltd. | . | £8,220 |
| Arthur Ballard & Co. . | . | £8,225 |
| Crowtall, Pocker & Son | . | £8,750 |
| Gallerton & Co. | . | £8,842 |
| Pockton Bros., Ltd. | . | £9,000 |
| Prendrill, Boot & Co., Ltd. | . | £9,105 |
| Bastien & Gallop | . | £9,500 |

A very level lot, but we are too low, by appearances, dropping £525 from the one above; and all just because of Arthur talking too clever to Spedder to have him price low, I've no doubt. Well, I am ready enough to be passed over *this* time, for I have no mind to be bit again on top of the schools; and also it suits me to be quit of Snadge and his row of winking pigs; but what I said to Arthur:

"How has it come about that Nibnose & Rasper have fallen into the same mistake we have, by appearances; and how is it they tender the same figure as us with only just £5 less? What's the meaning of it?" I said, "except Mr. Johnny Rasper has somehow got news of the figure we were about tendering, and then offered at the same with just £5 knocked off," I said. "Looks to me Mr. Dirty Johnny has done us a good turn this time, instead of a bad one, by getting a contract away from us at a price that means losing money," I said, and Arthur agreed.

"Like enough," I said, "he thought he would be safe following our price and could save himself the trouble of pricing out the bills of quantities until after he knew that he had landed the contract; but who in our office?" I said to

Arthur, "or who out of it?" I said, "would get to pass on our figure to N. & R.?" I said; and Arthur could only shake his head and stare at me, the same as I did at him; and so we stood and couldn't make head or tail, no more than I can now.

Spedder's letter covering the priced bills arrived four days in advance of date for posting the Tender; but it was only on the morning of posting me and Arthur agreed to knock off £49 to make a round figure; and Arthur says he didn't fill in the Tender on day of posting till after dinner, and it lay on his table till past four, when he signed covering letter and handed Tender to Smith; so whoever came by the knowledge to pass on to Mr. Dirty Johnny, must have come in Arthur's room between two and half after four, or been about when the letters were put up in the back office, later.

Well, perhaps nothing is wrong and all just a "coincidence", as they call it; but by what I know of Mr. Johnny Rasper he'd come creeping to spy down the chimney if it was only ninepence to be had. I don't forget, and am not likely to do, either, the time he was on with that garage next door to where we were building the Saint Julian's Hotel. Before we knew where we were, everything was growing legs and walking off the job. Fred was in charge, and he was properly worried thinking some of the men we had signed on, special, were playing it off on us. It was half a score of scaffold boards one day; and then three drums of roofing mastic and two of putty and thinnings skedaddled, until we didn't know what we'd got or what we'd lost.

Fred cleared away all he had laying against the boundary wall and things got better, so it seemed Mr. Johnny had been fishing with hooks and slings to catch all he could over the wall, nights and Saturday afternoons and Church, Sunday, for we never caught any at it; but old Fred got a suspicion someone had managed to fit a key to a lock-up store

111

he had where was a rare lot of copper service piping and screwed unions, special for the job; and he set a booby trap with a three-quarter bucket of white-wash mixed up with dirt and nastiness to make it an extra nice treat. Someone got the white-wash all right, though the police never could tell us who, but the thieving being found out, and Fred putting new lock and bar to the store, stopped the game.

It is not like us to have suspicions going about; but putting two and two together there is certainly the smell of something fishy in this Sausage Factory business. However, I'm well content to have Nibnose & Rasper fall into the hole Spedder dug for us with the helping hand of young Arthur; and I dare say they are feeling things a bit draughty now they see they are £500 below where they'd like to be.

## NEWS

This is a cutting from our weekly "Sentinel" newspaper I have gummed in as a record, for there is something lays behind this Gasholder business that we shall hear more about later on, clear enough. It is taken from the report of Plans Committee Meeting of the U.D.C., Thursday.

"The Surveyor, Mr. F. Plimsol Bargate, F.S.I., F.I.S.E., reported that he had that day received plans from the Gas Company for extensive buildings proposed to be erected on land South of the Company's works. He had not yet had an opportunity of examining the plans, but he noticed that it was intended to erect a Gasholder on the line of the sewer from Gayton. The Surveyor was instructed to write to the Gas Company calling attention to the oversight, and to point out that it would be necessary to change the proposed site of the Gasholder."

Well, Bargate's letter will not bring any fresh news to Parkin or the Directors, that's certain; and what the meaning of it all is I cannot make a guess—unless to use up a bit of time so as to ease the dreadful worry it is to everyone having such a wonderful lot of it to spare that they don't know what to do with it all.

## A TRAVELLING COMPANION

It is too much for me going down to Dorchester, for Belhampton, and back home on the same day by motor—or either if I change at Clapham Junction or taxi across to Waterloo and travel by train; and I felt so used up when I got back to Waterloo last night, that I put up at the Strand Palace, and have kept quiet at home to get rested, to-day.

Mr. Spinlove fixed it, by my idea, for this William Barnacle, the new appointed Clerk of Works, to travel down along with me so as I could smooth over his rumpus with Fred and see them settled down together. I thought he had missed the train; but when, at last minute, I was hanging out of the window at Waterloo with umbrella held by wrong end, handle up, for him to know me by—like I told him I would do over the 'phone—there he was, as I guessed at once, with a porter and his luggage on his heels; a thin, bald, sloppy, red-moustached fellow of forty-five, with a round face on a long neck, and more than six foot tall, that came shimble-shambling, toes in, flip-flap, flip-flap along the platform, raincoat flying open each side and his trousers looking to be wearing holes in one another by his knees rubbing together. In he got—first-class for a treat!—and was soon settled down comfortable opposite.

He seems to be a cute, knowledgeable man, spite of his hunched shoulders and great bony wrists and knuckles as if he had set out to be first-class hefty but couldn't get to cover his skeleton: a queer sort of affair altogether, and a sly one, to my thinking, and not to be trusted for honesty. It seems he was "apprenticed" as he called it, to his uncle who was a builder in the Midlands; and, after a spell in the office and doing estimating and costing and evening classes, he went outside to learn bossing up, and so was never a craftsman at the bench, or to follow a trade on the scaffold, like the best Clerks I have known began.

He seemed pretty sharp on Bills of Quantities and prices; but I don't know what he'll think when he finds his copies are blank, with no prices filled in, for he'll get nothing from Fred unless he steals it. Mr. Spinlove is strict on the Contract Schedule being kept under seal, and the Quantity Surveyor, only, to have any business with the rates and prices; and so ought all architects to do, in my opinion, to set up a standard of right behaviour and give the contractor confidence he will be treated fair, which he cannot always be sure of when there are variations ordered. The Contractor is willing to face the risk of *well*-priced work being cut out, and that put in being *under*-priced, and to take the fat with the lean and trust to good luck; but if the Architect has the Schedule of Prices always under his eye to learn them off by heart, the Contractor's luck is likely to run out by the Architect trying to "practise economy"—as he calls it—by taking advantage of the prices; or, if he should chance to feel in a fright in case he won't be able to purr loud enough to make his client pleased at the Bill of Extras, as will now and again happen—or so I've been told—he may, if he is made the same as some, use all his best wits to see how he can substitute low-priced labours and materials in place of the good-priced work that the Contractor looks to for covering the other and seeing him safe through.

There is far too much of the idea abroad among young gentlemen just setting up for architects that they are specially-appointed, like policemen, to see that the Builder gives more than he is paid for, and that he makes everything just as nice and clever and pretty as the Architect has in mind to have it though he never thought to write it out in the Spec. and the Quantity Surveyor has described something different. It would be a good thing, to my mind, if some of these clever masters for giving lessons to the young gentlemen, had them to read in a few of the law books that lay down how the duty of an appointed Architect is to hold the balance fair between his Client and the Contractor, like he might be an Arbitrator set up to decide on the rights of the case. If they knew that lesson off by heart, they would put a drop or two of hot wax on the Schedule of Prices to keep safe and show it has not been broken open when the Final Account comes to be settled or dispute arises—the same as Mr. Spinlove always does. I don't say anything about the Quantity Surveyor giving kind advice to his dear friend the Architect to help him reduce the cost of the work by the knowledge he has of the prices, but I dare say I am not the only one who has found his luck running thin on that account.

Me and Barnacle got along together all right, going down. He is shy of a bit of fun, and one of the cautious distrustful kind, or I'm much mistaken; but he opened up about Sir Ezra Gotsnitz, talking as though he was a kind of ogre for making everyone frightened of him; and couldn't tell me often enough how brave a man Mr. William Barnacle was to carry things off the way he did with his employer, just as he might be some lion-tamer letting on what a dangerous life he led, and spluttering with it to make me hear better—spite of his great red moustache hanging down in front—till I felt I'd like a change—which was soon enough—and made pretence to go to sleep; on which he puts on his spectacles and had out his Spec. for the rest of the time.

When we got to the site, there was old Fred civil as he knows how, and he and the other shaking hands like they had inquired in the meantime and found there was nothing amiss with each other's mothers, after all! Fred had been quick running up an office for the Clerk along with his own, lined matching, and with everything thought of as comfortable as any could wish; but lanky Barnacle would have a telephone all to himself!

"That's out of reason," I said. "Here is Mr. Bloggs can let you have the use of his any time you want. You won't have any need to be telephoning all day, right away out in the country here," I said.

However, he kept at it; so at last I told Fred enclose telephone in a lobby between the two rooms so as to make it private; and, having a talk over, aside with Fred, for him to keep things running smooth with the Clerk, I had the idea for Fred to put the door between his office and the lobby with glass panel so as he could see through if the other door to the Clerk's place was shut. It was a queer idea to get hold of, on a sudden, for I have never thought to do such a thing before; so it shows I have got a notion or two in my head more than I know the reason of, not to fancy Mr. Lanky pushing his neck round the corner, like it might be a giraffe's, to overhear what was not intended for him.

## A LAUGHING MATTER

Here is one of the queerest chances come about I ever heard of, that has kept me at laughing and slapping my leg, off and on, ever since I got the letter this morning; and Arthur laughing when I told him so as he had to sit down to it, though he only knew of Pollard's visit by me telling him. I was made so above myself by it that I passed little Rumble a tenner out of the good nature I felt, but a fiver would have been the better thing, or even just a pound for good luck, instead. I had him promise, sacred, he would not breathe word to any, or we shall have expectations and discontent all round; and not even tell the Missis, or it would break out "Caw, Caw, Caw," like a colony of rooks from door to door and up and down the street, before ten minutes was passed—but I didn't say it that way to Rumble or let fall any complaint of his good lady who would be only doing like the best of them when it comes to a bit of good news to brag about.

First, was yesterday afternoon, when Mr. Spinlove asked for me on the 'phone to know how things were at Belhampton for him to write the gentleman; and then at the end he asks, casual, have I had a letter from Mr. Blenhasset? I answered him No; but we were expecting any time, as I had sent in a tender to him over-night; and why had Mr. Spinlove asked, I said. "Oh, nothing particular; no importance," he says, and rings off.

Then, this morning, came the letter from Mr. Blenhasset, and our tender for Priors Franklyn is accepted. That is good news, for it is the sort of work I can take a pride in; but the fun is in the list of tenders—only four invited in with us— that goes like this:

|  | £ | s. | d. |
|---|---|---|---|
| Arthur Ballard & Co. . . | 5,998 | 9 | 6 |
| Blackington & Pollard Ltd. . | 6,000 | 0 | 0 |
| Prenderly Bros. . . | 6,182 | 10 | 0 |
| Gambol & Stedd . . | 6,650 | 0 | 0 |
| V. C. Rollart & Son . . | 7,225 | 0 | 0 |

So there is Mr. Pretty Pollard passed over just for the price of a fresh pair of petticoat-pants for wearing, change and change about, with his wife; and we shall have him round to hand in another of his visiting-cards in a day or two—or I am much mistaken—got up in a red collar with his hair permed—just for a change—to say his managing director would like to be informed how it all came about, and what we mean by it!

It came about by Rumble bringing over his pricings-out for me to fix the amount of our tender. The total he made was £5,512; but, after looking over, and by what I made of the drawings in the architect's office, and of the site—that I thought well to run out to Hertford to see; and by the awkwardness of getting our stuff laid handy; and the different parts, scattered about, being hard of access, and protecting of lawns, and one thing and another;—well, I thought Rumble had drawn it too fine and I judged best add £500; and so I told him, and said I would tender £6,000; on which he makes the little groaning noise under his breath when he is not satisfied that starts my backbone creeping by hearing it too often.

"Well, what's the matter this time?" I said. "You can't be discontented I have added on near 10 per cent to your figure, I should think!" I said.

118

"It's a very round sort of figure, sir, isn't it?" he says.

"Well, what if it is?" I said. "It's a round figure the same as a bargain generally is," I said. "What's wrong with you this morning?" I said. "Did the bacon go the wrong way at breakfast?" I said.

"I thought, maybe, another might fix on the same, sir, if they had a mind to offer at a round figure," he says.

"All right, all right, all right!" I said. "Have it your own way if that will make you feel happy," I said. "So we will knock off thirty bob and a sixpence extra for luck," I said; and that is how it came about our tender was £5,998 9s. 6d., and was why I made Rumble a present by him using his wits instead of just treading round and round the mill—like the donkey I saw somewhere in Isle of Wight—year in and year out, as the half of them do, and so never get beyond clerking-work for another to overlook and approve, however long they keep at it.

To-day, when there was a message to go through to Mr. Spinlove's office, I asked to have a word with him to answer his question, yesterday; and then it came out that he had recommended us to Mr. Blenhasset to be invited, and that Mr. Blenhasset had rung him up, yesterday, to ask a special question or two about us, and that is how Mr. Spinlove came to be interested to know had we been successful?

Well, I don't know when I've been so pleased and tickled: I dare say not since Nibnose & Rasper had their old steam wagon blow up and scare the whole town and knock down the beautiful new urinal—all glazed brick in colour-patterns for drawing attention—they had just finished top of the High Street, and lucky no one killed into the bargain!

119

# THE LOST, FOUND

Now, after nearly a fortnight gone, Saunders must follow after me—seeing me crossing the yard through his window, no doubt—to say Snape has found the pound lost out of the Petty! Saunders was pleased all over his skin like some dog wagging his tail to show master what a good dog he is; but I just gave him a grunt for answer and passed along, instead of clapping him on the back and dancing a jig which was what he expected—by the look of things. Later, after thinking over, I went into the cashier's to see into the meaning of all the nonsense.

"So, Mr. Snape," I said, "I hear from Mr. Saunders you have discovered the whereabouts of the pound that went astray; just by persevering and not losing hope, as some might do," I said.

"Yes, Mr. Grigblay, I have succeeded at last, as you can see for yourself, Mr. Grigblay," he says; and he holds up a note out of his drawer as though no one could ever believe it!

"Well, that's a wonderful thing to have happen, after all this time," I said. "How did it come about you were so smart?" I said.

"Yes, Mr. Grigblay, I kept at it and, right at the end, just by a mysterious lucky chance that might never have happened, Mr. Grigblay, I found out it had slipped over the back of the drawer and right down behind the books, in the cupboard under, like this, Mr. Grigblay," he says; and so he ran on with his gabbling, and must pull out the drawer, and there was a space—a quarter-inch, I dare say—between the top of the back and the under-side of the desk-top; and then he opened the cupboard to show the books ranged along the top shelf, standing an inch or two away from the back lining to leave a gap where the note had fallen down behind.

"That's how it came about for certain, Mr. Grigblay," he says, "and the proof is: directly I went to pull out the M.14 Req. file, just like this, Mr. Grigblay," he says, "there was the note laying, like I put it now for you to see, Mr. Grigblay; so it must have slipped over the top of the drawer without my ever guessing it could do, Mr. Grigblay, and it was just a lucky chance me taking the M.14"—and so he ran on until I had had enough, and said:

"Well, Mr. Snape, now it has happened the once, you will not have the same trouble when it happens next time, by knowing where to look first start off," I said.

"Yes, I will do; you can be sure of that, Mr. Grigblay," he says.

"And you might have a try to see if you can prevent it happening next time," I said. "There is a clever thing invented to prevent notes from blowing about if the door should chance to be left open or the wind come in at the window," I said; "and that is a paper-clip or an elastic band for holding the notes together, so that if one goes astray the whole lot goes together and is more easy to find by not getting down behind if there are any narrow cracks waiting to catch it," I said.

"Yes, Mr. Grigblay. It is a good idea, instead of just putting them under the bowl for safety, like I do, Mr. Grigblay."

"Well, keep at it," I said, "and we shall get things straight soon and, I hope, no more trouble for you by accidents that can be prevented," I said.

"Thank you, Mr. Grigblay," he says. "You can rely on me to be careful, as I always try to be, Mr. Grigblay," he says, as I walked out.

Well, there it is! It is not in nature for such accidents to happen twice over inside six weeks; but none can say the one note might not have got shut in the book, or the other pushed over the top of the drawer by catching in some

121

splinter when the drawer was pulled out, considering all the skirmishing and disorder there always is handling the petty cash and subbing money; and the books pulled away to make a space at back, might just be anyone's fancy to see them lined up with the front of shelf instead of pushed in. Unless Mr. Oswald Snape makes a guess I am the twin brother of Simple Simon, he will be warned, by the style I carried on with him, that he is on dangerous ground with his losings and findings, and will have a better care in future.

# CHRISTMAS

Here is Christmas coming round again, and I had a word with Smith to-day for him to get out the list. As long as I last I will have the old style kept up, and that is: a turkey or a first-class fowl to the heads and leading foremen; and a prime joint of pork or beef to every man, whether tradesman or labourer, that has been with us five years or over. Smith gets to know what the families are, so that the weights are made according, and all can choose whether pork or beef, as they fancy. The order is given and all is laid out on a trestle-table in the hardwood loft, with a sprig of holly and the names and a word of good wishes written on a picture-card with each, and me and Arthur go round and say a friendly word before they pack up for the holiday with three cheers and one over. For them that are away, the wives like to come and fetch it or it is sent over, as Smith thinks best; and if any of those away don't come home, Smith has the foreman in charge see to it. That is how it has been in the past, and so I keep on; and I won't say I don't please myself, on the quiet, where there is illness or distress at home that I hear of, whether a man has put in his five years or not; but, by the changes there are all round, I dare say Arthur will have things different some day, for I know he doesn't see things the same as I do, though he acts up to please me like the good lad he is.

Then there is presents to architects and quantity surveyors and one and another—more than I can remember, sometimes—that is my business to arrange about, and I don't relish; for things are different from what they had used to be when it was just a bit of conviviality and jollity out of good nature, and no-one thought any different; but now commercial competition has given things a new look, so that, even if it is which shall pay for a bit of lunch on the train, there is awkwardness, as if the one was out to fix an obligation on the other to do him a favourable turn in the business way; and many a time, in the past, have I been hurt in my feelings, or bothered to know what the other was thinking, whichever way I acted; and this I will say, that no one now seems to bring out a half-sovereign without he has in mind an investment for profitable return in the future. I like to feel it a mark of respect when I accept anyone's hospitality, and to so value that any should accept mine; and as for taking a present off anyone!—why that's as high a compliment as I know how to pay, for, if I did, it would be only out of my affectionate feelings.

# A REMINISCENCE

The worst I ever felt was when Mr. Spinlove was married; and I dare say it would hurt me too much to call to mind, even now, if I hadn't had the better of him and if he hadn't made joke of it with me more than once since as though the laugh was all against him.

It was half a year after we built Honeywood Grange, when Mr. Spinlove was new set up for architect, that he married Miss Phyllis, that was, the owner's daughter. There had been a rare to-do getting the job finished and out of the way; and it looked, at one time, I should find myself in the Law Courts over the wonderful patent decorators' paint I objected to, but was ordered to use, that went wrong so as it all had to come off and be done over again, fresh, and a nice business that was! However, it all ended pleasant enough with everyone good friends, and Sir Leslie Brash not able to be polite enough to me, and wedding bells getting ready to be pulled and everyone happy; so when the young man was married to the young lady that had been running all over the job with her friends, like the slip of a chattering laughing girl she was, I felt warmed up by the prettiness of the whole business and bought a nice lot of cut table-glass that anyone might be glad to have by the money it cost, and had it sent to Mr. Spinlove's office—not knowing what other address he had—with just my card and good wishes laying on top, inside; so he had to open the case to see who it was from and would know what was in.

Well, the first news of kind thanks I had was when I walked into my office one afternoon off the train, after two days away, and there was the case staring at me with the lid off and my card on top and the hay and paper scratched away for any to see what was inside! I can remember the way I stood and stared, by the queer kind of jolt I took at seeing it. There was a letter, of course, but marked "Private", and, so, sent over to the house, that I knew nothing of it till later. It was in his own hand and went something after this style, as I remember:

Dear Mr. Grigblay,

I have received your most kind greetings and much more kind and generous wedding-gift you sent along, and I need not say how much I appreciate your kind generosity and all the more by the difficult times we have had together. I needn't say how much I want to keep all that nice pretty glassware you were so very kind and generous as to offer, and how hard it comes for me to communicate that it is impossible for me to do so by being an architect not allowed to take presents of any I am related to in business on behalf of clients, as you will remember now I put you in mind; so I am regretfully returning your kind and generous case and fully esteem your most friendly idea in thinking to send it,

Yours most sincerely.

Well, I was in a proper rage at him and his priggy ideas of minding what people might think if any ever found out; when all was open and above board with my card to lay on top for all to see when the presents were spread out in the house and under the very nose of the gentleman he had acted architect for, and who was the only one to be concerned by me giving his Architect a present. What made me so particular irritated and mad with it, was to remember all the trouble I had been put to by Mr. Spinlove not having enough experience to keep things going straight—spite of me giving him a hand to help him along or Lord knows where we should all have been landed—so it was not exactly planned in my head to do something to make sure I should contract again where young Mr. Spinlove was in control to direct the business. I felt so sore with it that I sat down, on the spur, and wrote him this style:

Dear Sir,

I have taken to heart, to always remember, your kind remarks in your letter just received. I offer my humble apologies to yourself, the future bride, Sir Leslie Brash and Lady and all concerned, for falling into the mistake of expressing my good wishes for your marriage in the usual style without remembering that everyone would easy see the purpose for bringing about another pleasant and profitable contract under your wise guidance and direction; with the building-owner always close at hand to give a bit of extra help and advice, when needed, so as to keep things running smooth. The case duly to hand and signed for.

Thanking you again for your consideration in writing me your kind remarks.

I am, dear Sir,

Yours faithfully.

However, I thought better wait and see in the morning; and then, sitting to tell Louie after tea and a romp with the children, it all looked to be different; and we got to laughing together over the young man trying to learn how to behave strict; and then Louie had one of her sudden bright ideas, and says:

"Why not send it to the young lady? You've often told me about her": and so I did, very first thing in the morning; and all the message Mr. Spinlove ever had from me was when he saw the glass, with my greetings to the bride, among the wedding presents—and after he was married, like enough. It was a dam' good smack in the eye for him that he could do with at the time without taking any harm.

Now here is her letter for pasting in, that I came across in that lot Louie left behind, and have kept for remembrance of her being so pleased and tickled at the way it goes, and at the scrawled writing by the hurry and excitement of the young girl, just as she felt at the moment, no doubt. Le dernier cri is in French, and means the same as writing "latest fashion"—or so Louie told me.

My dear Mr. Grigblay,

You really are a perfect *darling*! However did you guess? It is le dernier cri and the very poshest of the posh so that Mum is *quite* green. Even Snooty—you know! The one with the carroty shingle—fell to it *absolutely*, and said I was a dirty little digger. You will see it all set out when you come. No time for more.

Ever yours sincerely,

PHYLLIS BRASH.

Inside there was an invite to the church and, after, at Honeywood, with "Mr. and Mrs. John Grigblay" filled in; but we thought not to accept for the party with all the Swells crowding; and, on the day, I was tied up and the car wanted, so we did not go to the church, either—and not missed, I dare say!

It was two or three years before I saw Mr. Spinlove next time, by our tender for Kedlington accepted; but, the very first thing, he made outcry of the sly one I was that no one knew what he wouldn't be up to next, and a lot more nonsense and joking; and, also, he has remembered it once or twice since then, so all came well in the end.


## A RIDDLE ANSWERED

It is out, at last, for any to read in this Friday's *Sentinel*; close on two columns of it with great headlines in big letters to call attention like it might be an earthquake happened:—LOCAL SENSATION. DEMAND BY THE GAS COMPANY; DISORDERLY SCENES ON COUNCIL, and cross-headings, all down, as well, to keep up the excitement in case any

should begin to feel they didn't want to read to the end:—
MR. BLACKMAN CALLED TO ORDER. "WHY NOT BUY THE
GAS WORKS?" COUNSEL'S OPINION TO BE TAKEN, and so it
goes on; and it clearly explains that the Company sub-
mitted plans of new buildings with the Gasholder shown
where it would cut through the sewer, when there is no
occasion for any new buildings except to make pretence
there is no other site for the Gasholder—the most scanda-
lous swindling of the public that ever was heard of; for the
Company is out for compensation and nothing else, as is
clear enough when one knows something of what Parkin
has been at behind the scenes!

First, was when the Secretary read out a letter from the
Gas Company replying to one Bargate had written pointing
out to them that the Gasholder was sited on top of sewer,
and would have to be shifted; and, lo and behold! they say
there is no easement on the land for the sewer to run across,
but that the owners of seventy-two years ago just gave a
grant of leave, consideration £50, with limitation not to
interfere with enjoyment of the land; no-one ever supposing, all those years ago when Gayton was a separate village,
that the land would ever come to be built on; and now the
Gas Company say they regret it is necessary to call on the
Council to remove the sewer off their land forthwith, so as
they can have full enjoyment!—just as if you can pick up a
24-in. brick sewer and lay it down somewhere else like it
was a scaffold board!

Well, first those in Council said: why had not Bargate
laid the letter before the Plans Committee for their report?
And Bargate said he judged it was a matter to go to the
Council direct; and then they had an argument and shouting over it till someone proposed that the letter be referred
to the Plans Committee, and they decided unanimous—all
but two votes—not. Next, Bargate was asked, and said he
had ascertained the facts were as stated in the Company's

letter; and so far as he could see the only way would be to scrap the sewer—which was an old brick and lime-mortar barrel—and lay a new three-foot, spun-concrete pipe-sewer to pick up branches in Gayton, and come down Hill Road under the Railway Arch and turn across; and he said his rough estimate was twenty to thirty thousand pounds! That was when the real shouting began; and then a bit of politics got mixed in to make the time pass a thought more quickly and pleasantly; so, in the end, there was nothing settled except the Clerk is to get George Trencher, Solicitor, to take Counsel's Opinion, so they will hear all about it, some day—with a few more lawyers to tell them what the Opinion means—and will know what to start shouting about next; but, as I said to Arthur, it will soon be time for us to think about our Contract being broken and make a claim ourselves, I said.

## AN ADVENTURE

Going for a walk with Effie, Saturday afternoon, and coming along home by the field-path from Broddle and up the drift under the Railway, there—just short of the archway—was the road puddled right over and swamped in mud and grit, by a nine-inch, clay-jointed, temporary drain pushed through the hedge and running three-quarter bore, with real thick water, faster than the ditch could take it; and the "piff-paff" of a gas-engine sounding away off,

We picked our steps through—by me giving Effie a lift over —and I thought no more till we took the turn into Station Road and came to hoarding-gates with Nibnose & Rasper's name on; so, clear enough, they were still on their New Loco. House for the Railway Company, and having a job to keep water from making on their foundation-work, during the week-end.

Next, passing along by the side of the Old Loco. House that lays right up against the footway, my eye chanced to light on a crack running all down through the coping to the plinth; and new-opened, clear enough, $\frac{1}{8}$ in. wide—and more, in places—with crumbs of mortar laying in and actually slipping down, here and there, under my very nose for me to see it happening! So there was Mr. Clever Johnny Rasper, pumping, pumping, pumping—to keep the water under in his Loco. pits, no doubt—and pumping the whole of the dam' place down on top of himself instead! just by not having the sense to remember that—when you keep on at pumping nice, thick, soupy yellow water for blocking ditches so as they won't drain, and plastering roads so as none can travel them—there is sometimes just a chance of taking away sand and loam from where it may be a bit more useful laying quiet to support buildings, like it was before, even if they might be a quarter-mile away.

It was no sense letting the harm go on and grow worse by keeping at pumping right through to Monday morning before anybody came to be the wiser; so we went along back and banged and kicked for someone to come. I had to half kick the boards out of their shoddy old botch of a gate —good enough for preventing chickens, I dare say—before an angry fellow came to see who the hell was breaking the place up! He was a stupid heavy chap with a thick slow voice, special-selected by Mr. Johnny—I've no doubt—as a smart man for sleeping up against the engine and coming awake soon as it stopped running.

130

"Hullo!" I shouted, by the way he put his head out to see what was up. "Is there anyone about?"

"They all cleared off, one o'clock."

"You'd better send for someone to come right away, or you'll have the place tumble down," I said.

"What's that?" he says.

"You must stop pumping, and 'phone for your Foreman," I said.

"I got my orders," he says. "Keep regulator at five and half; them's my orders." So I had him come up the road—thirty yards or so—to see for himself.

"That there arn't nothing to do with me," he says.

"Have you got a telephone, inside?" I said.

"I haven't got no orders to interfere with no telephone," he says; and off he straddles back to carry out his orders and earn his money like a steady, reliable, honest workingman; so I judged best save time and ring up Mr. Johnny as we passed along by the Station, to see if he was in; but he was up in London and not expected home till late, being out to do a kind action for the holders of Brewery & Distillery shares—I've no doubt. On that I went in the Station-Master's office, as I thought there might be just a chance the Railway Company would be interested. The Station-Master listened to all I had to say, but didn't seem to know what to make of it; and then he had a sudden bright idea, and looked at his watch to see if that would help things, but it only made him more puzzled what to think.

"It's the Permanent Way Engineer's job, if you ask me," he said. "He'll be back Tuesday, and can have a word with you then. They wouldn't pay any attention to me," he says.

However, when I followed him out, there was a young fellow waiting for the London train that he spoke to, and who came over and said he was on the Engineer's staff; but, when I told him, he said he didn't see what he could do as he was only a draughtsman for laying out sidings, and had

131

no authority; but he gave me the name of N. & R.'s manager he had seen once or twice about lay-out of track, who I found in the Directory and got at once—out of his easy-chair for a nice Saturday-afternoon snooze by the sound of him.

"Well, what is it?"

"Is that Mr. Kilmorton?"

"Who's speaking?"

Then I told him what I'd seen of the water pumping and settlement started.

"Who's speaking?"

"Did you follow what I said?" I asked.

"Yes, I heard. Who's speaking?"

For answer, I hung up, for I don't want any truck with Mr. Johnny, who, like enough, would find cause to make trouble of some kind; or else he would be so extra grateful to me for all my wonderful polite and kind-hearted behaviour, that the only possible way he could hit on to show his great thankfulness and make adequate return for benefits received, would be to offer me a nice easy chance to finance him without security, or to lend him our new fifteen ton lorry for him to forget he'd ever had it.

There is one rule that I have found come true time and time again, all my life, big and little things the same, sorry as I am to remember; and that is: that so sure as ever you go out of your way to do anyone a good turn with no idea of any advantage or favours to be gained, so surely will it bring you in return—sooner or later—a slap in the face to teach you not to meddle next time: which is just the same as it means when the proverb says: "Virtue has its own rewards." I do not hold there is any virtue in keeping back from acting malicious; but, in case Providence should think any different, it is only polite manners not to reach out after the appointed reward by letting Mr. Johnny Rasper know I was the one that gave him the friendly tip, and which, like

132

enough, might prove to be no smack in the face *this* time, but a real, hefty, first-prize kick in the backside—just for a change.

However, now I come to think, it seems there *was* a bit of virtue, after all, in me meddling in Rasper's business; for, by the delay, me and Effie thought to have tea at the Café Magnolia; and, after, it was the cinema; and, when we got home, if Henry Curt hadn't come special, all the way from London, to see us—after 'phoning to learn we would all be in—and only gone ten minutes after sitting with Meg more than two hours!


## AN ANNOUNCEMENT

Here's a jolly bit of news to-day about that sly old Fred when he was home, Christmas; and all the men, and the office staff as well, making a great joke of it to-day from the paragraph in *The Sentinel* that Smith called my attention to this morning—for I never noticed last night when the paper was delivered—and that I have just now cut out for pasting in. It reads like the fashionable news, and very nicely put, as well.

### FORTHCOMING LOCAL CELEBRATION

Readers resident in Jubilee Street and Porchester Avenue neighbourhoods and others, will be interested in the information just forthcoming that we understand a local wedding has been arranged to be shortly celebrated between Mr. Frederick Joshua Blogg, of Farm Cottage, Porchester Avenue, the well-known and popular president of the Trident Pig Club and leading member of the staff of Messrs. Ballards (Builders), and Mrs. Susannah Penelope Tippits, of 42 Jubilee Street (General Dealer), relic of the late Sergeant

Major Tippits, M.M., our late respected and popular townsman and well-known late drill-instructor, for many years associated as successful late Captain of the Town Tug of War in opposition to the Fire Brigade and Police at the Agricultural Show, as very few will forget to remember. Our readers will join with us in offering our hearty congratulations to the happy couple to be on their forthcoming local matrimonial celebration and which we hope will soon eventuate and long continue.

Old Fred never said a word to me when he came round to the offices, morning after Boxing Day, before he started off back to Belhampton, being a bit shy to tell me, I dare say, knowing I should joke him; but I remember he looked very smooth and quiet in his face, and not so much of his stammering and anxiousness talking over arrangements, and brushed up more than usual, as it might be a Sunday, almost, the simple old fellow!

Well, it makes me feel happy, for I have somehow come to love old Fred who would never put his foot in it and make a mistake; and his lady-love is a hearty little roundabout, well on the right side of fifty, and always like a new pin and ready for a laugh; and she has a bit put by, no doubt, from the buzz there always is in her little corner shop where I go in, passing to the Station, sometimes; and have my papers sent up to the house and the girls' weeklies sent also:—how to be more killing than ever before and catch 'em, certain, every time. Fred was pretty smart about it; for I have never heard gossip of him dangling and there have been plenty after her, I understand. Well, I have written to the old fellow to joke him and wish him good luck and what would he fancy for a wedding present, so I shall be getting one of his special-marked "privit" letters in a day or two.

## A NEW ARCHITECT

Yesterday I made acquaintance with Mr. Rupert Blenhasset, A.R.A., when I called to sign the Contract for
Priors Franklyn at his office at Burlington Street, just off
Bond Street near to the scent shop; and a wonderful place
for an Architect's office it is when you get inside; with a
gentleman's servant, as he might be, to open the door after
the lift attendant has pressed the bell in case it should
trouble you too much to reach out for yourself; and then,
within, it is all thick carpet, and pictures of his architecture
hung round the walls, all in colours like real life—though
some a bit overdone, if any should ask my opinion—and a
waiting-lobby at the side—for his Dukes and Duchesses, no
doubt—with more Architecture pictures like a shop for
selling them, and statues on the mantelpiece, and a great
pot with glass leaves on a corner-stand; and a rare Cuba
mahogany table with silver inkstand ready; and fancy-
carved chairs and settee, with footstools, all upholstered in
pale, shiny, green morocco to make you feel too shy to sit
down, and a lot else, besides. After a minute, the gent's
servant came back and took me off by a side-passage to the
drawing office he has, up a private stair, in the roof; and
the chief draughtsman—Mr. Mooney by name, from what
he said—laid out all for me to sign; and, after, we had a talk

135

over the drawings, and a handsome lot they make, I will say.

Well, it will be a real lovely thing when done, for certain, to judge by the sample bricks there: greeny-buff and pale rose broken-colour mixed facings, that are special out of Cambridgeshire under a p.c.,—and they will let us know the yard later—$1\frac{7}{8}$ in. thick, for laying with $\frac{5}{8}$ in. mortar joint squeezed out and cut off with the edge of a trowel—a nice thing, if we don't have any frost come and take it out! The Edge Hill stone is specified for copings and some bits of dressings there are—the same I used all those years back, Banbury way, and do like the look of most particular with its quiet buff-white colour, marked over, pie-bald style, with green patches as it might be camouflaged for the war, almost. It is to be Llanywrwyd Rustic Slating—that I recall the look of better than the spelling—half-way to stone, almost, like the Cotswold, but with a nice green colour and rough face, though a bit greasy-looking when the sun strikes on them. It will be a rare nice job, and no mistake; nothing for size, of course: just the terrace, flagged, and a terrace wall along where the grass bank now is; with a little "Garden House", as it calls them on the plans, backed into the rhododendron shrubberies to close the terrace, one each end; and then, in the middle, facing south across terrace and over the lawn and garden, is the "Pavilion", laying open, with front pillars, for having tea in, as I fancy by the door in the back opening to a narrow path through the shrubs to the kitchen-end of the house. Right in front are fancy steps down, seven on each side of a pretty little cascade gathered from a natural spring to discharge out of a fine bit of carving on the face of terrace wall, and end in a lily-pond on the lawn below.

I will have old Snoop down to look after the brickwork. Those half-domed niches in the walling of the Pavilion, each side of the columns, for setting a statue in, will keep him happy and, when he's finished, make everyone feel proud. There is a separate contract for the garden—day-work account for monthly settlement, as I understand—let to Sprewitt & Trott, who I never heard of before but are, likely, one of these commercial firms always ready to act as consultants to direct and advise on their own contracts; and give service to the owner by placing the special highly-skilled technical knowledge and experience of their numerous staff of experts at his free disposal entirely without any charge; and not asking so much as a sixpence in fees for very strongly recommending him to buy whatever they want to sell, for them just to charge at their usual prices and make a bit of easy money, nice and quick, before the "What Ho!" is sounded and the shouting begins. However, the gardeners following close on us, we can work in along with them to know where we are, and make a tidy finish.

## IN THE SANCTUM

While I was looking into things with Mooney, the gentleman's servant came in and says: "Mr. Blenhasset will see you now, sir," and he took away my hat, coat, and umbrella without a word, before I knew what he was at, to hide them away somewhere as if they were things not proper to be seen. Then he conducted me over the soft carpet to a door, and asked me my name, fresh over again, so as not to make any mistake; and then he announced me, standing straight up, side of the open door, like some officer in uniform, as though the Lord Mayor was giving a party inside. It made me wish I had my hair cut last week, like I meant to do; and had slipped on my clothes for going to Church in, as well.

Mr. Blenhasset, A.R.A., is a very agreeable gentleman by

what I saw of him, that stood up behind his knee-hole table when I came in, and made a polite wave of his hand to a chair, with a bit of a bow for me to be seated. He was very quiet and serious in his manners, and not one of the confidential sort like Mr. Spinlove—always ready to return your smile and pass you one on his own account, as well.

I was surprised Mr. Blenhasset is just a little broad, thick fellow, with a small, fat puggy face and nose pushed a bit sideways; but he made up for it by his dark hair plastered down, very shiny, low on his forehead each side of a wide middle parting like a path over the hills; and little close-clipped whiskers as far down as the front of his ears; and a queer arrangement, I never saw before, of a black satin tie going a half-dozen turns round like the influenza, with a broad square bow in front, same as Miss Sniggit, that was, had her prize cat to wear—except pussy's was blue and slewed all to one side.

It was a beautiful room he had, with fine pictures hung round—none of his architecture *this* time; but no one would ever guess any work was done in it, by the style of the drawing-room carpet; and the rich-carved mahogany arm-chairs; and the pedestal table with great silver boxes for cigars and cigarettes—all like it might be some show room of an Art Furnisher's, at Olympia. There was just a great portfolio-stand, five feet high, pretty near, all fancy-shaped mahogany and brass rods, to hide his drawings away, no doubt; and a fine polished dinner-table with three flower vases set along it, for spreading them out, by appearances.

Well, Mr. Blenhasset is a wonderful man that knows his business all right; and, if he doesn't work *there*, he works precious hard in some other place at another time, for he knew about Priors Franklyn inside and out, and didn't need to have his chief draughtsman at his elbow to tell him the answers, like one or two famous architects I could name. He is all in jerks for quickness, and talking the while in a low voice it is difficult to follow. He whipped a quarto pad of sketching-paper out of his drawer, and slapped down in pencil, for me to see, sooner than he could have had the drawings laid out: plans, elevations and sections—no matter what—just as far as he wanted for his explanations; and bits of detail, too, as quick as lightning—the most remarkable knowledge and skilfulness I ever thought to see in an architect, and the whole cram full of sense and value, and no time lost by it.

Well, all was clear enough to me, with nothing new that I didn't feel sure about; and it always warms me up when I know an architect has his heart in a good bit of work so that I can join in with him and make sure he is satisfied; but one thing troubled me, and all the more now I have examined spec. and drawings and gone over the Bills, and that was: all he had to say about where materials should be deposited, and paths protected, and how to arrange access so as his Lordship and family shall not be put to inconvenience, and no harm done to the gardens by a geranium come to be snapped off or any other terrible accident happen. I didn't reply to it at the time, except to make sure I understood his meaning—and, if it comes to that, we can take as much care as anyone, and a lot more than most, I dare say; but two things are pretty clear: first, there will be a rare lot of wheeling, and a rare lot of planking over paths and of planking raised clear of killing the grass, by all the coming and going and barrows running backwards and forwards; and, second, the Quantity Surveyors—Previous & Frogg, that I have heard of but never seen their work—haven't measured near enough to cover, if the Architect's ideas are going to be put into practice.

It was good enough, before bills of quantities were the regular thing and we tendered on spec. and drawings, for the spec. to say: "The builder is to include for all necessary

139

planking, etc., for protecting paths and lawns from damage, and make all good at completion"; and "The Contractor is to have access by the back drive and to deposit materials where directed", as Mr. Blenhasset has it worded in his; but, now that the practice of London quantity surveyors is to measure and bill every separate item of labour and material necessary for completion of the work, the contractor looks to be properly secured by the Bills, and not have to take a chance and add on a round sum to cover. If the Q.S. knows his business he will find out from the Architect exactly what the Contractor is to provide against general clauses in the spec.; and if the Architect knows *his* he will see that the specification is completed *after* the bills are finished, so that the descriptions in each agree and there will not be the rare old mix-up there often enough is when the Spec. says one thing and the Quantities say another thing; or the Quantities and Spec. set out to describe the same details in different words, with the idea, no doubt, to make things a bit clearer for everyone all round and prevent any misunderstandings or disappointments coming about! I have been waiting these many years for the law-case where the spec. and the quantities are "taken together", and the Judge has to decide which is binding when they both say different. I have not heard of any such yet, and I dare say it is because the muddle is so thick that people are kept out of court by the lawyers splitting their heads over it till they can't say what day comes next after Tuesday week, and so decide—"better settle".

Well, I will have Rumble do a bit of measuring on the ground; and if Previous & Frogg do not show me where I am covered in the bills—which they can't do—I shall write the Architect, before we make a start, and ask authority for the extra, unless he should fancy changing his mind and directing different instead. I will go down with Tolpenny—who will be in charge—and Rumble this week. I can't go

next, by it being fixed for me to meet Mr. Spinlove, Belhampton.


## FRED RETURNS THANKS

Here is old Fred given me the best laugh I have had for
many a week past, with his reply to my letter congratulating him on his marriage engagement :—

                              Jitty Cottage
                                  Pash
                          Dorchester (Near)
                          Wensday 7tht
                                    (January).

Mr. Grigblay.
My dear Sir,
   I have the pleasure to acknowledge receipt of your
esteemed favour of the third inst., and beg to thank you for
your kind expressions as per same. Thanking you for past
favours and soliciting the continuance of same re your last,
I herewith beg to transmit all best wishes to your good self
and family and remain,
                    My dear Sir,
              Your obliged and humble servant
                 FREDERICK JOSHUA BLOGGS.
(Privit.)
   Something in the garden way wd be most like has waht I
feel the need of thanking you kindy.

                              FRED.


   It was too much for the old fellow to tackle, by the look
of things ; and perhaps he was a bit overcome from seeing
himself in print like the fashionable news ; at any rate, it's
clear enough he had someone who knew everything about
how to write letters to do it for him the polite style, and

then copied it out in his very best hand by himself. The rare part of the joke is that he sent the same letter—but with a word or two left out, and not done so careful—by the same post to Arthur, who had written him a line to show there was no ill-feeling, but with the bit marked "privit" out, of course. I must ask him what it is he wants—a mowing machine or a cultivator, I dare say.

## A JOURNEY

When I got to the station for the 7.37 up—which is a bit early for me, nowadays—there they were waiting on the platform to come along to Prior Franklyn and see things ready for making a start: Tolpenny as new and fresh as if he was just off to a Union Meeting, Central Hall; and little Rumble just out of church to be married—by the look of him—with a new red tartan tie ready for pulling off his trousers and dancing to the bagpipes in hairy knees as is his way soon as he gets North—or so they say. They had brought along umbrellas, attache-case, five-foots, level, tripod, staff, ranging rods, chains and arrows, as though we were out to survey for the new Jerusalem.

"Good morning!" I said, "but we shan't want that lot to-day, except tape and rods," I said. "Get along and stow in the Cloaks, sharp," I said.

Off they went, but it was over the bridge, which I had forgot; and then the train must run in while they were on the other side, so there I was hanging out of the window to see them come, till, of a sudden, the whistle went and I had a scramble to get out in time and nearly came down over it by their umbrellas and the rods and the roll of drawings I had brought along, getting mixed up with my legs; and then if Mr. Johnny Rasper—that I had not noticed sooner—wasn't standing by the bookstall, all of a grin, to see me! The same minute came a hullooing and shouting on the far side, and then Tolpenny—"Get in, sir!"; and there he was at the door with the train moving off! I chucked the things inside, and got hold of the upright with my left, and went hopping along—one foot on the step—reaching out with my right to Tol. with the Station-Master and three porters lending a helping hand by shouting as loud as they knew how, till Tol. caught my arm and the two of them dragged me in, flat on my face, as I might be any old baggage-bundle, and my shin barked something cruel.

Oh, I was angry with them!—crossing the down line and climbing in on the near side against the Company's rules, like any pair of schoolboys, without letting me know they were about it; and so pleased with themselves as if they had done something clever, to say nothing of that fellow Rasper looking on to split his sides and make a joke against me at every hotel and private saloon in the place! What with puffing and sweating and rubbing my leg, I dare say I forgot to take special care to behave in the polite style and be particular agreeable and friendly in the remarks I passed; but, after a while, seeing them sitting so glum, and turning over the figure I must have cut, I couldn't help but start laughing with it, and that soon cured the dumps.

At Liverpool Street I had plenty time to go out to a Chemist's and have a cool iodine-bandage put on my leg that was a sight to see—all bloody, and coming up, blue, the size of an egg, as well. It had made me feel a bit tired, and I should, rightly, have taken a First, by myself, to get rested; but I didn't like to stand away from little Rumble,

143

and I couldn't mark him off from Tol., so we all went down to Hertford in a rare old fusty, grimy Second-class, with cushions put in, special, for the people of those parts to clean themselves against until they have to give over by the cushions coming to be as dirty as *they* are; and there was a funny old black-smudged notice up, saying not to put your feet on the seats, et cetera, that belonged to the time before the cushions were made ready for dirtying your boots, instead. Plenty of tunnel-smoke, to make a pleasant mix with soap-boiling and glue-baking and bone-manure-frying, came in as we passed along; and then Tol., after asking leave, must light up so as to be chummy and join in; but whether he smokes hairdresser floor-sweepings, or hoof-parings, or just horse-droppings and rubber, I couldn't truthfully say.

## AT PRIORS FRANKLYN

Well, we got to fresh air and Hertford at last, and drove North seven miles on the Sempling road before we turned off, with fields white in frost and a clear sky up above, though misty looking ahead. The butler opened, and went to inquire, and came back and said it was all right and we could get to work. I had brought Mr. Blenhasset's sketch along, and all was clear enough; but the Extra was just what I thought for, and a bit over and above, too! I had Tol. and Rumble to get in their heads what was the matter, and left them to their job of measuring, and had a walk round with the drawings; and then, after a while, there was a tall, fine-looking, lean gentleman, with dark eyes and a hook nose and scrubby moustache, dressed in an old cloth hat and riding cords and scrim-shank leggings by his legs being like two sticks—out of his high breeding, I dare say—

that had four or five mixed kinds of dogs running about on his heels. Up he came and says:

"Am I addressing Mr. Grigblay?" So he was Lord Blades, sure enough, that I recognized, when he was close to, from his picture in the papers.

"You are, my Lord," I said. He nods very friendly and says, in a pleasant style, that he was glad a beginning had been made; and then he changed to a loud, snarling voice— "Ah, get out of it, you ugly old devil," and so he went on, talking at the dogs to keep them off from sniffing at my legs, just in the style the huntsman does to his hounds.

Then, we got talking of this and that in a general way; and what a fine view it was when clear; and had I noticed the front entrance because it was said to be by some Mr. Jones; and how annoying the frost was, coming just when he was free to have a day or two's hunting. After, I got him talking about the way we should tackle the job to protect paths and lawns and unload out of the way; and it didn't seem he was much concerned but:

"You will, of course, take care not to spoil the gardens," he says.

When I asked him upon a particular point and he couldn't say:

"Come along, we'll ask her Ladyship," he says; so we went aside till there was a kind of rock-garden above, with a lady in big gauntlet-gloves and a trowel amusing herself; and he calls out—"I say, Toto!" and she looked round, and he asks her; and she smiled and bowed very pretty to me, I will say, by guessing who I was, no doubt, and answers him that she does not think any harm, and gives me another smile before she turned to her trowelling, and all very kind and friendly it was.

Well, it's clear enough they don't set any great store by Mr. Blenhasset's special ideas for protecting lawns and paths, et cetera; and it just means: we shall have letters written, and estimates made, and the Quantity Surveyor asked to explain to us and then to the Architect; and the Architect explaining to the Owner and the Owner saying "Oh, Hell!" and having his Architect arrange just as I could have settled in a ten minutes' talk with his Lordship; but that does not mean I have any mind to tell Mr. Blenhasset how the land lays. If it was Mr. Spinlove, now, I would get him on the 'phone, first thing, and say all I knew; but with a *new* gentleman for Architect—and specially a gentleman who has his own particular fads and wears all the frills Mr. Blenhasset has about—I should, likely, make a peck of troubles if it seemed I had been asking questions behind the Architect's back.

Well, his Lordship was wonderful easy and pleasant, which made me more than ever glad to have a chance to see him proud and happy. He shook hands like we were old friends, in going off; and then he turns and says: "You'll take lunch before you go?"

I felt a bit shy of being in the way, but he wouldn't have it.

"No trouble whatever," he says, and off he goes, whistling his dogs.

Half after twelve, Tol. and Rumble came to say they had been invited up to the house for dinner; and a little after the butler came out and it was—"Your luncheon is served, sir," and he leads the way, by the side-door out of the garden, to a room with guns and fishing rods cased along one side, and a rare lot of stuffed heads, and specimen fish and birds set up, where was a choice of cold dishes for the butler to carve, with salad and apple pie and a rare blue cheese—Lancashire, by what he told me—and a glass of port to set it off after the bottled ale I had first named. We got away at three, and very pleased and comfortable I felt riding First-class—*this* time—with a good cigar to keep me from dropping off.

## AT BELHAMPTON

Me and Arthur went to Dorchester overnight, to see into things before Mr. Spinlove met us on the site, yesterday. It is three weeks since I was there, and old Fred has got things pushed on in fine style: the farm pulled down and the sheds ready; foundations of the house near all in; pulling about of old walls ready for making good to new, well in hand; picked stone from the ruins being wheeled, with the masons fairly at work getting out the ashlar; but a lot more men about than I cared to see—as I wrote to Fred after looking over his wages sheets, to-day. Lanky Barnacle was in his office, where, passing the window, I saw his bald head at work taking off from the drawings—to find out mistakes in the quantities, I dare say, and cheer everyone up in case time should chance to hang heavy on our hands! Fred said the Clerk gives him no trouble.

"I have him mind his own business, sir," he sings out; so it's clear enough the Clerk has had to learn to be underdog, for a change, which is a state of things that had not ought to be, and would make me uneasy if it was any other than Mr. Spinlove, Architect, or I had not Fred Bloggs to rely on.

A little before 12 Mr. Spinlove drives on: "From Richmond in two hours 51," he says, looking pleased; and then he tells me the gentleman is coming on the site, and, sure enough, quarter before one, there was his limousine and out he gets and stands looking about. Then he comes hurrying with his man on his heels—ready to catch him in case he threw a fit, by the look of it—with such snarling and braying as I never heard the like of, and couldn't have credited. We stood there staring to know what the row was about that made Barnacle pop out of his office and come flip-flapping across with his mouth full, not to be late. At last, when the gentleman was quiet, Mr. Spinlove calls across, loud and slow, without moving a step: "The men are all at dinner."

On that he looks at his watch and shouts out:

"It wants twelve minutes yet; they've no business to sneak off before the time. Understand? I'm paying, and I mean to have my money's worth; understand?" And then it was that nothing was done or being done; and he meant to have his rights; and we would soon learn who he was; and he would 'phone his solicitors to take action, directly he got back, to have a new contractor take over, that would attend to business and carry out orders and do as he was told; and he would go to law to have the penalties for delay under the contract awarded, for the reason that we were not making any attempt to complete by the contract date— and goodness knows what else he wasn't going to do; with —"Understand? Understand?" and screaming higher and higher like some squalling child and the slipper mislaid. The most silly raving nonsense that ever was heard, with no sense in it from start to finish.

Then, when he came to a stop, puffing and mopping his forehead, Mr. Spinlove passed across from where we stood together staring at him, and had him turn and walk a dozen paces away; and we could see him explaining to the other, and him arguing and waving his arms; and then Mr. Spinlove takes a quick step up to him and says something short

148

and sharp right in his face, with a bit of a nod for earnest, which seemed to cool the other down; and after a few words he went off and got into his car again, and Mr. Spinlove came back with his mouth pretty grim and a queer shine in his eyes.

"I'm going to get something to eat," he says; and he passed across to his car, near at hand, while the footman opened a great basket and began serving his master through the window of the limousine, on which me and Arthur got out *our* nosebags, too.

Twenty minutes later the game began over again by the gentleman climbing out and brushing the crumbs down; and then the large pink-and-yellow treat that he had with him before—but in a cherry-colour dress and green-trimmed hat all to one side, *this* time—was handed out: a most respectable lady, I make no question, but one I wouldn't care to go about with myself, by too many saying "Oh my!" Also, there was a neat little hospital nurse, for giving him his medicine—as it seemed. However, the other one found old Fred's beautiful ballasted path didn't agree with her pretty tootsies, judging by the fussing there was, so in she got again; and him and his nurse, with the servant following behind, came, single-file, up; so, counting Barnacle and Fred, there were seven of us like a lot of farmyard hens following round after a bantam cock, and he kept  s for near two hours, asking questions to try and understand, and then questioning the answers; and if by chance he understood any answer he got, he wouldn't credit it, and Fred and Lanky had to line up and tape through to prove the dimensions were the same as on the plan, because he said he wasn't such a stupid ass as not to know better.

"I'm afraid you haven't paid yourself a very pretty compliment," says Mr. Spinlove, when he was taught how to read the tape for himself; but the other only stared at him and then started off about some "balcony" or other he had got in his head, though Mr. Spinlove explained twice over there wasn't any "balcony" and could not be one.

"But I *want* a balcony—Understand? Understand?" he says. So it went on, and the nurse, with his medicine poured out, dodging round to have him take it; and, when he drinks it off, he looks at his watch and says:

"Four minutes late, ought to be on the half-hour—Understand?" and no other thanks to her!

Well, round about three, back he goes to his car at last, with Mr. Spinlove and Barnacle attending; and after saying good-bye to them he calls Barnacle back to have a private talk through the window without Mr. Spinlove being at hand to know what—the most irregular behaviour I ever heard of; and it was clear Mr. Spinlove didn't mean to allow it, for, looking back and seeing what the Clerk was at, he stood a moment and then started to go down again just as the car went off with Lanky left standing as though he had had a present of a flea in his ear for a parting gift.

It was the most exasperating and teasing afternoon I ever spent on any job; for the whole air was poisoned by the gentleman's way of carrying on, and we all felt like killing somebody—if the rest were like me—and glad if an earthquake would come and blow the whole dam' job to blazes —excepting my old Fred, who seemed very pleased with himself.

"We're all right, sir," he says.

Next, Lanky Barnacle comes flapping up with

"S'Ezra is not satisfied. I've got to see you get along quicker."

"Oh!" I said. "Is that really so? Well, we must think about it," I said, and turned aside; on which Fred comes across and whispers:

"Shall I drop him a word, sir?" So I nodded, and then I heard a bellow:

"Now then, Daddy, you just dance your legs along inside and go on at your adding-up sums,"he says. "There's nothing to keep you outside in the cold," he says; and the other goes off looking pretty sick with one thing on top of another; and when I glanced his way, there was Mr. Spinlove, with his back turned so as no-one should notice laughing and laughing as if he couldn't stop; and, when I went up, he looked at me with tears in his eyes:

"Did you *ever*! In all your life! Grigblay?" he says.

"No, sir, I *never* did," I answered him; and we had a good laugh together, and I made bold to ask him what it was he said to the gentleman before lunch, that made him quiet down.

He looked at me as if he had only half a mind; and then he told me that the gentleman has been at him, all the time, to promise he will have the Earl—Lord Rainsport, that we built for at Dulkington—to pay a visit, when the job is near done, for the gentleman to show him round: and what Mr. Spinlove said was: "If you don't behave yourself there shall be no visit of the Earl here," he says. Then he says to me:

"No stick is too dirty to beat that kind with, Grigblay," he says, quite fierce for him!

Well, we must hope for better times when the walls go up and the gentleman can see things happening for himself; but it makes me a bit uneasy to see the style Fred orders Lanky B. when, by rights, it had ought to be the other way round for Lanky to direct Fred, and say what the Architect will have, and what he will not have. However, Mr. Spinlove knows Fred's ways well enough by this time and, as he laughs to hear him, he cannot think any harm; and if all goes right, as I intend it shall do, it would be a mistake for me to take notice, for old Fred would be terrible cast down if he thought I was not pleased at the way he is carrying on, and I should likely be making more trouble than I prevented.

151

## WORDS WITH ARTHUR

Arthur tried to put me down, to-day, over the Gas Company asking us to hold off with the Tank for a few weeks, just to oblige, till now nine weeks is gone by, which, added on to the five of shilly-shally getting ready, makes fourteen weeks since Contract signed and no start made, or likely to be made for months yet, by reason of the dirty game the Company has started with the U.D.C. Young Art. considers the job as his special responsibility, after pressing me to agree he should have a bit of Engineering to play about with, for once; and no doubt that was why he got so huffy at me telling him something he had not thought of for himself!

"When you are dealing with the shrewd, hard-headed business man," I said to him, "it is only polite and friendly to behave in the shrewd, hard-headed business style yourself, back in return," I said, "and not to ask for fair and reasonable treatment when it might mean the whole of sixteen pounds fourteen and ninepence less money to divide among the Shareholders, next year, if you got it," I said.

"The Directors of a Limited Company", I said to Arthur, "have to brush their hair flat down once in a year to answer the Shareholders without any mistake, like good boys learnt their lessons off by heart; for if not, Mr. Catchit, and Mr. Snatchit, who retire by rotation but beg to offer their kind services again—looking at their boots the while—may *not* come to be re-elected, at £100 a year, to sit at tea at a Board Meeting once a month," I said. "That is why the Directors will grant you no more than you can enforce," I said, "or else Mr. Johnny Rasper, or some other thoughtful friend, will pass word for a Shareholder to stand and clear his throat at the General Meeting and ask: 'Is it a fact the Contractor is using the Company's entrance and gate? and, if so, what allowance is he making for not being required to provide his own gate and entrance? and, if none, will the Chairman explain why this concession is being paid out of the Shareholders' dividends instead of out of the Directors' fees? Hear, hear, and applause.' You can see clear enough," I said to Arthur, "that as the Gas Company does not do as they would be done by with the Council, they will only expect to be done by as they would do, by us," I said.

Well, it seems Arthur had no mind to listen to sermons away from church, just then; and, of course, he has more of a fancy for the special brand of new young wisdom he invents for himself, instead of for the fine old-matured brand, offered free, second-hand, by his Dad; so what must he do next but get out his rag just as if I had said something beyond reason!

"What's all the talk about, Dad, that makes you so sour and angry to listen to; and all for nothing, so far as I can see?" he says.

"It might help you to see a bit further if you stopped asking questions till I have finished telling you," I said.

"You started off to say what was best to be done, Dad; and there's no sense going on as if I knew what you were talking about when you haven't told me," he says.

"It will be time enough for you to talk about sense when you have lived long enough to learn what sense means," I said; "but you can take a lesson from me, now, just for a first start off," I said, "and that is: I am telling you the reasons for my proposals, first, so that you will not be nag-

153

ging and haggling to know why this and why not the other, soon as I tell you what the proposal *is*," I said.

"That's putting the cart before the horse," he says.

"Before the jackass, more like," I said.

"Most people would be ashamed to say a silly thing like that," says the smart young man.

"Stop your yar-yaring," I said.

"Stop it yourself," he says. "I never saw such a rotten temper as you're in," he says.

"I'm *not* in a temper," I said, giving the table a pair of bangs with the flat of my hand to have him know I meant it, that made Smith put his head in to inquire—and pull it out again pretty sharp, too.

"There's precious few would keep their tempers the same as I have kept mine these last weeks with all the dam' jawing and muddling over this blasted old Tank of yours that's not fit for a sewage-contractor to touch, let alone a proper builder; when I told you all along, clear enough for any fool to understand, what it would all come to with you going down on your knees and near blubbering to get me to allow it; and now fourteen weeks gone by, with nothing but jaw and upsets and silliness, and no knowing how much more of it yet to come; and a nice stew you would have been in, twice over, if I hadn't pulled you out each time; and now you're trying your best to get into a worse one and drag me in along with you instead, with your dirty friend out for cadging bribes and nothing else, and conspiring to swindle the ratepayers; and all these botherations come about just because he is the Captain of your cricket and you want to make sure he will put you in third wicket down every time," I said.

"That's a dam' lie," he shouts out. "I won't have you say it. You know it's not true," says the boy, all upset with it by getting a bit more than he bargained for, I dare say.

Well, I should not have said it, I admit; and it happened

154

just by the way words will fall from my lips, when I am worked up, that never were in my mind till after I've said them; and so I told the boy, and put my arm across his shoulder by being sorry I'd hurt him, for he is a real good lad, is Arthur, and only a bit too fond of his own ideas; and of having his own way; and not ready enough to listen, by being too set on saying what *he* thinks, instead. So then we sat at the table together, and I wrote down to have it made clear, what we would write the Gas Company, which was:

(1) We much regret to have to call attention to the fact that fourteen weeks has transpired since Contract signed; and we now have to notify you that it is our intention to determine the Contract under Clause 21 of Conditions, and claim £750 in damages, unless within ten days of date at head you agree proposals below. (I wrote it "passed", but Arthur says it should properly be "*transpired*"—him being more new-educated than I am.)

(2) Fix a date for us to start some day previous to June 1st, and agree to pay us extra to cover increase in labour rates and cost of materials that have happened since Contract date (20th October), or that may come about any time before the new date for completion.

Arthur says he doesn't see how we can make good a £750 claim, considering we have not done any work; but I said to him:

"Nor I don't see either, my Son," I said, "but we can show that £750 is the reasonable-expected profit and overhead; and we can show how shrewd and hard-headed and businesslike we know how to be by having a dam' good try to get it," I said; "and, if we don't know how to set about it, there's likely some twisty lawyer or another can tell us," I said.

So I will have Mr. George Trencher, the Solicitor, to draft a letter for us to write the Company in case we might write something for the lawyers to find out, in a year or two, that it means different from what it says; but I will have

Trencher to leave out his aforesaids and whereases and hereinbefore afters—just for the once.

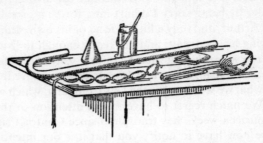

## THE VICAR IN TROUBLE

Our good Mr. Peebles seems to get all the bad luck that's going!

"I am afraid the Bishop will not be coming after all!" he says, shaking his head at me when I passed him, going up the Crescent, Thursday. "His Lordship's secretary has written a most kind and charming letter, oh *most* charming," he says in his queer style; "but there seems little hope for a visit to us, alas! so I fear your kind efforts have been wasted, Mr. Grigblay," he says, and he looked at me, in the style I know so well, for me to help him in his troubles by letting him off from paying the balance (£39) for his "convenience".

However, if it is to be no convenience to the Bishop, it is a rare convenience to some others. That decent old body, Mrs. Bunch, that does the scouring and cleaning in the church with the help of her poor half-baked second girl that lives at home with her, soon found out a better way than going outside in the rain and cold to empty the floor-water down the gulley; and they hadn't been at it a fortnight, I dare say, before the two of them together managed to block the trap, which I got to know about by a letter

156

from Mr. Peebles saying: "Kindly send a man to clear it at once, and leave it in proper order so that such a thing cannot happen again"—as if it was *our* fault!

Well, we do our best but, short of keeping a policeman inside, it's difficult to know. Haggit had quite a job; and, from what he told Arthur when he came back, it seems old Mother Bunch and her daughter, in the excitement of getting done, quick, while no one was looking, poured a scrubbing brush and floor-clout into the trap along with the dirty water; and then one, or the pair of them, got hold of the clout to pull it out, and pulled so hearty and strong between them that they wedged the scrubber across the trap and got the clout fixed solid as well.

Then Mother takes fright, and tries to push the lot down the drain with the handle of the broom so that no one should be troubled; and she worked so hard at it, good old soul, with her daughter to heave all her weight on the end whenever Ma called "Hoi *Hup*!" that at last they gave over by not being able to ram it up any tighter, and then slipped away, on the quiet, on the chance no one would find out. So there was 4s. 9d. and the price of a new clout and scrubber for Mr. Peebles to appeal for; and, next, lo and behold! if it wasn't a sixpence, three threepennies and fifteen coppers wanted out of the collection to pay for the lav. flooding over.

Mr. Peebles fancies having ladies to play about and make busy in the Church—"workers" he calls them—and it seems that some of these "workers" were working in the vestry to change the chancel flowers, when, "Oh! look, darling!" for what could be more fascinating and delightful than to have a lovely dainty lav. basin all handy to knock the bottom out of first time anyone lets slip one of the earthenware linings of the altar vases. So they got to work with their flowers; and, after the first time, the water didn't seem any too glad to run away down the drain; and

157

after the second, it decided to stay where it was and wait, instead, except what ran over on the floor—for some reason; and so then it was: "Will you kindly send someone immediately?" over the 'phone. It was because of petals and odds and ends choking the waste, and nobody ever supposing there could be such a thing as a clearing-eye to put things right.

Well, well! We shall get straight soon, I dare say.

## THE VICAR BESET

I read in the Parish Mag. a little while back, that Mrs. Rudolph Broadbench is giving an aisle window in the memory of her dear departed who was the most objectionable old fraud in the place when he lived here, and the same somewhere else, no doubt, after they left. However, it seems his good lady has an idea to celebrate herself, the same as others do, by having it written up on a brass plate —or all in coloured glass to last for evermore—something after this style:

*This Window is given*
*to the Glory of God and in Sacred Memory of*
RUDOLPH BROADBENCH, ESQUIRE
*by*
*the kind generosity of*
MARIA JANE BROADBENCH
*his dear, sweet little broken-hearted widow,*
*beloved by all,*
*who never slapped his face*
*and*
*called him a dirty toad when*
*he behaved polite,*
*Hallelujah*
*Amen.*

158

"Or words to that effect; or words to that effect," as the old music-hall song used to go.

I thought no more till our good Vicar must stop me today, in passing, to say: could I give him some of my kind help and guidance to advise him how to decide about the New Window, because he didn't know what best to do next —which is always his way, to go ahead till he is full of troubles instead of taking advice beforehand so that there shall be no troubles arise for others to try and pull him out of after it is too late.

He took me along to the Vicarage, when what was there but a gentleman pacing up and down, in front, like he might be waiting on guard; and that took off his hat at Mr· Peebles as if he was his lady-love; and turned and kept in step by his side like some shopwalker showing the way to the pyjamas, but that Mr. Peebles didn't seem to have any use for, just at the time, though not able to get him to take the hint; and the other:—

"I trust you received our last letter quite safe, sir," and Mr. Peebles:—

"Oh! Thank you! Yes, yes, I think so, yes;" and opposite the front, he says: "Thank you! Thank you! but nothing settled yet, I regret to say. Thank you; but I will certainly think over and write to you at once in due course. Thank you," he says.

"Just exactly as suits your convenience, Mr. Peebles, sir," says the other. "We shall be honoured to be allowed to beautify your fine Church, sir," and holds the gate open and takes off his hat again with a bow and: "Always at your service and ready to oblige in every possible way, Mr. Peebles," and so we left him closing the gate after us in most polite style; but, lo and behold! directly we got inside, if there wasn't another of them sitting there in the front hall —like he might be some collector called about the gas for the very last time—that Mr. Peebles was fretted to see, clear enough, but didn't know how to get quit of by the affable style the other smiled in his face with his head on one side to show how patient he was in giving Mr. Peebles his kind services without any thought of the trouble he was putting himself to; but only too glad to make every excuse for Mr. Peebles's not treating him the way he had hoped and expected by what Mr. Peebles led him to understand, previously; and he was quite sure Mr. Peebles would never for one moment mean to behave unfair; and might he remind Mr. Peebles that time was passing? and would Mr. Peebles be so good as to say why so much hesitation? for he was only too anxious to meet Mr. Peebles's wishes in every possible way, and would send one of his firm's fleet of beautiful motor-cars, always waiting ready, any day and hour convenient, to take Mr Peebles's good self and friends to the Arto-Glasso Studios at Shoreditch to see for himself some of the lovely fine windows just got made; and his Managing Director would consider it a wonderful honour to have the great pleasure to entertain Mr. Peebles and friends at luncheon before motoring them back home; and so he went on with head to one side without blinking, like some bird, and the Vicar not able to decide which of his legs was best for standing on, till at last he settled it and came out with :—

"Oh, yes. Thank you! Thank you! Most kind I'm sure; Oh, *most*, and I will certainly think over very carefully; but I must just look and see first, and then I will write to you at once as soon as ever possible in due course. Thank you! Thank you!" and he made a move to get to his study, but the other put his hand across with :—

"Just one moment, sir!" and would have fixed him again, like a weasel with a rabbit, if I hadn't walked forward to push between and march him along and shut the door; on which he made a loud sigh, poor gentleman.

"Oh dear, Oh dear! It's like this more days than not, and

letters nearly every post as well, Grigblay; and I don't know whatever to do, for, if I say 'Yes' to one, the others will all be at me," he says; and he rang the bell—to have the maid show the tout the way outside, I suppose—and hung his coat and hat in the cupboard he has there, as if he was quite weary with it; and then he got out a great armful of papers to lay on the table, with his hands trembling—and truly sorry I was to see him almost worried crazy with all the goings on.

Just then the maid knocks to say: "Please, Mr. Blornidge's compliments, and would the Vicar kindly spare him a moment before he goes back to London, as there is a particular thing he forgot to say";—and there he was, followed her, and standing beyond for smiling through, expectant, at Mr. Peebles! Lucky I was at hand to push the door to, or the fellow was all set ready to prance in and start it over again.

"Say the Vicar is engaged, and will write in a day or two," I told the girl, and shut the door after her; on which Mr. Peebles looked across and says "Thank you!" as if he meant it.

Well, it seemed no sooner the announcement in the Parish Mag., than they had begun at him, with callers and letters, like blue-bottle flies to run about on his bald head; and fast as one was brushed aside it settled somewhere else, for a change, and others came as well. He couldn't understand how it should happen, till I told him there was a place for combing out the Church and Provincial Papers, and Parish Magazines, so that each tout should be ahead of others on the cadging lay. Mr. Peebles listened to what the first two said, and thought it very polite of them to take such a rare lot of trouble out of their kind ideas to help him; and then he found it was all too much, by not knowing which way to turn with all saying something different, and, especially, by the letters to answer; for it did not help if he took no notice, they only came to sit on his doorstep and follow after him, instead, so as things were made worse.

When he had told me *that* far, if the maid didn't knock again! and it was a card on a salver, *this* time, and the tout —that I caught sight of before I signalled the girl to shut the door—standing just as he had done before. On the card was "Arto-Glasso, Ltd.," with "Representative, Mr. Carlo Blornidge" in the corner, and "P.T.O." scrawled across in pencil—as I noticed when the girl passed beside—so I had her to stand.

"It's a written message *this* time; do you special want to read it?" I asked of the Vicar.

He shook his head; so I took and dropped it in the fire. "No answer," I said to the girl; and I went to whip the door open and shut—the same as the tamer does at the Circus—to prevent the lion getting through to finish up our Vicar.

The Vicar had eleven different coloured-in pictures, special-made to suit, that were got up the same as those hung side of the stairs down to the basement at the Civil and Military Stores, to catch the Clergy on their way to buy a garden roller or a rose-squirt; that made the fellow bagging onion-seed at the counter to get pink in the gills, when I asked, because of the chance of a commission coming his way, poor devil! But he hummed and hawed and wouldn't say who was going to make the pretty windows, all to order, for the Stores to sell and put their label on to prove everything was their own work.

By what Mr. Peebles showed me, there were seven firms competing: one with three designs, for choice; and two others with two each, besides letters and proposals from others—one with gold crest and heading to make it more important; and specifications with red typing to show them off; and correspondence "Adverting to our last" without end; and catalogues with coloured pictures and prices, and

Mr. Peebles not knowing which belonged to which or what way to turn next—and no wonder!

The lady had said £300, which was good enough for a proper-made window of that size, in my opinion; but Mr. Peebles thought it would be clever not to let any of them know, and that is one of his troubles.

"Here is the highest, £480; and the lowest, £225; and the nearest, £275; but I don't like that one, Grigblay, and, if I did, what am I to do with the £25 left over, in any case?" he says in a tone of voice I could not help but smile to hear.

While we were turning over and sorting out, there was his telephone went.

"Yes?" he says. "Yes, speaking! Who? Oh!" and then he looked across at me, with the receiver held as if he didn't know what to do if I didn't help him; so I took hold, and blessed if it wasn't Carlo on the job again, waiting for his train at the station, no doubt.

". . . quite the usual thing, Mr. Peebles, and our Directors always willing to pay five to ten per cent as private personal commission when they are indebted to the kind services of gentlemen placing orders; so please understand, sir, we would be only too glad to oblige in your case, Mr. Peebles . . ."; so then I chipped in, giving as low-down and gruff a tone to my voice as I could manage, just to satisfy him and make an end:

"Nothing doing. Go to Hell!" on which the Vicar, sitting in his chair, must fair jump in the air.

I had to make my apologies and explain what was up, which he was properly shocked to understand after I had made clear the meaning of it; and I had him put up Carlo's pictures and correspondence, without any letter, for me to post the lot back on my way; so Carlo will find himself on the carpet to-morrow to learn to keep at it; and be a bit more genial; and cock his head further over; and have more care to be affable in his manners by giving better attention to smiling in the glass, for practice, mornings and odd times, in the future.

After that I had a talk with Mr. Peebles to settle what best to be done; and, when I asked, he said the lady was gone away to New Zealand and wanted him to have all done before she comes back next year. Well, in the end, I had our Vicar agree to send the whole of the pictures back, with letters just thanking with regrets but all now settled; and said I would send him a list of proper, private window-artists, with work handy for viewing for him to choose from; and then he could write for the one he thought best to call and agree ideas and settle for the price; and, if not agreeable, he could try another till he was satisfied; and then the artist would send him a picture to fix the bargain by:

"And," I said—when Mr. Peebles started humming and hawing—"he is more like to fuss with it and put in more work and better material, than to leave out from his bargain; for that is the way with these artists," I said, "never able to do anything well enough to please themselves, or let be when finished," I said, "and he will carry out according to his artistic notions that mark him off from others; and so, in the end, St. Andrew's will have a fine window with the best feelings and handiwork a man has to give, and," I said to Mr. Peebles, "if anything less than that is good enough in a place set aside for the worship of our Lord God," I said, "I do not know what use there is in any man ever doing a job of work in first-rate style for the sake of having it first-rate, as all decent men love to do if let alone and given a chance," I said. "Nor I do not understand," I said, "why the Almighty has set it deep in the hearts of my old trusties, and all right craftsmen and tradesmen, to get joy and pride in giving themselves to skilful work in honest materials—which is the same as acting the artist—if He doesn't set store by such doings; and it beats me," I said, "asking your kind pardon, Mr. Peebles," I said, "how clergymen can allow any other kinds of things to be set up in their churches, as they do," I said, "or have dirty traffickers, with lies in their hearts as well as in their throats, scrambling to plant their shoddy pretences for the sake of making a bit more money than another would; and charging as much for their touting and advertising and pushing to cadge the job, as there is left over to spend on the job when cadged," I said.

Mr. Peebles agreed, of course, as he always does when I carry him along with a bit of talk, just by not having time to settle what he ought to say next. It was lucky he had me in, as I know something of the ways of the window manufacturers from Mr. Spinlove when we were on with his church, Waddering, Hants; so it was time well spent, if it was all of two hours, for we shall see a bit of colour-work we can feel pleased about at St. Andrew's, I have no doubt; instead of something to keep everyone ashamed for a few hundred years.

## THE GAS COMPANY AGAIN

Mr. George Trencher obliged with a very neat draft letter for us to write the Gas Company, and they replied fixing May 25 as date for us to commence, and will pay all extra wages and materials like we said, but no reference made to our claim for £750 damages if we are prevented, again; so I had Trencher draft a letter acknowledging and making safe for us. It now looks—judging from

the report of Council Meeting in *The Sentinel*, Saturday—
that the Company is out to agree with the Council, right
off, so as to keep clear of our claim, by the delay, if they do
not; for they have very kindly and considerately offered to
"forgo their building programme" and grant easement to
the U.D.C. to maintain the sewer over their land, for
£2,000!

There was a rare old hullabaloo, by the way it reads: Mr.
Vint saying the land itself is not worth that much money, it
being not above nine acres in extent; and several arguing
the same, and others disagreeing, till Bargate had them to
know it was close on eleven acres and grown to be worth
three times more money, as building land. So then it was:
"Buy the land for putting up more council houses"; and
that started the same old political back-chat and calling
names over again, till Bargate told them the line of the
sewer comes very awkward for a lay-out; and so it goes on
for near two full columns, and, in the end, nothing settled,
as usual, but wait for counsel's opinion, and the Clerk to
write and refuse "this monstrous claim"—and quite the
right words to use, too, in my opinion.

Well, to-day I dropped in to have a word with Bargate,
private and confidential between us two—with his new
clerk sent on a message out of the next room to be away
from the door, Bargate being a bit deaf—to let him know
the inside truth about the Gas Company's game so that he
should give the Council advice to call the bluff. It is not the
kind of thing I care about doing, but, as one that is "an old
inhabitant" and has been a ratepayer and well-wisher of the
town for near on fifty years, I hold I am only lending my
weight on the side of public right and justice not to have the
people humbugged and robbed.

Bargate laughed a rare lot at the Company asking me to
hold off with our contract "just to oblige" while Parkin got
busy at his drawing-board sharpening his pencils and stay-

ing late to fake up plans of new buildings, that are not wanted and could not be used unless the present lot got wiped out by an explosion, and which the shareholders would never sanction, and would mean new capital subscribed, in any case, if they did. Bargate seemed in a proper muddle between one Act of Parliament and another; and with the Law of Easements, and Rights of Local Authorities, to mix things up a bit more thick; and, on top of everything, he tells me that that old 24-in. brick barrel sewer is nothing but common Gayton bricks—not now made—set in lime mortar, and is grown to be pretty well rotten after eighty years; and, also, it has more than it can do to carry away flood water; and it backed up so bad that a small river came down Gayton Hill and washed the side of the road out on the day of the "cloudburst"—they called it —summer before last. However, he was quite jovial about it all, as is his way; for Bargate always manages to keep on top.

"It is not for me to settle," he says. "The Council will have to say, soon as the London lawyer's opinion is known about," he says. He was glad enough to have me tell him the rights of the case, and shook hands most cordial, as he always is to me.

So there it is! and, if counsel's opinion is on side of the town, maybe the Gas Company will get an opposite opinion from another lawyer and go to law for a Judge to say the Council is right in its arguments but wrong in its facts, and give a win to the Gas Company for the same reasons the Council's lawyer argued that the Council ought to win. Then, if the Council keep at it, three fresh Judges will, like enough, decide that the first Judge made a mistake by his reasoning after lunch being different to what he felt like before, and so there must be a new trial to make quite certain; and if the Gas Company thinks best to inquire at the House of Lords, then it may befall that three Judges out of

167

five will decide against a new trial and the decision of the first Judge to be turned round the opposite way to make it a win for the Council; while the fourth Judge complains that the other three are wrong and votes in favour of a new trial; while the last is strong that the whole seven are balmy and the first Judge right all the time, from the very start!

I know things have got to be straightened out and made clear by the judges, so that people will understand better next time and not go to law about it; and if half the lawyers are taken up with arguments to decide the meaning of what other lawyers have said before, and in providing plenty for arguing about after they are dead so as to keep things going and prevent unemployment creeping in—well, it is only what we must expect where each is as clever as the next; and if they come to divide up the whole of £10,000 between them, over Parkin's bright idea, we may be sure the money will be well earned.

## A CHANCE MEETING

Passing up High Street to the Cameo with Effie, last evening, who should be coming along—hooked on to a girl friend, with his head fresh-permed and greased for pushing up out of a brand new raincoat so as none should miss catching a sniff—but Master Oswald Snape, Esquire, that, soon as he saw me, must remember, of a sudden, to close-examine a fine tin brush-pan hanging in Coggin's window that he had noticed in passing a day or two before, but forgot about in the meanwhile. The lady stood staring round to see if her boy had hooked on to some other, by any chance; and she and Effie exchanged nods as we went by.

"Who was that?" I said, having a notion I had seen her before.

"Gwennie Rasper," says she. "You know her? The one you upset her tea over at the 'Save our Wild-flowers' party, Church Hall, November," she says.

"If people holds cups of tea behind my elbow when I don't know," I said, "I may knock over when I don't know, same as anyone else might do," I said, remembering the fuss there was with the girl's dress all messed up and a cup broken that I paid for (6d.); and then it came in my mind: what was going on behind my back to make the young fellow ashamed I should see him? And then: how about Master Oswald passing word of our Sausage Factory Tender to his pretty little peach, so as her dear dirty Dad should come by secret information for cheating me?

Well, the young girl is out to please everyone with wonderful fine black roots and peroxide tops; and nice, sharp-pointed red nails as she might be just come from scratching someone's eyes out to serve them right; and lips like she fed on nothing but the most delicious juicy raw meat; and eyebrows plucked clean to leave plenty of room for a pair of lovely Garbo's painted on, instead; and if she has tried to be a bit extra-pleasing to me by passing over to her Dad a Contract to save five hundred on before any profit can be seen, I ought to be the last to complain, *that's* certain; but it will be a new world for me when I suspect disloyalty among those I employ, for such a thing has never been yet, nor shall it ever come about while I have a leg to stand on and another to wear a boot for kicking into the street.

I cannot help but get the idea that Mr. Johnny has set his little pet tabby to play at pusscats—one on, t'other off— with our Oswald, to have him steal tit-bits out of my larder; and it rather takes my fancy to lay out a nice bit of jalaped liver to spoof Mr. Oswald Pusscat and give Mr. Johnny Rasper a first-class bellyache for him to remember where it came from and keep away in the future in case of catching a worse. However, I dare say Mr. Dirty is feeling he has been dirty enough, just for the present, by the last bit carried to him giving him the indigestion; and besides, it wouldn't be in my nature to lend myself to that sort of game, for it's no use fighting to do worse than your nature however it may be to fight to do better. On the other hand, it would be a "judgment" on Rasper, as they call it, to pay him out in his own coin and teach him right conduct; and, also, it is clear enough we must somehow put it to the test to know, for certain, if Snape is playing Rasper's game; for it would be unfair to sling the young fellow out just only on suspicion of what he has been at. I must have a word with Arthur to hear what he thinks. It was him that brought Snape in against my ideas; for a first look at the fellow was enough for me, and it would have saved the lot of bother there has been, and save some yet in store, maybe, if I had had my way at the start.

## TRIBULATION

Here is the awkwardness that came about a year ago at that nice little house we had building, Keston way, for Dr. Sylvanus Craske, F.R.C.P., M.D., of Harley Street— Seth Grainger and Paul Perverse, Buckingham Street, Strand, Architects—settled at last! I feel sorry for the trouble the Architects got in and will have to pay for; and I was a bit uneasy myself, at the time; but when me and

170

Arthur called at their office and talked things out, they hadn't a word to say of it being any fault of ours, though Mr. Perverse seemed inclined to be nasty at the start—if he could have found a way out! However, the pair of them are both gentlemen when it comes to putting blame on a Builder that has only done as directed and approved and cannot be held responsible just because the Architects have made a bloomer. The Owner has behaved handsome, in my opinion —though not a wealthy gentleman, I understand—like enough by bearing in mind that if he claimed his rights with lawyers, as another might, his Architects would be fair ruined in pocket and in reputation, for they are only just set up on a little Public Wash House Comp. they won working overtime at home when assistants to Mr. Jasper Raddish, R.A.

It is just the old trouble that most architects learn about once in a lifetime, and that is underburnts—or "Place Bricks", as it calls them in the Spec. Ours came from the Hallops district where facings have been made before anybody knows; and it beats me how the Hallopian Brick Company, that has been burning slop facings thirty-eight years for using all round about for everyone to see them and judge, can let underburnts go out of their yard when they must know the truth about them. It is a pity Buckle— who was in charge—did not have those selected, out of samples, marked by the Architect to make sure and prove it; but that was none of his business and—cautious, careful man that he is—I make no doubt that the K2, P, & T, so marked by the Company, were the same Mr. Perverse picked out to give the broken colour-mix he wanted, as Buckle wrote us and as we ordered; to say nothing of both Architects seeing the facings in bulk on the site, and the walling going up, many times, too, without objections made and only satisfaction expressed.

All went beautiful till the pole-plate was on and we had

171

that sharp frost, and skating, after the long wet spell last year, and then:—"Seen this, Gov'nor?" from one of the men, and there was the face coming loose on the pale reds, in flakes and splinters, blown by the frost almost as it might be by lime, and falling all round against foot of walls, and showing powder for rubbing off with your finger, underneath.

Well, there it was, and getting worse as time went on by the face crumbling to make a hole where the brick should be; and everyone coming to stare and ask each other "what next?" and the Owner worried, sad to see; and the Architects in a stew and not knowing what; and preservative experts sent down to say what *they* thought, and some ready to have a try, but none to give any guarantee; and, in any case, all that soft dusty face would have to be cut back before they made a start, so what was the good of that! Then it was: "roughcast the lot"; but the Owner wouldn't have it. "I hate that kind of house", he said, and he meant it, too!

The end is we are to start and pull down the whole outside $4\frac{1}{2}$ in.—or, rather, pick it down, brick at a time, so as to keep the ties in place; and if anyone asks me how we are going to dodge the heads and cills and this and that, I'm damned if I know, though, lucky, them and the jambs are in the picked, dark-colour ones, hard and sound.

However, we shall manage somehow; and the Brickyard is going to supply the extra bricks free—for near one-third are in the pale reds—and pay one-third of labour costs; and the Architect one-third, and the Owner one-third, and I am going to help by charging only our prime cost. For one thing, the sound bricks are hard, and the mortar will come away just by tapping with a gavel, so perhaps things won't be so bad now we have got done with all the jawing and disputing and haggling which has taken five months to get finished, with more distress and annoyance and dis-

172

appointment and indignation and sour disgust for every-body than could be credited; and all, like enough, because some slacker in the brickyard wanted his beer too soon for the fires to be minded; and because some foreman quar-relled with his wife and was too sulky to be bothered to make sure for that day, since all the other days when he bothered to make sure there was nothing to bother about, after all:—just the same old story of accidents that come about when no one could possibly expect they would do; and that are nobody's fault; and that could not possibly be foreseen or prevented because of happening by their own accord! Well, it's a song I have heard sung often enough in my time; and if it ever sounds in tune it hasn't been when *I* was listening.

## A SKIRMISH

Here is our Priors Franklyn claim settled after a spot of bother that need never have been. Rumble made it £260 more than Previous & Frogg allowed, at our prices, for wheeling and protecting lawns and paths according to the Architect's ideas; and when I wrote them what work the Architect had directed, for them to please be so very kind as to say where they had covered for it in the Bills of Quantities, they sent down young Mr. Billington out of their staff, who couldn't settle it with Rumble in an hour and a half because of Mr. B. having been the one sent to measure on the site, and so he was all for keeping himself out of trouble. Rumble brought him in to me when they were stuck, and I had Mr. B. to know what *I* thought; and then, looking at the Architect's sketch and by what I saw on the site, I had this idea: instead of unloading in the back yard and wheeling all that long way round, why not use the road to the gate serving the kitchen garden, and make our yard inside? It would only mean pulling down some rotten old potting sheds, better gone, and re-building, new, after; and dismantling some frames easy put back again; and then, after we had excavated the slope and carried the terrace wall up to terrace level, we would wheel through the wicket along where the gardeners will make good after us, without any traffic whatever over lawns and paths; and we can hoist the barrows with a hand-jib up on terrace where we shall do no harm, for that is to be flagged at the finish.

Well, Mr. Billington really couldn't say, though I offered to do it a bargain against what was provided in the Bills—and a pretty good bargain for us, too! So off he went back; and, as I heard nothing more from P. & F., I wrote the Architect making claim as required by Conditions of Contract, which is not a pleasant thing to have to do, first start off, with a new Architect so eminent and praiseworthy all round as Mr. Blenhasset is held out to be by everybody —not forgetting to include himself.

The next was a letter:—would I please call and see Mr. Mooney? who is his Manager as well as Chief Draughtsman, it seems. Mooney was moony right enough! He didn't know what Mr. Blenhasset had ordered, but it seems Mr. Blenhasset is too fine an artist to be troubled with estimates and extras. He expects Builders to do what he says and give no trouble; and the Quantity Surveyor to settle what is to be paid, and the Owner to pay it, with Mooney just to make note of how much it is so as he can add up the Architect's charges correct.

Mr. Blenhasset's clients are always grateful any time Mr. Blenhasset thinks well to have them know how much it has all cost for a bit of fancy building made to suit Mr. Blenhasset's high-art tastes; and if it is not quite pretty enough to please Mr. Blenhasset the first time it is finished, and he decides to pull down and try if he can't alter it more agreeable to his ideas, his clients are delighted to pay for that, as well; and a second time over, and more if need be, till they have made certain their Architect is satisfied he can't make it any prettier, and is not merely holding off from pulling down—just for a last try to make quite sure—out of any sentimental consideration for their pockets, by any chance —or so I gathered by meeting some friends last week. I told moony Mooney, in parting, that I would understand I was to carry out Mr. Blenhasset's directions as an Extra unless I heard to the contrary; and that was *that*, far as I was concerned.

Next was by telephone message for me to meet the Architect on the site; and, when I went in the garden, there he was on the terrace with Lord Blades and her Ladyship, talking and waving his arms as if he could never get it all out in the time, and dressed up in a black felt with special wide brims, and a black cloak lined dark green silk with a chain across at the collar to show off his influenza-bandage, till he didn't look like real life at all, but more as if he might be out of one of those foreign pictures of someone just going to be murdered. He was too busy talking to throw me a nod on seeing me, so I stood a bit away; but her Ladyship gave me a bow and one of her pretty smiles with it, which made her Lord turn to look, and he stepped across.

"I see you're getting ready!" he says.

"Yes, my Lord, we shall be making a start directly we have the Architect's orders," I said; and he nodded and offered me a cigarette before helping himself and going back to where Mr. Blenhasset was waving his arms in a new direction with his cloak flapping like some bird ready to take off; and then they all moved away, round the far end.

Well, I'm not used to going where I'm expected to hang about as if I wasn't there, and not given even so much as a nod after being asked to travel all that distance to oblige; so I stayed where I was, to have him run round and search after me if he liked; or would it be just blow a whistle, instead, like some dog was lost and wanted back to heel? After a bit I strolled round to go through the kitchen garden and have word with Tol. who was marking time in the back yard with three lorry-loads of plant for getting ready with; when, soon as I got to the wicket into the kitchen garden, there were the three of them just in front, with the Architect explaining all the ideas I had passed to Billington as if they were his own notions!

That is all as it should be, no doubt; but I didn't care for his style of holding up a finger, without stopping his talk, for me to go running to him; so I made pretence he must mean someone else at back of me, and looked behind as though to see who. However, he started nodding his head backwards to beckon, so I went forward not to have any unpleasantness happen while the lady was by, but save it for some better time when I would, maybe, have a chance to come down got up as a Beefeater, or a Knight in Armour, to show what a fine fellow I am, and have him pay attention to me.

When I was close up, he jabbers away to lay down all the same orders I had told Billington would be best, but in such a quick voice no one could follow except they had known it all before. I just said: "I understand," with no "Sir" or any other word to him: but to the other I said:

"I hope his Lordship understands that I am not accountable for the fortnight of delay there has been," on which he smiles and nods:

"So you will be able to go ahead now?" he says.

"Yes, my Lord, next week we shall make a start, I hope," and I took off my hat at him and his lady, and off I went with no more notice taken of the great A.R.A. than he had taken of me; and, after a word with Tol., I went straight back to London for Mr. Blenhasset to play hide and seek to find me, if he had the mind, not feeling in a very pleasant temper to be dragged all that way just for the fellow to show how superior an A.R.A. is to a "common Builder-man"— as I heard said on the train one day by a fine satin lady very strong on the eau-de-Cologne, to another with gold bangles pulled on over her gloves.

Well, if Mr. Blenhasset thinks he can make fame for himself without a Builder to help him, he is the only one who doesn't know different; and there is another thing it would be no harm for him to know, and that is for him to get inside his Lordship's skin for half a minute to find out who it is Lord Blades thinks to be a better man than his dressed-up, jabbering, shopkeeper Architect; for I knew in my bones, first start off, that me and his Lordship belong to the same pack, to understand one another better than words can help to explain; just as our forebears have been ever since England began—*his* proud to command and *mine* proud to do their bidding; while this Blenhasset, with his eyes a bit too close together and a lift at the corners to make you think of the Koy Lang Tea poster—well, he doesn't exactly belong where me and his Lordship belong.

# A HAPPY EVENT

Here is one of the jolliest occasions come about that I can call to mind, and that is:—old Fred married, Easter Monday! There was such cheering and heartiness with church bells ringing as never was; and the people standing in the streets and looking out at their windows, on the grin, to see them go by; and a crowd waiting ready with rice and confetti; and old boots flying enough to make you look out where the next would land. What they fastened on the back of the taxi for mascots, and had trailing behind by strings, I couldn't have counted on my fingers, for all I have seven and two thumbs left.

I heard what was to do, week before last, when Rube Johnston came to me to ask could they have use of the hardwood loft for the wedding dinner, Bank Holiday? I don't know how they managed, but everything went first-class, with a trestle table laid out with flowers and all sorts in the fashionable style, by some of the wives giving a hand with things from home; and cold joints and pies and a barrel of beer, not forgetting port for the ladies; and the cake in middle, all white ribbons with a fat young child in nothing but a wreath across and pretending to shoot an arrow out of a bow, set on top as if he was all white sugar like the rest.

The wedding was at noon, with flowers out of their allotments set in pots against the altar; and the Vicar seeming quite sunny, for once—like enough by having his hair new-trimmed round—standing front of the altar to tell them—waiting before like a pair of good children—all about the State of Holy Matrimony; so as it made me smile to see old Fred's broad square back listening to hear as though he didn't know a dam' sight more about it than our Vicar could say.

Fred's brother, Harold, out of Hackney, with a white

178

rosette and silver horseshoe, same as Fred's, was Best Man; and a fusty old chap—Uncle of the bride and that gave her away—had come from Birmingham special for the job, and got squiffy, later, by taking charge of a bottle of whisky and keeping it hid between his legs, dinner, so as no one should know where it had got to—as Rube told me after—and then had Rube to lend him ten bob—by offering to cry if he did not—just to see him safe across London from pub to pub as far as Euston, because he had no more than his return ticket left over. After the service they had me in the vestry for a witness; and then off we went to the Yard. All was arranged by Rube, first-class, I will say; Fred and the Bride stopping at my house to walk across by the private way at a quarter after one when we were assembled ready for them in the loft.

There were thirty-two sat down to dinner; and it made me feel proud to think all these decent fine men and their wives were like one family with me, and looked to me as one that had given them an honest way of work and homes they could stay by and security and self-respect; and the whole of them considerate in their manners, spite of their freedom and laughter and jolly fun, as no gentlefolk could be more so. It is a thing for me to remember when my time comes, that there are a many the better for the way I have got through life and no one the worse that I know of. They had me sit at top with the girls, and Arthur and Ellie at the bottom. Fred and his new wife—that was all smiles and ready for the next joke—sat middle of one side over against the cake.

We had rare fun, and there was not too much of asking and handing about, for Rube had three there that had offered to wait at table. Then at last it was the cake to be cut; and there was a great shout and laughing when the lady couldn't manage, and Fred put his hand on top and drove the knife through like it was so much dough and he didn't know there had been anything to hinder him. Oh, it did make me laugh to see the old fellow, after all the years we have been at it together, and me knowing his ways of carrying on so well and the thoughts that pass across his mind almost as if I read them. He looked all smooth in his face and a bit pale with it, if anything; taking their joking in good part but letting it go by with none of his back-chat for *that* day. They kept at it that he must kiss her, and blessed if old Fred didn't come over more pink than the lady, with it!

Then, of course, it was me to propose the bride and the bridegroom. I said a word of the long years me and Fred had been together, and the times he had helped me out when things came awkward—and that fetched a lot of laughter to hear told; and then I said how it had been a happiness in my life to have Fred at my side, till I saw it was a bit too much for the old chap, so I ended up with a laugh for Fred to join in with: how, the next thing, we should have him goalkeeper of the Pirates so as no more balls got through into the net!

Then Rube must make a speech congratulating on behalf of the hands, and there was plenty of cheering and clapping to carry him through till it was "For He's a Jolly Good Fellow" and then "Auld Lang Syne" on top, for some reason, and I thought time to make a shift by there being a touch of Saturday-night creeping in. Then we had a look at the nice lot of presents they had laid out on a side-table, and Fred and his bride went back to the house, where I had a word of business with Fred while the lady put off her fallals; and then their luggage was carried down and out they went for cheering and pelting, and into the taxi and along to the station for another send-off with the porters joining, this time, and passengers with their heads out to see the fun —so I'm told.

Well, there they are, settled down in a furnished cottage

180

they have taken, for the time, at Pash Village, close by Belhampton; and I understand Tippets's General Shop is being run by the lady's daughter—that always used to help
her—along with her young husband out of Salisbury's
Chandlery where he was manager. I make no doubt Mrs.
Bloggs keeps the direction of things where her capital is
locked up, so old Fred looks to be in clover for the rest
of his days, and glad I am to think it.

## OLD FRIENDS

It was Thursday Mr. Spinlove wrote that Sir Leslie wants
me to build a little house with hangar, and level over
bottom field, so as Lady Brash can have her own private
'plane and a pilot, under her husband's orders, to take care
of her and mind what she's about; and, to-day, Mr. Spinlove arranged over the 'phone to pick me up on his way out
to Honeywood for us all to meet on the ground and get
things settled for a start, as Sir Leslie wants everything done
at once, to his orders—an idea I have seen something of
before—him having his flying man already engaged and the
'plane near ready for delivery. Mr. Spinlove brought along
sketches and I was wanted to start the levelling, right off,
while the drawings are being got out; and to do the whole
work at prime cost plus 15 per cent. However, I asked that
the buildings should be carried out under a schedule to be
agreed with Tinge, with him to measure and price at the
finish; for I have seen something of the frowning and dis-

content of owners at Daywork Accounts; and of the way they keep watch to see if the men are going ahead, piece-work style, without resting; and are trotting their barrows all the time so as to be quicker; and running up the ladders like they were sailors, and sliding them to come down; or whether, by any chance, the builder has agreed for the men to work "ca' canny", to take as long as they can manage over it, so as the builder will make a bigger profit by the work costing more! Sir Leslie is a man of business in the City where they know all about how to make a profit where another would a loss; and I wouldn't for the world be saddled with business-like City ideas where friends are concerned, besides having seen something of Sir Leslie's queer ways of thinking in the past; and so I thought well to have all measured and valued by Tinge, which Mr. Spinlove agreed and advised his father-in-law accordingly; and he says to him:

"The quantity surveyor's fees will be paid by the builder," he says—by which he meant to pull the other's leg, clear enough, from the funny twinkle in the corner of his eye; but the old gentleman seemed quite satisfied, by reason of his mind being otherwise engaged, I suppose, for Sir Leslie is no fathead by any manner of means.

Mr. Spinlove's lady was in the car with us to see her Dad and her Mum; and a jolly family party they are, I will say. Sir Leslie does not look to have aged so much as fifteen years since we last met; but he was always the old gentleman in his ways of going on, and at all times had the appearance of his boots pinching more than he could bear. He is now grown to be remarkable podgy and bloated in the face, as if he might break out any day—but to-morrow most likely—which has happened, no doubt, by him doing himself too well at the restaurant-lunches where some of these City men meet and stand each other treat, every day, so as to carry forward their business at the time when they

182

feel dear-old-fellowish; and can forget about never trusting anybody; and can each think he has found the soft side of the other.

Lady Brash is come to be so shrivelled up and apple-wrinkled as I do not think I ever saw anyone more so—unless it would be Mrs. Draper, Pornish Almshouses, that has her birthdays in the London papers by being 106 last time—and the lady has grown to be so thin in the figure that it would make no wonder if she rattled, moving about. However, she is quite spry in her manners, and active as a bird hopping round and back along a twig; and she seems to have quite forgot to be perplexed at what is going to happen next, and does not get all tangled in her mind by taking hold of the wrong end of everything and pulling at it without letting be—as I remember her doing in the old days. They were all most friendly to me; and Mrs. Spinlove had me talking so much about bygones that *he* got a bit impatient at her.

"Do let Mr. Grigblay alone for a moment, Puddy," he says. "There is such a lot we have to settle," he says; so she puts out her tongue at him in the humorous style, to let him have his way.

"You will not be free to do that at him when he's an R.A.," I said to her aside, for Mr. Spinlove is winning a high reputation among the artists, so I am given to understand.

"Oh, *won't* I!" she says, laughing; but pleased to hear me say it, as I could see clear enough.

The Pilot is Captain Spruce, with medals and a stiff leg, poor fellow, out of the war; and spruce he was at knowing his mind beforehand, and making all clear to Mr. Spinlove; and he had no complaints except three elms would be better out of the way. Two in the south hedge are ours; but the other, just West, belongs next door by the ditch being our side. It seems the present owner is Witspanner, that we had

all that trouble with when Honeywood Grange was building, and that has grown to be all the more crusty now he is
not as young as he was, and because of Sir Leslie keeping
his own dairy instead of going to *him*, and so it is no good
asking Witspanner to agree to anything. However, Sir
Leslie is giving up his dairy to have the field clear before his
lady wife makes a new start at billiards with a try at can-
noning the cows; so I said:

"Better make an oversight and throw *that* one first of the
three," I said, "for Witspanner couldn't make us put it
back again, even if it did him any other good than keep the
sun off his oats," I said; "and, after, offer him the timber-
merchant's price for the standing tree, which will be anything from price of a pint to 7s. 6d., by what I have seen,"
I said; "and then hold out the olive-branch of him having
a regular customer, to keep him sweet and out of mischief,"
I said to them, and, in the end, it was so agreed.


## LADY B. WANTS ALTERATIONS

Later, we went up to the house where was a hot leg of
mutton at lunch, with two or three glasses of port to
make Sir Leslie feel comfortable after his "follow"; and
then it was the good idea for alterations Lady Brash has set
her heart on so as any coming in the front hall can see right
through into the garden by a pretty, five-light, leaded casement window, same as to the outside, fixed in the $4\frac{1}{2}$-in.
partition wall with the stays to stand out for catching you
in the guts as you pass to the stairs. It seemed to me so silly
an idea as any the lady got hold of in the days we were
building the house, for, as Mr. Spinlove says to her:

"Everyone coming to the front door will see straight into
the drawing-room, and you won't like that, will you,

184

Mum?"—for so he calls her. "The maid cannot say you're out while you are sitting there, right in front, for everyone to see you at tea with your friends, can she?" he says.

But, No! The lady, it seems, visited in some house where it was arranged to see through; and she has got the word "vista" fixed in her head, and why can't she have a "vista" like other people? However, no one paid more attention than if it had been so much talking, which is the best way to treat her, no doubt; and, if she gets depressed, she can go for a flip round looping the loop till she feels better, instead of making herself unhappy and crying with it, poor lady, as I have many times seen her ready to do.

The house has stayed in rare good order, I will say; not a joint opened anywhere, nor cracks come in the ceilings or stud partitions, by what I saw; and so I said to her, and asked after the aquarium she was formerly so much taken up with that she must have h. and c. laid on to the drawing-room for it, though all is now gone.

"Oh! a most terrible thing happened, Mr. Grigblay!" she says. "Didn't you ever hear about it? They all dried up to nothing, poor little things! Wasn't it simply *too* dreadful for them?"

Well, I didn't question her how it came about, for I know better by this time! but I suppose the water was run off by some mistake while the house was unoccupied. However, she is now all taken up with pekinese dogs that she has everywhere for treading on or stepping round. They are the big blue-eyed cream-colour sort, with faces made flat— for licking their eyes clear—like someone had fetched them a swipe with a cricket bat while soft; and looking the same as old men that have been on the loose all their lives to make you ashamed to see them—not the kind to take my fancy, by any means; but the lady can't have enough of them, by appearances, and, when she came to the front gate to see us off, she was running about all over the highway calling out to have them come to her so as she could gather them in her arms out of danger; and she would have barged straight into a motor, by never looking to see it, if the gentleman driving hadn't stopped to wait till she was quite finished before passing along. She is all feather-brains still, clear enough; but a kind, nice lady with it all, and one that was always friendly to me, and I ask no better than to help see her made contented.

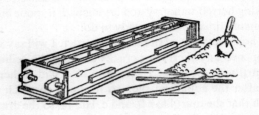

## BARNACLE GETS BUSY

By what Tinge writes me, here is Lanky Barnacle started his games! I got the idea something clever was afoot some time back, when Fred told me nothing would suit Lanky but he must measure the whole of the foundation-concrete—as if it wasn't laid, with no variations whatso-ever, exactly as figured in the drawings! Fred thought best to agree measures with him, not to have disputes arise after covering in; and the next was Mr. Lanky taking advantage to get scant measures everywhere by holding the tape where a corner was knocked away, or on the short side when not quite square, et cetera; and actually arguing to deduct where he had before noted big stones in the bottom, better left in, that stand up to make the concrete less!

Well, Fred got tired of running backwards and forwards along the tape to see what Lanky was about; so, at last, he fell to gathering up a few inches of slack to hide in his hand, *his* end of the tape, to strike a balance with what Lanky was cheating us of at the *other*—a dirty trick when played dishonest, but it made me laugh to hear of Fred playing it off to diddle the other at his own game, for any C. of W. that knew his business would tumble pretty quick. Old Fred was cheerful enough telling me; so all Mr. Clever Lanky has done is to bring us more full measures than if he had set out to act on the square from the first.

The next thing Tinge talks about is what Fred also told me of at the time; and that is: Lanky holding out there is an omission to come off from the punning of the trench-bottoms—by the bottom being, in general, a lot harder than any punning could make it—the most fatheaded ignorant twaddle I ever heard, when we have taken a chance with our price, not knowing what we should find, and might have had to pay six times over what we have allowed for the punning, if the whole ground had been like we found it in one or two places—as old Fred had Lanky to know in a bit of the real, choice, special British language he knows how to get his tongue round when he wants.

However, that has not been enough for our brainy Clerk, it seems; for he has been out to curry favour with his master—to let him know what a conscientious Clerk he has got —by having him write to Tinge to complain that the Bills show about twenty pounds' worth more of foundation-concrete than is wanted for the job; and that the punning of trenches is quite unnecessary, except in a very few places, and please to be so very kind as to say at once how this has all come about and what deduction will be made to correct the error. I suppose this is the style Barnacle carries on in supervising the alterations to the Gotsnitz Co.'s shops; but was such a thing ever heard of as the Clerk going behind the Architect's back to complain to the owner, and the owner going behind his Architect's back to complain to the Quantity Surveyor? to say nothing of the complaints being all a silliness, for we have not asked to be paid for more concrete than we have laid; and, in giving a price for the punning without knowing what the ground would be like, we did no more than lay the odds—so to say—and, if *we* have won our bet instead of the owner, we can no more be called on to hand over our winnings to *him* any more than we could claim to have him reimburse *our* losses if the *other* horse had come in first!

Well, I have no wish to be mixed up in any such nonsense; and so have written Tinge that we have nothing to say, and to suggest he sends all correspondence to the Architect to hear what *he* thinks.

## A BATTLE ROYAL

We had as fine a set-to as any I remember, yesterday afternoon in Sir Ezra's private room at the Gotsnitz Coy's offices, Queen Street, arising out of Lanky Barnacle's clever notions of the Quantities being got out too full; but, as Mr. Spinlove said when I called at Mount Street to go to the City with him: "I have not arranged the meeting because of this nonsense about full Quantities," he says, "but in order to settle matters so that there shall be no more interferences in the future," he says.

Well, I have built for Mr. Spinlove these many years, ever since he was new-hatched out of the egg to peck about and learn where he'd got to; but it was a new thing to see the style he went ahead and took control to have his own way with "the old toad"—as Henry Curt, his butler, calls Sir Ezra; and enough rudeness and ugly behaviour to make us forget there was such a thing as polite manners, till we got outside to signal a taxi, and had the driver apologizing at not being able to take us West because he was obliged to go East, back to his garage.

Mr. Spinlove told me he had directed Tinge to answer Sir Ezra's letter by asking him for the measurements agreed between Barnacle and Fred and lo and behold! when he got them, if they didn't show foundation-concrete to be £12 14s. 9d. *extra* over what Tinge had taken, and the omission of "about £20" claimed by the Owner, to be deductions made by Lanky, on his own account, for stones standing up in the bottom to make the concrete less, which he must have measured on the sly and made note of, secret, without Fred knowing he had done, unless it was Lanky's clever guess-work after everything had been covered in and no check possible! On getting this piece of news, Mr. Spinlove had Tinge write the Owner that there was an extra to be added on, instead of an omission to come off; and, also, that the amount for punning trench-bottoms, that Lanky complained about, was correct, and so there was nothing to come off that, either. Mr. Spinlove also had Tinge send him copies of the letters, so as Mr. Spinlove could write Sir Ezra that a meeting was necessary "to settle this and other more important matters"—for so he told me his words were.

I ought to know well enough, by this time, about the rare old mix-ups and disputings, never to be decided, that may come of measuring-up digging and foundations after all is covered in; but nothing of the kind has happened at Belhampton, by reason of Mr. Spinlove being most careful and exact in all his ways; and Tinge, too, is more safe for close pricing than any Q.S. I know of, and he also understands Mr. Spinlove's ideas, through and through, by long experience of them. Mr. Spinlove had four trial-holes sunk to judge the ground before he designed his foundations (dirt and rubbish it was, laying on top of chalk, carted for filling in and levelling over the stones, and all sorts, tumbled about everywhere, thick, from the ruins) which Tinge saw for his taking off, the same as me and Spedder did for our pricing; and, when we got to work, we found nothing to bring about any alteration from what was fixed in the contract, except it was a rare job for us getting a level bottom, and not reasonable to be done with great stones out of the castle walls—six foot content, and more, some of them— rooted in the ground and only to be got out with crowbars for filling the hole with concrete no harder than the stones we took out—so what was the use of that? Fred had Lanky to pass every bit of trench before concrete laid, according to what Mr. Spinlove had approved and directed on the spot; and, now, here was Lanky claiming to deduct the stones rising above the bottom, out of the measures of the concrete, without taking account of our evening-over the bottom with concrete, where pitted in holes; and of the extra cost to us of great splinters of the Purbeck slabs, off the old roofs, standing up for digging out or sledging off, which were never reckoned on or allowed for in our pricings!

When we got to Queen Street, there was Tinge and Barnacle reading advertisements from pictures on the walls of the waiting-room as if neither could make a guess who the other might be; and then the four of us were shown in where Sir Ezra was sitting at his kneehole, back to the window, with a secretary set ready to take down—and to make all as Sir Ezra would have it to read, according to Mr. Spinlove's ideas, it seemed, for he outs with it first thing, soon as we were settled down, and so the rowing started.

"It is quite unnecessary to have any record made, Sir Ezra," he says.

"Well, I choose to have him do it:—Understand?" the other snaps.

"And I choose not:—Understand?" says Mr. Spinlove, giving me a proper surprise to hear him.

"I'll have you to know, Mr. Architect," the other squawks, giving a bang on the table with the flat of his hand, "that when——" but Mr. Spinlove reaches forward and hits *two* bangs on the table, heavier than the other, and shouts, top of his voice:

"And I'll have *you* to know, Mr. Owner, that I'm not here to be browbeaten and bullied:—Understand?"

It was as queer a thing as ever I saw, the way the other took it from him. He stared as if he had never had one to answer him before, and didn't know how to behave next; and when I looked at Mr. Spinlove staring back at him, I could see clear enough, he was just play-acting by his mouth shut tight to prevent any smiling, and laughter in his eyes to see the shabby figure the other cut. They were set like two dogs for, I dare say, all of ten seconds, before the other seemed to remember, of a sudden, and waved his hand aside to his clerk and told him: "Ring up Mr. Cohen to come round at once."

"I'll clear you out," he mumbles, looking this way and that and fingering his papers on the table as if he didn't know what he was at.

"I won't go! I'll fight you," Mr. Spinlove says.

"Huh!" the other grunted, like he might be some pig. "You'll soon find out. I've sent for my Solicitor," he says. "He'll be round in five minutes to let you know," he says, fidgeting his hands about over the table and not looking our way.

"I shall be delighted to meet your solicitor," says Mr. Spinlove. "If you'll listen carefully to what he tells you, it will save me the trouble of trying to get you to listen to *me*."

"What's that you say?"

"I've come here to tell you the rights of this matter and get things settled so that we shall have all running smooth in future."

"Nice and smooth, ain't it? Nothing being done; the men——"

"You're wrong! Mr. Grigblay is ahead of his time. All well, he will finish by the contract date. He has taken special steps to press the work forward. The site is crowded with men——"

"Why don't they make a showing, then? There's nothing to see, only holes all about——"

"You're wrong! The walls are up three feet. In four weeks they'll be as high as the first floor."

"Time enough, too, when I am asked to pay for what isn't done nor wanted. Tell me the meaning of *that*, Mr. Clever? Barnacle has it written down in notes, for evidence; so you can't make out——"

"Be civil! Mr. Barnacle has got to learn to make his reports to *me*, not to *you*."

"What's that? Not tell me, when I am paying him to see I'm not rooked!"

"You'll find yourself sued for slander if you don't take care, Sir Ezra. Will you read where I have marked in the margin?" and Mr. Spinlove pushed the Conditions, spread out, under his nose.

"What's all this you're showing me?"

"The contract you're bound by."

On that the other put on his tortoise-goggles, made with a spring to sit a-straddle his nose. However, he didn't seem able to give his mind to reading so as to know what it meant; so Mr. Spinlove pointed him:

"You can see, here, that the Architect is to decide everything to do with the building; and, on this other page, that the Quantity Surveyor, Mr. Tinge, will decide the sums you must pay the Builder. You have no power to interfere."

"Oh! Stand aside, is it, and see you fellows do what you like and make me pay what you choose? Who says so? Eh? Tell me that!"

"*You* do."

"Talk sense!"

"Behave yourself! You engaged to it when you signed the Contract."

"I am not such a stupid ass as to pay for all that ramming the earth Barnacle says was not wanted and not done; nor for all that concrete spread out too wide, just to bring up the cost, and steel rods in it, too, that never were wanted:—Understand?" So Lanky B. had his own ideas of how the Architect ought to design, as well!

"Yes, you *will* pay. Mr. Tinge has decided you must:— Understand?"

"You'll learn I don't do business that style, Mr. Architect! As if the law would fix me so as I can have no say in how I spend my own money, and no way to protect myself from being cheated and robbed!"

"You're wrong again, Mr. Building Owner! You have the security of my, and Mr. Tinge's, reputation; and of our capacity and integrity: and, if we fail in either, you can sue us for negligence or fraud, or both, and get damages awarded and ruin us professionally."

"Oh, yes! Of course! I've never heard of that sort of thing before, have I? So that's the game, is it? To have me put up with any house you choose, and pay twice over for it into the bargain; and then go to the law to settle it for me after the harm's done, when I know, all the time, by what Barnacle tells me——"

"He has no business to meddle."

G : N                    193

"No! That doesn't suit you, my boy, does it?"

"Keep a civil tongue in your head. Barnacle won't meddle in future, for I shan't let him go on the site."

"You shall this, and you shan't the other! Wait till Mr. Cohen comes. He'll soon show you different, you stupid ass," on which Mr. Spinlove—that I could see was for laughing if he had let himself go—must bang with his hand on the table and shout enough to be heard in the street:

"You shall apologize for that:—Understand? Apologize at once. Apologize! Apologize!" with a fresh bang every time he said it, to make the other sit back in his chair as if a lunatic was at him; and, same moment, Mr. Cohen must walk in.

## A SOLICITOR INTERVENES

Well, that is all just as it happened; and it is remarkable how I can recall the words of it for settling down.

Mr. Cohen was a fattish, dark-haired, short gentleman that might have been brother to the other; with a black-rim monocle on a wide ribbon fixed in his eye to hold it round-open and push down the lower lid so as to show how nice and red it was inside, as it might be the eye of one of these St. Bernard dogs that pant and hang out their tongues at you like they were dying of their own stink—or so they always seem to me. He marched in with quick short steps not to be too late to get us sacked, first go off, and next, put us all in jail for a month or two—or so it looked like from his style.

However, it didn't happen quite that way, after all; first, by Mr. Spinlove insisting he must have his apology before a word more of anything else, till at last he got a mumble from the other by the Solicitor saying: "A little unseemly, perhaps, with others present, Sir Ezra": and, next, by Sir Ezra starting off thirteen to the dozen—with Barnacle dropping a word, now and again, to thick the muddle—till at last the Solicitor would hear only Mr. Spinlove, who refused to discuss measurements of concrete, and punning and foundation-design, but held to it that such matters were for the Architect and Q.S. to decide about, and no other person; so, at last the Solicitor got things straight in his head to explain to his client, leaning over to talk to him, sotto, for the other to have a good stare close into his round eye to see it magnified nice and big, for a special treat.

Last of all Mr. Spinlove had it up against Barnacle pretty stiff, for the Solicitor to agree, that a Clerk of Works must carry out the Architect's orders and no one else's, with Barnacle sitting to hear him and get it inside his head at last; and when Sir Ezra was for chipping in, the Solicitor would not have it. In the end, Mr. Spinlove acted generous and said he would agree for Lanky to stay Clerk of Works, as a last chance, so long as he kept to the rules and gave satisfaction. After that Mr. Spinlove made to shake hands on leaving, and Sir Ezra gave his, looking aside with a bit of a shrug and the corners of his mouth pulled down the while, like he had had a dose he didn't fancy the taste of; and so the four of us came away—with nothing spoken by me or Tinge, first to last—leaving Mr. Cohen to have a last word to make his Client feel a bit more contented in his mind, let us hope.

Mr. Spinlove seemed cheerful enough when we got outside; and was laughing with it after we got clear of being seen out of windows—and lucky he waited, for I caught sight of one of them peeping round the curtain as we passed along, under.

"I don't think we shall have any more trouble," he says, "but I never thought I should come to shouting and slapping a table to have things settled my way," he says.

## CONFUSION

Yesterday afternoon our good Vicar called at the house to ask for me, and was all of a hesitation with the worry of not knowing whatever to do next when Meg told him I was gone to London; and then he must wander across to the office, it seems, to ask again, as though such a thing was beyond belief and there must be some mistake.

I made a guess some dreadful new trouble was come about; and, sure enough, this morning—me in my slippers reading the paper, comfortable, front of the fire, and breakfast clearing away—there he was hurrying in as though it was too important to wait; and, lo and behold! he has managed to get himself mixed up in *another* pickle over his new aisle window for me to tell him how to get clear *this* time!

Well, I dare say I wasn't any too glad to listen to him, at the moment; nor I couldn't make head or tail of his rigmarole till he handed me a letter: "Dear Mr. Peebles, I really must protest . . ." and so it went on; and, when I turned over to see who from, the signature read "Gervase Triconnor," that was one of the Window-Artists I had put down on the list for Mr. Peebles to choose from. After, I read some other letters—but none of his own, for he has not the habit of keeping copies—and, by asking questions, I got the hang of how things are, at last.

196

Our Vicar, it seems, acted according to what I said to be best; and he asked Mr. Triconnor down from his Chelsea Studio by taking a great fancy to the West Window he did at Saint James-the-less Church, Croydon, that I had made note of; and they settled it between them on the spot, right off, for Mr. Triconnor to do our window according to a sketch he made there, at the Church, in agreement with Mr. Peebles' ideas. Fortnight later, Mr. Triconnor sent in a proper picture, in colour, of what he was about; but Mr. Peebles did not think to acknowledge it because it was just exactly what was arranged for, and all according to his tastes; so there is nothing in writing, let alone any form of contract, but only word of mouth between the two of them to fix what has been agreed!

Ten days after, the donor must send a cable from Colombo—on her way to New Zealand, I suppose—that read: "Let Primstake do window Broadbench"; and, very next day, there was a p.c. from Mr. Vicat Primstake—that I never heard of before—dated from Norwich, that he would come and take particulars "soon as practicable"; on which Mr. Peebles wrote Primstake to go ahead so as not to have any delay; and, same post, wrote also to Triconnor that another had been appointed to carry out the window so would he please be so very kind as not to trouble himself any more.

That was when Triconnor wrote to protest—and no wonder!—for, by what he says, he has the cartoon finished, and his cut-line for the glass laid out, and has been to Birchingtons, Lewisham, to order special glass he has in mind to use:—"so I am afraid I must decline to retire at this late hour after all has been agreed and much of the work done and the glass ordered" he says—and properly put, too, in my opinion: so Mr. Peebles has got two engaged to do the same job, the one well ahead with it, and the other made a start, as well; for it seems Mr. Primstake came—without notice—all the way from Norwich to take particulars on the same day Mr. Peebles was gone to Portsmouth to lend a helping hand at trying if a happy pair couldn't somehow be got safe-married, because—by appearances—*one* clergyman, all alone by himself, is not many enough to tie the modern fashionable-style knot properly tight, so as it won't come undone too soon and make the wedding presents all so much waste.

It was from Bunter—who has care of the clock and the bells, and looks after the heating as well as acting Sexton—that Mr. Peebles came to know Primstake had been to the Church, by asking to find out who it was called at the Vicarage without leaving any name; and it seems Primstake had Bunter to point him which window, and help with a tape and a ladder for noting the particulars. Whether Bunter told Primstake the money for spending, and told him right; and, also, whether he approved his artistic ideas —which is like enough by all the muddling there is—I did not inquire of Mr. Peebles by feeling properly tired with the whole rigmarole; and when I said: "Cable the donor, that all is settled and too late to change; and tell Primstake the same; and write Triconnor to go ahead as it has been all a mistake," he couldn't make up his mind to do it by not seeming able to find the right place for biting on his finger: and then it came out, by me asking, that he had no written word from the donor stating cost, or even saying she was giving a window at all; and, of course, none directing him to order it, but the whole business set going by Mr. Peebles on no more than what passed in talk one day between the two of them. However:

"There cannot possibly be any mistake," he says, "I am certain of that; perfectly certain! Oh, perfectly! There was no misunderstanding whatever. Oh dear me, No! Such an idea has never once entered my head," he says: and when I said to him:

"Get the lady to write it down in a letter to you," he didn't favour the idea because it would make seem he didn't trust her; and when I said:

"How if the lady should die and the executors require legal evidence of the gift?" all he says is:

"God forbid!" and started at biting on the side of his finger, again, to see if that might help; but nothing came of it.

## A SCULPTOR AND OTHERS

Well, there it is! and *I* can't help our Vicar, and *nobody* can help him; and so the only thing is for him to muddle himself out same style he has muddled himself in, and which I dare say he will manage well enough by all his long practice doing it before: but I feel sorry enough for the poor gentleman that always means to act for the best; and I am sorry for Mr. Triconnor, also, though it beats me how these Artists cannot learn to be more careful when it comes to matters of business, and try and use their common sense to keep things straight so as they will grow up to take care of themselves same as other people do.

There was that poor young fellow Hibbert Callington,

now dead, with his sculptures in the R.A. Exhibition and that did that fine piece on the front of Biggington Institute we built, all those years ago, under Mr. Stanley Paragon, A.R.I.B.A.,—as he then was —who won it in the Comp, that started him off to make a name for himself.

I have a rare liking for a fine, clean-cut bit of white sculpture, and I fancy this group by Mr. Callington, I must say. It is a great, fine female with pretty-done hair and a crown on top made like a castle, sitting with just a sheet, as it might be, looped up to hang round for her arms and feet and one leg—as far up as above where her stocking would come—to show bare, all as like as real life: and then there is another smaller-size figure of a fine-looking naked blacksmith—though he would be the better for a hair-cut—with a tongs and hammer in each hand to show who he is meant for, leaning up against the female's other leg, affectionate style, for you to see his back; while his striker—taken off his clothes as well, but with a bit of apron put on, after, out of politeness—is standing opposite for a front view, and tilted backwards, far as he can manage, ready to bring his sledge over, full circle. He is a hefty one, and no mistake, with great muscles standing out all over, wonderful to see and good enough for knocking the beak off the anvil standing in front, as has been done before now and which he may be having a try to do, for there is no iron laying on the anvil for any to see:—a very nice piece indeed, to my way of thinking, that I go and have another look at whenever I get the chance, by it seeming to be part of my own work; and the meaning said to be—by those that understand such reasoning—"Commerce the Mother of Industry," which shows that the two smiths are brothers, and sons of the female; so no wonder they are a hefty pair, if on the small side, for their mother is a remarkable large handsome woman—although I never heard of any smith that chose to work naked with bare feet, and would think it a queer business to have mine start that game, even if they do, at times, pull their shirts off to be easy in the hot weather.

Well, the Architect picked on Mr. Callington for the Sculpture-work, and the Institute Council agreed, and the Sculptor's sketch-idea was accepted; so then it was for the Sculptor to say what the cost would be; and what must he do but send a scale sketch, in plan, section and elevation, to his stone-merchants, and will they please say the cube necessary, and the price in selected Whitbed; but he never thought to write any scale on the drawing or figure any dimensions to fix it, and he can't have shown any joint-lines, either, which is hard to understand. Whether it was he just asked rough information to oblige, as seems likely, with no quotation invited, or how else it happened, I don't know; but by some carelessness they read the sketch as scaling 1 in. to the foot and all in one stone—by no jointing being shown, no doubt—instead of $\frac{1}{2}$ in., and close on eight feet high, as it was drawn to be; so their figure of cubic content was only one-sixth part, more or less, of what was correct. Meanwhile poor Callington had got out his own estimate for pointing and boasting and handling and all the rest, and when he got the Merchants' estimate he must have simply added it on to his own total to arrive at his Tender. How any first-class Sculptor, however young—and Mr. Callington was twenty-six at the time—could accept a measure of 80 feet cube for stone to fit in with labours estimated for 500—for that would be near the proportions— only a true Artist could make a guess, and he would have to be a very great Artist, too, with long experience in making muddles for himself.

No one guessed anything was amiss, the stone being not a fifth part of sculpture costs; the Architect was no doubt glad enough to recommend a wonderful low tender, and the Council pleased to accept it; and Callington never found out where he had landed himself till he got to laying out his jointing for ordering the sizes of the different stones he would want. I do not know what the Architect had to say about it; but Callington faced the music and did a piece that would have been his making if he had lived; but I would judge from the amount of his tender that, by the time he had paid the high wages of masons and pointers and finished the work, he had given the whole of his time for nothing, and was lucky if he came out, other end, free of debt.

The fact of the matter is that the average Artist, by what I have seen of them, has no more sense of where he is than the next bullock going to be poleaxed; big things or little, it is always the same. There couldn't have been a more little thing, for an instance, than that bit of a cup for the "Waterboys" Club, here, two years ago:—and what happened that time?

I came to hear the "Waterboys" had whipped up £15 among them for a loving cup to pass round at their dinners twice a year, and of course the Committee must dispute over catalogues for choosing one of these humbugging spun cups, polished up like any mirror and stood on a velvet cloth to bait a mug-trap in Goloshes' or Spankums' front window, that are priced so wonderful cheap and reasonable at only two and a half times the cost of the silver and labour to make it, that it is a perfect marvel to tell of. They listened to my ideas, and decided for me to arrange for a real bit of silver-smith's work that would be different from any other, instead of out of some "very popular special new line" to make sure it was the same as next door.

The first I wrote to was Mr. John Spender Forton, by taking a fancy to his work in an Exhibition at that time, and seeing his name and address in the catalogue; but John had come over so bashful and shy, in the meanwhile, that he couldn't bring himself to answer my letter; and, as he was off the telephone—so as to keep himself more secret and out of the way—I didn't think it kind to travel over to Wimbledon and, perhaps, give him a fright. Next, I had Mr. Mervyn Prepense make me a first-class picture of a £15 cup that the Committee agreed to; and I fixed it for him to go ahead, with four months to get finished in before the special anniversary Club Dinner when the cup was wanted.

After six weeks I wrote to inquire; but, getting no answer in a week, I sent a wire, and then Mervyn wrote he had got the silver all right, but the money was not enough for all the work there was to do—when he had made his own free offer at £15! Next, it was a drawing for an altered idea he wanted to follow; and when I wrote that he must keep to the original, I got no answer from him and couldn't come to know what he was at, until there was less than a fortnight of the four months to run. When at last I got a letter, it was all to do with the dreadful trouble he was put to getting finished not to be late; and the next letter was how the Goldsmiths' Coy. had refused Hall Mark because the handles were made in two pieces that ought to have been in one piece, so that he would have to make them new after all the time and trouble he had been put to going from Guildford to London to settle it—just as if it was *my* fault and I ought to have told him the Goldsmiths' rules, beforehand, and not left him to find out for himself after he had made the cup wrong! The cup arrived, just two days in time' with a new packet of grumbles instead of the stand, and, only three days later, there came a letter—but without any invoice:

"When am I going to be paid for my work?" and "I have had to pay cash for the silver and I cannot afford to be kept waiting" and "It is not fair to expect me to wait indefinitely" and a lot more—the whole business, from first to last, being so much silliness and muddling stupidity as is beyond belief, and that I would not myself credit if it hadn't all happened in my own experience.

# THE YEARLY AUDIT

The Auditors have been here a fortnight; and to-day I heard that Mr. Blackington was down again to see what his two clerks are about sitting together in Smith's room, put at their disposal, with Smith to have his table in with the typists, meanwhile, who make him so irritable with their rattle and talking that it shakes up his wits so as, seems to me, he would be better, all ways, in with the Gas-engine or at a desk in the machining near where the saw is running, for a change, to smarten him up and get the best out of him, good little man! I saw Blackington going off in the afternoon, and had a word with him. He said there was some matter to do with the Cash Sales that has got to be cleared up; and then he said he thought perhaps better if we arranged a bit different so that a record was kept in the Prime Costing of the prices charged for goods sold out of Store, but he would tell me his ideas later.

Well, I don't know what more check is wanted. It is the same way we have had things these many years without complaint from any auditor, first to last. It is a long time since I got in the way of obliging small local builders and jobbers that are in need of something out of the way or find themselves short; and, also, it helps me get rid of odds and ends, left over from Contracts, that lie in the yard, years, for any chance I have of using them except to break up for hard-core or rubbish—like those 700 special-moulded Basingstoke splays I sold to Sutton only a week ago by passing the time of day with the man in the street, and learning how he was fixed. Those bricks laid a dozen years, I dare say, and would, likely, have laid another twenty if Sutton hadn't had a use for them.

However, I don't hold out to be a Builders' Merchant, and I won't run an account with anyone. Those that want what I have to spare can come and pick it up and carry it away after paying cash down; for I don't know who they are, and don't want to know—as long as it is not Johnny Rasper—and so "no cheques" is my rule. Rasper knows well enough I will oblige him soon as he has learnt how to oblige others, which he hasn't yet started to do unless it was a first try when he picked up and carried off—as I have a good idea he did—the pair of sheer-legs that rolled off our lorry coming from the schools last month; and then, for all we could get to hear of them when we began to ask questions, passed them to the saw for firewood, no doubt, in true Johnny Rasper style.

It was smart of Fred, a year back, when that fellow no-one had ever seen before, O'Brien he called himself, came to inquire for a 12-in. interceptor with clearing eye wanted in a hurry; and, when he found we could oblige him, went off back to get something to carry it away in. Fred heard mention of it, but who would be wanting a 12-in. interceptor? so he asked questions in the town, dinner, and lo and behold! if Johnny Rasper hadn't been assing about with a Traction Engine to drag a tree out of the way, other side of the sewage-farm; and was in such a hurry to get done that he hadn't time to see where he was going and must break through some sewer or other and tumble the old Traction, with the tree on top, through the hedge and into the ditch to make a finish, just for the day—so that's where our interceptor was wanted for! but, when Mr. O'Brien brought two labs. pushing a hand-cart with the name smudged out, to fetch it, he had to go off home again with his empty barrow to have Rasper's name cleaned back; and 'phone Sankey's, I dare say, to have a 12.-in interceptor sent at once, nice and cheap alone on a truck by itself, express, by passenger!

Well, what Blackington has to complain about I don't know. Colbert, storekeeper, makes out the voucher, and the buyer takes it to the Prime Costing to have the price put on; and, when he can show it receipted by the Cashier, he is free to pick the stuff up and take it away: so there's the Storekeeper's book and the Cash Sales Book for check and record, and it beats me what more Blackington would have us to do just for a simple little bit of side-business that only runs to four or five hundred in the year, I dare say. It comes in my mind I might start cocking my nose in the air to smell better if I thought Mr. Oswald Snape was anywhere about; but the Cash Sales Book is just a counter-book that Saunders takes care of, and nothing to do with Snape who only has it to post up the Cash Book once a week.

## THE WINDOW SETTLED

Entering up the offertory in the vestry after morning service, Sunday, the Vicar must ask me round to see Mr. Primstake's picture for the new window. It is a fine big picture, all coloured up and pretty enough to look at, of a fine sturdy Saint Peter, in pink, with a bushy ginger-colour beard, and hair standing out, frizzy, all round below where he is bald. He is holding out a great key in a very simple style for an old fellow, almost like some child just given a rattle that does not know what it is for; and, facing him in the opposite light to look across the mullion at him, is Saint Paul in green, more thin than the other and a lot balder, with a grey beard more long and straggly. He is rather a dumpy old man by his head being made same size as the other, though his figure less; but a wonderful close likeness, in the face, to Ben Harris, that formerly had the drapery opposite the old Fire Station, when I went to see him for the last time after he was ill.

In his right, far side, Saint Paul has his sword, but it might be his umbrella by the style he carries it in and had ought to be altered to make it more like, in my opinion; and in his left is an open book, held close up to cover his chest where poor Harris was so bad. Both have on their halos, back of their heads; and their names—to say which is which—are set out on yellow ribbons below their feet with the toes spread out for you to see them clear, done remarkable true to life. The pair have their heads twisted round to show you their faces better, and their eyes rolled up to try if they can't see in the trefoil-tracery above, where is one of these cherub affairs of a head with solid goldcolour hair parted in the middle for standing out all round, and blue wings—more duck-shape than chicken—growing out at back of the ears by there being no room for any shoulders to set them on;—a bit too far from nature to my tastes, though others may like such fanciful things.

Well, I didn't feel I cared over much about these ideas of Mr. Primstake, pretty-done as his picture is; for it is all too much like the stale commercial lines that one knows all about without looking at, by seeing them so often before, and would take no more notice of, passing by, than of the next lamp post. Also, Mr. Primstake has made his figures look a bit comical, to me, by not caring enough what he was about, so as it has got in my mind they are the same as two performing dogs sitting up opposite as they might be in some Music-Hall turn. No doubt it will be nice enough when done, and Mr. Primstake will give us a bit of coloured glass to make us all feel happy; for it is not the pictures in a window that matter so much as the silvery light, and the pattern of jewellery-colours, as they might be precious stones, the artist makes play with, just as it was in the kaleidoscope—they called it—Auntie gave me when I had the chicken-pox, and that started me hankering after a nice bit of coloured glass-work ever since.

## ALTAR DECORATION

Mr. Peebles seemed well satisfied with Mr. Primstake's picture: but when he untied the string made ready for sending Mr. Triconnor's picture back (Mr. T. asking for it so as Mr. Peebles should not have another to copy it for nothing, I suppose, as, like enough, he might do out of his simplicity in never thinking of any interests but his own) it was clear enough he liked it the better of the two,—as I did also—by it being more of a pattern, with the figures only seen when you look close instead of made to jump out at you, in Primstake's style, like it might be a story-book for children to look at; but it beats me how Mr. Peebles could go to Chelsea and wheedle Mr. Triconnor to cancel the order for his window, by holding out a commission for a new altar instead—with riddels and hangings and three pictures painted in panels to fold over for setting at back— when Mr. Peebles cannot get the money together to pay for it, in years, by having everyone bled white already, and by the overdraft at the Bank got to be cleared off without the help promised by the Bishop coming to dedicate the roof. However, that is what he did, it seems; and he showed me the picture-sketch of it in colour and gilding that Mr. Triconnor has just sent in; and Mr. Peebles asked me how did

I like an idea he had seen somewhere in an Artists' Exhibition and taken a fancy to, because Mr. Triconnor would not put it in when he told him; and that is: to have strings of glass beads dangling from the riddels to stand for Angels' Tears?

Well, Angels' faces slobbered in tears seems an ugly notion to me, though others may feel different by being able to guess what is happened to make them cry; but, as I said to Mr. Peebles:

"If you think pretty to have strings of beads hung on the riddels, I see no harm," I said, "but, seems to me," I said, "it would be better not to shout about 'Angels' Tears', in case too many should decide they are nothing else but just a parade of crocodile tears for making a pretence of extra fine feeling that no one feels," I said. "To my way of thinking, asking your pardon, Mr. Peebles," I said, "it is no harm for people to get sentimental ideas in their heads, private, if they want;" I said. "But to push sentimental ideas at them when they *don't* want, only sets their skins creeping, like they were ashamed, by showing other people's silly insides laid open for gaping at as if supposed to be their own," I said, being a bit hot at him talking the kind of nonsense that scares more wholesome folk out of Church than it draws other sorts in.

## RUMINATIONS

Sitting to doze after dinner Sunday, it being too stormy for going out, I got thinking about this Angel idea, and remembered those pictures of them in Mr. Dore's book about "Paradise Lost"—it is called—that Meg brought home a bargain out of Crutcher's Auction, and that I was turning over a little time back. Mr. Dore shows all the good

Angels like pretty young women got together in a crowd for slinging their brothers and husbands—or whatever else they are—out of Heaven to fall through the clouds into a volcano and be the same as devils in Hell; and also he puts them into bats' wings, for a change, instead of feathers, although they are as fine a lot of athletic, good-looking fellows as you could see anywhere, except the whole are frowning a bit ugly—and no wonder! Then, it came to my mind that, by the way the artists will have it to be, it is *always* the women that are pretended to be Angels and the men that are the Devils, which is all just so much nonsense besides being unfair to us. A woman was the first to tempt, and will be the last, too, *that's* certain, by the way they keep at it; and the worst devils for real wickedness in making mischief I have come to know about in my time, have been women, and not men.

Well, no doubt it has all just happened because of Mr. Dore, and all the other Artists of any account, being men, with the Women-Artists just for copying their ideas; and so the men made the women into Angels and themselves into Devils just out of politeness not to be rude; or, maybe, to curry favour by flattering the ladies to please them, and so make more chances for themselves. It is a queer state of affairs to my mind; but, by the style women are going ahead to compete with the men, like enough there will be some woman painter happen before long that is big enough to strike out a line for herself, and have the men for Angels and the women all Devils, just out of the same proud feeling not to be second in politeness, that makes them say "Gentlemen and Ladies" where a man would say "Ladies and Gentlemen".

## A ROW WITH ARTHUR

Here is a finish made with the pesky old Tank Contract
at last! and also a finish made with Arthur's haggling
and nagging to have his own way fooling with Engineering
ideas to get us into a new lot of troubles soon as we are out
of the lot before; but him slamming the door and swearing
at me is more than I will put up with from anyone, as I will
have him know, for I am not yet grown to be one of these
dodderers for sucking pap up the spout of a teapot—like
old "Shakey" Fender—as might seem by the way Arthur
carries on; even if I do, at times, come over queer by the
blood rising and buzzing my ears and no wonder! when I am
worked up by a young fellow making believe he knows my
business better than I do myself just because he is my son-
in-law; to say nothing of a whole packet of bothers coming
about by him not minding what I told him, first go off, but
getting on my soft side to have his own way, instead!

Everything happened in a bunch, by Counsel's Opinion
being laid before the Meeting of the U.D.C. the very same
day—June 1—fixed as date when our Tank Contract would
determine if the Gas Coy. did not notify us to make a start
beforehand—which they have not done so now will have
to pay us £750 damages for breaking our Contract; and it
does not look that they will get 1d. out of the Council, let
alone £2,000, as they schemed to do, which is a dam' good
slap in the eye that they well deserve to teach them a lesson

ready for the next time Mr. Friendly Parkin has one of his clever ideas to make them a byword and a disgrace in every public house in the place, and also in the First Class going up to Town of a morning, as I'm told; everyone knowing, by this time, the dirty trick they tried on of putting forward plans of pretence buildings, never intended, to humbug the Council and lift £2,000 for themselves out of the Rates.

*The Sentinel*, Friday, prints how, at the Council meeting, Wednesday, Counsel's opinion was read out with Mr. Trencher to say what it meant. It all seems a rare old mix-up to me, by the great London lawyer (after no end of talk about the Law of Grants and Easements and about Acts of Parliament to mean one thing, with others to make them mean different) saying the Gas Company have the right to determine the Grant allowing the sewer to run across their land, but no right to interfere with the sewer; and, also, even if they *could*—by what it says in the Grant—make the Council pull up the sewer, there is an Act of Parliament to say the Council can lay another sewer, same as now, or different if they choose, in same place or anywhere else they like—so what would be the use of doing that? Also, it seems, there were ditches when the sewer was laid, by it being all fields in those days; and the sewer was, maybe, part-made to carry the ditch-water, by what the Grant says; so the Gas Company cannot interfere with the sewer for carrying away surface water, in any case,—although it now comes more from streets than fields—even if they can object to it taking sewage—as if anyone could filter out the one from the other to know whether it came out of a wash-basin or a R.W. down-pipe! However, the end was: the Council told Trencher draft a letter, for the Clerk to write the Gas Company, that the Council will not have any interference by building on top of the sewer, and will not pay compensation; so now, perhaps the Gas Company will get another lawyer in London to tell them *his* ideas about it all, and then we shall see!

What has put the Gas Company in the soup is the time it has taken the London lawyer to decide on an opinion that would be too clever for any other lawyers or Judges to decide different about; for the Company could not tell us to go ahead with our Contract, without they withdrew their claim against the Council, and so they were in a fix. Like enough, the Company thought to talk us round, if things went against them with the Council, and agree a new Contract after June 1 was past; but we are not going to be talked round, because I will not have any more talk—never mind what young Arthur fancies.

When I had Arthur come in my room, to-day, to settle for Trencher to notify the Gas Company they had broken our Contract, and to lodge claim for £750; the very first thing the boy must say is:

"Why not wait and see if they won't ask us to go on, Dad, now that the Council has refused their claim?" he says.

"Because the Gas Company has behaved disgraceful," I said, "and I'm not going to have us lift them out of the hole they have put themselves in by their dirty cheating ways, and that's why," I said—just to have him know.

"I don't see what that has to do with it, Dad," says the wise young boy, out of his long experience of life.

"Well, if you don't, it's *your* fault and not *my* fault," I said.

"That's just argument without any meaning in it, Dad," he says in his quick style, as if he couldn't wait. "Why shouldn't we meet the Company in a new arrangement, if they want?" he says, always out to make argument, whatever it is.

"I'll tell you that, too, if you'll give me a chance to get a word in," I said. "First we were held back five weeks," I

213

said. "Next, just to oblige, we agreed to let the work stand over another nine weeks, to make fourteen; and last, we had Trencher draft a letter for us to fix June 1st as limit, or else we would claim £750 for breach," I said.

"I know all that, Dad," says young impatience, that made me so irritable by him keeping at it, all the time, that I felt near to getting impatient myself.

"Then you had ought to know something else by this time," I said, "and that is: it is not my style to shilly-shally and beat about the bush to agree different, any minute of the day, after things have all been settled beforehand and written down by lawyers to fix them," I said.

"I don't see what harm it would do, Dad," says Arthur, never content until he thinks he has had the last word.

"If you would wait half a minute to think, instead of being all out for hearing your own voice," I said, "you would understand without me telling you in so many words, that it is not a question of what *harm* it would do, but what *good* it would do," I said.

"What *good* would it do, then?" he says, trying on a bit of sulkiness.

"It wouldn't do any good without you think better to chance getting 6 per cent net profit if we're lucky, with nothing, or less than nothing, if we are not lucky," I said, "instead of $11\frac{1}{2}$ per cent certain, with no risk and no work to do for it," I said, to make him look silly.

"I thought you set first store by the work, and only second by the profit," says the boy, to see if a bit of cheekiness would help.

"I don't want any lip from you this morning, so keep it for some other time," I said, straight. "You ought to know, by this time, the difference between a Builder and Contractor and the next Road or Sewage Contractor out to get done and make a quick profit, and then scratch about, like some old hen, for another chance to do the same over again," I said, "if you ever had enough sense to use your eyes and see for yourself," I said, "instead of waiting for me to tell you and not bothering to listen when I do," I said; on that he has the face to out with:

"Don't be so dam' rude," like as if he had touched off a gun at me, that made me so wild at him having the sauce to do it, that I gave it back to him, straight, to teach him to behave next time.

"Stop that game!" I said, pretty sharp, "I didn't take you in for partner to have you cursing and swearing at me any hour of the day that suits, even if I am your father-in-law," I said, "and old enough to be your father, as well; that have had over fifty years' grown-up experience of life while you have a bare fifteen; and that had more knowledge of building before you were born than you have at this moment, sitting there to damn me that picked you out from under-manager at Swurts' to be a full-blown builder and good as head of a business that has as high a reputation for right building as any in the country; and, come to that," I said, "I can let a swear good enough to take all the wind out of *your* young sails any time I choose, so you have a care, Arthur, not to fire off any of your girl-school drattings at me," I said, "or else you'll hear something you'd rather not," I said:—and there he was, sitting with his elbows on his knees and his face in his hands to show it was a bit more than enough for him.

"If you'd wait to hear me out, instead of thinking to push your own ideas down my throat and choke me off," I said, "you'd soon learn the reason why I think well to be quit of the Tank Contract," I said. "At the very first start off, as you know well," I said, "I told you, clear enough for any to understand me, that there would be nothing but trouble made if we tendered on that humbugging engineer's blue-print that had enough left out to make only guess-work of what was put in," I said; "and on that shoddy mug-trap of a Specification, without any quantities, got ready by your wonderful kind cricket-friend Parkin, to put us in the soup so as he might offer to pull us out—by swindling his employers—if we oiled his works to make it worth his while," I said. "and now what has happened?" I said. "First," I said—and then, of a sudden, without a word, Arthur jumps up, flings out of the room and bangs the door on me!

Well, I'm not going to have any slam doors on me, or the whole lot will be at it—but there it is! Soon as ever you go out of your way to do a kindness—the way I did letting Arthur tender for the Tank—it is certain you will get a knock to make you sorry; and it worries me having upsets with Arthur, for there's nothing wrong with the young fellow if he wasn't so full of his own ideas he can't listen to what anyone else has to say, first. However, I'm not going to be put down and have doors slammed on me by anyone, and so I will have Mr. Arthur know, to-morrow, for good and all, or it would be a nice state of affairs for me to arrive at after all these years, and I shouldn't know how to look anyone in the face.

## RECONCILIATION

I was a bit cast down after writing in this Journal, last thing, by feeling alone in the world, with life all rushing past me as if I didn't belong—as it comes over me to feel, now and again, these days; and I wasn't too happy getting up this morning, either, being wild to have it out with Arthur and let him know who I was; when, early after breakfast and me settled down with the paper, Ellie must come in for a surprise, at that hour, and settle in a close-up chair and start in her affectionate style—but very serious, for her—how Arthur did not sleep for fretting all night; and so she got him to say what was the matter; and there she was, putting her arm round and beginning to cry—not like Ellie!—by her sorrow that we couldn't agree without quarrelling; and then it was: what a dear good fellow Arthur is, and how happy they all are at home by his kind ways and always thinking of her and his little boys to play with them and have them grow up proper little men, and so pleased another is coming—as I know it all well enough; and there! she might have been her Mother come back and sitting to put me to rights, in the old days, to make me see things different; and then I felt: what did the blasted old Tank matter to make us all unhappy and come between me and that straight, energetic, healthy young fellow—if he does think he is more clever than he is—that is taking the load off me every day so as I can know things are right without looking into them to see?

And I dare say it is true enough, as Arthur sees it, that I an grown to be a bit crotchety and impatient; for it is certain that things hang in my mind, and fret me, that I should have thrown aside and forgot all about in my younger time; so I gave Ellie a kiss and walked straight over to the office and into Arthur's room—who sent the clerk away directly he saw me—and I told him, straight out, what my true feelings were, which might have been a difficult thing enough, except the boy was so frank and handsome to me as no one would credit; and blamed himself for taking things to heart, but all come about from the feeling he had for me that made it hurt real bad when I was put out with him; and so nice and kind to me, he was, in his feelings and his manners, as no son could be more so, till at last there was nothing between us but the Tank Contract that I said he should carry on with as his own affair, with me to stand aside and just keep an eye open; but Arthur said he didn't want any more to do with it, and agreed with me to take the profit and be quit; which I did not like, because he might look back and regret it, after, and remember it was me that disappointed him, and so I said to him. But, no! He said he had been thinking over and decided my ideas were right and he wanted to forget all about it; and he meant it, too, sincere and genuine from the heart, clear enough; and so we had Trencher come along and take instructions, and a lot of laughing with it; and I don't know when I have felt so light and spry as I have ever since, for I would do anything for that boy, as he knows well, and nothing can change.


## THE AUDITORS' REPORT

The Auditors have certified the accounts, all right; but there is a letter from Mr. Blackington to recommend us to "tighten up" the Cash Sales by having the Prime Coster to book up the prices he puts on the Storekeeper's "out order"—used as invoice for Cash Sales—for check on Cash Sales Book. Blackington writes that, as things are, there is a "hiatus"—he calls it—so as no one can say that the Cash Sales Book shows the same prices fixed by the Prime Coster —all of which has no sense to me at all, for why wouldn't they be the same when the buyer only takes the invoice down the passage to pay and have it receipted for authority to the Storekeeper to let him pick up, and to the Gate-keeper pass to him out?

The other thing to be "tightened up" is the Petty Cash and Subbing, which is signed for in the Receipt Book by whoever receives, and the carbon copy torn out and given to him. Mr. Blackington says the carbon had ought to be handed to the Secretary for filing away—the meaning of which I do not for one moment understand. Doesn't the Petty Cash Receipt Book discharge the clerk? and isn't it laying there for check against the Petty Cash Book, any time? Unless I am too old to know the way people are made we shall have a nice job getting them to pass their carbons to Smith; they will forget; or lose them crossing the passage; or think they have handed in to Smith when they have handed in to the Bookmaker's runner, instead, by writing the name of a horse on the back—but I suppose we must make a try to get things arranged the way Blackington says.

At any rate, Blackington finds nothing amiss, except there are one or two matters that might be small discrepancies, but not to be explained except by asking the Cashier and Prime Coster if they can remember—"which," writes Blackington, "we do not feel called upon to do; but perhaps," he says, "you may think well to examine the Cash Sales Book and Petty Cash records, for your own satisfaction," he writes; so I will have Sennock, out of the Prime Costing, that formerly was in with Saunders, to see if we can find anything for me to take notice of.

I have heard plenty of ugly stories of the losses to Builders by dishonesty; but that has not been in the office, but by Foremen entering false names on the wage-sheets and putting it in their pockets, instead; or by conspiracy, inside and out, to have goods taken where they are not intended; for I dare say it is easier to get away with a lorry of bricks than it would a gold watch, though few may credit it. I have never had that sort of troubles myself, by always taking good care not to give the easy chances that make thieves of men that would stay honest enough without them; but there is always the worry of the old custom going too far, by which the men think they can pick up anything that is not wanted, and particularly waste wood, so that if it was a scaffold pole that got broken across, it might be gone before you could look round by being sawn in fire-logs for tucking under their arms when they go home; and so with any old stuff, especially when we are clearing up.

219

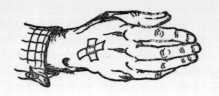

## AN OLD RETAINER

Last night, past nine o'clock, there came a ring at the front that made me to wonder; and then I heard the door shut and the girl knocked to say Mr. Wallace to see me; and, sure enough, it was old Bert, my foreman mason seventeen years, before he went groggy in his legs and had to give up. He was looking well enough, though a bit pink and chubby in the face and short of breath with coming up the front steps, poor chap; and it was sad to see him— always such a hefty man and not yet turned of sixty—dragging along with his legs swinging between crutches and only enough stiffness left in them to prop him while the other props step forward. I took his hat, held against his crutch, and a heavy parcel hanging by a string to the other, and had him sit in my chair to be comfortable; and down he went pretty heavy by me not being quick to easy him, and I thought the springs would have gone—as sure enough one of them has—by him being grown such a heavy old chap. He said he kept pretty middling except his legs were getting more and more weak all the time, and he reckoned it had come about by a fall he took when a lewis slipped and threw him off the scaffold.

That was before he came to us, for I never had any lewis give out on me except only the once when that new young journeyman, Piper his name was, had the Corsham Down key-stone of the great central window-arch, Coggleswild

Institute, drop back on the float and smash up £30—it cost me—of twice-returned and mitred Architrave-ears; and might have smashed himself, too, if he hadn't been nippy, and poor Rattleston, his labourer, as well, that had his eye put out by a splinter flying. Oh I *was* angry with the fellow making me so ashamed!—right in the main street for all to see and gape at, and me just made a start to establish myself! I gave him his money, same day, to let him have a chance to get along off, quick as he fancied, to be Professor of Assing with Lewis-bolts at the Technical School, where —as I suppose—he learnt how to tell me all about my lewis being made wrong, and start off with his ideas about "incline planes"—he called them—to show me on the back of an envelope.

"What the hell did you use it for if you know such a bloody lot?" I said—being more free in those days than what I am now; and that shut him up, for it happened they had forgot to put the answer to that one in the back end of the book he learnt from, where it has all the answers set out so as you can be first in the examination without the trouble of learning anything for yourself.

Well, there was old Bert pleased enough to be sitting with glass of sherry wine to his cake that I had the girl fetch in; but not a word of what brought him; and then he had me reach him his parcel, and if it wasn't a four-pound paper-weight of a fine great toad he had cut from nature, all by himself, out of a bit of statuary, for a present!— remarkable clever-done for a man that was not a carver though always a rare good hand at rustics, which the carvers make such a fuss to meddle with. There were his toes turned in, just in the comic style they squat, all blown out, to think what next; and his back pimpled over, wonderful true to life; and given an egg-shell polish, same as it might be ivory, and a rare lot of work in it; but the eyes are coloured in pink to be like some white rabbit, which is a bit

221

too much of an improvement, to my ideas, though no harm to the kindness of the old fellow thinking to do it for me, and that I shall always take a pride in to remember who made it, and Arthur after me—and so I told him.

At last, after a lot of shyness, by not finding anything else to say while he couldn't bring out what he wanted, he let fall he had come to see me about Sydney, his youngest, that I put in along with Saunders, to make a start, last year. I couldn't gather what was up, by his humming and hawing and saying he hoped I would not be annoyed at him; but it seemed the good little lad was fretted by not being happy in his work and, his mother noticing, Bert led him on to be confidential, by making light and teasing the boy without letting him guess what his father was about—a difficult job, too, with these young creatures just coming to be men and shy of their voices cracking and down coming under their noses; and then Bert started to say about young Syd always being such a good boy at home, instead of telling me what it was all about.

"And so he is at the office, too," I said. "Your boy is shaping the way I would have him, and is right-thinking, and intelligent, and stays by his work and will be a credit to you, Bert," I said, "as you deserve he should be," I said.

The old fellow liked me saying it, and then he got out that the boy is unhappy by Snape always being at him with—"you want to know too much", when he asks some question, and—"keep your eyes to yourself, Pongo"—he calls him—and, "have a care what you're about or the Governor will catch you"—that's me; and scaring the lad with tales of young clerks jailed for mishandling the cash by mistake; and pulling his ears as often as he has a mind; and tweaking his hair to hurt him where it is short behind; and chopping him across the back of his neck, of a sudden, the way they go to kill a rabbit, all for nothing, and gave him a headache, once, doing it too often:—so Master Snape likes

222

a bit of bullying when he is not the one that gets it, as I can well believe it of him!

"What does Mr. Saunders say to it?" I asked; but Bert says it is done on the sly or when Saunders is out of the room, and Sydney has not told him.

"No; your lad is too much a chip of the old block to go telling tales," I said; and Bert said he would not have him to do; and, also, the boy had no notion of his Father running to me, "So please don't let him know, sir," he says.

"You can be sure enough of that, Bert," I said; and then I poured him out another and one for myself—though I never do at that hour, as I have to take care, these days.

When we had sat staring at nothing for a while, I said to Bert:

"Soon as I can manage," I said, "I will give your boy a raise—1s. 6d. a week, maybe—and put him in with Smith to learn posting up the Letter-book and charge of stamps, for he has got all he wants in the Cashier's," I said; "and later, he can go in the Prime Costing, or Estimating, to get the hang of things to decide what line he fancies before he takes up with evening classes which I would not have him do for a couple of years yet, Bert," I said, "for these young limbs are better jumping about at Scouts, or cricket, or whiptops, than doing classes after hours," I said, and the old fellow was a bit too grateful in his feelings because I had a care for his boy—but so I do with all of them, or else clear them out, for I feel a responsibility starting these young ones in life; so, next, I had Bert all grins.

"You were a useful one with your maulers, weren't you, Bert, years back?" I said. "What was that I heard of you and Fred exchanging a few clips to pass the time down at Warblington where you went, first go off?" I said.

It made the old chap laugh so as he jumped up and down, sitting there, to think I had ever come to know.

"That was just a bit of misunderstanding, sir, before I got to know Fred," he says, "but I was ready to put on the gloves with anybody, when I was apprentice," he says.

"Well, Bert," I said, "your Sydney is a stout boy for his time of life, so why not have him to know that he must fight his own fights, for himself, and not allow any to pull his ears unless they have the right?" I said: "Why not take the boy in hand, Bert, to have him learn the one to the mark, straight from the shoulder, full lunge: and how to cover up; and the knock-out, too, if you think he could reach as high up as that fellow Snape's chin; but," I said, "one-two of your son's best, straight to the bread-basket when he don't expect, is all Mr. Snape will want to make him lean over the back of a chair so as to be more comfortable groaning and make it more easy for Sydney to fetch him a swipe, full bat, in the right place, with that long ruler Saunders has, to have him stand up again, quick, ready for another in front in case Sydney should like," I said.

Well, we laughed over it; but we agreed it would be the best thing, for I know Bert would never put silly conceited ideas in the young boy's head.

"Tell your son," I said to him, last thing, "say his prayers and then go, straight, and land Snape in the guts for all he's worth, just to bring the Kingdom of Heaven a bit nearer and push the other place further away," I said, "and let him do it when Saunders is there, just in case!" I said.

So off he goes down the front steps with a bottle of my sherry wine done up in a fish-bag, feeling his way as if he might topple over any minute; but he wouldn't have me to help him—the proud old fellow.

# RETRIBUTION

Bert Wallace didn't lose much time showing his son how to shape, nor the boy at learning his lessons; but the old fellow went a bit too far by taking for serious what I only meant joking, though all for the best, I dare say, to make an end for good and all.

It was only five days since Bert called when, to-day, Saunders must come in my room, at the office, without knocking, as if the place was afire and he scared half out of his wits.

"A dreadful thing is happened, sir," he says, all out of breath with it.

"So!" I said. "And what may that be?" I said, making a guess directly I saw him.

"That young Syd Wallace has broke out and hurt poor Mr. Snape cruel to see," he gabbles, with his eyes staring and his mouth open to hear if I would tell him 'phone the police, no doubt.

"Oh dear!" I said. "However did that come about?" I said.

"I was sitting to check over last week's reqs, sir, and not taking notice of the other two writing up the bags at the side, behind me, when there was a kind of scuffle and a stool fell over, and I just turned my head round to say 'Not so much noise,' sir, and that very moment, young Syd, away from his place, rushed across at Mr. Snape, standing there, and hit him with both hands, one on top of the other, as fast as you could see him, right in the middle, sir; and when poor Mr. Snape doubled up and swung round with the pain of it, the boy made a jump to my other side before I knew what he was about, sir, and grabbed my rattan walking stick and lammed Mr. Snape such a whack, sir!— as fierce as a young demon; Oh dear!—right on his—on— on——"

"All right! I can make a guess," I said. "Get along."

"Yes, sir; and when poor Mr. Snape stood up with a shout at the surprise it was, Syd hit him in the stomach over again, sir, fierce as a tiger—Oh my!"

"What did Mr. Snape do then?" I said, scarce able to keep a straight face at the way the boy had got it in his head to act up to my funny idea.

"He went straight down on the floor, sir; and there he is, all curled round on himself and groaning terrible, and his face turned dreadful to look at."

"And you left him alone with Sydney, with no one to protect him?" I said.

"I thought best to tell you, sir, at once," he says.

"Have them come in to me, here, before more mischief is done," I said, and off he went like some wasp was on his tail.

It was all of five minutes before they came; first, Saunders to hold the door; next, Master Snape, good as six feet tall if he hadn't bent himself down with one hand over his stomach-ache and the other over his arse-ache so as to look sorry for himself, and with a rotten colour and no mistake —as if he was in two minds whether green or yellow would suit him the best for his complexion; and, last, was young Syd, that came inches short of the other's shoulder, carrying himself like a proper little man, but a bit white in the face and half-way to a blub, as I could see, clear enough, poor boy. Then the door was shut and they stood front of my table for me to look at them, with Saunders to the side.

"Well, what's all this Mr. Saunders is telling me?" I said. "You, Mr. Snape! How came you to let a young boy half your size, hurt you to make a fuss about?" I said— "and don't stand to gape at me bent all crooked, like you were some gorilla monkey out of the Zoo holding yourself together not to come in pieces," I said; so then he made a shift to stand straight and take his hands away, pulling a

226

face the while, to make pretence it hurt him to let go; and then he starts off:

"Mr. Grigblay, sir, it was simply by him hitting me twice over, before I could possibly know, Mr. Grigblay, right in the very middle centre of my abdomen, sir, to hurt me something awful, so that I do not know at this very minute whether he has damaged my inside organs permanently for life, Mr. Grigblay, as I think he has done, for me to get damages off him as I have the right to do, as you know well, Mr. Grigblay, without me telling you, sir, and shall do, certain, and he can mark my words, Mr. Grigblay; or else you may be sure it is not like me, sir, to have a little whipper-snapper like him hit me, and as if that wasn't enough, Mr. Grigblay, he must take the first chance, when I was not looking, and fetch me one right across the posterior locality of my back, sir, as hard as he could lay on and far worse than School, Mr. Grigblay, to leave me black and blue and hurting enough to keep me standing days and days, Mr. Grigblay: and then the young hooligan, for so he is, sir, hit my abdomen again, as hard as he could, to make it hurt me worse than before till I did not know how to breathe with the agony of it and thought my last minute had come, Mr. Grigblay."

"Did you hit him first?" I said.

"Oh, Mr. Grigblay, however could you——" he begins, but I'd had enough of his whinings.

"Come on! Out with it! You hit him first?" I said.

"Well, Mr. Grigblay, I did perhaps give him just one or two gentle little pats across the back of the head, to teach him better attention to his duties, the way you would wish, Mr. Grigblay; but all out of kindness so that he would remember better in future, Mr. Grigblay," he says.

"So! I see! Just one or two gentle little pats!" I said, and I looked across at young Sydney that looked back at me without a word spoken, but with his mouth a bit puckered by holding in—and Oh, it did make me feel in a proper rage with the other.

"Well, Mr. Snape," I said, "you showed Sydney *your* idea of just one or two gentle little pats, and Sydney has shown you *his* idea of one or two little pats in return," I said. "The one that gives the first little pat cannot complain at the little pats the other hands back in exchange, to strike a balance," I said. "But," I said, "it is not my style to stand aside when there is any patting going on in the office; and my pats will be for the one that gave the first little pat. My pats are not little pats with the hand, but little pats with the boot along the passage and into the street," I said. "So that's all, for the present," I said, "if Mr. Saunders and you, Sydney, will wait in Mr. Smith's while I have a word with Mr. Snape," I said;—and my word with Snape was:

"Mr. Snape; I have put Sydney Wallace to help in the Cashier's. He is a willing enough lad, and if you can't manage with him, it's likely we shall find we can't manage with you," I said. So then he starts off:

"Mr. Grigblay, sir, you know without me telling you, Mr. Grigblay——" but I had had enough of his grating voice by that time, and came over all fierce and buzzy in the head, of a sudden, at the whining, greased-up lying bully the fellow is, and I chipped in to make an end.

"You're quite right, just for once, Mr. Snape; I *do* know without you telling me," I said: "but there is something *you* don't know without I tell you," I said, "and that is: if I hear a word of you haseing young Syd Wallace, in the office or out of the office, I'll show you what it feels like to be licked by one that is bigger than you are, so as you can find out the difference now you know how it feels to be licked by one that is little more than a child—*Get out!*" I said, loud enough to make him jump; and off he went as if he thought I might set about him, any moment.

I had young Syd come in, then, and stand close up alongside my chair, that looked as if it was as much as he could do to hold up.

"I don't think any the worse by what's happened, Sydney," I said, "but it wouldn't do if we all started at punching each other, would it?" I said. "How came you to do it?" I said.

"My father showed me, sir, and told me I might if . . ." and then he stopped, too proud to say what the other had put on him—the way a true-bred gentleman would feel!

"You didn't hit him below the belt, did you, Sydney?" I said.

"Oh, no, sir! I hit him where father showed me; just here," he says, laying his hand over his young mark.

"That's all right, then," I said, having all I could do to make sure he wouldn't see I was near laughing. "As long as you behave the way your father would have you, Sydney," I said, "that will always please me too," I said.

"Yes, sir."

"Well, run along off home, and tell your father I am well satisfied with the way you shape at your work; and you can stay away after dinner for a half-holiday, to start fresh in the morning," I said.

"There are the bags to be finished, ready for to-morrow, sir!" he says.

"Well, I dare say Mr. Snape won't mind stopping late, just to oblige," I told him; but there was something about the quiet, modest style the little fellow carried himself going to the door, that made me feel almost as if I wanted to say my prayers; and it gave me a happy notion, too, just as he was about turning the handle.

"Have you got a set of gloves, Sydney?" I said.

"No, sir."

"That's a pity, now you're growing up, not to practise at boxing. Would you like to?" and on that his cheeks went rosy by him being too pleased to say it out; so I wrote an order to Chillingham's to supply him a set on his way home, and off he went trying not to be too quick for good manners except his legs were running away with him before the door was fairly shut.

## COMMENT

Young Sydney is just the sort I like to have about and watch while they grow up—a real English-hearted boy that will be all the better for knowing how to knock out a brother Christian in proper style, if none the worse for never having to do it; for the being able gives a man firmness in his mind to know what he means and have others to know; and a straight man that can use his fists, stops more mean conduct than he ever guesses, and prevents a lot more fighting than he will ever bring about. Besides, bruising is British, along with betting and beer; and what's British, so long as it's in reason, can't be beat, in my opinion; and what is natural to an Englishman is better than any laws to make him different.

What is it keeps the bus-conductor, and the railway porter, and the whole lot so cheerful and friendly all the time? Just having a bob on—or going to have—or a tanner on Saturday's Pool, of course! And what so friendly and jolly as an hour or two of an evening in a good old pub, with no harm to anyone? There's more good nature in a firkin of beer than there is in all the namby-pamby and "Oh, how wicked!" yar-yaring of polite ladies who don't know even the different taste of mild or bitter, and couldn't put down a pint if they tried: "Oh, no, Darling! Thank you *so* much; I'm sure it's not nace. I couldn't, reely, or I should start spewing all over the droaring-room"—or however else they go on in private.

230

Boxing belonged to England before there was any other argument—or so I've been told by those that know; a clean, decent, humane way to settle differences and leave friendliness after, instead of the biting and kicking and gouging and knifing that other countries go in for, to start it all over again, first chance, next time. It is the proper sporting thing to be clean and fierce and strong, so as not to be dirty, cruel and cowardly—like those Germans in the Great War—and the easy way to get at proper sporting ideas, by what I have seen of things, is to know how to box; for a man has got to learn to be strong before he can stand out to be good, and three months under a first-class bruiser, to take the count once or twice and hand it to others, would be the making of our Vicar, though he *is* turned of forty. That new curate at St. Bartholomew's has the scouts, and all young fellows, hanging round him to listen to what he says; not by buns and sugared tea and "How's Mother?" but by holding his own with the scoutmasters—and a good deal more, too, if he did all he knows, judging by what I saw at the boxing tournament they had.

Then there was the Revd. Cuthbertson, senior curate at the same church forty-two years ago—Lord, how time flies! —that had the people, both young and old, crowding to hear him preach because of the high style he carried it off with George Blimber, that was a bricklayer with Nibnose before Rasper joined him. Mr. Cuthbertson was passing down Tanner's Lane one day just when Blimber happened to be slinging his wife out of their front door into the road. Whether she deserved it or not I can't say; but, when Mr. Cuthbertson went to pick her up, Blimber told him leave her alone and was for laying hands on her, which Mr. Cuthbertson prevented by getting between and talking to be reasonable; but, because of a crowd collecting and bad language starting and Blimber swinging to the head and missing, the Reverend Gentleman socked him one—in the

231

ear-hole, as I understood at the time—and knocked him over; at which he climbed on his feet to ask for more, got it, and went to sleep.

Mr. Cuthbertson had him carried in and waited till he came round; and it did him no end of good, for he was not a bad sort though a remarkable tough customer. Mr. Cuthbertson became friendly with them, after, and they with him; but the business got round for people to talk about and if there was a man that everyone admired and would listen to to mind what he said, it was Mr. Cuthbertson; and a pity it was he got his call only two years after. If I had things my way, I would have the Bishops proper trained, when young, so that they can put on the gloves with the deacons to test them, before passing them for priests, to see if they can take it and hand it back in good style; or, if not, go away and learn better for the next try. To my thinking it would be the easiest way to fill the churches which there is so much talk of standing empty just now.

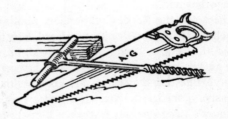

## LAID OFF

Here have I been laid off by a great, angry, tender place swelling up in the thick of my leg, topside of my knee, that made me to walk lame by my trousers touching and hurting me; but I thought nothing till Meg had Doctor to it, who made me undress and get in bed, straight away, to lay quiet with hot cloths applied every hour. It was lucky

Meg sent, by it being a touch of phlebitis—not a nice thing to have, at my time of life, by a clot chancing to get loose and kill you in a twinkle or leave you good as done for. However, I felt cheerful enough laying there to see in the Yard by the bed pushed against the window; and all went well by it coming to the surface for Doctor to ease me, and then I was free to sit with my leg propped; when, what must Arthur do very same day to be ready for me, but move in one of these patent chairs made to slope the back to suit by winding a handle as you sit; and leg-rest to set at any height; and arm to open out like a gate for getting in and out; and table and book-rest and lamp-stand to swing across, all so as I might sit at ease and live there, too, rest of my days, by the rare convenience of it—a most kind idea for the boy to think of, and cost no end of money, I'm sure, all in pretty green-colour Utrecht velvet that is just my fancy, and that I have now had shifted downstairs instead of my old arm that Bert Wallace broke the spring of.

Well, this makes five weeks since I had the old Journal out, and three days since I went round to the office, first time, for an hour. Arthur didn't tell me anything to think about when I was ill; except Blenhasset's office rang up to have me go to Priors Franklyn very next morning! so perhaps H.R.H. Prince Rupert will try if blowing through his fingers will bring me running to know his gracious commands. However, Tol reported all well.

Arthur went to Belhampton, fortnight ago, and found everything first-class and a wonderful showing for the time we've been at work, as I must go down and see for myself soon as I feel a bit more brisk. Fred told him Sir Ezra Gotsnitz was there the day before, when no one expected, and pleased enough, *this* time, except he never stopped yap-yapping at Lanky. Nothing would do but he must go back to fetch his large pink-and-yellow piece out of the car to see it all—but Oh dear, No! Pretty couldn't think of walking

233

on the horrid nasty dirty paths and planks, by her feet being all dressed up for killing like they belonged to some French tart: so then she must be carried sitting on a cushion laid on one of the mason's hand-barrows, like Mrs. Guy Fawkes. According to Fred they have a joke she weighs all of sixteen stone, and it was a job for four labs., one at each hand-hold, to take the strain, for of course they couldn't ask her to stand. They had half an hour of it and, at the end, not so much as a "Thank you", or 9d. for a pint among the four of them. Fred says they talk of letting her drop, next time.

## A TRAP FOR MR. SNAPE

Another thing Arthur told me is that Johnny Rasper has taken on the Tank Contract at our price. That set Arthur wondering, and, by a question here and there and putting two and two together, it is clear enough Parkin has misled Rasper by having him believe our price covered risks of water, and running sand, and sides caving in, and grubbing up necessary; whereas we had a letter attached to our Contract for the Gas Company to handle those risks. Rasper would feel safe taking on at our price by knowing our rates always run higher than his because of us putting in better work than the shoddy stuff he deals in. Arthur took sides with me against Parkin, *this* time; and, also, agreed with what I said—just for a change!

"Rasper is a Builder," I said, "that belongs here and pays rates; and, if I haven't joined the Federation I dare say I can act up a bit more particular than some of them do," I said. "It's not my style to let personal feeling stand in the way of acting fair by another of my trade," I said, "even if I might show him I can behave as dirty as *he* behaves, every chance," I said, "so we must find some channel for letting the fellow know where he is, without risk of him having cause to show his gratitude by asking favours of us," I said: but neither me nor Arthur, sitting together, could hit on any idea how to work it, till, next day—me comfortable in my big chair and my thoughts far afield—it dinned in my head of a sudden, as it might have been that brick-bat I caught all those years ago at Barney Towse, to have Master Snape blab it to his pretty little catch-'em-alive-'o Gwenny, and so kill two rats with the same clod. Arthur agreed it should be so, and we laid our plans to get at it, soon as I felt up to the mark, so that Rasper should raise hell and get things put right betimes; and to-day we brought it off, first-class.

We seated ourselves—Arthur drawn in, end of my table with papers spread between, as is his way—and then sent word Mr. Snape was wanted by Mr. Ballard, in Mr. Grigblay's room. Soon as we heard his step, we started talking about the Tank Contract for him to hear before he came in, as is his way whenever there is a door worth listening at—by what I've noticed. When he knocked I said "Come in", but we were so wonderful busy together he had to stand and hear it all.

"Well, anyhow, it's a rare good job we're quit of our Tank Contract," I said to Arthur.

"Yes. It's a good end to a bad business for us," says Arthur. "I hear Messrs. Nibnose & Rasper Ltd. have taken on the Contract at our price," he says.

"So!" I said. "You surprise me!" I said. "I suppose Mr. Rasper knows we made it a special condition that the Gas Company should take on all risks?" I said. "You remember we wrote it when we sent in our Tender, and had the letter attached to the Contract, after, to make clear our price covered no risks," I said.

"Yes, I remember," says Arthur; "but what arrange-

235

ments Mr. Rasper has made is no concern of *ours*," he says with a bit of a laugh. "Mr. Snape, I want you to get on your bicycle . . ."—and he sent him down to the Railway goods-yard with a demurrage charge to be explained; and off goes Master Snape with his ears spread out to catch the wind and help him along; so now we must wait and see what happens.

## A CALLER

To-day I went across to the loft to see this Spanish Mahogany, selected by Mr. Spinlove out of the stuff put forward by Rollins & Pinkards, Stepney, and just delivered for the Belhampton doors, etc.—as fine a lot as ever I saw, and the stuff for panels cut out of the crutch of the tree and the figure good enough for veneer. It is Cuba, right enough, by the little chalky pinholes when you look close, and will be a sight when it is worked up and dark-polished, with the touch of gilding, that is specified, to show off the sunk bosses where the solid-struck panel-mould breaks round; and the ormolu lock-plates and furniture and Lord knows what and all. It is a queer notion for such a little bit of a house as it will be when finished; and it beats me how anyone can want such richness about him just for holiday-making out in the country.

When I went back to the office, Smith met me to say there was a gentleman, name of Princeton, waiting in my room; so I had Smith give me a brush down, seeing the lot of dust I had picked up, and in I went wondering if it was some Architect I did not know, come to make sure before having me tender—as London Architects, building locally round about, have done from time to time, before now—and, when I got inside, there was a young gentleman very politely dressed sitting with his raincoat laying across his

236

knees that did not look like any kind of Architect I ever came across, by a pale yellow-colour fluffy beard hanging round his chin as if he had been careful to never shave it for a try if he couldn't manage something as pretty as the one Barnum's bearded lady put up for show—enough to make some joker set a match to it when no-one was looking. His hair was smooth-brushed back, sticky, over the top of his head to stand out, back of his ears, like quill pens, and come down over the top of his collar, behind; and he had a tall forehead with no eyebrows for any to see; and eyelashes like the housemaid had been at the pearl-powder again while the missis was out; and his mouth held a bit open over big beaver teeth, by his nose being too long for breathing through without whistling—as queer an affair as I ever saw, and I couldn't make a guess who he might be except he was some kind of sucking Artist, clear enough, but he did not put on a bit of swank with it. He seemed sad, as if he couldn't help it and knew I would feel sorry for him.

He got out of his chair, soon as I came in—a thin straight gentleman well over six foot tall.

"Oh—er—is this Mr. John Grigblay?" he says.

"Speaking," I answered him.

"Oh, yes! I've just called in because of Mr. Peebles telling me you would see about everything," he says.

"And what may those things be, sir?" I said.

"Well, Mr. Peebles hasn't got them, and said very likely *you* had," he says.

"What are you speaking of, sir?" I said.

"The cases."

"Oh! Well, there are a good many cases come here, sir, taking one year with another," I said. "So what would be inside these particular cases?" I said.

"The window for St. Andrew's," he says.

Well, it came out that this was not "Princeton", as Smith got it, but *Primstake*, the Stained Glass Artist our

Vicar commissioned; and it seemed he had travelled from Norwich, that day, to arrange for someone to fix the window; and Mr. Peebles had told him come to me!

"No, sir," I said. "We can't undertake the fixing. Such work is always done by them that supply the window," I said; on which he gives out an "Oh!" to sound as if someone had pulled the valve from his tyre to let the air out.

"I thought Mr. Peebles would put it up," he says; on which I shook my head at him.

"How do you generally arrange, sir?" I asked.

"Well . . . er . . . in fact . . . I mean, this is the first window I have designed—*so far*," he says, "and I didn't know I should have to pay for putting it in"—so I suppose he has been cadging socially to have some friend write to Mrs. Broadbench to say what a nice clever boy he is, and that is why she cabled to have him appointed.

"You'll have to do more than pay for the fixing; you'll have to direct and take the responsibility, sir," I said. "I can supply scaffolding and labour and a mason to sink for and making good saddle-bars, under your orders," I said. "But where would this window be, sir, if you have come from Norwich to fix it?" I asked him.

"Oh! Haven't you got it? I thought Mr. Peebles said you would have it," he says.

"Why should he tell you that, sir?" I said.

"I don't know—unless he gave it to you. I had the cases addressed to him."

"To his house, sir?"

"Yes. St. Andrew's Vicarage."

"When was that?"

"Three days ago."

"So you had them sent by aeroplane, did you, sir?" I said.

"No. Of course not. Why should I?"

"Well, sir, the Railway wouldn't complete delivery of them in three days, would it?" I said.

"Not in three days! Why it only takes . . ."

"Not in three weeks if you're a bit unlucky," I said.

"Well, where are they then?" he says, spreading his arms out as if I ought to be able to tell him.

"Likely they're at Norwich, sir, getting ready to make a start; or perhaps they have gone off down the line and got blocked up in some goods-sidings for a few weeks; or, maybe, they are on the way to Nantwich by the 'Norwich' chalked on the returned empty only getting half cleaned off and come to be read as *destination* Nantwich; or maybe they are puffing off to North Wick by this time," I said.

"Oh, dear!" he says. "Ought I to inquire, then?" he says.

"Yes, sir," I said. "You might inquire. I've done a rare lot of inquiring of the Railway in my time and you couldn't find a more polite and cheery lot than their people, anywhere," I said. "They are never rattled or put out however long you keep inquiring of them," I said, "and the answers they send by post are done, polite style, in clear print for easy reading, and all put ready in pigeon holes beforehand for licking their thumbs and picking out the one that suits best, so as not to waste time," I said.

"But, sir," I said, "I don't think you need worry to inquire just yet. Allow the Railway Company three weeks to see what they can do in the time, first; and that will give the cases a fair start before beginning to trace them," I said. "Don't get disheartened at it, sir; no goods have ever gone away on rail but have turned up again, by being *traced*, some time or other, just by when it may happen someone notices them and says: "Hullo! What's this little lot?" and, likely enough," I said, "the very same day you get a printed letter to tell you your cases have been traced and are held up at North Wick because they can't get any further, they will be unloaded on Mr. Peebles's front steps," I said.

He took me for serious, being in too much of a hurry to catch his train back to Norwich to attend; so now we shall have to wait until something else happens, I suppose!

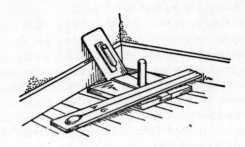

## MR. BARNACLE IS ROASTED

I had Baker run me down to Dorchester, in the saloon, day before yesterday, for me to sit quiet in the back seat with Meg, who does not get about much for looking after me and the house. I enjoyed being out and about once more, with Baker told to keep to 40 to give us a chance to look about and feel pleased at all the pretty country and that nice bit across the New Forest from Romsey to Wimborne, instead of cutting in at 60, and coming near to skidding every time, if he didn't brake, at the corners; but it's no good telling him it is not the proper way to drive, for it only makes him look down his nose as if I didn't know how to handle a car. Like enough, I shall have to send him packing, as I have told him often enough I will do very first time he tips me out: however, he is young and wonderful nippy; and if he *does* like to cut a dash to show the girls, I dare say all will be well till he comes up against another that thinks he knows how to be more dashing than Baker does, and then—What Ho! I had him keep to 40 by watching the speedometer and tickling his ribs with the point of my umbrella, every time, to keep him in mind; till, at last, he must go sulky with it and drop to 30, which suited us first class.

Taking it easy, Thursday morning, we went on the site half after eleven, where was old Fred expecting me; and it was nice being there in the sun, after nine weeks, to see the house up to the window-heads of first floor, and a good start made re-building old walls and the guard-houses— that were; and that mucky old pond dug out for the bath-ing pool, and ready for puddling and concreting for Callen-ders to come and lay their bitumen. First, I went in Fred's office to see the last masonry details passed us by Lanky. Fred makes out that the top string-mold under the oversail will not die on the bulge of the tower the way the Architect shows, and, clear enough, he is right and Mr. Spinlove will have to alter it different by a self-return, or one of his pretty ideas, to stop it, though it looks an awkward business to settle by what I can see. Fred said that Lanky held the drawing three days in his office before he handed over, which was time enough for anyone, except Mr. Lanky, to check the work and find out it was wrong. Fred says Lanky won't settle things so as Fred can go ahead, but is always shilly-shallying not to make himself responsible; so I thought just as well roast the fellow a bit, to put him in mind of what he is for, and I had Fred bring the drawing and tell Lanky to follow along.

"Good morning, Mr. Barnacle," I said when he came up. "This mason's detail you handed Mr. Bloggs won't work," I said.

"No," he says, "so he tells me."

"Well, how is it," I said, "for you to have the drawing laying on your board three days to keep warm under your stomach like an egg under a hen, and then pass it over to Mr. Bloggs as "all correct" for him to have the masons set out and find it won't work only just in time to save pulling down for putting right?" I said.

"It's no business of Mr. Bloggs' to tell the Architect he has made a mistake while you are sent down here special, to check details with the old work for Mr. Spinlove to know all is as he would have it," I said. "We've got to make good *our* mistakes," I said, "but there's nothing in the Contract for us to nurse-maid you, and clear up *your* messes," I said; but he had not a word to say except crack his knuckle-joints.

"Well," I said, "we can make all the muddles we have any use for ourselves, without you lending a hand," I said; "so next time, I will ask you to initial the drawings before you pass to Mr. Bloggs, to show you have checked and found correct," I said, "or else perhaps the Architect will say how he would like things arranged," I said; hearing which Lanky pulled at his moustache to make sure if it wasn't coming loose, and nodded his head.

Next, it was a silly little question that didn't matter one way or another, and so Lanky couldn't decide it; and that was: which joint it should be to carry the damp-course under the parapet-coping where it ramps?

"I told Mr. Bloggs he could suit himself," says Lanky.

"Mr. Bloggs knows that his proper business is to suit the *Architect's* ideas; and that your proper business is to say what the Architect's ideas are, and find out if you don't know," I said, "and not keep the masons idling while you stand to pull at your moustache," I said. On that he settled the damp-course, while we waited and stared at him; and so we had him to do with another silly little matter of dodging one of the old quoins to suit the new work, that any mason could have said straight off. Next, I had him get along off to his office to write down what he had settled for a signed order to Fred; and also write the Architect, with sketch, to have it decided whether to set back the face above the oversail, or alter the mould projection, or stop it, or

242

return it, or whatever else it was to be; and I told Fred be careful have Lanky write down and sign, for record, everything he decides, "for if you don't," I said to Fred, "he'll get you down," I said.

"Oh, I don't take any notice of *him*," says Fred.

"That's where you make a mistake, Fred," I said. "These flabby men with no personality and no guts, that daren't say Bo! will get you down sooner than a crooked one bent on mischief will do," I said; but I felt sorry for old Lanky flapping off, toes out and knees rubbing together to make his breeches squeak as he goes; with his employer biting him all the time; and Mr. Spinlove telling him off; and Fred haseing him; and now me, the Builder, roasting him; and all because he is made the way he is instead of different—but there! We must all look after ourselves, for no one else will take care of us except to get the advantage, that's certain.

After, I had Fred back in the office to run over his diary and one thing and another; and next he must look at his watch and hurry off to hammer with a horseshoe on an old copper he has slung there on a gallows, out in the middle, to raise a din, like the end of the world, for dinner and knocking off—just the sort of good idea old Fred will get hold of, to cost nothing, and do the job in first-class style, for, with the hands all scattered, the wind might take the whistle and the half of them not hear it.


## VISITORS

While he was away I noticed how wonderful orderly Fred had his office arranged, with colour-wash and a picture or two; and a bit of curtain front of the far window; and a table with a white paper cloth and daisy-flowers in a

243

mug laid out for dinner, other end; and a screen knocked together to stand out half-way across; and a cosy smell of something nice to eat; and it all tickled me, no end; so I walked down till, round the end of the screen, there was a little paraffin cooker with a pair of pots boiling; and next, a little wash-up rigged; and last, when I got level to see round, blessed if Fred's wife wasn't sitting there, sewing his pants!

Well, I suppose the surprise had something to do with it, but I laughed, and went on laughing, and that started her off; so there were the two of us, like a pair of children, without a word spoken, when Fred came back. Fred is not much of a laugher, and he was a bit troubled in the face and stammering with it to hope I wouldn't object by no-one of any account knowing.

"Sooze"—he calls her—"just comes over and gets dinner, and clears up," he says. "It's a bit lonely for her all day, up in the house, sir, with all strangers round."

I joked them, and said I always liked to see ladies about; but, after, I told Fred no harm, this time, right out of the way where he was: "but it won't do when the Architect or the Owner are about," I said, "nor as a general thing," I said, "for I can't make exceptions, and it's not to be thought of for the foremen to have their wives about; and the washing hung out; and the children making mud-pies in the mortar," I said.

I thought surprises were over for that day; but me and Meg were scarcely settled in the car with a nice bit of chicken and salad, put up at the Hotel, when a gentleman passed along near by; so I put my head out to see who, and there was the back of a big fellow in a grey lounge, and stick, and bowler set at an angle like he might own the place. I gave a call. "Have you come to see *me*?" on which he turned, and if it wasn't Henry Curt!

It turned out he was travelling round on his holiday, and,

putting up for a day or two at Weymouth, had walked over to see what we are about.

"Weymouth is no dam' good," he says, pulling a funny face; and, when I asked, he told us he is giving notice at end of the year, or when it suits, and is going to set up Hotel Proprietor at some likely place, and that is why he is travelling, to look about. He wants to be where it is a round season.

"I don't mean to stand staring out, middle of the front bay-window, with my hands in my pockets, eight months of the year," he says; "but Brighton and Bournemouth are 'overdone'," he says; and Torquay "all bath-chairs"; and Ventnor "an out-of-doors hospital for sucking in milk," he says. Weymouth he thought of to help Navy officers run through their pay when they made Port; but "Navy officers aren't any good," he says, and pulls a face at them, too; and so he went on, just in the old style, till anyone would think the whole of England wasn't good enough to please him! He said Sir Ezra had gone off to Clerichy for his cure.

"What's that?" I said.

"So as he can eat more without dying of it," says Henry. It is a dozen different water springs, in France, hot or tepid, strong or weak, to suit yourself, either to drink or bathe in, or for gargling as well, he told us, as he knew all about from going there when he was valet to Lord Pladdon.

"His Lordship's cure was gargling in a park they had there. He was like a blooming song-bird in a bush," says Henry, "and I ought to know by the times I have carried a towel to put round his shoulders while he was at it," he says.

He told us there might be three hundred at it together on a fine morning, and the half of them blowing it out at their noses like they were horses sneezing, by being taught the trick of it at some college or other they have in the place.

"The beastliest row you ever heard," Henry says, "spite

245

of the Band kept going to drown it," he says—as I can well believe it would be.

This was all many years ago, and Henry said things were greatly improved, the last time he went there, by the strong water they gargle with poisoning all the grass and starting to kill the trees as well; so then they built a fine great gargling hall—only they call it in French, "Sallder" something or other—with sinks, to take two together, set against the side walls, and facing each other down the middle; and statues in niches and, at the end, a platform with palms set about for the Band; but, according to Henry, the noise of it was terribly loud by the echo there was—so the Architect was at fault in his acoustics again, as the most of them always are, from what I have seen.

When I asked Henry did he try what good the water was for him:

"No fear," he says, "I got to know too much," he says; and then he told us the people that have learnt by belonging to the place will have nothing to do with the water; and, when any fall sick, the doctor shakes his finger in their face and says, first thing, "*Have you been using the waters*?" —which is just the way people always prefer something they have not got, and think nothing of what is at their doors.

Well, it was all new to me; but so the talk went, with Henry sitting inside for a bite and a bottle of Bass; and then Meg showed him round while I fixed up things with Fred, and, after, we dropped him at his Hotel, by going the Weymouth way round instead of Dorchester. He is a pleasant gay sort of man, if he does draw the longbow in his talk; and he looked wonderful young and gentlemanly considering the pompous behaviour he kept up at Tallons Dyke. He had Meg very playful with him, and laughing no end at his nonsense; so altogether it made a pleasant outing for her, who is too much given to staying in and looking after the house, by my ideas.

246

# EXIT MR. SNAPE

Here is Master Snape got the sack for a good riddance; and time enough, too, if he is to make a fresh start to do himself justice at some place where they like 'em extra high-greased and scented—which I do not.

It came about by Arthur taking the chance to nip into the same carriage up to town that he saw Parkin make for; and so they got talking, and it came out Parkin is in hot water with his directors by Rasper making trouble for him— which is just what we were waiting to hear and all we want to know to prove that Snape is hand in glove with Rasper. Arthur agreed that the one that fetched Snape in had ought to show him out; and he had Snape sent for to my room when we were sitting together, so as I could take note of what passed.

"You can come in, Snape, and shut the door," says Arthur, when our young gentleman stood holding it open with the blood settled in his sticking-out ear-flaps to make them better for hearing anything not intended for him.

"Yes, Mr. Ballard," he says, and comes in and stands holding one hand in the other like "What's the next article, please?" while I sat too busy with my papers to pay attention.

"We are making new arrangements in the office, Snape, and we cannot fit you in, so we think you had better look about for another billet," says Arthur. Then the other starts off:

"Oh, Mr. Ballard, you are in a very great error, sir, if you suppose for one moment I am one that would stand in the way of any different arrangements you may desire to create, Mr. Ballard. It would not be like me, for one moment, as you might know well by this time, Mr. Ballard, not to accommodate myself in every possible way, sir, to give you

247

the best satisfaction as I always have done in the past, Mr. Ballard," he says.

"I am afraid, Snape, the decision is already made that it would be best for all parties if you got a job elsewhere," says Arthur.

"Then am I to understand, Mr. Ballard, that someone has been making a complaint against me that I do not know about, Mr. Ballard, and am not allowed to make so much as a guess at by you not telling me, sir?"

"No complaint has been made against you. There is, simply, no place for you here, and you must look elsewhere for work."

"And what about poor Mother, Mr. Ballard? How am I to tell her you have sacked me with no reason given, Mr. Ballard? She simply would not believe it of you, sir, after all your kind-hearted words to her! It would break her heart, Mr. Ballard, if you knew her as well as I do, sir, and her rheumatism is so bad just now that I dare not tell her, or it might make her fret right away into her very grave, and that is the truth, Mr. Ballard, as you ought to know without me telling you, after the time you saw her laying on the sofa not able to move, Mr. Ballard."

"I will go and see your mother, Snape, and let her know there is no complaint against you," says Arthur, that made me hold a paper close up in front of my face by my eyes coming over so terrible hard of seeing, of a sudden!

"But whatever have I done Mr. Ballard, for such terrible unkind injustice as you to tell poor Mother you have turned me out for no reason whatsoever, right on the spot, just as if it was some low dishonest behaviour I had done for everyone to talk about and wonder at me, Mr. Ballard?"

"I am afraid I have nothing more to say, Snape. I am sorry, but there it is," says Arthur.

"Yes, and all done on the sly behind my back by that fellow sitting there that has always turned against me, from

248

the very first day, to make the worst of everything I have done; and, even when I found the 10s. some of you sneaked off me for a private temporary loan and then put back on the sly, he was ready to think I had taken it to spend it—which I might have done, too, and no one the wiser, and is proof I never would take a single penny; and most likely that fellow did it himself to trap me if he could."

Well, it was sad to hear him talk so ugly, for I wouldn't have credited such a thing, even of him.

"Mr. Snape," I said, "you are *entitled* to one week's notice from Friday. You will receive notice at *four* weeks from Friday, but, if you like better, you can take a week's money and walk out this moment," I said. "You have spoke more than enough, and can go," I said.

"Mr. Grigblay . . ." he starts off.

"You have heard me!" I said. "If I have another word I will have you shown off the premises to call round for your money, pay day," I said, and off he went, hang-dog style, as ugly as I ever saw.

## AT PRIORS FRANKLYN

Mr. Blenhasset thought well to write, last week, just for a change, to appoint a day, instead of a last minute message, over the 'phone—as if I spent my time toeing the mark with running-corks, ready for when he liked to shout "Go!"—and yesterday I met him at Priors Franklyn. Tolpenny had mentioned the house was going to be empty, and, as there would not be any to notice me making a fool of myself, I dressed up in tails and my high hat, and my white waistcoat with gold Albert slung across, and spats, like it was Fred's wedding over again; and also I got out my lavender kids and malacca with the gold knob they gave me when I saved George Butcher from drowning; and would have fixed myself with an eyeglass, as well, if it had come to my mind earlier—all just for a joke to see how the A.R.A. would take it. The queer thing was, he seemed to think I was a somebody, for the first time—like enough by seeing I could make myself look nearly as big an ass as he knows how, when I have the mind—and so he kept to better behaviour. However, he didn't find his Lordship and the Viscountess there to strut round them and spread his tail at, for they had gone off the day before after the grouse—"the glorious 12th" as the grand folk call it—but, my word! Didn't Mr. Blenhasset carry on!

He was togged up all in summer grey, this time, hat to match, and had on a cape—lined lavender silk for a change —till he came to perspiring with the fret he got into; and then, laying it over a bush, a sharp bit of wind caught it and lifted it into the middle of a banker where lime for the plasterers' putty was just starting to boil nicely; and that threw him into a worse stew than he was in before, for I have never heard tell that hot quick-lime soup is improving for lavender silk, if it is for superfine light summer cashmere suiting; and, from the polite gentlemanly cursings we had, I gathered he had never heard it was, either. It was a comical sight when old Sam Gordon, acting mudman, ran in such a hurry to rake it out that he must rake it *in* and then fork it out on the end of his pole, by a prong going through the skirt and tearing it worse, like some old sack had got mixed in with the white-wash.

What fretted him, particular, was a mistake made in his office—by Mr. Mooney mooning too much, and I shouldn't be surprised. The drawings they send us are a wonder to see for detail and their style of get-up; the whole work being drawn to $\frac{1}{2}$-in. scale, and every brick-course, with the joints, shown and numbered every time; but that did not prevent the old mix-up brought about by the detail drawings not agreeing with the $\frac{1}{8}$-in. scale.

The front of the Pavilion is open 30 foot, in front, with adzed oak beam, carrying pole-plate, supported on four axed Farnham columns with Edgehill caps and bases. Each side of the opening it is 7 feet of brick wall from jambs to angle of return wall, with semi-domed niches with Edgehill keys and moulded cills for taking lead statues, as I understand. The $\frac{1}{8}$-inch drawing is figured 2 ft. 9 in. from return angle to angle of niche, and 2 ft. 5 in. from opposite side of niche to the angle of jamb, so that centres of niches were 2 in. off the centres of the brick walls. However, the $\frac{1}{2}$-in. detail only showed one half of the niche, and, there, the dimension from angle of return to angle of niche was shown and figured 2 ft. 7 in., which made the distance from niche to jamb also 2 ft. 7 in. (instead of 2 ft. 5 in.) and brought the niches to centre on the brick walls.

Well, there was the Pavilion carried right up, with the carpenters making a finish with fixing the rafters; and the Architect was pleased enough—as he had ought to be with the fine job Snoop has made of the brick semi-domes and the columns with their entasis set out more intricate than I ever saw—and he was strutting about down in front like he was admiring himself in the looking-glass, when, of a sudden, he comes charging up on the terrace and lays his ivory two-foot against the work; and then he rushes off to Tol's office to see the drawings. Of course he found it was *us* that were wrong; but Tol was too many for him without me saying a single word. So then it was—"pull down the lot!" and when I inquired of him the reason why? he jabbered that he wouldn't have the niches on the centre, they must

251

be 2 in. off centre, the way he had designed they should be.

"But, sir," I said, "that would be a pity, wouldn't it? now it is so nice-finished and will never look quite the same after, if you do," I said. "There is plenty of bearing for the beam if you just pull down the face of the jamb and rebuild four inches back so as to bring centre of niches 2 in. off, as you want, to make dimensions 2 ft. 7 in. and 2 ft. 3 in. instead of 2 ft. 9 in. and 2 ft. 5 in. as you first intended," I said. "The space between jamb and first column is 1 ft. 6 in. less than space between columns, so there will be no harm making it just 4 ft. $7\frac{1}{2}$ in., instead of 4 ft. $3\frac{1}{2}$ in. as you have shown it," I said.

But no! That would not be nearly artistic enough to suit, it seemed; and he wrote an order out to shore the beam and pull down five feet wide of 1 ft. $10\frac{1}{2}$ in. brickwork twice over, from the plate right down to 3 feet above terrace level, just to build it back two inches different; with the semi-domes to build all fresh, over again, and bonding-in that will never make it look quite as nice as it does now, any more than a mold-profile looks as nice on the paper if you rub it out, to what it does if drawn slick off, first go—for I have done a rare lot of setting out in my time, and so it always seemed to me.

When the Architect was on the site last time, he had a new idea, it seems; and he had brought along the drawings to talk about; and the idea is to have seven columns set along the terrace wall from the garden houses, each end, up to where the steps go down off the terrace opposite the Pavilion; all to be same as the columns in the Pavilion and ranging with them, for the floor of the Pav. is 2 ft. 3 in.— same as coping of terrace wall—above terrace, with five steps laid out semi-circular to a landing in front. They are to have Edgehill bases and caps carrying a great adzed oak beam scarfed and pegged over the columns; and the Edgehill coping of terrace wall will have to be pulled about—and a fussy little lot of extra stone ordered—to finish the dies for the columns to stand on, which are to be bonded to terrace side of wall.

Well, it will be a pretty thing, I dare say, when done; "but", as I said to the architect, "this is an exposed position, sir," I said. "Those columns will be only stayed one way," I said, "and do you think, sir, it will be safe when the roses and creepers someone is sure to set, grow up to be like a sail to catch the next Sou'-wester or South-easter?" I said.

"No, no, quite all right; quite all right. I've done it before," he gabbles, looking about as if he couldn't attend to a silly little thing like that!

"Perhaps it was a sheltered place, that time, sir," I said, "or perhaps it was only a little while back, and the greenery not grown thick yet," I said. "Or perhaps they fixed the weather-cock so as to prevent the wind from blowing across," I said.

"You're wrong! Quite wrong! It was a long time ago. I want the work built as I have shown it," he says in the "Haw, Haw, Haw" style, to put me down; but "Hee-Haw! Hee-Haw!" would have suited better to my way of thinking, by him looking to be one of these Arty fellows I have come across before now, who fancy mortar to be an extra-special fine brand of glue for sticking bricks together properly tight, so as they can never come apart again.

"Then you will have to get someone else to build for you, sir," I said. "I don't care over-much for being cross-examined at Coroner's inquests to settle if it's manslaughter or not," I said; "and I am far too modest a man, sir, to want to see my name advertised in the newspapers as a thoroughly safe reliable Builder for setting up what the wind will throw down," I said.

It made him give attention to hear someone who knew

his own mind, and that could tell him something he had not thought of himself; and, after a lot of talk, he agreed to my idea; and that was: have three ½-in. rods upset in the concrete foundation of the dies, and carried up, spread wide apart, in the core of the columns for filling round, solid, in 5 to 1 fine concrete, and anchoring to beam on top.

"Oh! Yes? Well! So you think that will make everything safe, do you?" he says.

"Well, sir," I answered him; "I am not a Consulting Engineer," I said, "for calculating the effect of the wind-pressure on different kinds of leaves with a slide-rule to seven places of decimals, so as to get it quite exact, and then multiply by five, for factor of safety, to make sure the answer is correct," I said; "but" I said, "I am willing to so build, sir, if you take the responsibility of ordering me to do," I said.

I do not know whether the great architect liked feeling grateful to so humble a person, but it made him forget himself so far as to offer to carry me into London—which suited me first-class—and off we went to the garage. Going along, there was the first of the Llanywrwyd slates just unloading off the lorry, and he stopped to have a look, and handled one or two while his great black limousine was fetched out; but when he made a motion for me to sit up beside the driver—to look, in my top hat, like some undertaker on a hearse—I suddenly remembered I must go to the 'phone, to be a long time. "So good day to you, sir," I said; and my 'phone message was to the little Hotel they have near by, for a hire-car to the station, for if I am not fit to sit alongside any A.R.A. in the country, I am not fit to sit alongside anyone else. I dare say I am getting old and touchy, though always ready to give place to my betters and respect rank; but there is no rank in an A.R.A. to prevent him from coming of a marketing mother and carrying fleas about in his shirt like any other might; and there is also a respect due to age, in my opinion; and if an A.R.A. has not learnt it in forty years there is still time for him to begin before he finds out by growing heavy on his legs, and his hair turning white, and his breath coming short.

## A CLERICAL VISITOR

Our Vicar rang up to know would he find me? and, soon after, he walked straight in on top of me at the heels of Smith, when I was close-engaged with Wallington and Pember's representative about our timber discounts; and he upset my applecart, for I had good as got my way till Mr. Peebles interrupted; but, by the time I had said "Would you kindly mind waiting, sir, in the outer office till I am free"; and he had asked how long it would be? or should he go away and come back after he had seen whether they had done mending his garden-roller? or else he might be too late by it being early closing; and when I had told him to go to blazes—in proper church language, of course —W. and P.'s man had recollected himself and was of a new different mind, and so I got nowhere with him, after all!

"Why did you allow Mr. Peebles to march in on top of us?" I said to Smith, after the chap had gone.

"I told him 'take a chair', sir; but when I came to tell you he followed before I knew,' says Smith.

"Well, next time, show him in your big lock-up cupboard and turn the key on him," I said, being properly annoyed at the nuisance the man is; and a pity he doesn't get married to some sensible woman to show him how to behave with a few pounds of damp sand in the foot of an old stocking, to cob him across the side of the head with it any minute—which is the only sort of thing that will ever do him any real good, in my opinion, and would improve his sermons too, judging by the sort of slop he has been piddling onto our heads over the edge of the pulpit, Sunday mornings, lately. I never saw such a man! He's like some plaguey dog all the time jumping into your lap to be petted fast as you heave him off, just as if no one was any use in the world except to make a fuss over *him*; and bringing his old bones and cods' heads, and the drowned kittens he's unburied, for you to wonder at them; and the stink of the last muck he's been rolling in to see what *you* can make of it.

Writing that last, makes me laugh to remember all those years ago when I had just taken over the Yard and was beginning to go ahead; and a great lady of those days, Mrs. Klimber—widow of the London Dentist that made his fortune by saying "Open, please—thank you" so gentle and pretty to the ladies, that he became the first fashion, and had Duchesses and all sorts clamouring to be first for him to "fit them in" in his diary at a quarter before eleven in the forenoon—or whenever it might be.

Mrs. Klimber had The Evergreens—now altered to Blagdon Nursing Home—and wrote to me to cure her roof leaking spite of it always being under repair. So I had a ladder taken over, and, of course, there was the old trouble of iron nails rusting away and loosing the slates for them to slip down and blow about, for any water that got in to trickle down the rafters and drop off somewhere else so that no-one could say where it came from. I dare say there was a half-ton of lead up there in tingles to hold the slates that had been replaced. The roof wanted stripping, of course, and slates re-hung, for a rich lady must be made comfortable or there is no peace; so I called in to tell her. It is a great ugly house, but it would have suited me first-class, in those days, to have a nice safe paying job; and also to please a customer who might be useful by recommending me.

I was stood in the hall while the maid went to inquire, when a terrier dog, not worth the brick and rope to drown him—by the big size he was, and neither a smooth-coat or wire—came slowly along with stiff legs and his hackles up, to make *his* inquiries by smelling at me. Happened, I had calamine rubbed on my shin for a touch of eczema, and dear old doggie must have a sniff at *that* to try if he couldn't come by a touch of romance. I shoved him off with my leg, and then he set at me, dancing round me and barking to rouse the house and show what a wonderful clever watch-dog he knew how to be. The maid came back, and would I please come in the study; and she shut the dog out, by stooping to walk backwards dragging him by the collar, while she shut the door, and coming near to falling over her skirts with it by him barking and pulling for all he was worth.

Then Mrs. Klimber came in, short and thick, all in shiny blue satin very close fitting over the chest and tight-stretched behind—to catch 'the high-lights', as the picture-painters say—to see what I was like; and doggie came with her, dancing round to bark so as we should not hear each other speak. Mrs. Klimber did not like the noise, judging by her face, but didn't know how to prevent except by taking a lot of notice to pet the dog and calling him 'Darling Rollie Dear'. After a bit, he got quiet by being new-interested to sniff me; and he came up and touched my leg with his nose before I knew what was tickling me, so I pushed him off with my leg. Again he came, and again and

G : R                    257

again; poking his beastly nose—and Lord knows where he had had it last!—up against my trousers, and me waving my leg more and more to drive him off, with Mrs. Klimber standing and talking as if nothing could be a nicer treat for anyone than to have Darling Rollie keep at sniffing him. Rollie came again and got a push that made him growl; and a half minute later he came just once more, and, before I knew, took one of my best Association side-passes to drive him through the glass front of a pretty bookcase standing there.

Well, I didn't hear more of re-slating, by Mrs. Klimber forgetting there was any roof to re-slate with the row of the squalling dog, and the kissing he got on his dear clean sweet pretty nose, and the cuddlings and rockings to make him feel better. The dog was not hurt, and I went off leaving them at it; for Mrs. Klimber would not hear a word. However, I must have had a guardian angel, in those days, to see justice was done me, for, very next week, a motor-car came along—that were rare at that time—so Darling Rollie thought better set up his hackles and stiff his legs to inquire was it a lady, and, before he knew whether, the car took him and finished him. There is one good thing cars have done, and that is: clear the dogs away off the roads for them to carry on their ugly habits, private, like other people, instead of in public. Lord, how my pen runs away with me, to-night to make me forget what I was saying!

When Mr. Peebles came back he was holding out a yellow paper—I ought to know the look of!—as if he was for serving a writ. It was an advice note from the Railway that they would deliver two cases, glass, C.O.D., next day; and £2 7s. 10d. to pay.

"Well, that's all right," I said.

"Must I pay all this money then?" he says.

"Mr. Primstake seems to think so," I said. "What did you arrange with him?" I said.

258

Well, of course, they hadn't arranged anything, so they will have to settle by arguing it; and if Mr. Primstake has the better I will take off my hat to that young man, for he will go far.

Our Vicar wanted me to take charge of the cases and do the paying for it to be put down in the account; but he owes me quite enough already, and I shall only be making trouble for myself if I have any hand in his business, for the cases are not insured, so, of course, if I touch them and anything is broke—"Mr. Grigblay's fault!" I will arrange with Mr. Primstake to provide attendances, but more I will not do, and so I had the Vicar to know.


## FIXING THE WINDOW

Mr. Peebles rang up last week that the cases of stained glass window are set down on his front path; and will they take harm if it rains? and when is Mr. Primstake going to come? and what is going to be done next?—just as if *I* could tell him! Then, three days after, it was; please shift them in the church, by the grass being worn in a path with people going round, and stepping in the geraniums"; so we carried them to the Baptistery, as he asked us, and then, next day, it was: "please move them *out* of the Baptistery, as I had quite forgotten about Mrs. Norris' baby, and the verger wants to set out the chairs, and a florist is there getting things ready." Next it was Mr. Primstake come with his glazier and wanting us to set up a scaffold in a hurry, and provide attendance; and last was to-day, by Mr. Peebles on the 'phone, and could I come at once, please? as there seemed to be a little difficulty happened. I went over to oblige; and the little difficulty they are up against is, that when they had unpacked the cases and got all ready,

259

and lifted the windows up on the scaffold, tender and careful on a frame for slinging them, the glazier, out of his special skill and training, showed them how the windows would fit beautifully if the masonry was just pulled down and the jambs, arch and tracery built different, to suit!

They've got themselves in a rare pickle, by what I can see and the glazier seems to guess; for Mr. Primstake could think of nothing for listening to hear what everyone else has to say; and our Vicar was all the time biting the side of his finger, and then going off and coming back to have another bite whenever he could spare a moment for it.

Well, there they were! and had been over an hour at it, up on the scaffold, with rods and tape and two-foots and lines and a 15-foot straight-edge, to find out what I could have told them right off; and that is: the arch is not set out from *two* centres as Primstake—with old Bunter, the sexton, to help him think what he was about—made it out to be; but struck from *four* centres, so that the lower part of the arch-curve is quicker than what the upper part is, to make the arch come to be more pointed at the top; and a very pretty idea of the architect's, it is, I dare say with all those early-style deep-cut moldings he has running round —more than I ever saw, unless it would be Westminster Abbey, where, maybe, he copied from. The result is there is just room for the trefoil, above, to take its glazing, with a bit of faking; but the two big lights are over-big by 2⅜ in. full, each side, half-way above the springing, and come all of 4 in. too tall at top, as well.

The glazier, who is a fine knowledgeable man, knew too much to say anything except catch my eye, on the quiet; but Mr. Primstake's idea was to turn the church into a glazier's shop, with me to fix him up a trestle-table in the chancel where would be plenty of room to lay out his soldering irons and tallow and red lead and enamels and acids on the choir seats; and have his blow-lamp and straw and pack-ing-cases put handy for setting fire to the new roof!

"Well, sir," I said, "and how about the firing oven? and where would you choose for me to lay on gas and water and fix up a bin for the sand if the Vicar should be willing?" I said.

He didn't seem clear about the oven, by intending to send the glass away to be fired; so it seems he has had some Firm to fire his glass for him and lead up—not the right thing for one who holds out he is a Stained Glass Artist, in my opinion, or else any young schoolgirl that knew how to copy saints and angels out of a picture-book might set up to be one, if Mummy said "Very well, dear!" Well, I led Mr. Peebles aside and let him know my ideas; and then I told the Stained Glass Artist—by Mr. Peebles's not liking—that he would have to pack up and clear out and get his window shaped as he engaged to do, and then come and have another try to make it go in.

## A TRIP TO HONEYWOOD

Mr. Spinlove with his lady and their two boys—home on holiday—picked me up, first thing, Thursday after-noon, to go over to Honeywood where the run-way and hangar and little house are about clearing up; and I *did* enjoy myself and no mistake: first, sitting in the back yarn-ing with the two boys to have them laughing, and listening to their gay young happy chaff and prattle—if it *did* bring me near to the old sigh never to have had any son to my name. However, they got a bit boisterous with their joking, till one must slip down on the floor with laughing so much, and the other getting hold of his legs and making to open the door in pretence of slinging him out, till his Dad had a word to say over his shoulder, to calm them down. Next, when we got on the site, there was the aeroplane coming back with a brace of loops before it landed, and Lady Brash got out, quite pink and fresh, for kissings all round, as if nothing had happened; so then the youngsters started leaping in the air, like a pair of young goats, to be let go for a flip, and rolling on the ground with it so as not to keep still for a moment; and "May I sit with the Pilot?" till you couldn't hear yourself speak.

Father and Mother had a quiet word together, and then it was "one boy at a time", the elder with the lady, and the younger with his father, so as not to have those young limbs start their games up in the air, I suppose, for the 'plane is built only for three adults; but I got the idea there was more in mind with the parents, in case the thing came down quicker than was meant, for you can't measure the foolish tender thoughts we have when our young ones are growing up, if it is only the way a hen with chicks will pretend to run at a dog to frighten it with her feathers frilled out. I always hold that there is not much in our human nature finer than what belongs to our animal nature, when you think below the surface of things.

Then, nothing must suit the boys but that Mr. Grigblay must go round; so in I got—"but", I said to the Pilot, "none of your loops and Immermann's and dead-leaf stunts for me," I said, "I am an old man thought to be respectable, that would be ruined if any caught me standing on my head and throwing somersaults"; at which he grinned. "That'll be all right, sir," he says; and it was tame enough, except for the row, with the fields like postage-stamps laid out; and houses and churches looking like mean little fancy toys that made me feel ashamed of them, and would likely have driven me away from building alto-gether if I had seen what I was to be at from above, before I started in life. When we landed, there was Sir Leslie back early from the City; and the boys started shouting for *him* to go.

"It's no good asking Gaffer, he never does," says their mother; and the old gentleman shook his head and looked to examine had he dirtied his patent leathers walking across, in a style as if he had heard it said too often before.

So then we started off back, not having been there an hour and a half altogether, I dare say; and the whole party did me the honour to come in my house for tea on their way through. It was a pleasant occasion for the girls, too, who had heard me tell of Mr. Spinlove and the others so often; and what must Meg do—all her own idea and without a word—but tell cook: and when tea was laid out and we moved to the dining-room, there was a great hot Cambridge sausage, fresh out of the pan, set down opposite each of the boys. They *were* happy, and you can tell when a boy is pleased without him saying so. Those young Spinloves have a fine frank air with them and nice considerate manners, for all they are a bit free and riotous.

"Where are you going to sit?" says the elder, when Meg came in, last, from seeing about things; and pretty it was to notice the boy so thoughtful, and his sausage to think about at the time.

Mr. Spinlove wants to go down to Belhampton soon as he can see his way; and said he would like to have me with him now we are getting ready for the finishing. It was nice having him sit at my table, and see his lady all smiles and pleasantness; and to remember he was now a family man well-known in his profession and his work illustrated in the papers. It did not seem like reality when I pictured how he was when I first knew him:—slim of figure; a bit uppish and over-particular when it did not matter; and not too quick knowing where he'd got to, but always one with right ideas and kind thoughts to be fair to all, never mind how much trouble it made for him.

263

## SNAPE AT BAY

I don't know when I've ever been more upset than I have since Sennock came to me this morning. By the way he started at whispering for no one to chance hear in the outer office, I brought him over to the house. It is three weeks, as he could manage to find the time, that he has been examining into the Cash Sales and the Petty Cash as the Auditors advised should be done; and there it is, clear as a pike, that Snape has been sneaking money, regular, for months. I would never have allowed the fellow about the place except for Arthur shouting about the poor old widowed mother wanting her only son to live at home with her by her rheumatism being so bad—as if no one ever heard of an old woman getting the rheumatics, before! What makes me so ashamed is, after all these years of running a Business that is as well organized as any in the country—if not better—to have a young flap-ears walk in and help himself out of my till, often as he had a mind, with no one any the wiser if the Auditors hadn't been able to tell a rat by its smell without catching sight of it.

Reminds me of the Birkenpool Bank Frauds, years back, when a young simpleton, taken on for a junior counter-clerk out of some Provincial Scotch Bank, no sooner got smooth-fitted to his stool than, in six weeks, he put £90,000 straight in his trouser-pocket out of the cash, to hand over to a race-gang, without it being noticed, for the reason that everyone was so terribly busy posting-up and checking Cash Books and Ledgers for the Manager to sign them; and balancing to the last penny every evening to make certain; and writing up pass-books to send out, "with the Manager's Compliments"; till customers began to let fall that they had rather have their own credits than the Bank's compliments; and the day came when the Chief Cashier bolted out of the Bank, like a hare out of its box at Altcar, off to the Hotel where the Manager was at work laying out baits at lunch to catch new customers; so then the "Oh Hell!" was sounded in a hurry, and the Manager skipped off to count over the money so as to find out, quick, how much was left over.

How much Snape has taken no one can ever say unless *he* does; but it won't be as much as a hundred by what I can judge, if likely above fifty. His rule was "little at a time, but keep at it regular". We shall never know *how* regular he was, but, by appearances, he did not take more than 10s. at one time. His chief game at sticky-fingers was with the cash Sales, when Saunders was out of the room. The Buyer would bring the Stores' "out order" on which Jedbury, prime coster, had put the price to make it stand for an invoice; Snape would then take the cash, hand back the receipted invoice with "Thank you; a very nice day for the time of year, is it not?"—as I can hear him at it—enter up in Cash Sales Book at a *less* price, and slip the difference into his breeches. Sennock has found out three cases that are clear enough by what Jedbury recalls; (£2 19s. 4d., entered £2 9s. 4d.; £2 9s. 3d. as £1 19s. 3d.; £3 1s. 0d. as £2 11s. 0d.); but there are plenty more that look certain though not proved. One case may be as much as £2 by Jedbury saying he made a bargain for that lot of moulded

265

Basingstoke's we had left over, at £9 10s. 0d., which Snape booked at £7 10s. 0d. However, other big items are believed correct, so it is a good job Mr. Snape is a sly one, or he might have taken a lot more. Sennock has checked over with the counterfoils of "out orders", in the Stores, and all appear in the Cash Sales Book—so the fellow has never forgot to put down, by some queer accidental mistake, and bagged the whole, as he might have done. Then, with the Petty Cash, Snape altered the amount in the Receipt Book *after* it had been signed by the receiver, which comes pretty near to forgery, in my opinion. When Sennock drew £1 7s. 4d. expenses down to East Wrington, as he remembers it was and can prove, Snape had it recorded £1 17s. 4d. just by a stroke of the pen; and the dirty fellow was not above sneaking a paltry tanner or a ninepence, it seems, just by putting a tail, up or down, to an ought, when he thought clever—as is seen clear enough with a magnifier.

Sennock used his head-piece not to let any guess what he has been about, so as to leave it to me to make a full inquiry if I think well; which shows he is a young man that can take responsibility, as I got the idea of before and will remember—and so I told him; but it is clear Snape has robbed me, which is all I want to know. However, that does not mean I want *others* to know; and it does not mean I want it buzzing all over the town that I don't know how to keep my accounts straight, which would happen, certain— by them having nothing to think about if they didn't mind other people's business—if I went round to buyers and asked will they please kindly say how much they paid me for this or other of the odds and ends they have had off me, because I have forgot how much it was!

I told Sennock not to drop a hint; but it bothers me what to do with Snape. He's got his notice to clear out to-morrow three weeks; but when he asks for his testimonial, as he may do any day now he is looking out for another billet,

I shall be bound to say he has been embezzling off me, for, if he plays off the like trick on his next employer, I shall be held liable even if there wasn't our duty to our neighbour to mind: but if I write what he has been at, it will be the end of the young man, for a fellow like him will never lift his head again, but sink to be a down-and-out criminal. I must think over and have a word with Arthur before I decide to-morrow, and I wish it was someone else's job to see to instead of mine.

## A DECISION

I did not feel any too grand this morning after laying awake hours to think how best deal with Snape; with bitter feelings, difficult to get the better of, rising to set my heart going 'thump, thump' from my loathing and contempt for the fellow; and anger to think what a blamed old fool I was ever to let him under my roof. However, there it was! and got to be made the best of, according to my lights; and I had my mind made up, and felt more cheerful after breakfast, by Effie having the kitten pretend to walk about over the table on its behind legs, dressed up in hat and doll's socks, for Puss in Boots, to set me laughing with her like we were a pair of children; and, when I went across to the office, I had someone find Arthur and give him word I wanted him.

When Arthur came, and I told him what Sennock had put before me, he was properly shocked.

"Have a thorough inquiry, Dad, to find out how much he has taken, and then prosecute," he says, by it being more easy for the young man to decide before thinking first, than after.

"Well, Arthur," I said, "it will not do us any good advertising we let a fellow like Snape help himself out of our till without us being the wiser," I said; "and it won't do Snape any good to be prosecuted," I said.

"It will make a bad example of him," says Arthur.

"Yes, and it will likely make him go on setting himself up for a bad example," I said. "He's young yet; a brand to be plucked from the burning, as they say, if he *is* one scarce worth pulling out of the fire," I said. "There's just a chance to make him alter his idea of things; and, likely, it's the only chance there will ever come to be if we don't take it," I said.

"What do you propose to do then, Dad?" says Arthur.

"I do not propose anything," I said. "I have made up my mind and it's not going to be unmade," I said. "So let the old man have his old way without arguing, just for once," I said; and I dare say I sounded a bit broken, which is not my way, for the boy catches my hand:

"Of course, Dad," he says. "I thought you wanted my ideas."

"Well, perhaps I did, Art," I said, "while I was sure you'd agree with me," I said.

"Let me hear, Dad," he says.

So then I told him we must cancel Snape's notice so as he should stay on, at a lower wage, to make good and redeem himself, "until it is a thing of the past for everyone to forget," I said. "No one knows but Sennock," I said, "and I can trust him, and will show him my trust, not to let fall or tittle-tattle, so that Snape can hold up his head inside the office and outside the office, and find self-respect in himself," I said.

"Of course I'll back you up, Dad. I will do my best," he says.

I told him I knew I could rely on him. "You always see things right in the end, Arthur, my lad," I said, "if it does take you a bit of time getting there, now and again," I said —and we had a laugh over it.

268

I sent word for Snape to come to see me at the whistle Dinner, so as I could have him on the carpet with no one about to pick up ideas. I don't know what he was thinking, for he is so full of deceitfulness that if it isn't one thing he has to hide back of his mind, it will be another, so that it's queer to see his face when he does not know you are by. I motioned him to sit till the outer office had cleared off; and then I shut my papers in my drawer and had him bring his chair up close opposite, so as I could work on him, if so be I might, to help him out of his bad ways of thinking and doing, in hope that he might see a new meaning in life and walk with his chin up and his chest forward, not to be afraid of anyone or anything; and I won't say I was not a bit worked up and humble with it, to think of the trust laying in my hands for better or for worse, to him, and to generations after him, whether for courage and right-thinking, or for meanness and villainy, according to the power I might have to turn his mind to a better way of thinking and his heart to a better way of feeling.

It was so with me that I found my voice unsteady in speaking; and I do not understand how at the moment, a kind of love for the poor rotten soul that had ought to have been a proper man's, came over me beyond all reason; and there was a moment when I could have almost taken him to be one with me to understand what I understand for his strength and happiness. It was like some poetry-book that has caught me now and again in my life, that might be the poet Longfellow's, or another, if I remember; or it has come over me times when I was happy out alone in the country—a thing not to be understood by any talking or wondering about it. So it just was at that moment; but when I began to speak, everything changed at hearing my own voice, though I kept at it to do my best with the fellow.

Things didn't happen as I would have had them, by the young man being afraid, and with no other idea but catch at whatever would make things safe and easy for him, rather than confess, and face the worst, and take his medicine to feel purged and free for a clean start in life, as I hoped would be. However, there's hope he has good intentions to turn over a new leaf and act right in future, and we must be thankful for that.

It would tire me setting down what passed, for we were together better part of an hour; but, when I told him things were found to be amiss in the books, he went off this style:

"Well, Mr. Grigblay, it very likely might chance, now and again, that I would put down wrong by a mistaken idea in trying to think of other things at the same time; or what was young Sydney up to directly I could not attend to keep an eye on him; and so it would be just possible, Mr. Grigblay, for an accidental discrepancy to arise without me having any idea it had done, sir: but to my best knowledge and belief, Mr. Grigblay—and you know how well I am to be trusted for a very careful one, sir" . . . and so he went on while I sat and looked at him, feeling sad enough; but, seeing me just sit there, front of him, waiting for a finish, made him come over awkward and self-conscious, by thinking I knew a lot more than he fancied I could do, no doubt; and he dried up with—"and so that is just exactly how it must be, sir, if you take my meaning, Mr. Grigblay; and you may rely on me if there should chance to be any discrepancy happened anywhere, Mr. Grigblay, to be only too glad to be the very first to explain how it has come about, sir—if my memory should not fail me, which would not be like me if it did, as you know well, Mr. Grigblay."

The next was, I shook my head at him, and said enough was known of him putting money in his pocket regular, for months past. On that he admitted it was so; but said he had only taken it for a "temporary private loan", to pay back again, because of his mother being so bad that he was tempted to buy necessities to ease her; and he had put back

270

some of the money already, on the quiet, by adding on more than was paid in, once or twice, so as I should not be at any loss, in the end—all of which was lies, clear enough, and hard for me to hear him say. He could not tell me how much it all came to until I put it to him it was at least twenty-five pounds, which he would not allow; but, me pressing him, he admitted it might be near on twenty, which shows it is twice as much more, in the least, without question.

After that, I told him in solemn style just how he stood; with me to have the books close-examined, and customers to show their books for proof, so that everyone would soon know there had been embezzlement and forgery, perhaps, and who was the guilty one: and then, when all was known, the police would take him to go before the magistrates, and perhaps to be sent to jail against the assizes, for a Judge to send him to prison perhaps; and before I had done he was shivering and snuffling, and it was—"If only you will forgive and overlook just only this once like the good Christian Churchwarden everyone knows you are, sir, I will promise evermore on my sacred solemn sworn oath, Mr. Grigblay"—and so he ran on, till he must suddenly remember to get out his handkerchief; but it was, clear enough, all a bit of play-acting, by what I saw, to make a pretence of grief; for his shivering and snorting was from funk, and not a tear in his eye nor ever going to be!

Then I spoke earnest; and if my words had been fit to show him all the feelings I had to help him to a decent way of life, they could not have been wasted. I told him it was more to me to have him change his life to grow up a clean honest man, than any money I had lost; and that I had no intention of prosecuting him or letting anyone guess what he had been at. On that, because he knew he was safe, he brightened up and listened to me, instead of thinking to invent new lies to help himself; and also he was, as I hope, moved to gratitude and good intentions for the future, for he was so full of thankfulness that the whole could not have been put on in pretence.

Last, I told him how I was bound to report against his honesty in his testimonials; and I began to see an ugly look come over him till I said I would cancel his Notice for him to stay on and re-establish himself by good conduct, so that all might be forgotten about. That started him off again about his gratitude for my kindness; but I said to him it was no kindness that made me, but confidence that he would lay aside all treachery and meanness and folly, and come to be a clean straight man, trusted and respected by everyone, and with security and happiness laying before.

"So, Snape," I said, "I will give you a lower position where you can easy make good and win advancement, to carry you far ahead of where you are now, I hope."

"And what position will that be, Mr. Grigblay, sir?" he says, in a wheedling anxious tone of voice, and it pained me to hear him so eager to set a value on my liberality.

"That you will be informed about, later," I said; for I feared he would betray himself, worse, if I told him "cubing dimensions in the Prime Costing for three months at thirty bob" instead of the forty-eight he's getting now. Then I should have wished to lay a hand on the young man's shoulder, and take his with my other, to have him know I forgave him—for his temptation came of my own bad methods—and have had him to go away in some quiet place, and think, to strengthen his spirit and feel glad; but that I was not able to do by knowing, too well, he would only fancy I had a soft place for him to burrow in to his own advantage. Fear of consequences and a whip-hand, but nothing else, will discipline him; till, little by little, having him always under my eye, I may win his good feelings and lead him to go straight of himself.

## GOOD AND BAD NEWS

This morning there was a letter from Trencher enclosing the Gas Coy.'s cheque for £750, at last! and his own charges—£17 9s. 10d.—including 2s. 8d. for making out his own bill—and 1½d. for the postage tucked away somewhere we may be sure, by the queer way solicitors go to work. Well, he has earned his money! by the Gas Coy. wriggling this way and that, and offering first £500 to settle, and then £600. I have sent him twenty-five guineas, friendly style, for Trencher is a man I respect and is none too flush, with his invalid wife to care for, I dare say. Then, when Arthur came in, the first thing was: Parkin has got three months' notice—or so Arthur heard last night at the Cricket Club Smoker, though he didn't care to ask Parkin was it true. It looks as if Mr. Treadwell and the Directors are a bit sore at the bad blood Parkin has put them in with the U.D.C., with £750 damages to pay to us as well, and a lot more likely to be due on the Tank Contract than Parkin had them guess till Rasper blew the gaff.

The next letter I had Arthur to read, was from young Bruce, our Foreman in Charge at Mr. Christopher Quinger's little church, Great Widdlingford, which was not nice reading, though no blame on us, so far as we could see. By what Bruce said it looked as if the whole blame place might have come down in a run if he hadn't been uncommon nippy and served by a bit of good luck, into the bargain.

Bruce had 'phoned the Architect, he said; but I sent Arthur down, right off, to see what was up.

When Arthur got back after knock-off this evening, he came straight to the house to tell me what is happened. It bothers me all the time at the back of my mind, so as I keep wondering about it, for Arthur says—same as Tom Bruce wrote—that if Tom hadn't been uncommon nippy, and lucky as well, she might have come down right on top of his head!

This is the third time I've built under Mr. Quinger: first, that fine Ham Hill church, down Yeovil way; next the Humanities School—they call it—Cambridge; and now this little Widdlingford church; and if there is a gentleman I would choose out of all the rest to direct me in putting up a building, it is Mr. Quinger. His drawings are rough, may-be; but they're always full and clear, with no questions to be asked while we stand waiting for the answers! On the job, he's quick as a bird hopping about, and never at a loss for a moment; and all done and seen to and him off and away pretty near as soon as you know he's there, and which is often enough for us to be sure we are going ahead the way he wants.

This little church of his is in a fancy brick style different from what I ever saw before; and we have full-size details of all his oversails and undercloaks and of all his special crochets, sent us like it might be a stone church, though he's managed without a single axed or rubbed face, for all his cleverness and variety. The place holds 470 with nave 26 feet wide and aisle 12 feet and the whole roofed with Italian sand-faced half-rounds hung to a 30 degree pitch. Inside, the nave is a clear plaster barrel from chancel arch to west end; and the clever thing he has done is to carry this barrel high into the pitch of the roof just by braced 5 in. x 2 in. rafters covered with roof boarding, without any pur-lins, to carry the vertical tiling fillets: and the collar ties, braces, and struts off walls, are just passed and spiked without framing them, and form the right shape to take the cradling of the barrel. It was a tricky-looking affair in the $\frac{1}{8}$ in. sections and on the $\frac{1}{2}$ in. detail too, with only the 14 in. walls to take the thrust that it seemed must be something to take care of by all the heavy tiling on top and the distance the collar was pushed up by the barrel. However, that wasn't going to worry Mr. Quinger, for when he doesn't know for certain, he makes sure. It was set down in the Specification, and we so did, for two sets of trussed rafters to be set up 15 in. centres, as an experiment, with the feet of the rafters free to spread if they wanted. When we were ready, the Architect marked the bearings of the rafter-feet; saw weights equal to full roof-load put on; and noted the amount of spread. It came to about $\frac{7}{8}$ in. each side, only, so it was: "All right; go ahead" and "Good-bye" after he had directed us to knock back feet of rafters the $\frac{7}{8}$ in. so that there was no thrust left to come on the wall. It was the cheapest roof you could have—but it couldn't have been a sounder or looked better, inside and out, if it had cost as much twice over. Well, that is Mr. Quinger's way; and it makes me feel sorry he has got into trouble by being a bit too clever, just for once; and what's to be done I don't know yet, but the chancel arch is spreading—that's clear!

The crown of the arch is about a foot below the plaster barrel, but it is turned from a centre above the other so that its width below the springing is 19 ft. 6 in., and it has the abutment of the end-wall of the South aisle. At the crown, the arch is five half-brick rings with 1 ft. 6 in. sofite; and the spandrel, and the end-wall of aisle, is carried up close to underside of tiles.

Well, all is covered in and good as finished, and, last Saturday, half after twelve, Bruce came out of his office to blow the whistle for knocking off, and then he went in the church to see all clear for locking up when, quite by chance, so he says, his eye caught a crack through the crown of the arch—a quarter inch open across sofite and running up far as the line of the barrel before it petered out. Bruce says he had noticed a kind of hair-crack—the way they show up in new plaster—the day before, but thought nothing; so she was moving, clear enough, and he had just time to run out in the road and whistle to catch some of them before they had gone too far. He hadn't any big stuff to shore it, but he took four poles out of the painters' scaffolding and strapped them together with hoop-iron off the glazier's cases, with wedges driven to bind them tight; and there was his dead-shore for wedging up the crown by wedges driven under the foot as tight as they could swing the sledge; and Arthur says all is made safe till the Architect says what is to be done.

## A PERSONALLY CONDUCTED TOUR

Mr. Spinlove had me meet him at Belhampton eleven-thirty, Thursday, so I got along off to Dorchester, Wednesday afternoon, to take it easy and get across to the site from the Hotel, comfortable. When we had jolted along the approach road—which is in a rare state by the lorries we have had over it, and will have to be seen to, before the winter—there was old Fred down at the gate, guessing it would be me; and the gentleman's limousine was waiting there, too, for a wonder, with his hospital nurse inside reading a picture paper, but none of his fancy pieces *this* time, for a change.

"What's all this?" I said to Fred. "I wouldn't expect to have the owner come this time of day," I said.

"He's along above," says Fred, with a side-nod; and, sure enough, there was Sir Ezra away up; and a gentleman along with him; and his footman waiting; and old Lanky, behind, dressed up in new clothes like he thought he was on a beano.

"There's some great Lord coming to see over, sir, by what Barnacle dropped to me," says Fred.

"That will be Lord Rainsport, we built Dulkington for, without doubt," I said—from something Mr. Spinlove had let fall one day; but, as I had no call to pay attention, I took Fred in his office to get ahead with things, leaving the four standing together up above, watching the road like so many sheep with a dog over the horizon.

Fred was in a bit of a stew with the electricians and the heating people getting to loggerheads by each wanting first attendance for their cutting away; but he's got things fixed by a touch of his fancy language, no doubt, handed out right and left to one and another to make them look out what will be coming to them *next* if they don't give attention; and then I had the telephone account on the table to ask him about, £27 5s. 8d., just for the quarter! It had been a bit high the quarter before, and I let be; but this time it is out of all reason, and Fred told me Barnacle is at it, day in, day out; and by a word he has heard, now and again, it is the Specialist Sub-contractors Lanky is on with all the time. Well, I don't see the sense of that, and I don't think Mr. Spinlove will, either; so I had Fred copy out *his* tally—that amounts to nothing, scarcely—for me to call Mr. Spinlove's attention to what's going on and say if I'm to charge

277

the rest of it; and also I made up my mind to have Barnacle give me *his* tally, for check.

Eleven-thirty being past, I went to the door to look out; and there was Mr. Spinlove's car just coming in by the gate! and, following, a big smart saloon. Next, Mr. Spinlove gets out of his with Lord Rainsport, that I had not seen seven years, and who is aged a bit in figure by his shoulders more round, which seems to belong to his style better, by the soft fatherly kind-hearted gentle way he always had, as if he was pleased and grateful for everything and knew everyone meant for the best; though I must say he knows how to freeze when he wants, all right! I don't think I ever saw anyone so heavy put down as that garden contractor that tried on a bit of lying to see how far *that* would take him. He got his tail tight down between his legs in no time, and wanted nothing better than a chance to take himself off as fast as he could clear; and yet you couldn't say how his Lordship did it, he was so quiet in his manners and every word seemed considerate and kindly meant: it was just by the way his high nature stood out to make the dirty Commercial feel ashamed all over as in their deep hearts they must be if they ever let themselves remember; or else, you would say, they are not human beings at all, but come of mongrel dogs, and monkeys out of trees.

Well, the two came on up across, and there was Sir Ezra, like a little black-faced ram with his baa-baas on his heels, hurrying down. Mr. Spinlove turned my way, so I went across; and his Lordship was pleased to pass the time of day with me and remember me with many kind expressions; and then it was—"Ah! There is my old friend again! how *are* you, Bloggs?" So old Fred must get pink, shaking hands, and stammer with it as is his queer way when pleased.

Then Sir Ezra came fussing up not to be overlooked, with the gentleman that was his Secretary, it seemed, to carry a portfolio, and Lanky and the servant close behind;

and he barged in without any notice taken of Mr. Spinlove or a nod to me, any more than if we were not there; and takes off his hat, all grins and wriggling and dancing on one leg and the other, to be friendly and affable with Lord Rainsport, who took off his hat in return, and was very polite to listen to all the other had to say about the honour it was to show his Lordship the building he was doing, knowing how interested his Lordship was in building, after seeing his Lordship's fine house at Dulkington, where his Lordship had invited him a guest in his garden; but *this*, he was building here, was only just a little summer holiday-house for when his yacht was at Weymouth; and he hoped he would have the pleasure of including his Lordship in one of his week-end yachting parties next summer that he was bringing over in his turbine luxury-yacht, as he knew his Lordship was a yachtsman—and so he ran on till he led the way, with Mr. Spinlove on the other side of Lord Rainsport, to take him round the work; and must fuss to have his Secretary open the portfolio to take out the pictures Mr. Spinlove had made to show the building when finished, and Lanky to hold the plans ready unrolled, till his Lordship did not know which to look at first, or how to look at any for listening to all the wonderful things he was told, and how special it all was, and what a wonderful lot everything was going to cost.

"I shall be free in half an hour," Mr. Spinlove says to me, before they went off; so I went after, at a distance—in case I was wanted—and, also, I had Fred to get a pair of rods, just in case, and put on his coat and follow along with me.

Well, they went all over, and stood at the window, 1st floor landing, with the plan, to see how it was all laid out from above; and then they moved to go up to the great circular room, with look-out windows all sides, that is at top under the flat roof of the tower. Forty feet across it is, very near, and going to be panelled out Tudor style; with the binders, carrying the deck over, all worked out in panels for squashes on the plaster-work modelled, special, by Mr. Blackhurst, the well-known artist for such work. It is an oval stone stair-well with the steps built in and set dancing; it is three foot six from wall to the open newel, but the wrot iron fancy balustrade and stainless chrome-vanadium hand-rail is not yet fixed, though the steps are sunk for running in the standards, and the whole delivered ready.

His Lordship and Mr. Spinlove went up, and the others followed strung out to keep on the wall side, but, somehow, Sir Ezra dropped behind by being scared and, then, there he was stuck, seven steps up, with his hands spread out against the wall like he was a fly on a window pane, him being too scared—by not having a hand-rail 3 feet behind him—to know how to get up or come down. However, before I knew what was the matter, he got braver and ventured one step down, sideways; and then another; and so he gained courage and came to the landing where me and Fred were waiting to follow up.

"Why are there no balusters?" he says. "It is not safe left all open for anyone to fall over," he says. "I expect things to be finished ready before I come. Understand?"

"Well, Sir Ezra," I said, "that would be easy managed if we could do everything before everything else," I said; but Mr. Spinlove and Lord R. had got to the top, laughing together—it is only fifteen feet—and had gone through into the big room, with the others following. So then Sir Ezra must have another try; but he got up only five steps, feeling along the wall cautious style, one foot following the other, before he must change his mind and come down again, careful, but quick to be safe once more.

He was in such a rare stew to be left behind, walking about and looking up to think if he dare try it once more, that I said: "Take my arm, sir," I said. "It will be easy if

280

you have someone to hold on to. I shall take plenty care not to go over the edge," I said; and then he hooked his left arm in mine, without a word of thanks, and we started with him pawing the wall with his right to know he was safe. He came up four steps as light as a lady, and then he began to drag more and more till he got on the ninth, and there we got fairly stuck, just below a half-pace, by him trying to spread both hands on the wall with one arm hooked in mine. Well, the thing couldn't be done unless it would be by a pair of crabs taught how in a dance-school; so, after he had tried perching on my foot to see if that would help—but it did not, by our feet being mixed together so that we didn't know whose was which, without looking to see—I unloosed my arm, on which he started at trembling like he had lost his nerve in the Alps, and I had a rare job getting him down to No. 6, where he took better courage by the experience of doing it before, and climbed safe down, all the way home, by himself.

Well, he *was* vexed; tutting and dratting to himself, and walking up and down and hitting his fist in his hand. The others had gone on by the little oak stair, out of the big room, up on to the top deck to look out from the battlements, and see over the little observatory dome prepared ready for the 5-in. refractor telescope to be set up by Cooke & Watson later on. They took their time, and came down laughing together; till Lord Rainsport said: "Oh, *there* you are! We wondered where you'd hidden yourself," and then he looked at his watch, and had to be getting along home, so "Good-bye": but the other must hurry down to go with him to his car, and Mr. Spinlove went too, by his Lordship's turning to have him walk with him; and, the others following, I thought polite to bring up the rear.

Well, it was funny to see Sir Ezra try to get to travel with the lord both of them going the same road far as Brockenhurst. He had his hospital nurse get out like jack-in-a-box, and was for leaving her and his Secretary to get back any dam way they liked unless Lord Rainsport should ask him come in *his* Saloon. However, he did not; but made it seem as though it was out of regard for the other's convenience, and so as not to trouble him; and the end was, they said "good-bye" and Sir Ezra had his own car to follow close up, to keep near the other and perhaps have a chance to fuss about and do the affable if one of his Lordship's tyres should go.

I had three hours with Mr. Spinlove and things well cleared up and settled before he left; and then, before I got off to catch my train, I found time for a word with Mr. Lanky Barnacle about his little bill for telephone calls.

"I've been asking Mr. Bloggs about the telephone account charged to us," I said, "and looks like you have put through about £25 of calls in three months," I said. "I don't want to interfere with your personal habits or to push my nose into private matters you would rather keep secret to yourself," I said, "but, as I am the one that pays the bills, I would like to know what I am paying for," I said, "and just to inquire: is it a bit of romance with a lady friend up in Yorkshire, or somewhere else not too handy? or is it a dear old Aunty sitting tight on a bit of money away in Aberdeen that is made pleased her nephew doesn't mind how much it costs him as long as he may hear her sweet kind voice on the wire every day?" I said. That starts him at pulling on his moustache same as if he was trying to pull a dribble out of some old cow milked dry.

"They're all business calls," he says.

"Then what business is it," I said, "that keeps a score of girls plugging in and unplugging all over the country, five and a half days in the week?" I said.

"Well, there would be the Architect's office for one thing," he says, "and the Gotsnitz Company for another thing," he says.

"And what would the extra dozen things be?" I said.

"I shouldn't like to say, offhand," he says.

"Well, better have a good think to be ready with the answer by the time the Architect asks the question next week," I said. "I am ready enough to give everything in reason that is asked of me, but," I said, "I'm not the finest quality best selected special mutton-head that stands still for any that choose to put their hands in his breeches and pull out half-crowns, often as they fancy," I said:—which was enough for old Lanky, and he said he would copy out his tally of calls for Fred to send me. So now we shall see! and if he has been hob-nobbing with my sub-contractors, to have them think they must depend on his favours to get an easy passage among all the other specialists that will soon be pushing and shouldering each to get the advantage and let all others go hang:—well, I dare say Mr. Spinlove will get ideas that Lanky had rather he did not.

## A MATTER OF SLATES

Troubles never come singly, or so they say; and yesterday came a letter from Tolpenny that the Architect had dropped in to admire how his alterations were going on; and then it must be the slates that was wrong—after all finished and the slaters cleared off the job!

As I said to Arthur: "Why in the name of sense didn't the Architect say three weeks back, when I was by and he saw the slates unloading off the lorry, and handled them, too?" However, it's no good arguing about that, yet. The upset is: they are specified "Llangwrwyd Rustic Slates", and were so quoted for by Rollingham & Towster, slating contractors, when we were getting out our Tender; and it was Llangwrwyd Rustics, as quoted for by them, that I ordered; but now, according to what Tol. reports, they are not "Rustics", by Mr. Blenhasset's ideas, but ordinary Llangwrwyds, so the order has gone forth from His Majesty: "strip and re-hang with slates as specified".

Llangwrwyd slates are rather a special thing, and Tol. says he has never had to do with them before: but, in any case, he would not think that R. & T.—who we have had sub-contract to us for particular slating jobs many times before now—would cheat us; and, seeing the Architect satisfied—as he looked to be—would, naturally, be good enough for Tol., as it was for me, standing beside; for I can't keep Architects' specifications learnt off by heart inside my head, as some Architects seem to think I ought by forgetting what they have written down themselves! and so I never noticed—except that the slates were a likely-looking lot. However, one has to see Llangwrwyds laid out in bulk, to know whether they are the Rustic vein—or perhaps it is just a sorting over at the quarry to lay aside for "Rustic" those that have the rusty-marked patches, which all Llangwrwyds show, strong-marked over them so as to give that nice greeny-gold colour on the finished roof, when hung. Well, I have written to Tol. to wait till he gets instructions; and also I have written to R. & T. and to the quarry to know what slates they are, or whether the Architect has gone out of his senses!

Reminds me of when I was learning my business and we were building that great Cycle Factory at Coventry with acres of roofs to be hung with 2nd Bangor Countess. The slating Contractor made out he could not get that quantity of Bangors in the time, and so the Architect agreed to Portmadocs. The first delivery showed some cracked down the middle, and it was agreed that any a strong man could not break by gripping the sides with his thumbs behind, might be used. Well, the strong man we put on to the job was so strong that he broke the whole dam' lot!

284

# AN AWKWARD QUESTION

Tom Bruce reported the Architect had been down, day after Arthur was there, to see into this spreading of the Chancel Arch; and Tom said Mr. Quinger was satisfied all was made safe by the dead-shore Tom botched out of scaffold poles. Next, there came a letter from Mr. Quinger for us to prepare so as he could decide what would be best; and he had it all clear set out, with sketches, for us to have plumbs and blocks and a reel of fine steel wire, and a 20-ft. straight-edge and four buckets of tar, also—for some reason I did not guess—set ready for him, last Wednesday, when I thought well to go down myself and see what sort of a mess we were in; and had Arthur to come along, too, for he will have to see the job through when the decision is made.

We had a hire-car out from Brackley and found Mr. Quinger before us. He made no pretence it was any fault of ours, but had a word of praise for the smart way Tom had made all safe. He says the fault is not enough "haunching" on the North side of the Arch where there is no aisle with its East wall to act as abutment; by which he meant, as I understood, that there is not enough weight of brickwork above the arch-springing, by the crown of the arch being pushed up so high and the roof sloping close down over. He says she has taken her bearings, now, and will not move any more; but he means to get her back, far as possible, and make all ship-shape.

"With a tie-rod and screwed ends across the springing,

perhaps, sir, and anchors," I said, "and heat the rod by a match set to a twist of tow soaked in paraffin to expand it, and then tighten up the nuts to pull her back, quarter-inch at a time, as it cools," I said; but he laughs and says he does not care to have his church "skewered together with hairpins for all to remember me by; even if they hang up a rood to make it look as if it was meant for highest art," he says—for Mr. Quinger is a lively gentleman with his tongue. He told me the tie and anchors would be too rough-and-ready, by his ideas. "We should not see what was happening till the harm was done," he says; so he has special ideas of his own, that's clear, and we shall have to wait and see.

All this was after we had plumbed the outside of North wall of Nave; and the buckets of tar were for the plumbs to hang in so as they would come to rest, and not be set swinging by the wind—as I should have remembered. Then Mr. Quinger went up the ladders, and all over, to see for himself; and the N. wall is out at top, East end, 20 ft. up, $2\frac{7}{8}$ in.; and along the wall, going West at intervals of 10 ft., it is first, $1\frac{1}{8}$ in. and then $\frac{5}{8}$ in. and nothing to measure beyond. There is no crack—not even in the mortar joints—anywhere. When Mr. Quinger laid a straight-edge vertically against the wall, there was a bit of a hollow I could see clear enough when he called my attention, as though the wall had a bend in it by the top pushed over and the rest hanging back. Mr. Quinger seemed quite content it was not any worse; and there are no cracks in the plaster barrel, by the whole roof stretching gentle, all over, elastic style, no doubt; but the crack across the sofite of the chancel arch looks ugly enough. We did not get up to measure, but it seems to be all of $\frac{1}{8}$ of an inch, as Mr. Quinger agreed by a pair of field-glasses he had brought along for seeing better at a distance.

"It is always the little jobs that catch us Architects out, Mr. Grigblay," he says. "We cut down everything to economize cost as far as we dare, and sometimes we dare a little too much. However, all's safe here, and the Rector will have to bustle round and collect money for a little 'campanile'—he called it—which is just what the church wants for a finish, like a feather sticking up, side of a lady's hat," he says, and off he goes gay as you please; but he stopped and looked behind for me to follow, private; and it was to say he would write an order for the repair work, and would I please make it a separate account for him to settle.

"Oh, well, sir!" I said, "there won't be much in it, I dare say. Just the men's time and carriage of the plant we shall want," I said. So he thanks me and hurries off.

It is not every Architect would behave so fair-minded, but would more likely let the extra cost of making good his blunders be forgot by being buried with the new campanile, instead; and I must say that, considering the lot of trouble and time spent on supervision, for the very small fee an Architect gets on a little brick affair costing £4,630—for that is the contract sum—it is only fair, if he cuts things a little too fine in trying to save money, and has a mishap, that the building-owner should stand in with him and pay the bill, rather than see his Architect give money out of his pocket—as well as his time and trouble for nothing—as a return for him using his high conscientious skill. Anyone that had no care but earn his money and be clear, could have built with an iron tie-rod across the springing from the start, to make things easy and safe for himself.

I'm glad enough to notice that young Tom Bruce has his head screwed on and keeps his eyes lively and can act up in a difficult corner; and I said a word to him he was glad enough to hear, I could see. He is a nice quiet gritty young fellow twenty-six years of age and about ready to settle down now, that I have had my eye on for some time past while he was foreman bricklayer. As time goes on the old ones drop out and I like to know I have the right sorts coming along to take their places. This little Widdlingford job is the first where I have had the young man in charge; but I was pretty sure I was making no mistake. He is a bricklayer, which is not the most likely trade to find a high-class general foreman—or so they say; but Tom Bruce always kept with his evening classes, and what others may think is their own affair; but, by my experience of things, I have come to fancy that laying bricks gives a man toughness of character and a solid good sense that another trade will not. Look at my old Fred, now! His sort can't be beat anywhere, in my opinion.

## A SHOCK

I have met with as much dirty underhand trickery and cheating and mischief in my time as most, I dare say; but to think of a respectable firm like Rollingham & Towster—as I took them to be—that have had my confidence as sub-contracting Slaters and Tilers six or eight times in the last ten years, trying to play it off on me with their lying and deception just for the chance of an extra £70 with no one to be the wiser! Yesterday came their letter in reply to the one I wrote asking were the Slates same as specified? and they answer "Yes, they are the Llanywrwyd Rustics as ordered"; so naturally I thought Mr. Blenhasset had made a bloomer by not knowing a Llanywrwyd Rustic when he saw one! Lucky I wrote to the Quarry, as well, for to-day is *their* letter:

Dear Sirs,

Adverting to your kind favour of the 11th instant we beg to inform you that we duly received an order from Messrs. Rollingham & Towster Ltd. to supply our "Llanywrywd Slates", coursed, to particulars and quantities supplied. As we were some months ago in communication with Mr. Rupert Blenhasset, A.R.A., re our ability to execute such an order in our Rustic Slates, and as we know how particular this Architect is in his requirements, we wrote Messrs. Rollingham & Towster and queried would their order be for Llanywrwyd Slates (ordinary) indeed, or for Llany-wrwyd Rustic Slates indeed? We received reply from the Firm that their order was for Llanywrwyd Slates as stated by them, and would we kindly complete same without delay.

Soliciting a continuance of your esteemed favours,

We are, dear Sirs,

Your obedient servants,

for Llanywrwyd Slate Quarries Ltd.,

Lluellyn Trevredyn-Jones,

*Director.*

pp. F. Davis-Jones,

*Secretary.*


Well, I have written to Rollingham & Towster and told them I do not accept their statement, and that I must re-quire them immediately to strip roofs and re-hang with Llanywrwyd Rustics as specified and quoted for and ordered by me, to the Architect's satisfaction as contracted; and that I shall charge all attendances to their account. I have also written the Architect and expressed my regrets and told him how the mistake has come about, with no gain to me in any case; but it does make me in a rage to have anyone think I can't take care of myself not to be cheated. It's a queer chance the Quarry Company should have made a guess where the slates were intended, and so settled R. & T.'s hash; and it was lucky, too, that I only asked R. & T. were the Slates "Rustics" as ordered? without dropping word they had been condemned by the Architect; or else, like enough, they would have sent me their most sincere regrets and profound apologies, but they had only just discovered a purely accidental mistake had been made, and would use their best endeavours to correct the most unfortunate error that ever happened in all their experience, etc.—the sort of stuff I have heard a bit too often in my life, already.


## BLENHASSET IN TROUBLE

It was a rare old upset we had at Priors Franklyn, day before yesterday, when I went down to meet Mr. Blenhasset by Mooney ringing up to tell me, and it being six weeks since I had been down.

His Royal Highness was there, when I walked on the site, peacocking about in the sun and pleased enough with everything—not forgetting himself; and then, before we knew, there was his Lordship coming down from the house, who had travelled from Scotland by the night mail, as we afterwards learned, and was just out of bed before lunch when we thought he was miles away. He came round from back of the garden-house, West end of the terrace, while we were at the East, looking brown and lean and hard and full of vigour—such a handsome youthful gentleman as he is, though on the wrong side of fifty, I dare say. On he came with a wave of his hand to us; and then he stopped and looked about, as well he might do!

Six weeks he had been away, and he must have expected to find the work good as finished, no doubt, as it had ought to have been; and then, Hullo! There were the slates that he thought to find all hung, being taken off instead of put on; and the brick flank-walls of the Pavilion, he left built and finished, now half-way to being built over again—for those half-domed niches take a lot of time, beside axing the bricks ready beforehand, as I won't have any but old Snoop to touch them. Next, when he looked, left hand, there was a whole row of seven columns West of the Pavilion, and another row of seven, half finished, at East, that he had never heard of before and did not know the meaning of; so no wonder he stood and stared and did not look very pleased at what he saw. Then he turned and called—"Toto, just come here, will you?" for the Viscountess to join him; and then he steps forward to meet his Architect.

"Good morning," he says. "What the devil's going on here?" he says, a bit stern. "This Pavilion was built up before I went away; and now I see it being built over again! And why are the slates being taken off? I understood the roof would be finished long before this; and, in the name of goodness, what are all these columns? I never ordered them! What are they for?" he says—and I must say I felt a pretty big fool, standing there, although I was not accountable; but Mr. Blenhasset, who *was*, did'nt seem to give a damn, as though it was all in the week's work for him; but must step forward in his swaggering style, cloak flapping, pleased as you like, and greet his client, genial, holding out his hand, which the other took without seeming to know he did.

Then Mr. Blenhasset started his jabbering to explain what a very clever man he is; and how a little error had crept in the Pavilion as must often happen even with the greatest possible care, but he was making the necessary "rectification"—he called it. The slates were an inferior kind hung by the builder against his orders—which was a nice thing to hear said!—but he had at once detected the

291

irregularity and was having them replaced according to his original directions—Haw, Haw! The columns he found necessary for the perfect realization of his most lovely artistic conceptions—or some such nonsense.

Just then the Viscountess came up, and, while Blenhasset talked away, she was whispering to her lord to know what it all meant—as was clearly to be seen—while he told her, hurried style, and pointed her where to look; and they were both properly worried with it, as any might see.

"You will realize, Lord Blades," says Blenhasset, with a bow and taking off his hat at her Ladyship, "that an Artist cannot always envisage his complete beautiful design in all its pretty finished perfection first start off, by his inspiration always being so wonderful detached and abstract. The artist's conception is a very delicate style of flower, Lord Blades, until the opportunity comes for the realization of the desired beautiful effect to be comprehended by actual visual demonstration of the eyeballs to make him fully aware of the difficult problem he is up against, Lord Blades," he says, as near as I can recall his long words to hide any sense he might have to say.

"In order to visualize his conception in all its wonderful different diffused and detached aspects and clever abstract notions, the Artist must have opportunity for reconsidering and maturing his fine beautiful chaste ideals, Lord Blades," he goes on, waving his arms about to show how clever he was to have all his knowledge bursting from him faster than he could get it out.

"If you will kindly step down on the lawn I can show you how very superior and effective my design is, as I have now for the first time been able to envisage and interpret it to my entire clever satisfaction, as you will be glad to know about, I am sure, Lord Blades; for I may tell you, private, that this particular conception, with all its rare lot of rhythm, when clearly realizable to the visual eye, will stand

292

for one of my very most beautiful achievements," he says, modest.

"You will observe, Lord Blades, that from every point of picturesque view there is a varied but coherent impression of a superbly well-balanced pretty chaste composition to be enjoyed—although I say it who perhaps had not ought to do—Ha, Ha, Ha!—He-Haw! But we artists—as I need not inform a clever gentleman like you are, Lord Blades—are kittle cattle, Ha, Ha, Ha! We have to attain detachment. Our artistic conceptions are not a matter of thought and studying to learn. I can assure you, Lord Blades, that all inspiration comes from no man ever knows whereabouts; I am but the poor little vehicle by which the beautiful chaste ideas comprehended in my artistic conceptions become detached realizations. You owe nothing to me, Lord Blades, Ha, Ha, Ha. I am only a common dirty tool; but I may say that my wonderful lovely artistic ideas of your terrace and pavilions—now that I have this opportunity of fully realizing all their beautiful chastity—gives me complete satisfaction; and *that*, I need scarcely tell a smart man like you, Lord Blades, is a very rare thing indeed for any of us clever arty Artists to be able to say without telling a dirty lie," he says—as well as I can remember his jaw—and comes to a stop at last.

"That's all very well," says his Lordship; "but we are not going to spend our time sitting out on the lawn to admire your terrace and pavilions, Mr. Blenhasset! We want to sit in the pavilion, or walk on the terrace, and admire the lawns and the gardens and the landscape beyond," he says.

"Oh, quite so—quite so, Lord Blades; but my artistic convictions do not——"

"Oh, damn your artistic convictions, Mr. Blenhasset!" says his Lordship, in rather a high voice, that made the lady move away as if it was no place for her. "What are all these infernal things stuck up here like a row of ninepins? and what's that plank laying along the top for? What does it all *mean*? That's what I want to know."

"My artistic conceptions, Lord Blades——"

"I say, damn your artistic conceptions; what are the things *for*?"

"They complete my design in a perfect realism of the abstract notions which constitute the clever inspirational moment of my exuberance—as I have said before—by ocular confirmation of the imaginative inflate us" he says, or some such jargon that is beyond me.

"I don't understand what the devil you are talking about, Mr. Blenhasset," says the other. "I ask what the columns are *for*, and what the plank is *for*. I never in my life saw such an erection. Is it a pergola for growing creepers, or a gallows for hanging Architects?" he says, getting stiff, but holding his patience.

"Certainly, creepers; but tastefully employed, Lord Blades, to drape and festoon; to lightly clothe but not to veil the——"

"They must be cleared away; I haven't asked for them and won't have them," says the Lord.

"One moment, Lord Blades; I say they are necessary to the realization of my beautiful artistic conception——"

"I have already said—damn your artistic conception, Mr. Blenhasset."

"Lord Blades, you forget my professional reputation has to——"

"Damn your professional reputation, as well! Are we to sit up here behind a gridiron, frowsting among greenery—in defiance of our wishes and to the squandering of our money —out of regard for your professional reputation? Good Heavens! It's time Architects were packed away into an old liner and scuttled in mid-Atlantic. I wouldn't have your columns as a gift, Mr. Blenhasset. By the way!" he says, "who's paying for them?" he says.

"The completion of the design as a perfect rendering of my—er—of—of my visual idea, Lord Blades, is a part of the obligations attaching to my duties as your special-appointed chosen Architect. I might have found it requisite to *omit* certain pretty features embodied in my earlier fanciful conception, in which case there would have been a *saving* on the Contract. However, it so comes about to happen —just by a queer chance—that it has been necessary to improve all the rare beauty by *adding* to the contract sum," says Mr. Blenhasset.

"Don't you think it, my friend!" says the Lord, with a laugh. Then he says, loud, across to where I was standing:

"Mr. Grigblay! Kindly make a separate account for all work in building and clearing away these columns and render it to Mr. Blenhasset, from whom you will receive a prompt cheque in settlement; and now," he says to the other, "will you be so good, Mr. Blenhasset, as to explain to me how it comes about that the front of the pavilion, at the sides, has been pulled down for re-building?" he says.

Well, Mr. Blenhasset made a great to-do explaining how wonderful his cleverness was for making perfect even to the exact inch, which he noticed directly he saw the work by all the great gifts he is endowed with; and it just came about to be necessary by a little mechanical slip by a draughtsman, like a wrong letter struck by a typist, that would always happen now and again, to anyone.

"I see," says the other; "and am I paying for the mechanical slip you mention?—which must be costing money, I fancy," he says.

"No, that is all provided for, Lord Blades. There is included in the Contract a sum to cover unforeseen expenditure of this kind. We call it the Contingencies Provision, Lord Blades. It is my custom always to allow an ample sum for Contingencies," he says.

"Indeed!" says the Lord. "You interest me! Ah, yes! I

see! of course! If the sum included for Contingencies is not all expended by the Architect, the Contractor gets paid for work he has not done; but if on the other hand it is exceeded, then, in that case, the Contractor pays the overplus out of his own pocket—am I correct?" he says, and you could not tell whether his Lordship was all innocence, like he seemed; or pulling the other's leg, on the sly.

"Well, No! Not precisely, Lord Blades," says Mr. Blenhasset, beginning to sweat along his forehead with it. "It is an arrangement special to building contracts, of a rather technical nature," he says, "but, to put it simple style, if the amount fixed for Contingencies is not all expended, there is an omission in the settlement account; if, on the other hand more is expended than has been allowed, then, of course, an extra would be shown. I hope I make myself clear," he says.

"Perfectly!" says his Lordship:—"Mr. Grigblay! Please to be so good as to render another account to the Architect of the cost of pulling down and re-building the pavilion. Well, good day to you, Mr. Blenhasset. I have to go into the house, and shall not be at liberty this afternoon;" and he gives him a precious short nod for thanks, and starts to walk in my direction, but stops and writes in his notebook and tears out and hands it to the other, and says: "You may like to have the name of my Agent," he says; and then he came to where I was and shook hands, pleasant enough, but his eyes were thinking of something else.

"My Lord," I said, "about these slates!"

"But that has nothing to do with me, I understand?" he says, with his keen eyes piercing into me.

"No, my Lord; but I am ashamed to say I let myself be deceived by my sub-contractor. I ordered, and was paying for, the slates as specified; but, by the slaters secretly using other slates and my foreman understanding the Architect had approved them, the harm was done before I knew," I said.

296

"Unfortunate!" he says, "I'm sorry; the slaters will, of course, pay the piper," he says; and then: "I need not remind you, Mr. Grigblay, I hope, that at any time you care to mention it up at the house, lunch will always be served to you," he says; and off he goes with a nod, friendly style, looking at his watch not to be late. Now I take that as just a kind thought he had, seeing I am on the way to an old man, besides a bit tired in the face, I dare say, if I looked how I felt; so I just went and had a nice rest and a fine plate of Irish stew and Bass and cheese, by Mr. Blenhasset being cleared off somewhere. When I came out there he was! but with all the fizz gone off him as if his cork had been out too long; and after a bit, it seemed he had left without me having any idea he was going, or I might have got away sooner myself.

Well, I'm sorry for the man, for all I don't like his style of going on; for he is bent on getting everything nice and fanciful till he cannot make it more so, never mind the cost and trouble it is to himself—nor to anyone else, either, far as that goes! That is the way a true Artist will always behave, give him the chance; and why they are such a proper caution to have anything to do with. Of course, the great part of it is just vanity and conceited ideas—always to be more clever than any other would be, so as people will throw up their hands and shout "Oh, my" at everything they do; but what is it other than vanity that keeps the whole lot of us going? If you knock the vanity out of a man you knock self-respect out of him and spunk, too; and women the same, I dare say—only there is none that has yet knocked the vanity out of a woman, for if one of them takes on, and joins in to be a nun, that is just to have people marvelling at her and calling her pretty names, and to make her feel proud she is so wonderful humble and good; just as it is with a man that goes in a Monastry to worship himself because no one else will.

297

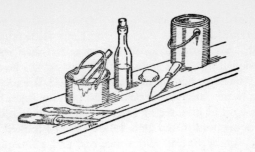

## ACHIEVEMENT

Primstake was down with his glazier, Tuesday, and by rasping and filing and chipping and squeezing with a bit of pully-hauley and one-two-three-and-all-together thrown in, they managed to get the altered window to fit—or so I gathered from the mason we sent over to fix their irons.

I did not go down to the church myself, but this afternoon, meeting Mr. Peebles, he invited me along to St. Andrew's; and there was the window with bed-spreads hung over so as none should see it before the unveiling. He is a clever man in his way, and has planned to leave his blankets hanging two or three Sundays to set everyone dancing with impatience to see behind; and so he will get a better collection at the ceremony when the Archdeacon is to come and rake in a trifle more by pulling the string with his very own extra-holy hand.

"What do you think of it, Mr. Grigblay?" the Vicar says, when we had got it cleared; and he backed away down a pew and set his head hanging over to one side to try if he couldn't manage to admire it a bit more—by the look of things.

"What do *you* think, sir?" I said. "You're a better judge than I am," I said.

"I seemed to like it at first, but I am not sure whether I do, now," he says.

"Well, I can understand that," I said, for I was properly sick to see the thing.

I suppose Mr. Primstake can draw and colour first class, if it is a picture; and I admit that the toes of his saints stand out well, careful trimmed as they should be; but other parts are decidedly a bit off, by him not being used to working in glass, no doubt. Saint Paul is crooked in the face like he was holding his jaw to one side to ease a bad tooth; and, if he was like poor Ben Harris in the picture-sketch, in the window he might be me got up in a beard and my head shaved for all the likeness there is left. Saint Peter's face is still more sad to see, for he looks as if he had had Joe Beckett at him and could never forget it as long as he lived. The hair of both—where they are wearing any—is just wet tow and nothing else; and the hands are the same as gloves when you put your mouth to them and blow out the fingers. Also, the pair are dirty-looking old fellows, carrying fleas or worse, clear enough, which is not a nice idea in a church window, to my way of thinking. The worst, however, is the cherub with wings growing out back of his ears;—except he won't be noticed to matter so much, up aloft, there, in the trefoil. His hair is wet tow, like the others, but carrotty yellow-colour and straggled out all round, unnatural, like flames; and the face is a terrible thing, that might be meant for Barnum's "Lion-Faced Boy", and enough to turn you sick saying your prayers.

That may be a matter of high art for Artists to know more about it than I do; but Mr. Primstake has not gone to work in proper style to alter the window to fit. He has crowded up the leadings so that there are bits of glass no more than the size of my thumb-nail. The window is buckled by being forced, as well; and there is no glitter of light in it. His white is just plain glazier's glass, and not as it should be; and his ruby and his blue—some of it—is good as black, and the whole a flat dull affair scattered over with places where the light shines through.

Well, it was not for me to say what *I* thought, till Mr. Peebles pressed it on me by being in two minds himself; but when anyone asks my opinion, serious, he gets it and nothing else, whether I'm right or whether I'm wrong, for so it always has been and so it always will be. In the end I told him that, in my view, the window was not fit to be seen in any church, and not fit to pay for either; and I told him that, if I was in his place I would have the Artist to take it away again as a matter of fair dealing, and supply what he contracted for.

"Oh, but—after the unveiling, you mean!" he says, as if I'd given him a scare!

Well, I can't make head or tail of the man. He's not a crank and he's not a fool by any means; and he's made me near to cry with his sermons, before now; and yet he can say a thing like that and, what's more, think it and mean it as if it was part of natural human nature.

When we first began to talk and I asked about the finances and whether Primstake had agreed to pay for fixing and carriage: "Oh, yes; yes!" he says. "Mr. Primstake was quite amenable to my suggestion; Oh quite! I told him I hoped to fix another window later, if he would let me have a design," he says—playing off the same dishonest trick he humbugged poor Mr. Triconner with.

I just said to him: "You'd best give it a think over, sir, whether to unveil before the Artist takes it away," I said. "It is a clerical matter that I have not been trained to decide about," I said, and I felt so glum with the whole muddle and ugliness of it that I didn't feel right till I had looked in, on the way, and tickled Ellie's boys; and while I watched those free, wholesome, frolicksome young creatures, I started wondering where clergymen came from and how they ever begin.

300

## DRY-ROT

Mr. Quinger was right when he said: "It is the little jobs that catch us out," and if he *did* mean architects, he might have meant builders, too, for the truth there is in it. I have never cared to have to do with these little houses, built all about, made extra pretty to let the water in so as everybody can be gentlemen and ladies on seventy shillings a week;—unless, of course, it might be a proper lay-out of a hundred or more, under a clever Architect like Mr. Richard Buckleton, F.R.I.B.A., that we built for at Carlingturn some years back; and even *that* job didn't pay over well with all the fiddle-faddling new dodges to do things different than ever was seen before. However, when the U.D.C. decided to build Council Houses, Upper Gayton, six or a dozen at a time, by advertising for Tenders—so as anyone who made the worst mistakes in under-pricing, or offered the most shoddy job, would get the Contract—I felt—as I have been in the place near forty years—I ought to stand in with the U.D.C., besides Bargate asking me to; and so, from time to time, I have sent in a careful Tender—so as not to be advertised in the paper as right outside every other—till, two years back, blest if we didn't come in lowest—by a bit of miscalculation—and get a contract for nine houses lumped down on us!

Well, the plans and the Spec. were sketchy affairs by Bargate, without any Quantities; and though he is a rare fellow for understanding about other things, he has only come to know as much about building houses as any cow, looking over the hedge to watch us, would learn in a half-hour's chew. However, we did a better job than asked for, and got out without dropping even so much as the whole of our overhead, for a wonder! and now, when all is finished eighteen months, there comes a letter from Bargate, end of last week, that dry rot has broke out in No. 91 and will we please uncover and see what is wrong?

It is a thing I would not have had happen for the world, right in the place where I live and carry on; however, we learnt the worst to-day, and I never in my life saw such a state of affairs as it is, nor would I ever have credited the blame stupidity of the tenants in the way they have let her run wild.

When I went round with a carpenter and another to open up, a nice clean young woman with four healthy children came to the door; and, directly she opened, you could smell it, plain. Her husband is a porter at the Station, and you would think he would be a sensible enough fellow; but when I asked where the trouble was, the wife said 'in the bedroom'! She took me up and, there, at the head of the stairs, the screws of the bedroom door were tearing loose from the lining that was rotted and crumbling away, bottom end.

"When did this happen?" I said.

"Sunday," she says. "We had to complain because we can't shut the door," she says.

Well, we had the lining off, and there she was! up and over the top and down the other side and into the floor, where seemed to be the end of things. So then we traced her back and, first, had the skirting of the stairs off, that was thin as cardboard in places, and broken in holes by traffic up and down. The rot was laying behind in a mat of damp strings and cobwebs that had got hold of the stairs as well, and so she went on down into the lining of the living-room door, but only a thread or two there; and where the main tangle of it stopped, one step up, we found she had actually come through the $4\frac{1}{2}$ inch just by two or three roots no thicker than pack-thread, and yet you couldn't say the brickwork was unsound, either, though of course only built in fat-lime mortar. Then, blest if she hadn't risen eleven inches from top of the living-room skirting by crawling under the plaster as if she knew beforehand just where she could get through the wall! The living-room skirting was all gone to pieces with the rot behind it; right across the end, she went, and along part of the back wall, as well; and they had nailed bits of tin boxes and packing-case wood and book-covers and all sorts, to hide the holes as fast as they showed.

"Why didn't you give notice when you saw all this begin, my dear?" I said to the woman.

"We didn't like, sir. My husband said best for him to patch it," she says.

So then we had the skirting off, and there was the deal wood-block floor as sound as a bell, when we brushed the mess of rot away, except only in the one small place where she ran up under the plaster to get through the wall. On that, we rolled back a bit of lino there was and had the wood-blocks up to trace the rot over the top of the mastic and in the bottom of the wood-blocks right into the very middle of the room, where she stopped in a mess of the stinking stuff. The next was: break through the concrete! though that seemed as dry as dry—if it might be a bit cold to the hand as I thought; and then, at last, there it was for all to stare at! the little thing, and nothing else, that had started all the trouble and would have eat the house to the bone let it alone to do its worst. It was just a brickbat—the half of an old slop-sandfacer—thrown in with the broken rubbish to lay on the damp ground and soak up the wet against the underside of the concrete for it to be carried up through, by the heat of the room drawing it, and so start the rot in some cranny or other under the wood-block where a dead knot had fallen out or a splinter got knocked off to leave a space for the infection to make a start; but if any were to ask me how the damp got past the mastic?—well, I just can't say.

So there it is! and we shall make good and hope there are no more bats been thrown about under the ground-spread. All seems right in the other eight of our lot that I inspected, to make sure; but it just shows what disaster may come about if a little thing is overlooked that might be no one's fault. It wasn't a job for a general foreman to be in charge of all the time; but I had Buckle keep an eye on it, while he was looking after Garling Road-house, and I shall be sorry to tell him what's happened, for he is a conscientious man if a bit slow and sure. It wouldn't have happened if it had been old Fred! None of 'em would have gone to sleep if they knew Fred might drop in, any hour, on his bicycle. They say there's twenty-one different kinds of dry rot. Well, that's just twenty-one sorts too many, far as I'm concerned.


## AN INCIDENT

Here is a little thing of no account happened, that sticks in my mind by the way it tickled me at the time.

The last few days there have come a terrible batch of proposals and Tenders from Specialists and quotes for fixtures wanted for Belhampton, against contract provisions, all in reply to instructions Mr. Spinlove gave me on the site, week before last; so—as I was going up to town, in any case, yesterday—I rang up Mr. Spinlove's office to ask would he rather see me with the papers to settle things,

304

right off? The answer was: "Thank you; and quarter past two will suit"; and me and Mr. Spinlove had just got all straight when, half-past three, the 'phone was put through, and it was Sir Ezra for Mr. Spinlove to meet him in twenty minutes, at a place off Sloane Street, to help decide electric fittings. Mr. Spinlove said he would be there; and, as it was not out of my way, he thought well for me to come, too, and take particulars; so we hopped into a taxi together.

The place was only one of these little fancy shops for ladies to choose pretty lamp-shades "to match my fascinating new curtains, darling"; and a slow graceful lady, finished off with one of these revolving heads out of a hairdresser's front window and an extra pure-tone voice, was there to show them off. We had not been inside two minutes before the shop went dark by a great limousine drawing up outside, and Sir Ezra must come in, same as if he owned the place, along with a young boy got up like he was a little man just stripped a dummy at Splincter's, with black hair, and eyelashes like artificial, and a conk on him to make you stare as if he was some young coal-hammer come alive.

Well, Sir Ezra started at fussing and snapping, till the lady didn't choose to come back for more; and then a little thick black-and-yellow fellow, wanting a shave, that was the proprietor, clear enough, came up out of the floor—by what I could see of it—and our bit of business got settled.

We went out, and Sir Ezra was standing on the pavement to consult with his boy where to go for their tea, while me and Mr. Spinlove waited to say good-bye, when a couple of errand lads came skirmishing and dodging each other up the road; and one, a long, freckled carrotty-head, without a cap, must spring on the path to dodge the other round the car; so Sir Ezra pushed out his elbow to keep him at a distance with: "Stop it! Understand?" On that the lad must pinch his nostrils together with his finger and thumb and say in a wheedling tone, at Sir Ezra:

"Vood you lak to puy a pewtiful cold vartsch?"—all up in the back of his nose, to the very life.

Sir Ezra hit at him with his umbrella after it was too late, and knocked his son's hat off.

"Oh Varder! What you at?" says he.

The two lads were off down the road, swerving like snipe, as if it was all in the day's play; but the queer thing was to see Sir Ezra getting in the car as if it was all in the day's round for *him* too, and he had just only driven off a blue-bottle buzzing round.

Well, I was properly tickled and couldn't keep a straight face signalling good-bye at him through the window, by the clever way the lad hit it off—good enough for the Halls, in my opinion.

Mr. Spinlove was laughing too—"An example of Jew-baiting in the twentieth century, Grigblay!" he says, as we parted.

## A CATASTROPHE

Here is a terrible thing happened, the like of which was never heard of in all the long time I have been at building, nor told in all the yarns I ever heard since I was born. Old Fred has been and got himself in no end of trouble, I'm afraid, and landed us, too; and Mr. Spinlove is more put out than I have ever seen him, and I don't know, to this moment, what he's thinking or what he would have us do. It's no good saying we're sorry—of course we're sorry!—and we don't even yet know all the harm that's done, except the nurse said she thought his jaw-bone is cracked, and it takes a hefty hook to do that—and it must have been a hook or he couldn't have reached round, standing side of my right shoulder, as he was.

I feel sorrier for old Fred than anyone else when I think of the way he was walking up and down, restless, after; with his eyes rolled round to follow me like he might be some dog that knew he'd been up to mischief and was in for a dam' good hiding—or how did his master feel about it? for, say what you like, it was just by instinct not to see me downed, and not because he had any mind to so misbehave or had intended to do it beforehand. And yet, when I was telling Arthur this morning—him standing with his mouth open to listen, and no wonder!—what must I do but break off spluttering with laughter though ashamed at doing it; and so it has been ever since :—me sitting and glooming and worrying, this evening, to let my tea stand and get cold; and then starting off to laugh low down in my bowels so as I sat jerking up and down without making a sound, and my mind at worrying all the time. It was like crying on one side of your face and laughing on the other—as they say; so no wonder the girls stared, and Meg says: "Whatever is the matter, Dad?" to set me off worse than ever, till I just sat and joggled at her; which made them both break out and fairly set me off, when there were the three of us giggling together and not one knowing why; for I felt more like cursing at the time, and all I told the girls was: "I'll let you know another day," I said, for I don't want to have any yap-yapping, with "Oh, my! did you ever?" and, "My word! what next?" and, "A nice way to behave, I *will* say!" to make a buzz, all sides.

It happened before anyone could know it had, yesterday

afternoon, when I met Mr. Spinlove at Belhampton with the owner expected on the site to say what *he* thought about things. I went down to Dorchester, night before, to take it easy. Mr. Spinlove drove on the ground just on noon. It was at two o'clock that Sir Ezra was expected; but it had gone the half-hour before he came frisking out of his car in his shiny patents, more lively than usual, as if he had had something biting him, sitting there. The nurse and the man-servant followed after him—he'd left his out-size dress-stand in the front window with the ticket on, for *that* day—and up they came to where me and Mr. Spinlove and Fred Bloggs were waiting.

Well, he had a liver on, clear enough—unless it would be the epileptic jumps, or something else, extra, the matter—by the way he went on as if he was angry with everyone and everything out of discontent because work has to be started before it can be finished; and it was why this? and what for the other? without waiting for an answer; and then he would have this done so and so, and the other something different to suit him, so that Mr. Spinlove grew to look pretty stern, for him, but always polite and very slow and clear and simple to be understood in all he said—if the other had listened to know; but all *he* wanted was to hear his own voice and feel he was cock of his own dunghill, by appearances. Then, it was the bathing pond had ought to be in a different place for some reason; and so he would have it moved where he had thought it was to be, after it is all waterproofed out, and rendered on top with that patent stuff, on wire mesh, with a polish to it like it might be marble, and the masons about finished with the fancy curb set round, too! till at last Mr. Spinlove had had enough by the other getting abusive, and he handed it back pretty stiff, and loud enough to drown the other and make him give over his rudeness. In the end Mr. Spinlove got real hot —and no wonder!—and says:

308

"You're the most disgusting person I ever had to do with; and I'll see you to blazes before I ever work for you again," he says.

On that the other pants with choking to get out what he wanted to say; and waves his arms and works his face something terrible to see till, before we knew, old Lanky and the flunkey had him, one on each side, under the elbows —by knowing what was coming, I suppose—and then the nurse asked Fred fetch a chair out of his office, and they set him in it, careful, and there he sat puffing and mopping as if he had been running in a race and been beaten on the tape. The nurse ran down to the car and came back with a medicine glass she had him take off, while we stood round and wondered at him. Then, after ten minutes, he stood up and put his handkerchief away as if he'd come to of a sudden; and next it was: "I want to see over the rest; show me!"

Well, we went round the walls where the old guard-rooms and the openings with the iron grills fitted, are just on finished by the good progress since after the masons came off the house; and then we went opposite the front where he must start all over again about some "balcony", he called it. So Mr. Spinlove repeated what he had said before, the last time; how there was not going to be any balcony because there couldn't be any balcony by reason of it being decided against at the very first beginning; and, also, that the same thing as a balcony was provided by having the range of casements in the lounge made hanging on runners to open, folding, right across; and he had Lanky bring the plans, and then it seemed that it was a "veranda" the other had meant to talk about.

"Let us look and see where we can put a veranda, Sir Ezra," Mr. Spinlove says; and he had the plans spread out —if Sir Ezra could have understood top side from bottom —but he couldn't say where he wanted it, except he pointed for Mr. Spinlove to tell him that *that* place would be against the stairs; and next, nobody knew what he was talking about by him starting to call it a "balcony" again; so Mr. Spinlove tried to smooth him by saying over all the wonderful things there *were* going to be, but Oh dear, No! that wouldn't do for our gentleman!

"I want a balcony. Understand? It's my house and I *will* have a balcony when I pay for it. Understand?" Then, when Mr. Spinlove began, over again:

"Well, Sir Ezra, will you say *where*? Here are the plans"; he must turn his back on Mr. Spinlove and call out to me, that was standing a few yards away.

"Here, you! I want a balcony. I've had enough arguing with this Architect chap. I *will* have a balcony. Understand?"

"Well, sir," I said, "I cannot act without the Architect's orders," I said.

On that he made a kind of a run at me, over the planking, on his little dancing feet, pulling a face like he was one of these Japanese masks, in his rage; and his mouth snarling and teeth gritted as he might have been some dog ready to bite me.

"Yah!" he says. "Yah! Yah!" poking his face into mine like we were in the same mad-house together, with his fists clenched and held up opposite his shoulders on each side, shaking with their tightness and suppression as if he was beside himself.

I didn't know what was happening at the moment, with his "Yah, Yahs" and his breath puffing right in my face, and pulled back; and then there came a sort of flash and a noise like a cork pulled out of a Bass, and there was Sir Ezra laying on the ground kicking and squalling same as a child bowled over, with his hands over his face and a trickle of blood running, pretty free, side of his chin, and down.

It was all so quick you couldn't tell what had happened

310

at first; till I looked aside, and there was old Fred standing with his feet apart and his elbows a bit squared, as if he was ready to shape; and never, while I can remember anythng, shall I forget the way Fred Bloggs looked at me, that moment. He was sorry and glad and proud and ashamed all at the same time, but not knowing whether I would be pleased at him, or the other thing. What it was, of course— and no need to ask him, neither—he thought Sir Ezra was going for me, to down me—as well he might do!—and the old fellow went off, Bang! like someone had touched his trigger, and he had floored the other before he knew he had. Directly after, he doubted if he had done the most wise thing he could have thought of; and he looked to see how *I* might feel about it without so much as a glance at the one he had blotted out. It's all a blamed nuisance, and no mistake; but the more I think, the more I can't feel angry with the old fellow; knowing well, as I do, the way he was feeling at the time, and how it is second nature with him to hand out clips.

I never could have credited the fuss the other made. He was squalling and howling and kicking, so that the men all stopped and came looking round from far off to see what was up, till Fred signalled them—"Get back".

Lanky and Mr. Spinlove and the nurse and the flunkey were all stooping over to give help, but he wouldn't have them take his hands away so that we could see what hurt he had taken. When, at last, he had calmed down, and was only whimpering and rocking with it and they could get to see; there was nothing but a red mark, side of his jaw, and the blood that was running out, corner of his mouth. The nurse felt with her fingers, and then tied him round with a knot at the top, like she was laying him out; and poured some stuff down his mouth that made him whimper with the pain of swallowing it. After that, they three-parts carried him and put him in the car; and he was taken off, slow and tender, like he might have been a funeral, to some hospital in Weymouth, as I understood from Lanky who seemed to think he had a better reason for pulling on his moustache than he had ever come by before. Mr. Spinlove went in the car along with the nurse—to hold his other hand, as I suppose; and as I didn't wait till he came back to fetch his own car, I haven't had word with him since.

I couldn't say much to Fred Bloggs, by wanting to catch the express back; but in any case he was too cast down and sick with himself for me to worry him at the time. All I said was:

"Well, Fred Bloggs, you've done a nice day's work for yourself and for me and for the Architect, too, by what I can see of things," I said; "but it's no good talking till we know what's going to happen next. You just look out sharp to keep the men off the scent," I said. "Tell 'em the gentleman had an epileptic, and make a great marvel of it all, so as they won't think anything is being hid away secret to start them mixing up a few clever guesses with their beer to-night, in the publics round about," I said. "That's the best you can do, Fred; and *all* you can do," I said.

"I am very sorry, sir——" he starts.

"Yes, we're all sorry enough, and shall feel a bit more sorry in a few days' time, I dare say," I said. "I'll just have a word with the Clerk of the Works," I said; so I went across.

"Mr. Barnacle," I said, "there's no one here but just ourselves knows what's happened," I said; "and Mr. Bloggs will take care the men don't get ideas," I said. "Sir Ezra would not care that any buzz should get about all over the country to make him feel ashamed before he has a chance to tell his own story; so I hope," I said, "that you will hold out that Sir Ezra was 'suddenly taken with bad pains' you say, for that is what it seemed like to me, and it had better seem the same to you, too, by *my* way of thinking," I said, "for if there is any Yah-Yahing for Sir Ezra to hear about, it will lie at *your* door and not at ours, as I will have Sir Ezra to understand if he has any complaints to make," I said, "and so you have a care, Mr. Barnacle," I said; and old Lanky stood there to look wise and nod his head as far as it would go without him loosing hold; so now we must wait and see what will be the next mischief to come about!

## RECOVERY

Mr. Spinlove's office asked for me on the 'phone to-day and, after I picked up, it was Mr. Spinlove wanted a word, and his secretary put him through.

"I thought you would like to know, Grigblay," he says, "that Sir Ezra was brought back to Tallon's Dyke by ambulance, yesterday, after three days in the Weymouth nursing home," he says.

"Dear me," I said, "is he hurt bad, sir?"

"Oh, Lor', yes!" says he. "Fractured jaw, and Surgeon-Dentist down from London to fit him with plates; and has to be fed through a tube," he says.

"It's a terrible thing to have happen, sir," I started off, but he didn't want to hear it, clear enough.

"It won't bear talking about," he says. "Of course you will replace your Foreman," he says—no "Fred Bloggs" *this* time!—"Sir Ezra must know he will never see him again."

"Yes, sir," I said. "I've arranged about that, and I'm writing for your approval," I said; and then I told him how I had taken steps to have the matter hushed up by giving out it was an epileptic touch; but, on that, the noise of a laugh, stopped before it began, comes down the 'phone; and he says:

"I don't think he will thank you for *that*!"

"Well, it was the best I could think of at the moment, sir," I said.

"Yes, I understand," he says. "He will probably prosecute your Foreman, I am afraid," he says. "Not pleasant for you, Grigblay, with all the Building Papers getting hold of it," he says.

"Well, sir," I said, "they will report my ideas about it, too," I said. "If old Fred is going to be put in the dock, I shall be in the witness-box to speak up for him," I said; "and I dare say you would, perhaps, say a word, too, sir?" I said.

"Me? Oh well! Yes, I suppose so! If I'm subpœnaed," he says—and so we ended; but it was not a nice thing for me to hear Mr. Spinlove talk so off-hand to me after these many years; and it surprised me, too—as if he thought I was responsible for the trouble! But there! It's just the way things happen in life so that you never know where you are from one moment to the next.

That was last evening; and this morning I wrote Fred Bloggs that he would have to change over with Tolpenny, and meet him here, Saturday, to see into the drawings, etc.; and I wrote Tol. as well. It's a blamed nuisance, but the best I can do at the moment; and Arthur will just have to get down to both places, often as he can manage, to see things are going right.

## DISCOURAGEMENT

It doesn't seem Snape is ever going to do any good, for all me trying to help him. I have a nod and a word for him if I go in the Estimating or meet him crossing the yard, any time; and I stopped to ask how he was getting along when I met him, togged up, in the High Street, Saturday evenings, just so as he shall remember I hold him in mind to see him re-establish himself; and Arthur, I know, has been extra nice with him, and called to see his crocky old mother, friendly. No word of any trouble arose between them—so he tells me—which shows Master Oswald has kept things dark at home; or else he has spun some yarn why he is less flush with the ready than he formerly was. He seems like he had turned sour against me as if he had some grievance biting him all the time, instead of feeling full of gratefulness as he had ought to be. I think it is because the fellow can't understand a generous purpose anywhere in the world, but thinks I am taking advantage to get more work out of him for less money. Rumble says he does his work accurate and without difficulty—and no wonder!—but when Rumble put him to a bit of abstracting, for trial, to get him better interested in the work of the office, he did not seem particular glad; and Rumble says he is all the time practising at juggler's tricks—tossing his ruler to make it land balanced on his hand, and other sillinesses like some clown out of a circus—as Rumble can see him at it by his shadow through the muffled glass in the door any time he comes back to the room, Snape thinking he could not see through, no doubt; and he is at it behind Rumble's back, too, by the many times there is his ruler falling on the floor, or knocking against the desk.

However, what has upset me more than anything else was two days ago when I happened to pass by the bicycle shed, quarter past five, after everyone had cleared off; and there was young Sydney Wallace with his tyre off and tube out for patching. The boy has just started a fine new bicycle for the first time—paid out of the extra money he draws, with his father to guarantee his instalments, no doubt.

"Hullo!" I said. "A puncture happened to your new bicycle!" I said. "That shouldn't be," I said. He stood up

315

and came over rosy by the surprise of seeing me and the nice respectful feelings he has.

"No, sir," he says, "and it happened twice last week, too," he says.

"Well, you're having all your bad luck in a bunch, to get it out of the way and done with," I said, and passed on; and then I had a queer idea come in my head by something that happened years ago with the girl typists and their jealousies, so I turned back:

"Was it all right when you brought it in after dinner?" I said.

"Oh yes, sir; and so it was the other times," he says.

"Well," I said, "you just take it through the back door in my yard, next time; and put it away in the wood-shed. It will be quite safe and, maybe, there will not be so many nails laying about to catch it," I said; for the idea came in my mind that Snape has been puncturing his tyre on the sly when no one could guess, just by noticing the pride and happiness the young boy has in owning a swell bike; and the idea stays in my mind, too, for all my wishing it would keep out by the ugliness of it.

There is something in a real bad heart that is beneath the most low animal, to my way of thinking; just as there is a greatness in a good one far above any beast. If there were any cure it would be the one they tried as a cure for Titus Oates—by my history book at school—and tie up Oswald Snape for a policeman to give him a dozen, would be the best day's work anyone could do for him—if I had the ordering of things; for he is a cowardly mischievous fellow that needs handling the same as they handle monkeys; and that is—jump at them sudden and grip them so as they know they are mastered, and who are their masters.

# BLOGGS ON THE MAT

I had old Fred in for a long talk, Saturday morning, him having packed up and brought his Missis home—for the change over with Tolpenny—after the men paid, night before. He was properly cast down when he came, by the pickle he has made for everyone; and by getting cleared out from finishing the rare nice job Belhampton is going to be; and not knowing but he may be hauled up before the beaks; and I dare say he didn't feel gladder by the time I had finished with him, either: but there it was! He is getting near to the age when they all have to jack up, and, though I would like to have him back in the Yard for a few years yet, it is no good thinking of that after the way he misbehaved before, to say nothing of the fine style Rube Johnston, with Billok to help in the Machining, has got things going—according to Arthur's ideas—so what am I to do with the old fellow? There is nothing laying ahead where I can send him when Priors Franklyn clears up in a couple of months' time, as I must leave things for Arthur to look after by getting too tired going afield myself and by always feeling ready for my nice arm-chair, waiting front of the fire, besides Doctor saying I had ought to take things more easy at my time of life; so, if Fred won't mind what Arthur says, what's to be done?

I told Fred all this, gentle as I could, with him sitting to look at the pattern on the carpet; and then, by having had ten days to think over, I told him that, after Priors Franklyn cleared up, I would keep him on the pay-roll at a pound, in addition to his Benefit, for him to hold himself ready to lend a hand at full pay, if called on; but he could always take on another job any time he liked, by arrangement, I told him. That pleased him, as I knew it would, by stopping the idea that he was going to be put on the shelf for good and all; though, far as that goes, I do not see what use we can make of him, and he'll never get in with another Firm at his age and being still so backward with his penmanship—according to the present ideas in the Building Trade. Last, I had another nice thing to tell him, and I shouldn't be surprised if it didn't make me more glad saying it than it did him hearing it!

It is years ago since I first had the idea, and it has often made me happy to think of since, though, now Fred has a wife who's well-to-do in the world, it will not count as much as I planned it should do.

That little old house, Farm Cottage—in Farm Lane, as it used to be, but now developed, top end, to be Porchester Avenue—Fred has had on monthly tenancy (£3 10s.) for twenty-seven years, or thereabouts. It belongs to Mrs. Skinner, a widow woman, that never has listened to any asking to buy the freehold because she was born there—her father being Dick Warren, the Dairyman, that I can remember—and she won't have the house pulled down and the land developed like the measles getting worse, for so the country all looks like these days, spotted over with those little shoddy pink houses Mr. Johnny Rasper is in such a hurry to put up when he gets the chance, so as to have the repairing of them—and the clearing of them away and the rebuilding, as well, if he lives to my age, I dare say!

Well, last week, knowing how things must be with Fred, I went and saw the old lady, who was wearing all her pretty smiles like she was sure I had come to make love to her, till she guessed what I was after and then, of a sudden, "Oh dear! No indeed!" and, after that, there was no sitting beside her on the settee to snatch a kiss from little 70-summer "Pussy"—as they called her at home—by reason of all the pins made to stick out to prick me, to judge by the way she pulled herself tight together, like a hedgehog, to keep me off her. However, by talking about old times; and having Pussy to laugh once or twice and call me a "naughty old man"; and by admiring of her cat; and being kind-hearted about all her reasons for not selling the property; and saying I would keep others from pestering her again—as they have been; in little more than a half an hour blessed if she wasn't ready to start Pussying with me in earnest! and I got her to agree for me to take over the freehold of the house and garden ($1\frac{3}{4}$ acres) and the $5\frac{1}{2}$ acre paddock beyond now leased to Flick the Butcher, for £1,000, just on condition nothing is ever to be altered from what it is now so long as she is alive, to know. Trencher is her Solicitor, same as he is mine, so Trencher is to make a conveyance to fix it; and I hope he will enjoy the job, for it would beat me to secure that my successor will act up same as I intend. To my way of thinking I am laying out the money to show a good profit in the future.

When I told Fred he would have Farm Cottage, rent, rates and taxes free, for him and his wife as long as they liked to live there, the old chap came over stammering by not knowing how to thank me; but I can tell the way he feels without him saying anything, so after I had told him he'd better go down, yesterday, to Belhampton to show Tol. round to-day—that is Monday—and then travel back to-night to get down to Herts first thing to-morrow, off he went; and if it makes heavy days for the old chap it will serve him dam' well right for all the trouble and expense he's loaded on me by not thinking what he's about till after it's too late.

That's the best I can do for him, and the last I can do; and if he comes not to like where he finds himself!—well, that's his own fault and he has no one to thank but himself unless it would be his lucky star, for who else would take care of him the way I have done?

# A SURPRISE VISIT

There came a surprise yesterday, Sunday, when who must ring up from London to know would we be in, but Henry Curt! and there he was, just in time for tea and hot muffins, looking no end of a swell and a bit trimmer round the middle than I thought—unless it is his tight waistcoat and starched front makes him to seem to stick out more when he is got up in the evening swallow-tails he wears, all day, when on duty. He had a rose in his button-hole, and one of these new green pork-pie American-style hats set a bit to one side like he was the Royal blood. He was nothing but grins to see us; and then it came out that it was because his master had got one in the jaw, and I couldn't tell him enough to answer all his questions—which was so much news to the girls, of course. I suppose the nurse and the flunkey had been talking for all the domestics at Tallon's Dyke to spread the good news; so that was all the use of me trying to keep secret!—except I stopped a buzz starting in *this* place.

Henry told us they brought Sir Ezra home from Weymouth after they had wired him together inside his mouth, and bandaged him outside as well. They call it "fracture without displacement" and he has had Sir Ramsden Scatterley down from Town to test him all over, since; and there are special nurses put to take care of him in bed, day and night; and Henry has no end of jokes about tubes for pumping his dinner up his nose—which I do not credit, for one moment—and about the trouble his cooks are put to making everything into different kinds of soup—enough to turn their hair grey, if true.

He was all the time pestering to see "the brave man that did it", as he called Fred; but that I would not have. However, round about half-past six Fred and Tol. must call round on their way starting off to Belhampton; so I had them in while Henry was sitting with me. He sat with his legs stretched out like he was a duke and grinned at Fred as a monkey might do, all the time; but Fred didn't notice after he had thrown his hand up to his forehead out of respect for the strange gentleman, on first coming in.

Then, when the time came and Fred touched his forelock —as the sailors say—turning to go, Henry must jump up and follow after to clap Fred on the shoulder with one hand and pass him a Bradbury—he must have had ready beforehand—with the other. Fred turned and stared; and then looked in his hand; and then at me—but I took no notice; and he went out, not knowing what it meant, clear enough; for he is slow in some ways though quick enough in others.

"You shouldn't have done that," I said, when the door shut.

"Why ever not?" says Henry, getting back in his chair.

"Because Fred doesn't understand such things," I said.

"Not understand! He's not such a fool as not to know a tip when he gets one!" he says.

"Well, it's lucky he didn't nap you on the boko before he thought," I said, "and then Jack would'a been laid out good as his master," I said.

"What are you talking about, John?" says he. "I ought to know how to tip by this time! Why, if that fellow likes to come down to Our Place"—as he called Tallon's Dyke— "we'd whip together a fiver for him in two shakes," he says.

G : X          321

"That's as you may think," I said, "but you don't know the man you're dealing with. I'd lay Fred has never taken money in his life, and I can't imagine any making the mistake to try and pass him any," I said.

"How's that? He's only just a working man, isn't he?" says Mr. Henry Curt. Oh, I did feel wild at his stupid ignorance!

"Working man! What the hell do you know about 'the working man'?" I said. "Fred Bloggs is as proud as any! 'Only a working man,' indeed!" I said. "Fred is a skilled craftsman and a front rank General Foreman of fine Architecture that works with his head more than with his hands, to organize and direct hundreds of skilled men at a time—not a pack of scabby flunkeys and kitchen sluts, to go round a table breathing on the knives and spoons to give them an extra polish," I said, to let him know I meant it; and then I came to a stop by the girl knocking with the silver salver and a little written message folded up small—as it might have been—that she handed me.

"Did Mr. Bloggs ask you to bring this to *me*?" I said.

"Yes, sir. This minute, before he left," says she. So I passed it over to Henry.

"There's your tip come back, and not taken long about it," I said:—so like old Fred to hand it me, to be sure he wouldn't make any mistake!

"Well, it suits me all right to have it back," says he. "You always were a queer lot down here," he says, which made me feel sorry; for Henry meant it kindhearted if he wasn't such an ignorant man; so I told him I was sorry I had broken out, and it was because I was getting on, and over-ready to get excited.

"Yes, like an old billy-goat, ready to put down your head and run blind at everybody," says Henry. "But that was always rather your style, you know, John," he says. Well, we laughed, and he was pleasant enough with it,

322

which makes me think he has got something up his sleeve if I could make a guess what it is.

When I told him Fred didn't feel too comfortable that Sir Ezra wouldn't prosecute him for assault, Henry burst out laughing and slapped his leg. "That's the best I ever heard," he says.

"What do you mean?" I said.

"*That* old toad?" he says.

"Well, why not him as well as another?" I said.

"*Why not?*" says Henry. "Do you suppose he would go in a witness box, on oath, to have lawyers ask him questions?" and then he laughs and laughs at the very idea. "If he does," says Henry, "you tip the word to yours truly, and *he'll* say a few things the lawyers would like to know," he says.

He stayed supper, and made a lot of fun with the girls; and Meg seems to think he is every bit as fine a fellow as he holds himself out to be, and next door to a Lord in Parliament to hear him talk about all the great people he has hobnobbed with in his time.

He said he had given his notice for the 1st of February, which will be time enough for getting his little Hotel ready when he has finished deciding.

"It would be about time for me to step off, in any case," he says, "by all this Belhampton racket in the summer; but now, if he hasn't been and bought the lease of a great house in Belgrave Square! and, through the London season, he is going to carry the most of the staff in a motor-coach he has, from Tallon's Dyke up to Town on the Monday for entertaining his London friends, and back, Friday morning, for week-end parties in the country. July and August will be his yacht and Belhampton, for a change."

"He must have a big holding in his Company," I said. "I noticed they are paying only 7½ per cent dividends on their Ordinary," I said.

"Well, it's going to be 20 per cent next time; and a prospectus coming out for new capital because of the way the business is growing," says Henry; "but that's only a little part of it," he says. "There's Kimbolds he just's bought—high-class sporting boots; and he is Jammerald & Tilbot, as well—the people that deal in all this special Indian brass-work. He owns seven or eight, all the same first-class names you would think of for quality; and then, soon as he has bought them, lets them down. *That's* where he gets his money. Take Jammerald's for instance. They made their name by selling genuine Indian craft work collected from all over India by their Agents; but our old man knows better than that. He has the brass trays, and such like, stamped out of sheet in Birmingham, and sent to some factory he has in Calcutta where his people put on imitation art-work patterns that are set up for genuine in Jammerald's window, as you may see any day you like to pass along Wistack Street. Of course people begin to find out the difference, but by that time the business that is bringing 150 per cent, instead of 30 per cent, is ready to be sold for our old toad to start it over again with some other reputable Firm."

"You do astonish me," I said.

"That's nothing," says Henry. "Did you ever hear of the East Droone & West of England Farm Produce Coy?"

"Yes," I said. "I think I have."

"Well, that's Sir Ezra's own special business that was never started first by anyone else; and the business is to import eggs from abroad, all over; have them loaded into lorries at Plymhampton, or wherever it is; and distribute them, at night, in Farms all about, that the Company owns, for the eggs to be sorted, cleaned, marked, packed and sold as 'English Farm House'."

"The police ought to be told," I said.

"Well, all this talk there is in Parliament just now about marking eggs, comes of our old Toad's goings on, most likely; and then his butter! If you like to travel West on the 6.43 a.m. from Paddington and keep your eyes skinned, you can see his trucks of Danish butter starting off, any Thursday, to the Company's Factory at Shanterton to be mixed up with a pat or two of British for 'Best English Farm House Blend'," says Henry.

Well, I don't know what to make of it all. It isn't the sort of thing Henry would invent out of his head, and he has plenty of chances to get to know Sir Ezra's private affairs if he has a mind. That is what he told us, at any rate, and he stayed so late he had to run if he was going to get to Waterloo in time for Brockenhurst. A decent sort of man, if he would give over his swagger and pretences.


## A LUCKY TURN

It was four weeks since the trouble Fred Bloggs made, and all was settled for the conveyance of the little house and the ground—except Trencher has arranged for me to *lease* with option to buy on the Vendor's decease—and I was expecting every day to have Trencher send me word to call in and complete, when, one day last week, as I was going up Station Road, there was a little fellow coming the opposite way that looked as if he was just from London, instead of going there, by the style of his get up; and then, when he came close to pass me, if it wasn't Cohen, Sir Ezra's Solicitor, eyeglass and all, but who did not remember me, or else he didn't mean I should think he had done. I wondered what would bring him to our little bit of a Town, but thought no more till, to-day, Trencher rang up to ask me to drop in; and after we had "signed, sealed and delivered" as they call it, Trencher says with a bit of a laugh:

"Well, you were only just in time," he says. "There was someone after it and pretty keen to get it, too, judging by the way he pressed me when I told him terms had been agreed. Mrs. Skinner sent him to me, it being too much for her to give him an answer he would take, I suppose," says he.

"So!" I said. "And who might that be?" I said.

"I don't know the name of his Principal," says he, "but it was a London Solicitor by the name of Cohen," he says.

I couldn't make sense of it at all; till, walking home, there it was, clear enough! That dirty fellow—by being afraid to give evidence to have it decided, fair, whether he deserved what he got, or not—must set his Solicitor on to find out, and buy old Fred's home over his head so as to enjoy the spite of slinging him out of it!

Well, seems that in my old age I'm getting into a world I knew nothing about before; so I ought to be the readier to get away out of it, that's all, for "we shan't be so long, now" as that cheery old fellow, Tillerton, was always saying when he was ninety-three, and more. I wrote a letter, private, to Fred to warn him in case they should set toughs to waylay him or try on some other ugly thing; but, after, thought better not to upset him, and so put it back of the fire, or we should have old Fred making more trouble for himself than any other could. No one has ever put Fred down except as Fred thought well to allow by his feelings for what was the proper thing; but it would be a serious matter if he got on the war-path, for he has none too much tact and, also, he is one of those that would never give in while there was breath in his body, if it was any cruelty or injustice—which is the way with the British, though not too much the way with those of different blood by what I have seen of things.

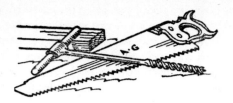

## A TICKLISH BUSINESS

We had a field-day at Widdlingford, yesterday, after getting all ready according to Mr. Quinger's directions written out in proper specification style, with a drawing, as well, to make everything clear. He wanted a rare lot, I must say; and it was a trouble getting to hire the three jacks, for he must have *oil* jacks, to suit his ideas, instead of hydraulic, to guard against frost and to hold the pressure. I didn't intend to go down myself, with Arthur there to see to things; but, night before, I remembered that old heads come in useful, now and again; so I took mine and joined Arthur on the 7.12—in the dark—as the Architect said he would be on the site at nine. He drove up just as we got to the Church, before his time—instead of after as is the way with too many Architects who think it no harm anyone should be kept waiting if it is not themselves. He had brought along the half-inch detail of the campanile for building on, extra, to give abutment—except the bell-hanging and finish, top end, that he wants to consider about a bit longer.

The drawing was careful-figured to place, for us to get the work started; but I thought well to first go on the roof with a two-foot, for these Italian half-round tiles are apt to butt awkward if not set out to suit from the start; and, sure enough, when I got up, that old campanile would have cut into the roof so as to make a fine bit of botching to get a finish of the tiles against it. I had the Architect to alter the position of the campanile $2\frac{1}{2}$ in. East, for making a neat job with a half-tile listing, so it was just as well my old head was there; for the way the tiles ranged wouldn't have occurred to anyone till it was too late, and it only came in my head because I " had been there before," as they say. Mr. Quinger was particular in thanking me; but it is a pity the public does not understand enough to know when they see a building that might be just out of hospital for a hare-lip or a club-foot or a double squint; for, if they did, we should have more Architects and Builders conscientious in their business, and fewer that are careless.

Well, Tom Bruce had all prepared ready, and Mr. Quinger examined into everything to make sure all was complete the way he intended; but, first, he would have us to nail bits of 2 in. by 1 in. tiling-batten, 6 in. long, to the face of the Chancel Arch each side of the crack, to pass each other, with a pencil line ruled across them for reading how much the crack might close up when the wall was pushed back. The arrangements Tom had made ready were three 2 in. planks, 19 feet long, set vertically to follow the curve of the wall outside where it was bent by being pushed over $2\frac{7}{8}$ ins. at the top. One of these planks was opposite the thrust of the Arch, and the other two were spaced at intervals of six feet to the West. These planks had each three heavy chocks bolted on at top, and 4 ft. 6 in. apart, to take the thrust of the ends of three 6 in. by 9 in. shores. At the bottom end of each plank there were 3 in. by 3 in. needles passing through the planks to stand 9 in. in wall with the heads braced against chocks bolted to the planks, which was done to prevent any chance of the planks sliding up the face of the wall when the load came on the shores to push the wall back to a vertical position.

Each set of three shores were led to 11 in. by 11 in. baulks, four feet long, laid vertically against the side of a hole, four feet six deep, sloped to give a normal base for the shores to thrust against. Each baulk rested on a deck of 2-in planks, laid on a bit of a concrete raft, to give a rigid foundation to push off. Each set of shores was distanced with boards nailed across at 5-foot intervals, and the oil jacks were seated on the baulk opposite to the Arch, with their heads packed up so as to bear on the foot of each shore, by wedges knocked opposite ways, under them. The shores to the two planks, West, had wedges (instead of jacks) for sledging those shores up to follow the jacks and keep the whole wall moving back equal.

The plumb-wires, with their bobs hanging in buckets of tar, were rigged; and a lime-whited board set up, far end and independent of the wall, to sight them against; which was marked, very careful, with a pencil line to agree with the ranging of the plumbs, so as to give exact measures of the distance the wall moved. When all was checked over, Mr. Quinger sent the men to 'stations', like he was the captain of a ship run on the rocks, that had to be warped off; and he had everyone rehearsed to know, and give, signals with right meanings. Then the men at the jacks had the order and started at pumping with Mr. Quinger to watch the dials and judge what load to put on each; and every now and again he would have the men hold off while he went to sight through himself, though Arthur was set to keep his eye on the plumbs and give a shout if she moved.

For a long time anyone would say that nothing was going to happen, except little creaks and crackings as the load came on more and more, till even that came to an end and Mr. Quinger was worried, clear enough, for it seemed she didn't mean to budge at all; when, of a sudden Arthur gave a call, and Mr. Quinger went over and I followed, and, sure enough, she was moving and had gone back a matter of a quarter-inch, almost in a jerk, as one might say; but Mr. Quinger said such behaviour might be expected at the start. After, by sighting through, you could see her moving back like she knew what she had got to do and was willing enough to do it when obliged! It was a nice thing to stand and see happen, and I could have watched her moving, moving, as gradual as you could hardly see, all day long, for the pleasure it was.

Well, in two and a half hours—by the great carefulness used—she had come right back to all but $\frac{7}{8}$ in. scant out of the perpendicular 20 feet above damp course, and no more would she come even with the jacks at full load; but Mr. Quinger said that it was as much as he hoped for and more than he expected; and the crack in the Chancel Arch, at the angle with the sofite, had closed the full of $\frac{3}{16}$ in., measuring by the tell-tales, leaving a bare $\frac{7}{16}$ in. open, which was better than he thought could happen; and the lab. set to sledge the wedges at foot of the dead-shore Tom had botched under the crown of the arch, said they had gone a bit more home, but he "wouldn't like to say how much" —which is just like a labourer!—but it shows the crown has eased upwards a fraction, too, which is as it should be.

Mr. Quinger waited while the bearings of the shores were chocked solid off the baulk-bed, so that the jacks could be taken out; and he saw the wedges spiked, too, against any chance of a knock starting them to slip. He checked the setting out of the campanile, and gave me and Arthur a lift back to town, which I was glad of; so now we are clear to go ahead and make things secure, and no harm has come to the church, after all; and when the crack is cut out, pointed, and plastered over, there is no-one to ever be the wiser unless it would be the architect to the Ecclesiastic Commissions to crawl over the building like some ant with telescopic eyes—but what more could *he* have us do to make secure?

# AN UNVEILING

Here is the beginning of our good Vicar's monthly letter in St. Andrew's Parish Magazine, just now brought, that I have snipped for pasting in:

My dear Friends,

All of you will be rejoiced to know that the longed-for opportunity to which you have been so earnestly looking forward for paying tribute in heart-felt gratitude for the generous gift of that dear old friend of St. Andrew's, Mrs. Rudolph Broadbench, who ever remembers us in spirit though regretfully removed in body seven years ago to a remote and distant parish, will at last be made forthcoming by a SPECIAL COLLECTION after morning service on the first Sunday in Advent, when our good and tried friend, The Venerable the Archdeacon of Tanchester, who never fails to step into the breach and succour us in our times of need, will attend and preach one of his memorable sermons we have all learned to so look forward to, and will afterwards unveil and dedicate the beautiful coloured memorial window that Mrs. Broadbench has so generously donated to the Glory of God and in memory of her late departed husband Mr. Rudolph Broadbench.

Though your first thought on this happy occasion will be of gratitude and thanksgiving, we all have to regret, as is so often the case, that owing to the need of "going to press" a fortnight before publication, the dedication ceremony above announced will unfortunately be a thing of the past before these words can meet your eye; but those of you who remembered to read the Notice prominently displayed in the Porch for your special benefit, had ample opportunity to make due preparations for the event; and after all that has been urged on this page in the past of your duty merely to *glance*, nothing more, at the Church Notices as you pass in or out, it is to be hoped that there will be a large attendance of freegivers and a more generous response than has been the case on too many previous occasions. It has often been pointed out how disconcerting it is to your Vicar, if, after all the trouble taken, our good friend The Venerable the Archdeacon is unavoidably made aware, on the offertory being counted in the Vestry, of the smallness of the recognition paid to his generous help; and how little his kind offices, freely given and often at great personal inconvenience, have served to break through the sinful crust of parsimony and self-seeking. It is hoped, therefore, that on this occasion, at least, there will be no cause for complaint especially having regard to the heavy debt still weighing on St. Andrew's.

Well, the church was three-quarters filled instead of half; and the collection was £6 17s. 8d., which is less than £2 more than the average, so I don't know what Mr. Peebles will have to say *next* month; though I don't know, either, that there was such a wonderful lot of good sense in writing to urge people to a thing that would be all done and settled before they could ever come to read.

The Vicar said a week ago, he thought better since the Archdeacon had agreed, to unveil and hear general opinion before he decides about sending the window back; him being in two minds about it—as he is about most things, unless it would be three! It was Sunday before last the Archdeacon unveiled by old Bunter running to get the pole for shutting the hoppers, and raking down the hangings by them not falling of themselves when the string was pulled. There wasn't any "Oh my!" like a firework gone up, that I could hear, though the whole congregation was crowded to see what would happen, and no wonder! for it was a dull misty day and the window, being in the North Aisle, seemed a dull, flat, ugly affair enough; to say nothing of the two old gentlemen looking to have been out on the roof to dirty themselves a bit more since last time, and to need delousing and a hard scrub with soap and hot water more than ever before.

Mr. Peebles told me he had written Mrs. Broadbench, to be forwarded, that the window was in, so as to have her send a cheque, which is something to have got done, at last! but if it is decided to tell Mr Primstake to take the window away and supply another in proper style, it seems to me, now it is formally dedicated, that there will have to be all the business gone through of securing a Faculty for removing it; so here is our Vicar been and tumbled himself in *another* hole and he will be running to me again, or I shall be surprised, to know whatever he had ought to do next?

## THE END OF PRIORS FRANKLYN

Here we are, getting to clear up at Priors Franklyn after a good deal of extra time allowed for the Architect's alterations, and for the special care we took not to have frost biting out the half-inch mortar-joints, which can never be re-pointed to look right when they are specified to be made by bedding the bricks and pressing down till the mortar is squeezed out, and then striking off, flush, with the edge of the trowel. I warned Tol. that, if the frost caught us, the Architect would have the damaged work down for rebuilding, so I am glad enough to get packed up and away, comfortable, before Christmas, which didn't look to be likely when we were rebuilding the Pavilion and starting on Mr. Blenhasset's idea for extra columns, which will run to four or five hundred pounds, including clearing away, according to what Jedbury's prime-costing shows, and swallow the Architect's fees, with his extras and expenses as well, and I shouldn't wonder. Mr. Blenhasset will have to put a fine picture of it all in the Royal Academy so as no-one will forget what a great Architect he is for never letting a paltry matter of L.S.D. stand in the way to prevent his beautiful chaste conceptions bringing about an addition no one expected—same as if the parlourmaid had a baby all of a sudden.

I thought well to go down, yesterday, for a look round before we packed up; and it is a nice job, I will say, now all is finished; and it made me feel proud when the owner and her Ladyship came along the terrace in the sun, and greeted me friendly style. They are well pleased, as they have cause to be; for it is a fine bit of building, with a wonderful lot of cleverness in the careful design of the details, that will show up better in the spring when the gardeners are able to make a finish, and things begin to grow up, and the new turfing takes hold. I told his Lordship he would not see a better bit of bricklaying craft, old or new, anywhere in the country, than what old Snoop has put into the niches and the arches over—for so I believe to be true. After he had shaken hands —and her Ladyship also—he stayed back and said to me, private:

"Mr. Grigblay; with regard to rebuilding the walls of the Pavilion, kindly include the cost in your account to *me*," he says.

"Very good, my Lord," I said.

"By the way, what does it amount to?" he says.

"Well, the Quantity Surveyors will fix that, my Lord," I said, "but I dare say it will come to between seventy and eighty pounds," I said.

"So much as that?" he says, and off he goes, whistling his dogs; so I suppose he is pleased with what his Architect has done, and has no mind to come down on him too heavy.

The result of clearing up Priors Franklyn will be old Fred laid off. Well, he's only got himself to thank. I've done my best to help him; but if I had my way, I would choose he should see the end of Belhampton, in any case; and it will be like the beginning of the end for me when old Fred is no longer on my pay-roll.


## ILL TIDINGS

There is an ugly thing happened that worries me for the trouble that may be coming to old Fred and his Missis.

Tippit's General Stores, which Mrs. Bloggs has her daughter and son-in-law to look after since she married, is on the corner of Jubilee Street and Station Road, in a little house where the bay in Station Road was taken out for a front window, and the five-foot strip of garden paved over where the buckets and brooms and coir mats are set out when the weather is fine; and the side window in Jubilee Street, next the door, is set out with newspapers and sweeties for children. It is just a humble shop, with no others thereabout, that is handy for the second-class streets laying at the back, and for folks passing to and from the station.

I noticed, a fortnight back, that Sutton, the shopfitter, had his board up on the row on the opposite side, by me coming to wonder how these sorts of small builders get away with it; when, if it was me, I should have the whole blamed place about my ears to teach me better ways. He was at clearing away the front window and door and the bit of wall between, and carrying the front, above on a little 6 in. by 4 in. R.S.J., bearing 4 inches, each end, on a couple of roofing tiles in cement, for templates, bedded on the old 9 in. window and door jambs as if there was magic in a bit of steel to make it carry any dam' thing without crocking; so no wonder Mr. Dorman Long makes them with factor of safety five—is it?—to keep our good friend Sutton, and his kind, in business—instead of in Princetown for manslaughter—and the building trade in good repute. I have seen a fellow lay his steel joist sideways to be more handy for a 4½-in. wall to sit in the trough between the flanges!

Well, to-day, lo and behold! if Sutton hadn't got all finished and "Newsagent PAUL GOMPERTS Chandler" fixed up in gold letters on a gaboon fascia with glass laid over it for modern style; and plate windows; and strips of mirror, back of the jambs; and the Area covered over with gratings and prism glazing; and any amount of swank in the showing off of galvanized buckets and household furniture set out against the 'return' of area railings of the house each side; and newspapers slung on stylish racks at the entrance; and a fine showcase for fancy sweets right along, bottom of the window.

I didn't think anything till I turned in at Tippits' for the vestas I fancy for my pipe, when who was there but Mrs. Bloggs behind the counter, like old times! There were other customers, and while I waited my turn a lady behind me wanted a feather duster, and was handling over.

"How much is this one?" she says.

"7½d.," says Mrs. Bloggs's daughter, that was attending her.

"Why, I can get the same over the road for 6d.!" she says, in a tone as if the other had tried to cheat her. So when I passed the time of day with Mrs. Bloggs, I said:

"Who's this fellow set up other side of the road?" I said.

"No one knows, Mr. Grigblay. He doesn't belong here," she says.

"I'm afraid he won't help your trade," I said.

"Indeed, No!" she answers me; and then she was minding a lady choosing a penny mousetrap, and I came away. In the street, looking across at the new smart shop where no one would think to find any shop, let alone one in

336

exactly the same line as that over the way, it came in my mind to have heard of big concerns freezing out the small trader by cutting prices next door till he puts his shutters up; and the fancy took me to cross the road and go inside.

There was a smart-looking young fellow behind the counter—that was all a sham of canary-wood got up with stain and polish to pretend to be mahogany—and, when I asked, he put his head round the pile of goods stacked end of the counter, when a lean grey-haired fellow with a hanging moustache and his bald forehead spotted over with pinpoints of black like his pores were too full of dirt to wash clean, and got up in a brand new apron just unfolded with the bib looped round his neck, came forward from behind.

"Has Mr. Cohen been in lately?" I asked.

"Eh?" he says, short and sharp, as if he didn't believe he'd heard right.

"Mr. Cohen. Will he be in, any time?" I said, casual. He looked at me in a queer style:

"Did he tell you to inquire?" he says. "He won't be coming here, far as I know. What name shall I tell him?" says he.

"Hookey Walker," I said, and went out, having heard all I wanted; and looking sideways as I turned into Pomfret Street—the way one does when someone is staring, particular, at one's back—there he was looking from his front, to make out who the hell I might be, clear enough.

Well, it's an ugly business, to be sure, and difficult to know what can be done: but it will be better not to drop any hint to Fred, for he won't have the right sort of tact to handle a matter of that kind; and it's no affair of mine in any case, except I would not have him put to any distress if I could prevent. However, there will be no harm me having a word with Trencher, to know Fred's right in the matter.

## A VEXED QUESTION

It might be the influenza broke out again for all the sneezing there is at Primstake's window; and those who never attend service; or who belong to some other parish; or even are chapel; are hurrying to St. Andrew's, weekdays, to see for themselves—like it might be one of Mr. Epstein's statues that London folk pay hundreds of pounds to see just because it is said in the papers to be so wonderful ugly it is enough to make anyone curse and break up the furniture.

First start off, everyone pretended to believe Primstake's window was pretty to see because of it being special-made by an artist all in coloured glass, and so it was bound to be pretty; till, next, the idea got about that it was a disgrace, instead, and that went like a house on fire. It looks to me it might be my Effie that scratched the match to set it off, by saying to her friends some of the things she had learnt of me; till now there is no one with a good word for it, and I hear from Vint that the Parochial Church Council were all in complaint against the Vicar at their meeting, Thursday; and him trying to calm them down to wait, because Mrs. Broadbench is expected back from abroad middle of next month, and then "all will be made right"—or so he told them.

Well, our good Vicar ought to know the way women behave by the years he has had them all about him, like some tramp enjoying to have flies crawl over his chest; but, to my way of thinking, by the time that fine big lady arrives back home in bottle-green satin—with a touch of Parma violet to keep you in mind she's by—and learns there is a proposal to turn down her generous gift, made special with her name on it by her pet artist, we shall be further away from getting things settled than while she is kept busy, a thousand miles off, nursing herself not to be sea-sick.

However, church windows are not any part of *my* business, and so I have kept quiet; but someone had ought to take the lead, or nothing will ever be done by everybody growing tired and ready to talk about something fresh; so that is why, when Mr. Spinlove drove in the Yard to-day with his lady wife, on his way to Honeywood, to look over that fine lot of mantel-pieces we have ready for Belhampton, I asked him if he would look in at St. Andrew's, since it lay on his road, and tell me *his* ideas—just to oblige.

I gave him something of the story as we went along; and when he got front of the window, he glanced aside at Mrs. S. and they had half a smile together over it. Next, he studied the window serious, walking this way and that for different views; and in half a minute he was away, off, and holding the door for us. In the porch he just said, quiet, over his shoulder, as he moved to get to his car:

"Hoof it out," and when I looked at the lady, she shook her head slowly, like she was sorry. Then "Good-bye," and a wave of the hand, and they were off round the corner.

Well, a nod's as good as a wink for me when it is Mr. Spinlove gives it; so I will set about to canvass the leading members of the congregation for drawing up a memorial to the Vicar; which will be all in friendliness, for he will be glad enough to know there are plenty behind to push him the way he wants to go if he could find the nerve to make a start.

Mr. Spinlove told me that, after three weeks, Sir Ezra was good as cured; and he has gone away, to a villa he has at Mentone, till the turn of the New Year, if not longer.

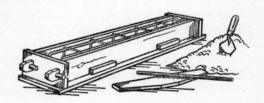

## THE UNEXPECTED

A thing happened this afternoon I would rather not, and that was Smith on the 'phone from the front office, to say Mr. Rasper had rung up to speak to me, and should he put him through? Well, it is always some kind of mischief when I have had any truck with the fellow—though that hasn't been for many years past—so the answer I told Smith was: "Mr. Grigblay's polite compliments but he is very much engaged; so will Mr. Rasper very kindly write what he has to say in a letter." Next minute, there was Smith again; and this time it was: "Mr. Rasper would take it as a particular kind favour if Mr. Grigblay would let him call this afternoon for a few minutes," so I said: "Tell him half-past eleven to-morrow morning," which will give me a chance to feel ready for him; and so it is fixed.

I have no idea what the fellow is after; but I hear talk that he is in difficulties with a shift of the ground at his Gas-holder Tank, which is a difficult thing to credit, for he ought to have the job good as finished and done with, by this time. They say the revetment is giving way, or some such nonsense; but that is the style they always get talking, with no one knowing who said it first; and no doubt it has all come about by my men and his mixing it up together in their beer so that the little thing gets bigger and bigger in the telling till there is a horse-race happens, or a cup-tie, to start them off on something different. The stories that were going round about Johnny pumping the foundations away from under the Loco-house—that I gave him a warning about—would have made you think the Railway Company was sunk; but I noticed he soon had the crack cut out and built up, which he would not do until he had made all secure below ground with underpinning or whatever was wanted.

Well, I shall know more about it this time to-morrow; but if he wants to borrow a derrick, or a lorry, or my motor-winch—well, he can try somewhere else instead, for I have had enough of his borrowings. How many years ago since he had the loan of that old twelve-hundred gallon tank of mine? that I forgot about till, eighteen months after, I couldn't lay hand on it, and then what must he do but make out he'd never had it! Next, one fine day a month or two after, there was my brave tank set up high on a staging, bold as brass, all daubed over so as no one could say it was the same. However, Mr. Johnny himself was on the ground, so I said:

"Hullo! What about it!"

"What about what?" says Mr. Johnny, all of a surprise.

"What about my tank, that you've got cocked up there to make you feel proud?" I said.

"Oh!" says he, as if it was a wonderful bit of news for him, "Is that *yours*?" he says.

*He'd forgot who he'd stole it off*!

Well, Mr. Johnny will find there are no flies can settle on me when he calls to-morrow.

# MR. RASPER CALLS

If any had told me the way I should be thinking and feeling, this minute, sitting alone after the girls have gone up to bed, I would have thought they were balmy; but it is just the way in life that, when things actually come about as, in your imagination, it would please you to have them—and to set you off laughing, as well—you find, like enough, that they take you in quite the other way to what you would expect. There is a thing happened to-day that would have made me split my sides to think of; yet the reality of it, with all the distress following on stupidity and dishonesty and folly, brings me nearer to piping the eye, instead; for here is Mr. Johnny Rasper good as shipwrecked himself, and proposing we should "amalgamate", as he calls it:—just as if a drowning man should offer to lend a hand at cleaning decks, when he felt like it, in exchange for being lifted safe and snug on board—by a boat-hook through the slack of his trousers—and given a quarter share in the ship with the grog-allowance of a dozen!

It was just ten minutes of my valuable time he had petitioned me to give him; but without any "by your leave" or "thank you", he helped himself to a full hour and would have taken another, I dare say, if the whistle hadn't gone, dinner, with all of them clearing off in a rush and me locking my drawer to have him know he'd got to shift; for it's always the way with Mr. Johnny, that anything he says is just what suits at the moment, with no other meaning whatsoever, nor intended to have.

I hadn't seen him close, to notice, for nearly ten years, I dare say, by me always looking the other way; and, my goodness, he *is* a sight! He wouldn't be forty-five, yet—forty-three most likely—and there he was all gone to pieces with booze, any hour; and by his razzle-dazzling up in London to come back tight in the last train Saturday nights, as everybody knows and talks about; so that, by his looks, he might be sixty, with his blotchy face and swimming eyes all blue and baggy underneath; and his fingers trembling till it was as much as he could do to hold a pencil, for all he'd had a rousing stiffener on his way—stiff enough to make me push back from my table the more he leant over to be confidential. He had spruced himself up with a new hair-cut and best suit and a smart tie, to make a good impression, I suppose; but it was a sad thing to see and it hurt my feelings, for it made him to seem proud he was the rotten fellow he looked, and prevented me having the kind helpful feelings that come for a man that is down and out. It is sad, too, to remember back to the time of old Nibnose that built up a sound business, all of himself, by forty years of keeping at it, early and late, day in day out, and putting every shilling he earned back where it came from; for, if he was an ignorant man and a third-class builder, he was keen enough never to let a chance slip him; and now here is Johnny Rasper, that he took in for manager and made partner when he started to crock up, taken five years to pay back capital and interest on his purchased share, and another five to clutter himself up with mortgages and overdrafts and creditors, and knock down all that Nibnose built up. That, at any rate, is what I make of his affairs, allowing for Johnny being first class at lying and out to make the best of things in the story he told me; but it was only at the end that he opened up with his amalgamation idea. He started off with flattering me to advise him—from my special clever experience and old age—how he was to get out of a trouble he is in with his Gasholder Tank Contract. His idea was, no doubt, that by sitting patient and admiring at my feet to learn off by heart the golden words of wisdom that would fall from my lips, he would put me in a right mind to listen to his "amalgamation" idea. Amalgamation indeed! Might as well harness up a kangaroo with the blind staggers to jump the wrong way against a cart-horse, and call it an "amalgamation"!

That old Gasholder Tank has made trouble enough for everyone, from the very start off; and Johnny Rasper's in a worse trouble than anyone else. I saved him from the trap Parkin set to catch him so as to keep himself from trouble with his Directors; and now here is Mr. Johnny fairly trapped himself by his greed and cheating to get a bit more money than he had any right to; and by standing in with Parkin to share the plunder—as is pretty clear, judging by the way Parkin tried to work things with us.

What has happened is, that no sooner had Rasper got the job finished, and had started at clearing up, when one fine morning, of a sudden, it was:—"Hi! Come here any of you blighters that can see straight this morning! Has something happened to the blooming Tank to make it cockeyed, or have I got them different this time from what I had them before?"—or it was somehow like that, as I suppose. At any rate, soon as they had rodded it this way and that, it was seen, clear enough, she was inches out of the circular by that great wall being crippled with the weight of ground at back—which beat me to hear told, for I know the ground in all that part, well, and I would wager it to stand on a vertical face fifteen feet, anywhere. However, that is how things are, according to Rasper; and they know just where she has moved, too, by setting up a staging and centring to the curb, when, lo and behold! she has moved in two places, to the North and North-West. She has come in $15\frac{7}{8}$ in. at the worst place and $7\frac{1}{16}$ in. at the other; but whether a foot or 6 inches is pretty much the same, for the Telescopic Gasholder has been ready, waiting for erection, these six months; and it and its stanchion-guides only allow very little play for packing up to the wall, so what's to be done now?

Rasper says there are no cracks: the wall is just bent over

344

and inwards—by being green as yet, I dare say, unless Johnny cheated the mortar of cement—and he says it is actually pushed *out*, more than 3 in. in the worst case, at the limits of the inward bulges; which would come about to make room for the length pushed *in*. Rasper says there are some wide cracks in the ground as far back as fifteen feet from the curb that he saw, before, but did not take notice of at the time! That, of course, ought to warn anyone the ground had slipped forward, and would have given me a rare fright.

"But how would that come to happen?" I said. "How could the ground make a start at slipping when it is held up solid by that great wall?" I said.

Well, it seems Mr. Johnny Rasper didn't think anyone would be clever enough to ask an awkward question like that; and "I couldn't say, I'm sure," was all he had for answer; but I would not have any of his deceptions and nonsense, and so I kept at it to get the truth out of him at last; by asking till he answered straight, and it is like this:

That sketchy specification botched up by Parkin, without any quantities supplied and with just a bit of a blue print of the section of the wall, said: "Backfill as necessary," which, of course, means "concrete fill" to bring the back of the wall up solid against the excavated face. Rasper went to work the same as Arthur's ideas, with a circular trench for strutting the face till the wall was built, and then excavating the rest of the ground, inside; and as the Gas Company was going to pay extra for any planking and strutting necessary, it would suit Mr. Johnny to make a thoroughly sound first-class job of it; and as it was agreed he should be paid for leaving the planking and strutting in, he thought he could make a bit more profit by pulling it out. That would have been right enough, and the soundest job too, if he had put in his concrete backfill—same time as he pulled out his planking—as the wall went up; but as he was being paid for concrete backfill—as was clear enough from what he said—he thought it would be a clever thing to leave that out, too, and make his backfill of "solid punned earth"—he called it—as he went up; and that was where the mischief began.

"What did Mr. Parkin say to 'fill and ram' instead of concrete backfill?" I asked him.

"Oh, Parkin was all right," says Mr. Johnny:—all right for a nice chummy glass or two, quiet, in the bar parlour, no doubt. "He was under notice, and is gone now. He didn't worry me," says Mr. Johnny—which is what makes me think there has been a bit of hanky-panky going on by what I know of Mr. Friendly Parkin, and can guess of the other.

"So Mr. Parkin was friendly to you, was he?" I said.

"Oh yes, I had no trouble with him," he says.

"Yes; and so was he always ready to be friendly with us, too," I said; and I went on at asking about his backfill til I got to understand just how things are.

The bottom section would call for ramming in little more than a two-inch space, by what he said; and the next section of the wall, going up, would give a six and a half inch space to be rammed, and above that 11 in., and, last, $15\frac{1}{2}$ in.; but he didn't seem to know what tools were faked to get at that kind of work; and the long and short of it is that even backfill with earth was scamped—instead of looked after, close, to make a particular job as should have been—until they came to ground level to fill against the curb, and that was punned hard and smooth to make a fine finish, so as everyone could see how careful and thorough the work was done, all through. However, there was the wall standing good as free of the ground it was pretending to support; and it might as well not have been there at all for any use it was in preventing the ground from slipping; for when that started—as like enough it did by the heavy rain we have had followed by the frost—and six tons

346

to the foot run, as it might have been, fell through eleven inches "*thump*" against the back of the wall in a wedge to lever it over, what sort of a wall is going to hold stiff? An engineer up in London would tell you the equivalent dead-load and overturning, to seven places of decimals off a slide rule, to get it quite exact; but he would leave out the friction and the natural flow of the ground because he couldn't put it in figures; and when he had been at it a week you wouldn't know anything compared to what old Fred Bloggs could tell you by walking round for half an hour!

Whether its solidified swill got in his head to push his brains up in the corner out of the way, I couldn't truthfully say; but, by the dull heavy style Mr. Johnny looked at me to understand what I was talking about, that is what has happened—to the best of my humble medical opinion.

When I asked him what the new engineer to the Gas Company, Mr. Charles Pole, had to say about the state of affairs, lo and behold! Rasper hasn't told him.

"Can't he see for himself?" I said.

"He's busy at the Works. I dare say he thinks the Tank is Parkin's affair," he says.

"Well, you've got to tell him," I said: and then it came out, clear enough, that the fellow wanted my advice to botch things some way or another so as no one would know.

"And have the Tank collapse after the Holder is fixed?" I said.

Well, I will have no hand in his cheating; and I will not go and see for myself, like he asked me, for I do not trust him and if I went he would, like as not, get it back on me that I had advised him to any kind of stupidity or trick he might have it in mind to try. All I said to him was: he must excavate, back of the wall, to the angle the ground will naturally stand at, which looked to be near fifteen feet back and not less than twenty feet deep; and to do it first at the places where she has moved; and be careful to start at once before more trouble comes about; and have the excavating complete all round before starting to pull down and rebuild at the places where she has moved, I told him—at which he made a kind of a groan and a hiccup, all in one.

That was where he began to tell me all about the financial hole he is in by all the big cost of making good the Tank, on top of the loss come about by him pumping the foundation from under the old Loco House; with more trouble, yet, by settlement started again—so he says; and by creditors and bad debts and mortgages and one thing on top of another; and then, by the drink drying out of him, no doubt, there he was actually starting to cry, and not ashamed at me seeing him—unless he thought a few drops down his nose and on to the carpet would make me bring out my books in a hurry to see if I could promise to put him straight, so as he might cheer up and dry his eyes.

Well, it's all dreadful sad; and if only he was a different sort of man I would look into things to find out what could be done to set him on his legs: for it is those working for him, and some that have been since Nibnose's day that are thrown out of work with homes broken up and distress for the women and children, that upsets me. But, being as he is, there is no one can help Rasper till he begins to know how to help himself—if then.

There is one thing I nearly said to him, but put aside as seeming to be just mischief: however, thinking over, I don't know what to feel about it. Rasper is a Builder, and I would always lend a hand to one of my own calling as, often enough, have I been helped, in a friendly way, myself; and if Rasper is a rogue—well, so is Parkin another rogue, and the Gas Company is a pack of rogues, too, by the style they tried to diddle the ratepayers out of £2,000, so one is as bad as anoher far as that goes.

Now, by my ideas, Rasper could easy land the whole

responsibility for the failure of the Tank on the Gas Company to let them get damages out of Parkin, as much as he's worth, though that will not go far to meet the cost of making good which, as I see it, may amount to all of £1,000. What Rasper had ought to do—but he should get Trencher to act for him—is: say to the Gas Company, "I notice your Gasholder Tank is starting to cave in, and will you very kindly oblige and say whether that is how you intended and I have completed the Contract to your satisfaction, or is there any further work you would kindly wish to be done before I pack up and clear off? Your wonderful proficient and conscientious private Engineer wrote in his fine accurate specification, 'Backfill as necessary', so as not to have any mistake made by nothing shown on his pretty-drawn Blue Print; and I took particular trouble to have him to say, exact, what backfill was necessary; and I acted on his orders to ram solid, back of the wall, and so did, to his full satisfaction and approval, him being about the job day in and day out, to make sure everything was according to the Contract as he would have it," Rasper would say "So now, please, will you very kindly intimate if all is completed to your best satisfaction and approval; or is there, by chance, any little extra bit of work you would wish to be attended to before I make a finish?"—he would say.

There is no answer to that, far as I can see; but I will not have part or parcel in Rasper's affairs, and so I will just write him to-morrow to advise he consults with Trencher to learn what his rights are; and I will myself go across and see Trencher, private, to let him know what I make of things. What Trencher will think well to advise I do not know, for I have no confidence myself and a Solicitor will always be careful—unless it is "Get Counsel's opinion"—or he may land himself in trouble; but a Barrister can advise as he thinks fit, whether he is right or whether he is wrong—as I understand.

349

# REJOICINGS

Here is Xmas come and gone again before you can turn round—or so it takes me; for, as you grow old, the years slip by the same as the telegraph posts go past the windows on the Railway. However, this Xmas we shall all remember, particular, by Old Father Christmas—so Arthur tells the boys—bringing their mother a present in his sack, of a fine little gold-haired girl! That's three they have, now, and all as well as can be; Ellie nothing but smiles and happiness, lying there, like it was her first; and Arthur delighted it is a girl, for a change, and Ellie, too, on his account—the prettiest thing for a picture of married life you could see anywhere. It will be nice to have the little one grow up with her brothers, for it's well for young boys to learn to be gentle and considerate; and first-rate, too, for girls to share in the boys' games and learn not to practise at the tantrums until they have a husband to tell them what perfect darlings they are whenever they try on the sulks or the vapours. There are more women spoilt by their husbands than ever were by their mothers in the nursery, that's certain.

Those two young limbs, Willie and Ernest, don't take any notice of baby; their new idea, now they can run about, is to get hold of heavy crooked sticks to go on the ice hockeying like they see the men. They are all over the place so as you never know where you won't find them next; but they've been told not to go in the machining, and it was Billock catching them there gave Arthur the warning. Last I saw, was Master Willie climbing, one foot at a time, half-way up that steep open-treaded stair to the hard-wood loft! These young creatures must find out everything for themselves, and there's no stopping them. Ellie's pair have fine head-pieces too. Arthur has a story about that big picture-book of animals, all in colour, I gave Willie on his birthday —and of course young Ernest must get it off by heart, too, not to be behind his brother. It seems the Lion is a calm majestic beast, looking out from a hillside to see what he'd like to be at next; but the tiger is ferocious and snarling, with great red mouth and shining fangs, ready to swallow you.

Well, Sunday afternoon, Arthur had them to sit quiet, for a change, while he told them the Bible-story of Daniel thrown in the Lions' den; and the boys were properly serious listening to hear their father. When it was finished, young Ernest says to his Dad:

"I 'spec that King will try tijers next time."

Now I call that real clever for a little bit of a chap, not yet turned of four and a half, to put two and two together in such a smart style, all by his own reasoning to end the bungling;[1] but when I told our good Vicar he only shook his head, serious, and "tut-tutted" with his tongue against his teeth.

Effie went over to dinner, Xmas Day; but I had my bit, quiet, at home with Meg, by not having felt over-well lately with headaches; and coming over red in the face for no reason; and my heart thumping going upstairs; and feeling always ready for my big arm Arthur gave me; and a touch

[1] This, then, is the origin of the anecdote vouched at third hand by Thomas Okey, in his "Basket of Memories." We seem here to gauge the limits of Grigblay's humorous perception, unless it is obscured by admiration for his little grandson's quickness.

of backache-kidney-trouble as seems to me by what it says, in these newspaper advts.; but we went round, tea-time and there they were rioting with some young friends from next door till you might think they could never tire. It would be a poor kind of a world if we were born all ready grown-up like flies, and such; for remembering how it felt when you were a child, and looking on to understand how it is with the young new generation, is the gladdest part of life, in my opinion; and if I came to be a great-great-grandfather I should get all the more happiness out of watching the young ones grow up. Is there any prettier thing in the world to warm you up and make you feel glad, than to have an infant pull out its thumb to laugh and crow at you, and kick off its little woolly boots in your face for a bit of sauciness, the clever way they find out how to do by rubbing their legs together?

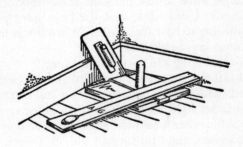

## A HAPPY ENDING

It looks to me as if our good Vicar would be quit of his window troubles at last, good and all; but of course it was I that had to show him, or he would be kept at it still like some fly struggling to get out of the treacle by working hard the best way to put himself further in. I never saw such a man! The more I learn his ways, the more he keeps me wondering at him. Thinking over, it seems to me it was a bright idea that came in my head while we were talking; for it settles the whole business for him, and he can feel pleased with himself once more and have Mrs. Broadbench and Primstake in to tea, all smiles, if he likes; but it tickles me to fancy what the Chancellor of the Diocese, who is some great K.C. lawyer up in London, will make of it all.

I had Arthur to draw up the Memorial to the Vicar, as he is cleverer at putting things into nice-sounding words than I am, by being more new-educated from school, and because of the better style of language taught now than was in my day. I had five leading members of the congregation to sign, and then sent it to Mr. Peebles by Registered—as I understand to be the correct thing in such matters—and Vint told me that the Vicar had agreed with the Parochial Church Council to apply to the Chancellor for leave—Faculty, they call it—to take the window out. I heard no more, not seeing Mr. Peebles to speak to, until I met him to-day in the Crescent and asked him; and there he was, all in a stew of perplexity and worry and not knowing whatever to do next, because the Chancellor had replied to him —"As it does not appear that you obtained a Faculty to put the window in, it is not necessary to secure a Faculty to take it out", which seems clear logic to me and good enough for anyone: but, as there was no hindrance to hoofing the window out—as Mr. Spinlove put it—which is what our Vicar asked leave of the Chancellor to do, it beat me to understand what all his finger-biting was about. However, by listening to him saying over again what he had told me before, and by putting a question or two, I made out that the Chancellor has asked for an explanation why he didn't apply for a Faculty before he put the window in, and Mr. Peebles' trouble is that the only answer he has to give is that he "forgot", which seems to me a good enough answer for anyone, though he is worrying himself to think of a better—by what I could make of it.

G:Z 353

Another thing is that he's scared to death of Mrs. Broad-bench, the donor, arriving back, as though she might be some ogress coming to eat him; but whether it is because she is such a remarkable tall out-size lady—him being just a little thread paper by comparison; or whether because of her deep-tone voice, like one of these special concert singers with a cold on the chest for singing bass with if they could go low enough without straining at it and hurting their insides:—well, I couldn't truthfully say which. He is scared stiff of Primstake having the Law on him, too; and scared of what people will say, whatever happens; and scared of the Parochial Church Council pushing him faster than he feels safe to go; and, by one thing and another, the side of his finger must be so callous by this time he had ought to get things settled quick so as to give it a rest.

Then of a sudden, there came the new idea.

"Well, sir," I said, "if you don't like the responsibility of telling Mr. Primstake to take his window away and put back the plain leaded-lights that were there before; why not apply to the Chancellor for a Faculty to put it *in*?" I said.

"But it *is* in," he says.

"Yes, we can all see it's in," I said, "but it can't *stay* in without you get a Faculty," I said.

"But, if I get a Faculty to keep it in, then I shall have to get another Faculty to take it out!" he says, so that I should get things clear in my head, same as he had them in his own. "I thought you were decided it must be taken out!" he says.

"And so I am," I said, "and so the Chancellor will say, too," I said. "He will ask the Diocesan Advisory Committee to report to him; and they will say 'Hoof it out' or other more polite words," I said—knowing what must be, by Mr. Spinlove's judgment. "The Chancellor will so order, certain," I said; "and you can tell Mrs. Broadbench and Mr. Primstake how dreadful sorry and disappointed we all are," I said; "and say to them, 'but what can I do

354

about it?' you can say, 'when our appeals to the Chancellor are jumped on and set at naught by a parcel of interfering busybodies like the Advisory Committee,' you can say; and," I said, "if Mrs. Broadbench and her window-artist have any feelings they would like to express, the Chancellor would be pleased to have them write and tell him, as you can have them to know," I said.

That made Mr. Peebles to rub his hands together all of a smile the same as if I was a Mothers' Meeting; and he chuckled low down like a bottle being poured—which is a very rare thing with him. But then he came over all troubled again because, by the rules, application for a Faculty must be unanimous of all members of the Parochial Church Council as well as the Vicar.

"Well, sir," I said, "The P.C.C. are unanimous that they want the window taken away, and you can easy get round them to agree that the best way to clear it out is to petition for it to be let stay in," I said. So that is what he is going to do, and it will put the whole burden off his shoulders and on those of the Chancellor and his Advisory Committee— except he has just got to explain, clear, why everyone is so very unanimous for the opposite to what they were so very unanimous for the week before!

It is a queer finish up, and no mistake; but to get the window cleared away will make everyone glad, for the more they try to admire it the more they wish they didn't have to; and those who have seen a picture about leprosy in Doctor's Waiting room—like me—must have the carrotty-head with wings growing behind the ears giving them the nightmare; and it is certain the two old fellows pictured below cannot be so dreadful holy as to look the old miserables Primstake makes believe to picture them.

# A CRUEL BLOW

There is a terrible upset happened that is like enough to land us in the ditch at last, and that gave me a proper shock reading the London Evening Latest, that I have sent in, last thing, so that I came over worse than I ever felt before, for the moment, by the great letters across the front page: "ARREST OF SIR EZRA GOTSNITZ, BART.," "APPEARANCE AT BOW STREET," "BAIL £20,000," "REMANDED IN CUSTODY," "A SERIOUS CHARGE," and so it went on in so many different-size mixed-up print to make it all the more wonderful, and with the same thing said three times over and the last put first and the first last, for extra excitement, that I might have been standing on my head till I got my *Daily Telegraph* this morning; and there it is, set out pretty clear, that he is wanted for fraud and misappropriation; but the Magistrate only took evidence of arrest, and he wouldn't accept Sir Ezra's own bail, but must have two sureties of £10,000 each; so it must be a big thing they have against him, and he was remanded in custody till his friends bail him, I suppose.

They can give the fellow twenty years for all I care, but it is a thing that will bring his credit down like a house of cards, certain, by everyone going for him like wolves to get what they can before it is too late; and that means bankruptcy, and two shillings in the pound, like enough, and where shall we be then? There is a certificate due to us round about £7,000 that I had a word with Smith about only two days back; and there is £3,000, and more, held in reserve on top of that, to say nothing of £2,000 in special stuff on order; and another £8,000, or near to, in sub-contracts we have let; and there is all that oak and mahogany joinery we have ready, but is not yet on the job and so not ranking for a certificate. Far as I can see, it would take £25,000 cash down, to see us straight, for what arrangements could we make with sub-contractors and specialists? What about all that fine marble floor-and-wall-tilings Gibb & Libberton have ready? and the gilded copper baths, all hand-made to special design, Ashcross has been at these three months to be in time? and all that wonderful hand-forged balustrading Sallowfield & Tuff are sending on the job? How can we make any bargain that will recompense those firms when the stuff is so much junk for all the chance there is of anyone having a use for it?

This morning, when I rang up and asked for a word with Mr. Spinlove to gather any news he might have; lo and behold! he hadn't heard a word, by being in too much of a race to look at the morning paper.

"You don't say so!" he says; and, when I told him, he was properly upset on my account.

"You must hope for the best, Grigblay. I will make inquiries at once, and let you know," he says: but there is no word come from him yet.

"You'd better keep on, Grigblay, till we know how things are," he says. "There'll be all kinds of waste and dilapidation if you let the work stand," he says.

"Yes," I said, "and the cost to us if we did! And then there are the specialists, and people starting to fix, or ready to! If I stop them, how will we ever get going again, to say nothing of breaking their contracts? I will take the chance of keeping on, sir," I said, "though it looks to be a precious poor chance; but directly-moment there is talk of liquidation, I will shut down and have every man off—sub-contractors the same—by my rights, under clause 26 of the

357

Conditions, to suspend the works any time there is legal restraint upon the Building-Owner preventing him continuing them," I said; which Mr. Spinlove agreed to. He is a nice-feeling gentleman if ever there was one;—not a thought about himself. His trouble is that he let me in by pressing me to give him a tender; but I would not allow it for one moment, and so I told him, serious, heart to heart.

So there it is, and I don't know where I am by the terrible state of affairs it is when every cheque I sign and every req. passed against the job-number, may be so much money given away out of my pocket. It is cruel hard on us, and no mistake; and Arthur, poor fellow, is glum enough, though not able to see all the mess we're in to honour our credit. Little Bellon, for instance, the clever working blacksmith down Croft's Jitty, that Mr. Spinlove let me past the order for his fancy casement stays! It was a nice job for the good little man though only £272; but how am I going to ask him to help us by abating his claim and taking over the stuff he has made that will never be any use to him or anyone else? Of course I can't. And so with others that sub-contracted for particular craftwork—if anyone should guess—to the specialist firms who sub-contracted to us. All those small men, that might be near ruined for want of a few hundred pounds earned, will be thrown in distress if we start trying to make things easier for ourselves:—all just by the dirty fellow's cheating to make himself more important among the shoddy kind he mixes with; and smother himself in his beastly unmanly luxuries that would disgust any clean Englishman;—which reminds me of the out-house there is at Priors Franklyn with a great tank of water in the floor, twelve feet long and six across or something like; and an old bench against the wall and coat-pegs and a bit of grating off a yacht, that I asked the butler the use of, dinner one day.

"Oh, the late Marquis, his Lordship's grandfather, had that made to jump in when he got in from hunting," he says; "and so did the present Marquis before he succeeded; and now his Lordship takes *his* plunge, soon as he gets back," he says.

Now that's what I call a proper healthy English gentleman, mind and body, and gives me no patience with these pulpy maggot-yellow alien mongrels, let in by the shipload to rot the blood and spirit of my country—but there! Doctor says I mustn't get excited, though it makes me wild to think of all the mischief and distress that fellow looks to have brought about.


## A BLACK FRIDAY

This is the thirteenth of the month come round—a Friday too!—and a black day it is for me, and Oh! I do feel so sorry for poor Arthur got to carry on for himself with all to rack and ruin—or good as; but there! I can't think about it, being all to pieces by not having felt well in myself these ten days and more, and no energy to face up to things.

I didn't hear any news from Mr. Spinlove, yesterday; and so I fixed it for Arthur to go up to-day, first thing, and inquire at the Gotsnitz Coy.'s Office, Queen Street; and have word, after, with Mr. Spinlove if he could manage; and then, twelve o'clock or just before, Mr. Spinlove himself, rang up to speak to me.

"I am very sorry to tell you, Grigblay," he says, "that a Receiver is appointed,"—just that and nothing else;—except he had tried all yesterday to get through, but the Gotsnitz lines were engaged; and when he rang the flat, it was "Please inquire at Queen Street"; and when he was put through, trunk, to Tallon's Dyke, the person at other end, soon as he heard the name and business, just hung up without a word uttered. This morning Mr. Spinlove went to Queen Street to find out for himself; and the place was choked with people pressing to ask questions; and the Secretary not to be seen because "Engaged"; and the clerks saying "nothing known yet" whatever was asked them—by instructions, as I suppose. Then, just as Mr. Spinlove was coming away, the Secretary passed through out of his office with a notice to put up outside the door, "Receiver appointed: Date of Public Examination will be announced in due course." Hearing that, I didn't wait for Arthur, but rang up Tolpenny to give all of them their notices from to-day, and warn Specialists what has happened; and then I had letters written, dozens of them, to sub-Contractors, Specialists and to Merchants where we have goods ordered, to say the Works are suspended by a Receiver appointed, and that formal notice would follow and that anything done after date "hereof", I said, would be at their own risk—which is all I can do until the Notice is in the Gazette and I can have Trencher advise me; for this terrible business is new to me and out of my experience.

Arthur was looking properly draggle-tailed, poor fellow, when he got back, close on four, to tell me the news. He heard it said that the Public Examination will open on 19th; and I will have Arthur attend with Trencher to tell him what questions to ask, for it will be beyond me, to say nothing of being all to pieces and not well in myself this last fortnight, though Doctor says there is nothing the matter only old age "and no cure for that"; and there is a bit of blood-pressure again, but "after seventy, we can't expect to be as young as we were, and must take things easy," he says.

# ESCAPE

Here have I been laid up these five weeks with a buzz-buzzing in my ears; and headache; and flushing in the face like I was angry when I am not: with Doctor putting his special bandage on my arm and pumping up, tight, till you would think something was going to burst, for him to read on a gas-meter-dial contraption fixed on; and keeping me upstairs in bed or in my arm-chair, carried up, because of it making me to pant and come over flustered climbing the stairs; and stuff for my backache-kidney-trouble, as well—but he says that is of no consequence—sour and nasty enough to make you want to gob it out each time you swallow! However, here I am downstairs again, and feeling all the better for my rest; and I have had Meg to bring me my old Journal, laid by, for writing down the wonderful bit of good news that has come about, and that Arthur did not tell me anything about before all was fixed, in case it would be bad for me to be strung up waiting to know for certain; but now here it is that he told me soon as he came back from London, three o'clock; that Belhampton, along with our contract to finish, is bought by another, all standing, lock stock and barrel; and we are out of the ditch almost as clean as if we had never got in!

It is a most wonderful thing to have come about, and no mistake; almost as it might be a miracle by Arthur's Guardian Angel, or the sweet little cherub that sits up aloft to keep watch for the life of poor Jack—as they called me at home—working in Mr. Oscar Belleview—such a name!—to make him smell a bargain; him being the one Fred told me came to Belhampton last Autumn in a great Rolls with radiator-cap and mascot and door-handles, etc., gold-plated—or so the chauffeur said—to be shown over, special, by his friend Sir Ezra; and he is the same too, I make no question, that Henry Curt named "His Royal Highness,

President of the Catsmeat" to set the girls laughing when he came to see us.

Arthur was in high feather to tell me, good fellow, and had no end more to say; but I told him to get along off and have Effie to know the good news; so away he went and I dare say I had had as much as I could do with, at the time, being not well in myself these seven weeks past.

## THE WHOLE STORY

Arthur was yarning with me two hours this morning, and again, tea, to have me know all that happened while I was laid off.

It seems our claim, at date of Receiver appointed, according to the figures Spedder got out with Trencher and a special London Lawyer, Mr. Polechat, Trencher brought in to help; was £34,235 3s. 0d. and was arrived at as following for a rough idea:

| | | | |
|---|---|---|---|
| Amount of Contract . . . | £66,987 | 14 | 7 |
| Balance of Extras over omissions . | 641 | 3 | 5 |
| | £67,628 | 18 | 0 |

### Analysis of Claim

| | | | |
|---|---|---|---|
| 1. Received by Ballard & Co. on a/c of work done . . . . | £30,500 | 0 | 0 |
| 2. Certified by Architect as due to Ballard & Co. . . . . | 6,535 | 14 | 2 |
| 3. Retention money on above items . | 3,703 | 11 | 5 |
| 4. Value of work and materials part prepared or ordered . . . | 21,545 | 18 | 0 |
| 5. Damages for breach of Contract . | 2,450 | 0 | 0 |
| | £64,735 | 3 | 7 |

Our claim of £34,235 was made up of items 2, 3, 4 and 5. Item 4 included the whole of our liability to Sub-Contractors, Merchants, etc., not included in item 2.

The Public Examination and Meeting of Creditors to try and get things straight—Sir Ezra being out on Bail and a dreadful sight by his worries, according to Arthur—had been going on, weeks, when Arthur had a letter, by hand, for him to please very kindly call at Messrs. Sprode, Punter, Sprode and Sprode, Solicitors, Craven Street, very important. Arthur took a taxi, right away, and one of their Sprodes—but which one, Arthur did not learn by the Clerk giving him to understand it made no difference—asked would we be willing to complete our Contract for a client of theirs in a first-class financial position, if he acquired the Belhampton property? Arthur fetched Trencher, straight off, and, end was, he signed a letter agreeing. Next day, or day after, there it was! An offer of £6,000 had been made for the whole property, as it stood.

A rare hullabaloo started at only £6,000 offered for property that had cost close on £45,000—which is the total of analysis items 1, 2 and 3 with £4,000 added on for value of land. However, Mr. Polechat, the London lawyer Trencher had brought in to argue for us, made things clear to them by his great knowledge and cleverness, till no one was left with a word more to say.

First, he said the land was worth £3,500 by expert valuation, which was more than the Debtor had paid, but the exact value was of no consequence, he said, and he would consider only the balance of the offer which was £2,500 for the house as it stood. On that there was more disturbance by the cost of the house being £40,773 (items 1, 2 and 3) and one of them called out, like an auctioneer might do: "Two thousand five hundred offered for property worth forty thousand; any advance on two thousand five hundred?" and so they went on laughing and jeering, till the

363

Receiver had them keep quiet, Mr. Polechat sitting down to wait till they had finished rowing.

He then said to them that the value of a thing was not what anyone might have paid for it, but the price it would fetch. He called Belhampton a "rich man's Folly"; and he asked how many rich men were there who wanted to own a Folly? and out of those, how many, did they think, would like to buy someone else's Folly "instead of building a Folly for themselves"? he said.

Next, he went on that, as it stood, Belhampton was nothing but a "stone quarry"—he called it; and he said a lot more clever things I should never have thought of like—"What's the value of a half-made swimming-pool with no water at a place where no one wants to swim"? he said. Belhampton has no value until it is made a finished building, he said, and if it was not finished at once, the Builders would clear off and the place go so dilapidated that no one would ever buy of it, and then fall to ruin, he said.

"As it stands now, it is worth £1,000, and no more," he said.

On that some bright man said there was £21,545 value of work and materials prepared (item 4) to be added on to make the total value of house £62,318, which raised laughter. Mr. Polechat answered that the only flaw in the gentleman's argument was that seven-eighths of the £21,545 was a liability and not an asset, and the eighth left over, was *our* property.

Next, Mr. Polechat said it was wonderful good fortune for the creditors that a purchaser had been found ready to complete the building for a "sentimental reason", he said; and so it came out that the purchaser was paying *us* the £10,238 (items 2 and 3) due for work completed; and on that there was a great disturbance, the meeting being unanimous the money should be paid to the benefit of *all* creditors and not by favour to one; but Mr. Polechat had them

364

to understand that any bargain the purchaser chose to make with *us*, had nothing to do with *them*. The only matter they had to decide was—could they get a better offer for the property? However, they kept at it and were talking together and all restlessness till Mr. Polechat had their attention to learn how things actually were.

First, he told them, if they could get no better offer and refused the one now made, the most they could hope for, later on, was £4,500, which would increase their dividends only by less than 2 per cent—the total deficit being about £250,000.

Second, if they accepted the offer of £6,000 then their dividends would be increased by nearly 2½ per cent; but in addition, our claim for £34,235 would be withdrawn, which would mean 14 per cent increase in dividend to other creditors, or 18½ per cent increase in all, as compared with a possible 1 per cent.

So, after that, they had nothing more to say; but were so sour and jealous against us as Arthur would not have credired, he says; and it was left for the Receiver to see if he could better the offer, which was open for a fortnight, and he had people go down to Belhampton to see for themselves; but now all is fixed, praise the Lord! and we have nothing to do but get things started up again.

Another thing Arthur told me happened when I was ill, makes me sad—though I feel too tired to fret over it—and that is he has given Snape the sack. It seems Saunders has the others clear out, dinner, and locks his drawer where he keeps the ready cash; and locks the door of the room, and carries both keys with him clipped on his key-chain, the spare drawer-key being in the Cashier's safe and that of the room in Smith's.

It happened one day, Sennock—kept behind after all had cleared off—passing the window on his way to get his bike, noticed the shadow of someone inside the Cashier's through

365

the muffled glass that I had put in the bottom squares to help them keep their eyes on the books, instead of staring out to wonder what Bill is saying to Harry, other side of the Yard. Sennock knew Saunders's ways, by being assistant with him before; so he stepped on a drum of thinnings lying there, to look over, and if it wasn't Snape fiddling to open the cash drawer!—or so it seemed. Sennock nipped round to catch him at it, but the other had seen him and they met in the passage. Snape tried to carry it off; but Sennock would not have it, and pushed him in the Typists and stayed, front of the door, till all came back, two o'clock. Soon as Arthur returned, Sennock brought Snape in and they had it out. Snape's yarn was that the door was open and he just went in to see if he had left a bit of rubber, and nothing else. He must have somehow got a key to fit the door, and was at picking the lock of the drawer, no doubt; but Arthur did well just to give him his notice and one week's pay and tell him not to come in again, so there he is! good as finished, after I did all I could to help him go straight.

Another thing Arthur said was, that from what he has heard, Rasper and the Gas Company are having a turn-up; and there was a letter marked "Private" came weeks ago from Rasper, Arthur opened, thanking me for kind advice, and he had been to see Trencher. Arthur had me tell him what the matter was—but Oh dear! I didn't seem to feel any interest in Rasper and his doings, and it made me so tired that Arthur noticed, and left me for a nap; which is the way I have of coming over, these last days, by all the anxiety and waiting to know what will happen next, and how soon? and not being able to start in and see to things myself; and all this wonderful good news, of a sudden, is a bit too much for me, I dare say; though I shall pick up again quick enough, certain, if I take it easy.

# A LION SPRINGS

I am grown so much better in myself that I have been out, days, for a look round in the Yard or down the High Street with the girls; and now, this morning, with the sun shining and the birds whistling for the nice spring weather that will begin soon, I had a fancy to see how old Fred was getting along, down home, especially as he had called several times when I was laid off, but Meg thought best not to bring him up.

Happened, I went by Station Road; and there, opposite Jubilee Street turning, was the new shop cleared out—except dust and litter—and a board up "To be Let or Sold" by the Receiver finding there was not much profit from "Newsagent Paul Gomperts Chandler", I dare say. After I had gone through Lawford Road to strike half-way down Farm Lane—or "Porchester Avenue" as it is now called by its nice polite new name—there was the back of old Fred himself, walking slowly and cautiously along opposite his front gate in a queer secret style, for him, like he was some cat creeping along to make a jump at something, with his elbows to his sides and hands in front so that I wondered to see him; and then he stopped and turned about, and blessed if it wasn't a perambulator he was pushing that I thought would be the washing, and him just waiting for the Missis to come along; but, directly I was closer to see his face, I knew it was something important and, sure enough, it was a mite of a sleeping infant he had snugged up inside, with its little hand—perfect down to its tiny pink nails— laying on the pillow ready for the thumb to go in, clear enough.

"Why what's this, Fred?" I said. "Do you mean you've started a family?" I said. "Well, that *is* a nice thing! When did it happen?" I said.

"He turned eight days only an hour ago, sir," says Fred

pushing the pram out and back, as he stood, like any nurse-maid born to it might do!

"A son and heir! That's a wonderful thing to have happen! So there will be another Fred on the pay-roll in twenty years' time!" I said.

"Well, me and the Missis favour the name 'John', if you will allow, sir," he says; so then it was me to stand God-father, and I shall be glad enough and so I told him; and then Mrs. Bull, that is helping them, came out and took the pram in the house; and all is well, and no trouble first to last, Fred says.

So here I am going to be Godfather to Fred's first, after I have always wished it was going to be a boy to carry on after me—and Louie too—and it never has been, but always a girl. Makes me wonder, if I had married again, whether things would have come different for me; but after Louie went I didn't seem to think of it in that way, but as though there could not be any son or daughter for me that didn't belong to her as well. Now, seeing Fred starting at just about the age I was when Louie died, makes me to wonder how it would have been if I had asked Mary Fosset—that might be here now if I had done, by not coming to be in the motor that killed her—but there were the girls grown up, that would not want another woman in the house, and that settled it.

When I walked down his garden, Fred had nothing to tell me except how he was turning market-gardener; and specially seakale, that is a rare paying crop, so he says, when you know how to manage as he learnt of some friend who was gardener at the big house, Grattington, when we were adding on. I was glad enough to find he was so con-tented in his mind, for I was afraid I should hear something of Belhampton, which would never do with Arthur to give him his orders! However, I wasn't so glad, when we got to the bottom hedge, to find the old fellow had fixed a gate

368

through, and had ploughed near half of the paddock!

"That's fine old meadow turf, and it's waste to bring it under plough," I said, which fetched him up short for he had no idea he was doing what he had not ought, so I just let be; but I never meant him to have use of the paddock at use at, and I dare say Mrs. Pussy Skinner will spread her claws for a bit of scratching when she hears of paddock use.

Old Fred with a son and heir! To think of Fred with makes me to wonder if I had married son again after again Louie went she would have liked if I liked if I married again with a son and heir after Louie went but in this life you can't life just I had a son grow up after Louie went to make life life if Lou . . .

THE HAND HAS GROWN TREMULOUS, THE LAST
LINES ARE SMUDGED, AND THE WRITING BREAKS
OFF THREE PAGES FROM THE END OF THE VOLUME IN
WHICH "GRIG" KEPT HIS JOURNAL

# GLOSSARY

**ATTENDANCES.** Services rendered by the Builder to Specialists; e.g. cutting away for Electricians, and making good after them.

**BAGGING UP.** Putting the wages of each man into a separate envelope. Each "bag" has the amount, with its computation, marked on it; hence "Writing up the bags."

**BENCHES.** Timber pegs, or other stools, the tops of which record a datum level.

**BUILDING CONTRACT** is set up by one party, the BUILDING-OWNER, engaging to pay another, the BUILDER (or CONTRACTOR), a certain sum for carrying out certain work. The former may employ an Architect as his "Agent" to design and direct the work, who will prepare CONTRACT DRAWINGS and SPECIFICATIONS defining the form of the building and the material and workmanship to be employed; and he may nominate a QUANTITY SURVEYOR, who is one versed in the measurement and valuation of building-work, to prepare BILLS OF QUANTITIES itemizing the amount of each separate kind of material and labour involved, so that when copies of these "BILLS" are distributed, Builders, by setting a price against each item, may readily determine the amount of their TENDERS. Contract Drawings, Specification, and (usually) the "Bills" together with CONDITIONS OF CONTRACT, are attached to a MEMORANDUM OF AGREEMENT and constitute the CONTRACT DOCUMENTS.

**CERTIFICATE.** A formal statement by the Architect that the Builder is entitled to payment, under the terms of the Contract, of a specified sum of money.

**CLERK OF WORKS.** One who represents the Architect on the works. He is paid by the Building-Owner.

**COLLAR BEAM.** A beam crossing from rafter to rafter above the feet of rafters.

**CRAFTSMEN.** Tradesmen, and others, whose work calls for Artistry! e.g., carvers.

**DAY WORK.** Work the value of which is, by the Architect's authority, to be estimated from records of its actual cost.

**ESTIMATING CLERK.** One employed by a Builder to measure and estimate building-work, and price Bills of Quantities, e.g. for determining the amount to be Tendered.

**EXTRAS.** Money expended, or work added, by the Architect's orders, in excess of the Contract amounts.

**FACINGS.** Facing bricks, i.e. bricks made for or used in the outsides of walls.

**FAT LIME.** Chalk lime, the basis of plastering, but "poor" for mortar.

**GAVEL.** A short-handled heavy hammer, used, e.g., by bricklayers.

**HAUNCHING.** The walling resting upon the springing of an arch.

**LEWIS.** A system of iron wedges which, packed into a sinking prepared for it, enables a block of stone to be lifted.

**LININGS.** Wood lining the thickness of openings in walls, e.g., to which internal doors are hung.

371

LISTINGS. Projecting fillets designed to throw water clear of joints where roofs butt against walls.

MEASURED WORK. Work the value of which is to be estimated by measurement.

OMISSIONS. Money saved, or work left out, by the Architect's orders, in depletion of the Contract sum.

OVERSAILING. Successive projecting courses supporting the carry-forward of a wall.

PAY SHEETS. Returns made weekly by Foremen showing the wages earned by each man.

POLE PLATE. The scantling of timber on which the feet of rafters rest.

PRIME COST. The NET cost. PRIME COST CLERKS are employed by a Builder to keep a running tally of the net cost of work as it proceeds.

PROVISIONS. Specific sums included in the Contract to meet the cost of special fittings or particular workmanship.

PUDDLE. Stiff clay reduced to a condition when it is impervious to water.

PUN. To ram.

RIDDELS. Curtained hangings about an altar.

RUSTICS. Stones in which a panel is sunk the surface of which is variously roughened (Renaissance).

SLEDGE. A heavy long-shafted hammer.

SLOP BRICKS. "Thrown" or hand-made bricks.

SOFITE. An under surface, e.g., of an arch.

SQUASHES. Decorations in plaster formed by pressing a mould into it.

SUBBING. The making of payments in advance of wages.

TINGLES. Strips of lead or copper nailed under, and clipped over the lower edge of slates, etc.

TRADESMEN. Men following a trade, e.g., Bricklayers